BEYOND THE SUNSET

But what could she, Jacqueline, do about it stuck here in Italy? Nothing, short of going to fetch her mother.

Her eyes opened wide.

She hadn't consciously considered it. They were just tired thoughts tumbling out of her brain. But slowly the thoughts took shape. It seemed quite a logical idea. She was a good driver. She had driven with Marco up to Nice and Cannes several times. This time she would just have to go further, but how much further? There were Michelin road maps in Marco's bureau.

She laid them out on the dining table, calculating distances, made notes regarding money, fuel and clothes. It was like being back in business – she had something to think about at last.

But wasn't she just playing? Wasn't this just a game to keep herself amused? Or was she serious?

The telephone rang.

That would be Marco. What would he think of the plan? She doubted if he would approve. He might even forbid her to go.

She picked up the receiver. 'Hallo?' She wouldn't mention the idea to him – then she could make up her own mind later.

But of course she had already decided to go.

**Also by the same author,
and available from NEL:**

JANTHINA

About the Author

Diana Bachmann was born in Guernsey,
where she worked in her family's
long-established jewellery business. More
recently, she moved to the island of
Eleuthera in the Bahamas with her husband,
a fellow author.

Once again on the move, Diana Bachmann
now lives on Spain's Costa Blanca, where
she is continuing her writing career.

Beyond the Sunset

Diana Bachmann

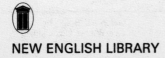

NEW ENGLISH LIBRARY

Copyright © 1985 by F. Beerman, B.V.

First published in Great Britain in 1985
by New English Library

First NEL Paperback Edition 1986

Second impression 1988

Typeset by Rowland Phototypesetting
Ltd, Bury St Edmunds, Suffolk

Printed and bound in Great Britain
for Hodder and Stoughton
Paperbacks, a division of Hodder and
Stoughton Ltd., Mill Road,
Dunton Green, Sevenoaks, Kent
TN13 2YA.
(Editorial Office: 47 Bedford Square,
London WC1B 3DP) by
Cox & Wyman Ltd., Reading

British Library C.I.P.

Bachmann, Diana
  Beyond the sunset.
  I. Title
  823'.914[F]   PR6052.A2/

ISBN 0 450 39494 8

December 1925

The North Railway Station in Bucharest was quiet and dark. It was close to midnight, and the streets, cut by an icy winter wind whipping down from the Carpathian mountains, were all but deserted. The few people who were about were more concerned with keeping warm than with the four motor cars which drew to a halt by the station's front entrance, and were prevented from pursuing any curiosity they might have had by the great-coated policemen who immediately formed guard squads at every entrance.

A group of men hurried on to Number One Platform, where the stationmaster and several other officials waited in front of a hissing locomotive drawing only five carriages. There were people already inside the carriages, valets and secretaries, bootblacks and footmen, but only one of the new arrivals would board the train to join them. He was of medium height, heavily built and inclined to stoutness for all his youth – he was only just thirty-two years of age. He had a little moustache, wore a quiet Savile Row suit and carried a soft hat. And was obviously more excited than sorrowful at the way he was leaving Rumania, and his birthright, in the middle of the night during the Christmas celebrations.

'There'll be talk tomorrow, eh, Bibescu?' he asked with a smile.

The police colonel, charged with seeing the young man safely out of the country, gave a tired sigh. 'Indeed, Your Highness,' he said. 'There will be talk tomorrow.' He glanced at his watch. 'There will be talk today.'

Prince Carol gazed at him for several seconds. Colonel

1

Bibescu was responsible not only for the prevention of crime in Bucharest but also for protecting the reputation of the Royal Family. They had come to know each other well over the past few years. Bibescu had had to hush up more than one incipient scandal arising from the Crown Prince's riotous way of life and choice of friends, and Carol was well aware that the policeman regarded him with contempt. He was for the first time realising that, having renounced the throne and accepted exile, he was no longer Crown Prince Carol, whose ailing father made him potentially the most powerful man in the kingdom. Now he was an ordinary citizen, while Colonel Bibescu was at least still the Chief of Police.

The Prince looked past the waiting men at the unlit doorway through which he had just come. He hoped, even now, that his mother – he knew better than even to hope to see his father – might appear, begging him to change his mind, to stay, granting him the only terms he had ever demanded of his parents, of the country. But there was no hope of that, Queen Marie had already tried to change his mind. She would not grant his terms.

'Well then,' he said. 'It is goodbye, Bibescu. Perhaps we shall meet again.'

The Colonel smiled. 'It will be my pleasure, Your Highness,' he said.

The Prince stepped on to the train, the door slammed shut. The stationmaster gave the signal, and the locomotive immediately began to move.

'See him again,' Bibescu remarked contemptuously. 'That would be a pleasure. Because if I do, I shall lock him up.'

'But it is romantic, is it not, Colonel?' asked the stationmaster. 'To give up a throne for love?'

'Of a Jewess?' Bibescu's disdain grew as he watched the train disappear into the night. 'Anyway, it is less his abandonment of the throne than his responsibilities that sickens me. He is abandoning two wives already. Did you know that?'

'And how many mistresses?' the stationmaster asked with a knowing smile. 'But come now, Colonel, would you not do the same, if you had the chance?'

A woman stood in the shadow of a shop doorway, as close to the station as she had been able to get, huddled beneath an expensive fur coat. She sighed as the train pulled away, and raised a gloved forefinger to wipe a tear from her eye. As she turned she almost bumped into another woman just emerging from the shadows on the opposite side of the street. They gazed at each other in surprise, and then spoke together.

'Anna?'

'Your Majesty.' Anna gave a quick curtsy.

They made a complete contrast, although their furs were of the same richness. Anna Dumesca, as befitted a once famous tennis champion, was tall and slender, while Queen Marie of Rumania was short and plump. Both women were fair, but where Anna's close-cropped hair was straight, the Queen's curled luxuriously.

Queen Marie's smile was as contemptuous as Colonel Bibescu's. 'You could not bear to think of him leaving, my dear Anna?'

'As you could not, Your Majesty,' Anna replied.

'He is my son,' Queen Marie said. 'And now he is gone from my side. He has turned his back on me and on Rumania. And he has renounced the heritage that was his. Should I not wish to see him a last time? But you . . . Perhaps you thought he would know you were there and that he would come looking for you. Perhaps you even thought he would take you with him. But why should he do that, my dear Anna? He goes to Magda Lupesca. Surely you knew that? She is waiting for him in Paris.'

'I know, Your Majesty,' said Anna in a low voice.

'She is the winner, and the winner takes all. So. What will you do now, Anna?'

She sighed. 'I do not know, Your Majesty.'

Queen Marie's nostrils dilated. 'You should leave

3

Bucharest,' she said. 'Do you not still own your father's home in Pitesti?'

'Yes, Your Majesty. But . . .'

'Return there,' Queen Marie commanded. 'You no longer have a place in Bucharest. Go back to your home. You can devote yourself to bringing up that child of yours. I suppose it is a miracle you have not yet put her in Carol's way. How old is she now? Fourteen?'

Anna Dumesca breathed heavily, keeping her temper only with an effort. 'You are correct, Your Majesty,' she said evenly. 'Jacqueline is fourteen and needs to be educated. She is attending the Convent of the Sacred Heart here in Bucharest.'

'The Convent. Ha!'

'I would like her to stay there, Your Majesty. Until she has finished school. And it may interest you to know that she has never met the Prince.'

Queen Marie gazed at her for several seconds. Then she said, 'Perhaps that is your mistake, Anna. Perhaps, had you introduced him to that lovely child, he might have taken *you* to Paris. With Jacqueline, of course. But perhaps, also, you have been the more fortunate one. Let the child finish her education.' She turned away, back into the shadows; undoubtedly there would be a car waiting for her around the corner. Then she stopped and turned back to face the younger woman. 'I have been rather hard on you, Anna, but I still think it would be best for you to remove yourself from Bucharest, at least for a while. And it is very beautiful at Pitesti, is it not? In the meantime keep me informed of Jacqueline's progress. You will write to me once a month, telling me of her accomplishments, enclosing a photograph.'

'Your Majesty is too kind.' Anna Dumesca sank into a deep curtsy, anger forgotten at the possibility that her daughter might receive the royal favour.

'Not at all,' Queen Marie said. 'Am I not the mother of all Rumania? And who can tell what the future may hold for your daughter?'

June 1927

Then nature rul'd, and love, devoid of art,
spoke the consenting language of the heart.

John Gay, *Dione*, prologue

'WE MAY conclude, therefore,' said Sister Veronica, 'that the revolution here in Wallachia not only provided the spark for the Crimean War, but also played an important part in reshaping the map of Europe, out of which our country was born.'

The girls shifted restlessly in their seats, and there was a distinct whispering from the back of the class. Sister Veronica, with hornrimmed spectacles and a faint moustache, was not at the best of times the most inspiring of women. When teaching history, she was definitely a bore. And on a bright early summer afternoon, with the end of term only three weeks away, the thoughts of the entire class were drifting through the open windows of the convent and out into the airy boulevards of Bucharest, encouraged by faint hints of a cool breeze arising from the River Dimbovita, winding its way through the heart of the city to penetrate the stifling heat of the schoolroom.

Sister Veronica glared at her charges. 'It is very important to understand the part our fathers played in making us what we are today,' she declared. 'Just as it is important never to forget what our *grandfathers* lived and suffered, and for what they died, under the rule of the Turks and the Greeks.' She looked from face to face. Rumanian independence was only fifty years in the past, and most of these girls' grandfathers, since they all came from the best families, had taken part in those exciting events. She had personally known many of them. The only member of her class for whom Sister Veronica could not name mother and father, grandfather and grandmother on both sides of the family was Jacqueline Stevenson, the half American. *She* ought not to have been here at all. Granted that her mother had been a famous tennis player in her day, and was in fact the daughter of a once famous house. But it was a house which had fallen on evil days financially – Anna Dumesca's father was reputed to have blown out his brains after losing his last fortune at cards. Now his daughter was a leading member of that social world which had turned Bucharest into a sort of Paris of the Balkans. Like her unfortunate father, she attracted rumour. No one knew anything very much about the mysterious Mr Stevenson, whom she had apparently met at the Wimbledon Tennis Championships in 1910, and married only a week after losing the final of the Ladies' Singles, and out of which union had swiftly emerged this sixteen-year-old irrelevance. Following which Mr Stevenson had somewhat conveniently died. His 'widow' had been left to pass from one protector to another. There were even rumours linking her name to that of Prince Carol. The fact that almost every beautiful socialite in the country had had her name linked with Prince Carol's at one time or another, the thin lipped nun considered to be neither here nor there. Since the Prince had chosen to renounce the throne two years ago and flee to the real Paris with the detestable Lupesca, most of his social set had prudently moderated their ways. Mother Superior had even been quite sure that Madame Stevenson – as she was recorded on the Convent books, although she preferred to be known by her maiden name of Dumesca – would have felt obliged to remove her daughter from the Sacred Heart. But the girl was still here, bold as brass, and as usual she was one of the whisperers.

Quite apart from her uncertain pedigree, her blonde hair and heart-shaped face, her straight nose and eyebrows, her soft and yet firm mouth, and her magnificent, wide brown eyes made her by some distance the prettiest girl in the class, and certainly did not help to make her any the more acceptable.

'I do not suppose, Jacqueline,' Sister Veronica remarked frostily, 'that Rumanian history particularly interests you.'

Jacqueline Stevenson sat up straight, squaring the shoulders of her white blouse, a faint flush creeping into the pale cheeks. 'I am very interested in history, Sister.'

'Then perhaps you will repeat to me the names of the leaders of the Wallachian Revolution of 1846?'

'Oh . . .' Jacqueline's mouth opened and then closed again. 'Count Cuza?'

Sister Veronica rapped her desk with her ruler, both a gesture of annoyance and to quell the giggles which rippled across the classroom. 'Count Cuza was the first *Prince* of Wallachia, you silly girl,' she snapped. 'Never a revolutionary. Really, I . . .' It was her turn to shut her mouth with a gasp, as she glanced at the door into the corridor and saw Mother Superior standing there.

At the same moment the girls saw her and hastily rose to their feet.

'Forgive me, Sister Veronica,' Mother Superior said. 'Jacqueline Stevenson, will you come with me, please?'

'Me?' Jacqueline looked from left to right at her classmates, who seemed to be withdrawing from her as far as they could without actually moving. Mother Superior had clearly been on the prowl and listening outside the door, and she was not above using her cane, even on sixteen-year-old fifth formers, if she felt they were not behaving like young ladies.

'Yes, you,' Mother Superior said, and turned back into the corridor.

Jacqueline gazed at Sister Veronica. Her knees seemed paralysed, she simply could not move.

Sister Veronica smiled contentedly. 'Off you go, Jacqueline, quickly. Be sure that your sins will find you

7

out. And if you keep Mother Superior waiting, she will be very angry.'

Jacqueline edged out from behind her desk, fingers wrapped in the blue serge of her skirt, and almost ran to the door. Mother Superior was already half way down the corridor, past the next classroom, so she kept on running. If she stopped, she wouldn't be able to move another step. Of all the terrible luck. But of course it wasn't luck at all. It was sheer dislike. All the nuns and the sisters disliked her, because they disliked Mama, and everything Mama stood for. If only she knew exactly what Mama stood for, or could understand any of the nuances which constantly swirled about her head and made each day at school an utter misery. Could it have been such a crime to marry an American? Theirs was the history she liked to read about, men like Washington and Munroe, Grant and Lee – but American history was not taught at the Bucharest Convent of the Sacred Heart.

'Ah, there you are, child,' remarked Mother Superior. 'You really should stop annoying Sister Veronica. Not that you will have the chance again.'

'The chance?' Jacqueline was so concerned she forgot to say the obligatory 'Mother'. Was she about to be expelled?

'Your mother has sent for you,' Mother Superior said. 'Go to your dormitory and pack your things. There is a car waiting to take you to the station. You are to go home at once.' She glanced at the girl with a certain amount of sympathy. 'Apparently there is some crisis which concerns you.'

The taxi growled its way slowly up the winding road towards the Chateau Dumescu that looked down on the town of Pitesti eighty miles northwest of Bucharest. Like all of rural Rumania, it might have been on a different planet. Once the wide tree-lined boulevards and the elegant villas and the great shops of the capital were left behind, the country reverted to the peasant farms, tiny

8

stone huts with grass or straw roofs which housed entire families and their domestic animals, which were all the average Rumanian could afford. Things would change, of course. So Mama always said. The country was just beginning to find its feet again after the horrors of the War, when Rumania had chosen to side with the Entente Cordiale of Great Britain, France and Russia. On the collapse of the Russian colossus into socialist revolution, it had been abandoned to the full vengeance of the Germans. Jacqueline had only been five years old in 1916, but still had vivid memories of fleeing north, sometimes on foot, holding on to Mama's hand. They had travelled in bitterly cold weather, often with not enough to eat, driven on by fear of being captured by the Germans, who, it was said, impaled babies and little girls on their bayonets and did indescribable things to their mothers.

In the end, though, Rumania had made the right decision, even if it had been disastrously timed. When the central powers of Germany and Austria had finally collapsed, Rumania had taken its place with the victors. Her boundaries had been enlarged, money had poured into the country, new industries and new resources had been discovered and were being developed – little more than fifty miles northeast of Pitesti were the great new oilfields at Ploesti, surely an inexhaustible source of wealth – but so far too much of the financial aid had gone to support the lifestyle regarded as necessary by Crown Prince Carol and his friends. Still, now that the Prince had renounced the throne and fled the country . . . if only she could understand something of that, Jacqueline thought, squirming uncomfortably on the hard seat of the battered Mercedes car which comprised the local taxi service. Why had Mama wept so bitterly the Christmas before last? And could the Prince's departure have had anything to do with their moving back out into the country?

Not that she regretted the move. Before, they had lived in town, and Mama had entertained lavishly. But Jacqueline had seen little of that, as she had been boarded

9

out at the Convent of the Sacred Heart, despite Mama's house being only a mile away. She had only gone home for the weekends, when Mama had been too exhausted to be much company. Since January 1926, however, they had moved from the city to the splendid old castle, once the seat of Mama's Dumescu ancestors, and which now reared up high on the hill, touched a gentle pink by the evening sun. It was an enchanted castle of high, smooth walls and copper-domed turrets. Seen from the road, the crumbling east walls and buttresses and gaping roof holes were not visible. At first Mama had not been at all pleased by their move. So much work had been necessary to make even the structurally sound rooms liveable. And for the first time Mama had complained about money. But, nevertheless, something wonderful had happened. Mama had started to discuss with her the redecorating and furnishing of the rooms they were to use. Suddenly, as never before, Jacqueline felt they were really close, united in a common interest. Together they had pored over books of wall-paper samples, materials and charts of paint colours. They had laughed and sighed together, consoling each other's disappointments when beautiful ideas proved too expensive.

And more, so much more. A real friendship seemed to grow between them. At last Anna Dumesca was treating her daughter as an adult, revealing to her the lively wit, clever charm and strength of will which had taken her to the top of the tennis world, had so swiftly captured the heart of Jacqueline's father, and had kept her for so long a leading figure in Bucharest society. Jacqueline had blossomed in the warmth of their new relationship to become a lovely and vivacious young woman. The lank hair and awkward bony limbs of adolescence had disappeared. Eager to emulate Mama's sense of style and grace, she had begun to dress carefully and tend her hair and skin. Newly aware of her femininity, she began to choose clothes which, despite the prevailing flat-bosomed, boyish fashions, re-vealed the gentle swelling of her breasts and lay gracefully on her rounding hips. Her skirts, like Mama's, came only to just below the knee and her long, smooth calves encased in silk stockings finished in daintily heeled shoes.

Whenever Mama entertained or went visiting, though she only did so very seldom now, Jacqueline was with her, enjoying the admiring glances and remarks she received. There had been one unforgettable occasion only last Easter, when mother and daughter had been invited to take tea with Queen Marie at the Cotroceni Palace. Overwhelmed by the exotic rooms, arches covered with exquisite mosaics, carved ivory screens and priceless *objets d'art*, as well as the number of very aristocratic ladies present, Jacqueline had been amazed and flattered at the attention and compliments paid to her by the Queen. Reclining on a crimson chaise-longue, the fifty-year-old granddaughter of England's Queen Victoria, strikingly draped in bizarre scarves and beads, had summoned the girl to sit beside her. There had followed something like a cross-examination. Between sips of fragrant tea from eggshell thin china cups, Jacqueline had been obliged to answer numerous questions. Did she ride? . . . play tennis? . . . read poetry? . . . had she any young gentlemen friends? . . . anyone special? Blushing furiously, Jacqueline had tried hard not to look gauche and was surprised and delighted when the Queen had turned to Mama and complimented her on her beautiful and charming daughter.

What a very happy occasion that had been for them both, she reflected, as the taxi turned through the outer gate and across the creaking wooden drawbridge – not that the bridge would ever be raised again. Old Anton the butler was there to open the door for her, and the footmen hovered to take her bags. Then there was Mama, at the top of the stone steps, waiting for her. A happy, smiling, exceptionally radiant Mama. And when Anna Dumesca looked radiant, she remained, even at thirty-nine, an utterly beautiful woman. She had strong, pointed features, yellow hair swept up and secured with a silver band, and a brightly lipsticked mouth. She moved with an athletic

11

grace retained from the days when her energetic beauty had swept the tennis courts of Europe.

'Jacqueline!' she cried, and hugged her daughter. 'Oh, Jacqueline. How marvellous to have you home.'

'But Mama . . . Mother Superior said there was some crisis.'

'Crisis? What nonsense. I have decided that you have done with school.'

Jacqueline stepped backwards to stare at her. 'Done with school?'

'Of course. You are far too grown up to wear gymslips and blouses any more. It is time for you to take your place in society. Besides, we are going away, you and I. Away, away, away.'

'Away?' Jacqueline looked left and right. 'Away from Chateau Dumescu?'

'Yes, thank God. Away. We are going to Paris, my darling. Think of it. We are going to Paris!'

Dumescu ancestors gazed disdainfully from the walls of the upper gallery as Jacqueline danced along to her bedroom, unbuttoning her blouse on the way. The long, dismal skirt was dropped to the floor beside her bed, followed by the regulation navy-blue knickers, round sausages of black stockings and the final horror . . . her liberty bodice with its dangling suspenders. What an offence to womanhood they had been. But never again. Paris! And with Mama, in Mama's world. Drawing a lace-trimmed negligee around her, she skipped excitedly to the window, flinging open the tall, double casement to take deep breaths of the cool evening air. Of course she was bound to miss all of this sometimes, she supposed, living on a Paris street. She turned to glance round her bright, pretty bedroom, so lovingly furnished and decorated to exactly her choice, in such contrast to the dramatic hills and forests beyond the castle. And this part of Rumania in particular was so very romantic, as much for its situation as its history. Looming in the distance, clearly visible from her windows, the dark peaks of the Carpathians were outlined against the evening sky. This was Dracula country, and if Jacqueline did not take seriously the legends of blood-sucking vampires brought to world renown by Sheridan le Fanu and Bram Stoker, she knew enough Rumanian history to be aware that the real Count Drakul, who had held this country in defiance of the Turks some four hundred years earlier, had been a terrible and formidable figure who had once had the turbans of Turkish envoys nailed to their heads because they had refused to uncover before him.

Tales like that made her blood tingle. But even if there had never been a single dark deed perpetrated in those mountains, they would still have held a special fascination in her mind, because out there, in the foothills, she had met Jean-Paul.

They had encountered each other entirely by chance on a narrow mountain road, and after a brief, shy introduction, had ridden together down to the village, tentatively arranging to ride that way again the next day. And again the day following that. He had undoubtedly found her attractive, and in her riding breeches and silk shirt she looked much older than in her school uniform. She had been fascinated by his knowledge of the infamous Dracula, and he had obviously been keen to learn that her ancestors had lived here during that time. 'Why,' he had said, smiling. 'You could be a vampire yourself.' The thought had seemed to delight him. It had certainly amused her.

On their third meeting they had dismounted to let the horses drink from a bubbling mountain stream, and she had wanted him to touch her, to look into her eyes, even to take her in his arms. From the way he had flushed, she thought that he must have experienced the same momentary desire. But he had then avoided her for several days, and when they had eventually ridden together again, he had been decidedly cool. It was only on the morning she had told him she was leaving for Bucharest the next day, to return to school, that he had looked closely into her face and touched her hands.

13

'School?' he had asked. 'I did not know you were still at school.'

'Well,' she had said. 'Not for long. I'm in the sixth form.' Which was stretching a point, but she would be in the sixth form that autumn.

His hands had slid gently up to her shoulders as he smiled and bent to kiss her on the forehead. 'I have enjoyed this Easter,' he said. 'More than I have ever enjoyed Easter before. And you did not sink your teeth into me once!' With which he had kissed her again, then quickly mounted and galloped away. On that journey back to Bucharest to start the summer term she had despaired of ever seeing him again. He had told her that he would be returning to France at the end of June, and the term would not finish until mid-July. But now . . . her eyes widened and her heart quickened; she had left school early, and it was not yet the end of June. She hugged herself with a new excitement. Oh, please God, she thought, please God let us meet once more.

She was quite sure that she was in love. Never had any of the charming young aristocrats or handsome, heel-clicking officers with whom she had danced at formal parties had this terribly disturbing effect on her. Only Jean-Paul had ever caused her mouth to dry and her thighs to feel weak. He filled her mind. But she had told no one of the darkly handsome French boy. Keeping secrets had always been part of her personality. She had no really close friends at the convent, and did not even keep a diary into which she could confide her thoughts. Her mind, that utterly private place, was where she dreamed her dreams and made her resolutions. Mama was the only person with whom she could discuss anything of importance, but just as Mama had never confided anything about her marriage or her gentlemen admirers, she did not feel able to confide her feelings either. Especially as she somehow doubted that Mama would approve of Jean-Paul's father, a jewel merchant currently engaged in developing custom in

14

Bucharest. Mama would never consider mixing socially with anyone connected with trade of any kind.

Jacqueline kicked Caesar into a trot, sent him hurrying over the uneven ground that rose slowly towards the first of the hills which marked the true beginnings of the mountains, several miles north of the chateau. It had been simple enough to convince Mama that she wanted one last ride on Caesar, one last canter to the mountains. Mama had no objection to her daughter being as romantically inclined as herself, even if she found nothing attractive about the forbidding, cloud-capped ranges. But Mama did not know that in the next valley, near the village of Chela, was the stud farm where Jean-Paul had been working with horses bred for the famous stables of the French National Equestrian College at Saumur, where, later this year, he hoped to start his training with *Le Cadre Noir*.

Jean-Paul was a serious young man whose ambition had always been for a military career with the French cavalry. A few kind letters of reference from some of his father's more influential clients, together with his own outstanding horsemanship and extensive knowledge of military history, had earned him the opportunity to fulfil his dreams. One of those clients was the owner of the stud farm, and had offered him the chance to stay and work with these magnificent horses while his father was in Bucharest. And he had told Jacqueline how delighted he was, also, having read much folklore as a hobby, to find that he was living in the Lower Carpathians: Dracula country. He dreamed of finding some clue that there really had been vampires in these hills, hoped perhaps to come across some secret grave containing a corpse with a stake driven through its chest. Jacqueline shivered as she reached the top of the slope and reined back – but the sudden chill was at least partly caused by the dipping of the sun behind an enormous cloud, leaving the summer morning cool.

Now she rejoined the road, Caesar's hooves clattering on the cobbles, and now, too, she could see the arched bridge and the houses beyond, clustered around the little church. Would he still be here? If not, there was always the thought that Paris was in France, and he, too, would be in France. But would he want to see her again? She would not be seventeen until next March, and he was a full year older. He was looking forward to starting his career, she knew, and probably had little time to think about girls. Girls? Did he already have a girlfriend waiting for him at home? Compared to herself he seemed very sophisticated, travelled and experienced. Would he really wish to continue seeing her in France, where his friends were no doubt equally sophisticated? Would he find her too boring?

The village was out of sight down the winding road. Jacqueline dismounted to open the farm gate, quite breathless at her own daring in coming here alone to inquire after him. As she led Caesar through she hesitated, almost losing her nerve, but she just had to know if he was still here. Determinedly she remounted, and rounding the old deserted lodge, turned to walk Caesar up the long straight avenue.

They saw each other at the same instant, some three hundred yards apart. Both urged their mounts to a trot, eager to be sure that the advancing figure was no trick of the imagination. Jacqueline's heart thumped so loudly in her chest it almost deafened her to Caesar's hoof beats. She reined in again to a walk, wanting time to collect her thoughts. How to explain her presence? She felt a flush creep up her neck to her face and desperately tried to drop her gaze. But her eyes were locked to Jean-Paul's as he drew nearer, back rigid, reins held low, effortlessly controlling the spirited prancing of his mount.

'Jacqueline!' She had always loved his French pronunciation of her name.

'Jean-Paul!' Her voice barely rose above a whisper.

'Our usual ride?' he inquired, smiling.

She nodded, speechless, and turned Caesar to ride back to the gate with him. No explanation was necessary. He knew why she was here, as she knew he wanted her to be here.

Jean-Paul's horse reared and snorted as they left the road for the open fields. Given his head, he bounded into the lead. Taking a great gasp of joy, Jacqueline slung her hat on to her arm and tossed her hair free into the wind as Caesar galloped to keep up. For a while Jean-Paul was out of sight as the path curved steeply up through the pines; and when she saw him again he was waiting for her by a high outcrop of rock.

'Have you ever been up there?' he asked, indicating a steep turning leading up from the main path.

She shook her head, panting.

'Come. I will show you. But we must go slowly and carefully. The path is very rough.'

For the next half-hour they picked their way in single file up the narrow stony track. Sometimes Jean-Paul would turn to smile at her, but they did not speak to each other.

Suddenly, Jacqueline was aware of the sound of water. Peering through the bushes she saw that their path ran by the side of a rocky stream, only half filled now, in early summer. The sound grew louder as the path became steeper, and, emerging through thick undergrowth, they were faced by a wall of rock some twenty feet high, over which the water cascaded. Jean-Paul turned to lead her up a winding incline from which they at last gained level ground and could look down over the waterfall.

'Oh! It's so beautiful. I never dreamed this was here,' Jacqueline said in awe.

'Don't stop yet. It is much better further on,' Jean-Paul urged her forward.

And he was right. A few minutes later, the trees and rocks were left behind them and they were on soft, green turf. The picture was quite breathtaking. They were in a magic, miniature valley. In the distance loomed the blue-peaked Carpathians, the steep, forest-clad hillsides and bands of lush green framed a wide pool at the bottom. Sky, mountains and trees were mirrored in its still water.

17

Silently they dismounted and led the horses down a shingle pathway through the boulders to drink. They stood gazing at their reflections in the cool liquid crystal.

Jacqueline stooped to scoop a handful of water to her mouth. It had been a long hot ride; her throat was dry and her clothes sticky. Leaving the reins on Caesar's neck she moved to a nearby rock where she sat to tug at her boots.

'I hope you don't mind, but I am dying to splash my feet in it.'

Jean-Paul laughed. 'Why should I mind? That's what the pool is for.'

Jacqueline let her toes ripple the surface. He watched her until the horses finished drinking, then led them to a small cluster of trees, dropped the reins over a branch and loosened their girths.

Jacqueline was startled by a big splash. A light streak flashed by under the water and Jean-Paul's head emerged, grinning at her from the far side of the pool.

'I hope you don't mind,' he mimicked, 'but I was dying to swim in it.'

It was her turn to laugh.

'Why don't you come in too?' he asked.

'I have no bathing-dress with me, and anyway, I can't swim.'

'Nor have I,' he said. But she could already see that as he drifted towards her through the shallows. 'And you don't have to go where it is deep.'

Her mind whirled. He was asking her to take off all her clothes with him there. He might look. She had never seen anyone without clothes on, even at school. And only her nursemaid and Mama had ever seen her. Yet she did want to be in the water with him. Waves of weakness spread from her stomach down to her thighs. Oh, yes, she did want to. And of course she didn't want him to think she was just a silly child.

'Go and look the other way, then.' Amazed at her own daring, she waited while he swam back across the pool.

18

She could not help looking furtively around as she started to undress, as if she felt eyes watching from behind every tree. Once she was sure Jean-Paul's head was turned away, she hurriedly scrambled down the rocks to cover herself with water. She shivered from the double shock of the cold and her nakedness. Moving to a patch of shingle she placed her hands on the bottom for support and kicked vigorously. Cutting silently through the water, Jean-Paul came up beside her.

'Is it not strange that we speak with pride of the progress of civilisation, and yet enjoy nothing more than to return to primitive life. Everyone likes to find a place where they can be alone . . .' he paused, '. . . except for one special person.' He turned to look into her face.

Once again their eyes met in a fixed stare. Again that strange feeling spread from her stomach through her whole body. Her breath came in short gasps.

'You are cold. Come into the deeper water and swim with me.' Jean-Paul took her hands and placed them on his shoulders. 'Just hold on to me and relax. Let yourself float. I will do the swimming,' he instructed, and, pushing with his feet, he carried them both gently across the pool with the easy motion of his arms and legs.

Jacqueline's fear left her as numerous sweet sensations flooded her mind and body. She was so aware of his muscles under her fingers, his feet touching hers, and more than that? She had seen nude male statues, so she had some idea of a man's shape, but had never imagined that the touch of him, softened by the water, could be so delicious.

'Come, we must dry in the sun before we get too chilled,' he said softly, as they returned to the shallows. He waded out, springing up over the rocks to throw himself face down on the grass. Jacqueline obeyed without hesitating and lay, likewise, beside him.

'Why are you not at school?' he asked.

'I have left school. Tomorrow Mama and I leave for Paris.'

19

'Paris?' His head jerked up.

'Yes. We are going to live there. Maybe we could meet there, sometimes?' she suggested tentatively.

'I don't know. It may be possible, but I don't live there, my home is in Bordeaux. I will be staying in Saumur, which is much closer, at least until I finish my training.'

'Oh. I see.' She nodded, trying to hide her disappointment. 'So we may not meet again for a long time.'

'Don't let us think about that now.' He moved closer and she could feel his warm breath on her cheek. As she turned her face to look at him his lips brushed hers . . . then she was in his arms.

Jean-Paul's kisses were soft and caressing at first, but then his tongue sought hers and her lips opened, their mouths crushed together, arms clinging tight, their bodies pressed hard against each other. Jacqueline fell back, at last, panting, and gasped as his hand slid over her breast. Excitement shot through her as his tongue circled her nipple and his mouth closed over it, gently sucking. Then he was between her thighs, that strange, hard part of him probing the damp hair at her groin, pressing, pushing. Her back arched involuntarily, thrusting up to reach him.

Sweet agony. Sweet, beautiful agony. But it doesn't matter that it hurts so . . . just let it go on, and on. There is more to reach.

It was finished. There was surely more to reach. But did it matter?

They hardly spoke at all as they rode back, down past the farm, through Chela. Jean-Paul slowed down only when they reached the path to the Chateau Dumescu.

'I will be visiting Paris more often, now,' he promised. 'It may be difficult to arrange at first. Might not be for at least a month. Do you know what your address will be?'

She shook her head in sudden alarm.

'I shall find you,' he said reassuringly. *'Au revoir, ma chérie.'* He leaned across to kiss her gently one last time. *'Bon voyage.'*

He watched her turn to wave three times before she disappeared through the trees. He couldn't see her tears.

The train began to slow, and Mama powdered her nose and renewed her lipstick. 'Prague,' she said. 'The train always stops for an hour in Prague. We will be able to stretch our legs.'

She realised that Jacqueline was not listening to her and clucked her tongue in impatience. But Jacqueline had hardly listened to her since leaving Bucharest. She sat with her elbow on the armrest, gazing out of the window of the first class sleeper. The journey she had always dreamed of making, the great escape from Rumania, westward, to all the glorious countries of which she had only read – and she was hardly seeing any of it. Suddenly, three days later, she could not be sure *it* had really happened. It had been a moment, no, an eternity, of the most utter, glorious sweetness. And she had wanted it to happen. It had hurt; only the memory of the pain was clear. All the rest had fuzzy edges, very like a dream, or like last Christmas when she had taken too much wine at luncheon and been half asleep all afternoon. But the pain had been entirely bearable, and in memory became almost attractive. It had been a necessary threshold to pleasure at some future date. Some future pleasure. The next time he held her in his arms? When he came to Paris. Then perhaps she might be able to touch him as he had touched her. She had wanted to, but had not been able to make herself, even though she had a feeling he would have liked it. But next time . . .

Would he come? She had not doubted it before. But now she remembered that it had been she who had gone to find him. Would he think her immoral for following her instincts? What nonsense. She had given herself to him, deliberately and gladly. She loved him. And he loved her.

The train had stopped for several minutes, and all around them was the banging of doors, the bustle of people getting off and getting on. Mama had apparently abandoned the idea of a walk, and was instead frowning at her. 'You are not feeling well?' she inquired.

Jacqueline concentrated. It was absolutely vital that Mama should not know what had happened – not yet, anyway. She had been terrified about the stains on her clothes. But she had left them in the dirty linen basket at Chateau Dumescu, and according to Mama they were never going back there.

Now she had to act as though everything was normal. 'I feel fine, Mama, really,' she protested. 'It is just that . . . I am so excited.'

'Of course.' Anna Dumesca's features relaxed. 'Well, so am I excited. By lunchtime tomorrow we shall be in Paris.' She leaned forward. 'Now, I must talk to you about that.'

'Yes, Mama.'

'In Paris, I intend to change my life,' Anna said. 'Back to what it used to be, in the old days. I have been a recluse for too long. In Paris I intend to throw many parties, dinners, receptions. We will entertain on a great scale.'

Now it was Jacqueline's turn to frown. 'It must be a large inheritance,' she said. Over the past two years Mama had been constantly complaining about not having enough money to do any of the things she really wanted.

'Inheritance?' For a moment Anna Dumesca looked bewildered, then she smiled. 'Oh, yes, it is a large inheritance. The point is, my dear Jacqueline, that I shall need you to help me. Oh, I know that you are very young. But you will be seventeen next March, and that is really quite old enough. But it would be best if you did not discuss your age with anyone. No gentleman is going to ask it, anyway. It would also be best if you did not admit to being my daughter, in Paris. You will be my young sister.' She gave another smile. 'We shall close the gap between our ages. Would you not like to have me as your sister?'

It slowly penetrated Jacqueline's mind that her mother was inviting her to enter *her* life, a life she knew little about. She hoped this would not entail much flirting. That

22

was impossible, as she had just given herself to Jean-Paul. She supposed she really should tell Mama all about Jean-Paul. But now was not the time.

Anna Dumesca was realising that what she had just said had not had the impact she anticipated. 'All this will mean,' she went on, 'that we must fit you out with some new clothes. Shopping in Paris,' she said, dreamily. 'We will go to Balenciaga. Oh, it is the most heavenly experience in the world, my darling girl.'

It did sound rather delightful. And new clothes, expensive adult clothes, would surely make her even more attractive to Jean-Paul when next they were able to meet. Until then . . . well, she would help Mama in every way, of course. But she was certainly not going to submit to any middle-aged lecher running his hands up her arms or across her shoulders. Besides, Mama could not really mean to allow that, she thought with relief.

The apartment was situated on the Avenue Georges V, not a stone's throw from the Champs Elysées, and in the other direction the Seine was hardly any further away. Even more exciting, to Jacqueline's mind, were all the famous restaurants and nightclubs with which the area abounded, not that she supposed she would ever be allowed to visit them.

The apartment itself was a place of high ceilings and elegant drapery, of high windows, too, which looked down on to the busy street below, or on to a secluded back garden. The furniture was of the over-stuffed variety, upholstered in reds and golds, so different from the delicate shades with which they had decorated the chateau. There were exquisitely carved occasional tables, on one of which stood a Buhl clock, a marvel of ebony inlay on a rosewood base. Jacqueline felt it might all be very difficult to live with.

'Worth a fortune,' Mama said. She did not seem so very excited about inheriting all of this. It was the fact of being in Paris that was making her happy.

Which was entirely correct, Jacqueline thought. It was this city, the being there, which mattered, not rich possessions. But the clothes! They devoted their first week entirely to their wardrobes, for suddenly Mama seemed to have an almost inexhaustible supply of credit, and could snap her fingers and buy whatever she liked. For Jacqueline there were voile summer dresses, printed chiffon afternoon dresses and neatly tailored gaberdine suits. She had silk petticoats and suede gloves, hats made of silk and hats made of heavy straw, suede shoes and leather shoes, light silk stockings and black stockings, handbags and purses, an exquisite black lace dinner gown with black crêpe-de-chine lining for the skirt and flesh coloured georgette under the bodice, which made her look almost naked from the waist up. Mama gave her a pearl necklace to wear with it, and several costume rings for her fingers as well as dangling ear-rings and a variety of brooches. In anticipation of winter, she had a black wool coat trimmed with grey fox fur, and a cerise felt hat. Jacqueline was quite overwhelmed, and spent hours before her mirror trying on clothes and then removing them again; she changed her dress three times in every day.

Her one regret was that to complete her metamorphosis into a sophisticated young woman, her golden hair had to be cut into the fashionable bob, which she felt left her face too isolated. 'But it is such a beautiful face,' the coiffeur said. 'So strong. Such a splendid bone structure. You would be entrancing, mademoiselle, were you bald.'

Which had Mama beaming her pleasure.

But new clothes and new haircuts were only a part of their new way of life. Mama had either inherited, or bought, or was hiring – she was very vague about the whole business – not only an enormous Renault motor car, which waited for them in the courtyard beneath the apartment, but also two horses, on which they took their exercise in the Bois de Boulogne every morning after breakfast.

'*Every* morning?' Jacqueline asked, on the first day it rained. 'But why?'

24

'Because that is what people do in Paris,' Anna said firmly. 'People who are anybody.'

With which Jacqueline had to be satisfied, although it seemed an awful shame to have her new riding habit soaked. This was no old-shirt-and-britches affair as in the hills outside Pitesti. For walking her horse in the Bois de Boulogne she wore a blue velvet jacket over a cream silk shirt, flawless cream buckskin jodhpurs, and a silk hat with a ribbon floating away behind her. 'You look exquisite,' Mama told her. 'Perfectly exquisite.'

Which left Jacqueline more confused than ever, because Mama had always, in the past, been far more concerned with her own appearance than her daughter's. But she also thought that she looked at her very best, and dreamed of the day when Jean-Paul would reach Paris, and come riding in the Bois. Because of course he *would* come riding, as he was very definitely somebody when it came to horses. Only another two weeks, or perhaps three, until he would come. Jacqueline could hardly wait.

So she rode with her mother every day, and smiled at all the people who smiled at her, and whom her mother also acknowledged, but with whom she never stopped to chat. Jacqueline was therefore quite astonished at the end of the week when they turned round a bend in the bridle path they were following and came face to face with another couple out riding. She was a dark, splendid looking woman, and he was a somewhat plump man, who wore a little moustache and had apple-pink cheeks, and whose face was definitely familiar. Mama immediately drew rein and signalled her to do the same, then cried out, 'Why, Monsieur Caraiman, how splendid to see you! And Madame Caraiman, of course.'

'Anna?' asked Monsieur Caraiman, obviously in total consternation. 'Anna Dumesca? Can it really be you?'

His companion's face had taken on a furious expression. 'She has followed you,' she snapped. 'All the way from Bucharest, she has followed you.'

25

'How absurd,' Anna said, calmly. 'I have come into an inheritance. You did not know that I have French relatives? So I have decided to come and live in Paris.'

Monsieur Caraiman was looking past her to Jacqueline. 'And this?' he asked.

'Is my young sister, Jacqueline,' Anna said.

'I did not know you had a sister either, Anna.' M. Caraiman raised his hat, which he had not done to Mama. 'I am enchanted, mademoiselle.'

'Sister,' snorted Madame Caraiman. 'Really, Madame Dumesca . . .'

'Sister,' Mama said firmly. 'It has been delightful to see you again, Charles. Now we really must be on our way. If you are ever in Rue Georges V, why, we are number thirty-seven, third étage. Good day to you. Jacqueline.'

'Monsieur. Madame,' Jacqueline murmured, feeling utterly confused, and kicking her horse to catch up with her mother. 'What a remarkable couple,' she said. 'I do not think Madame was pleased to see you, Mama.'

'Madame was horrified to see me,' Anna said.

'But . . .' Jacqueline bit her lip. Obviously Mama and Monsieur Caraiman had been friends at some stage. Why, he might even have been a visitor at the Bucharest town house in the old days, which was probably where she would have seen him. Because his face was most certainly familiar. 'Do you think you should have given them our address?' she asked.

'Of course I had to give them our address, silly girl,' Anna said. 'How else would he know where to find us?'

'Do we want him to find us?'

'Of course. Why else do you suppose we have been riding in the Bois every day for the past week, regardless of the weather? It was to make sure of encountering him. Now that we have done so, oh, Magda may scream and make a scene. She always did that. But we shall have an invitation. There can be no doubt of it.'

'I'm sure we can do better than the Caraimans,' Jacqueline asserted as they returned to the stables. 'Anyway, he's married.'

'Oh, don't be stupid,' Mama snapped. 'Married? Of course they are not married. Charles already has a wife, in Bucharest.'

'In Bucharest? You mean he is really Rumanian?'

'Of course he is Rumanian, silly girl. And how could we possibly do better than the Crown Prince Carol?'

The Crown Prince Carol! So that was why his face was familiar. Not that Jacqueline had seen his face very often, and in fact, she had not seen it at all for the past two years, since he had fled the country.

The Crown Prince had, she knew from the newspapers, been a source of worry and distress to both his parents and to those statesmen who were attempting to turn Rumania into a modern and progressive nation. Totally unlike his stern, German, soldier father, King Ferdinand, Carol had taken after his gay, brilliant, poetic mother, Marie – who had been so kind to her – only most of his brilliance and his romanticism had been directed to the pursuit of women. His parents had married him off to the Princess Helen of Greece almost as soon as the War had ended – having annulled an unfortunate earlier marriage with an adventuress named Zizi Lambrino. But although the couple had had a son, Prince Michael, the union had not been a happy one – they had not lived as man and wife, it was rumoured, since it was known a child was on the way – and he had soon fallen back into his old life, and surrounded himself with his old friends, of whom Magda Lupesca was the most famous. But could one of them have also been the almost equally famous woman tennis player, Anna Dumesca? Her own mother? There was an interesting thought. Was he really one of Mama's admiring gentlemen friends? A friend, or more than that? Why had the Lupesca been so angry to see her? Oh, no, surely not Mama. But Mama's departure from the bright lights and lavish parties of Bucharest for the solitary exile of Chateau Dumescu had almost

27

exactly coincided with Prince Carol's final quarrel with his parents, his renunciation of all rights to the throne in favour of his son, and his departure for Paris, taking the Lupesca with him. There was a lot of coincidence in that. Just as there was also too much coincidence for Mama to have inherited money in Paris from a relative she had never mentioned before, but who just happened to have lived in the city in which the Prince had taken up residence.

Mama and Prince Carol had been lovers! That would make Mama a courtesan; Jacqueline had read about such women in history books. A courtesan might occupy an important, even an honoured place in history, but she was still . . . Her mind refused to frame the word.

Undoubtedly he had sent for her. Without the Lupesca's knowledge? Jacqueline could have sworn that was so from the shock on the woman's face when they met. But then, she could also have sworn that the Prince had been utterly surprised to encounter Anna, and that did not fit her theory at all. Or he was a very capable actor, and the Lupesca might well be a very capable actress. Why adults had to play such silly games was beyond her. But it was incredibly exciting, to suppose that Mama, and perhaps she as well, were about to move back into the very highest society. What a tale to tell Jean-Paul. But then she thought it might be best not to tell Jean-Paul at all, in case he did not approve of courtesans. Better to wait until she knew him better.

How silly, to think of knowing a man better, when she already knew him better than any man in the world? Anyway, the invitation, when it came, would be very unlikely to include her as well.

But an invitation did arrive, only two days later. And it was addressed to both Madame Anna Dumesca, and Mademoiselle Jacqueline Dumesca, requesting the presence of them both at a soirée to be held at the house of Monsieur and Madame Caraiman on the following Saturday.

* * *

28

To Jacqueline's surprise, it was only after the arrival of the invitation that Mama became nervous. Hitherto her confidence and determination and her obvious enjoyment of their new life had been remarkable, but that evening she took three times as much sweet sherry, and spent supper staring at her daughter as if she were a stranger.

After the meal, she carefully closed the door and then sat beside Jacqueline on the sofa by the window. 'Now, my darling,' she said. 'We must have a chat, woman to woman, eh?'

Jacqueline put down her book, her amazement growing, and now accompanied by a faint unease.

'I know we have never had such a chat before,' Anna went on. 'I have not been a good mother to you, have I?'

'Oh, Mama . . .'

'Do not trouble to argue the point,' Anna said. 'I have had a hard life. For a while when you were very young I resented you. I know I lost the final at Wimbledon in 1910, but it was a near thing. I would have won it the following year, I am sure. But there I was, with a new baby. I could not play. I could never play again, at Wimbledon. The English are so stuffy about these things. Indeed, they are the most stuffy people in the world.'

Jacqueline did not understand. 'You mean they resented your marrying?' she asked.

Anna gazed at her for several seconds, obviously wrestling with an enormous decision. Then she patted her daughter on the knee and got up. 'I have never been married,' she said.

'*Never?*' She did not know what to say.

Anna arranged herself in front of the window, theatrically, facing her. 'I fell in love. Can that be a crime? He was a midshipman on an American warship. Oh, he was very handsome. Well, you can look in the mirror, can't you? So, we loved. I am only half Rumanian, you know. The other half of me is . . .' she hesitated, and Jacqueline had the strangest feeling she was deciding. 'French. Well,

29

that is easy to see as well, is it not? I am romantic. So I loved, and I paid the penalty.'

'You mean my father wouldn't marry you?'

Anna waved her hand, deprecatingly. 'He never knew. By the time I knew for certain his ship had gone, back to America. I was not going to chase a man half way across the world, begging him to marry me. I had my child, here in Paris.'

Jacqueline sat in stunned silence. She was illegitimate. Somehow she felt that she had always known that. The sisters at the Convent must have known, or guessed, which would explain why they so obviously disapproved of her. She was a child of love. She supposed that somehow that was romantic. But how could she ever consider marriage to Jean-Paul, who came from a most respectable family?

It was the first time she had considered marriage to Jean-Paul at all, she realised. But suddenly it had become very important.

'I had supposed it was all a secret,' Mama was saying. 'But of course the gossip columnists got hold of it. The following year my entrance to Wimbledon was refused. I could do nothing but return home. My mother was still alive, living at the chateau. Do you remember your grandmother?'

Jacqueline shook her head. She was still trying to think.

'Of course you wouldn't,' Anna said. 'She died in 1914. And then the War . . . by then I had made certain friends. Friends at Court. I fled with them when the Germans came in 1916. You came too. Do you remember 1916?'

'I remember 1917,' Jacqueline shuddered.

'Happy days,' Mama said, to Jacqueline's astonishment. 'It was then that I got to know Carol. Of course, he is a trifle younger than I.' She shot her daughter a glance. 'Only a trifle, you understand.'

A matter of five years or so, Jacqueline calculated. But she nodded.

'But then there were complications, his marriage to Zizi Lambrino – what he saw in her is a complete mystery to

30

me – and the quarrels with his father, the King, and then when they made him leave Zizi and marry Princess Helen of Greece . . .'

'But if he was married to Madame Lambrino,' Jacqueline asked in mystification, 'how could he leave her?'

'Royalty, my dear Jacqueline, can do anything. The King simply had the marriage annulled. Then Carol would have liked to marry me. I am positive of this. But a royal princess had already been chosen for him. And then along came this Jewess, Lupesca.' She suddenly gave a bright smile, and came back across the room to sit down. 'That is all behind us now. If I have told you all of this, it is because it is all behind us. There is nothing but the future to look forward to, because now neither of us has any past. Isn't that exciting?'

Jacqueline nodded, her mother obviously wanted agreement. She found the idea of having no past somewhat terrifying. Besides, she did not see how anyone could have had a more exciting past than Mama herself.

'So we must seize whatever opportunity comes our way,' Anna went on, watching her very closely. 'Now, I have never discussed any, well, intimate things with you before, because I have not considered it necessary. You are a woman, now, and, what is more important, everyone else can see that, too. I know you have had absolutely no experience with men, but this is all to the good. You are innocent, and yet obviously aware. On Saturday you will be moving into the very highest society, not only in Paris, but in all the world. You are beautiful, and you will be beautifully and expensively dressed. But you must also remember that being beautiful is a job of work. Beauty is wit and riposte as much as physical looks. You must concentrate, and have but a single glass of champagne. I want you to scintillate. Do that, and your future is assured.'

Anna had been speaking so fast that Jacqueline found it difficult to keep up with her. Obviously, as they were talking woman to woman, now was the time to tell her about Jean-Paul. 'Yes, Mama,' she said. 'But Mama . . .'

31

'Now,' Anna said. 'As to the matter of your virginity. A woman's virginity is her most precious possession. You must allow no man less than royalty the ultimate favour. Understand me well. A rich industrialist, a famous sportsman, or actor, may be permitted an occasional liberty. But nothing more than that. You must be very clear in your mind about this. To stumble now would be to throw away all of our hopes for the future. I hope you understand what I am saying, Jacqueline.'

Confessions regarding Jean-Paul would have to wait, and Jacqueline did not see that it mattered for a few more days. If Mama really thought there was some chance that she would marry an itinerant prince, she was going to be disappointed. But even if there had been, she had no intention of considering the possibility – she was going to marry Jean-Paul, and he was going to marry her, and the fact that she had yielded her virginity to him could only draw them closer together. Surely the fact that she was illegitimate would mean nothing to him?

She was beginning to get quite excited about the soirée. She wore her new black dress, of course, somewhat nervously, as it would be the first time she had appeared in public in anything quite so daring. She stayed close to Mama's elbow as they made their way along a sumptuously carpeted hall to the main reception of the Prince's vast apartment. The Prince's. It was incredible, but it was true, because there he was, with Magda Lupesca. Her undoubtedly pretty face twisted into dislike when she saw Mama, an expression which did not change as she greeted Jacqueline. 'Mademoiselle Dumesca,' she said. 'How good of you to come.'

'Mademoiselle Dumesca!' Prince Carol seized her hand and kissed it, and to her consternation touched her flesh with his tongue. 'Now my happiness is complete.'

Jacqueline glanced at Mama in alarm, but Mama continued to smile, while the Lupesca's face became even more twisted.

Then they were entering the huge drawing room, lost in a crowd of some fifty people. There were sportsmen whose names appeared in every newspaper, lean and fit and saturnine; industrialists of whom Jacqueline had never heard, but who were obviously very wealthy, if wealth could be judged by enormous paunches and gold watch chains on the men, by plunging decolletages and gleaming jewellery on the women; and writers, artists and poets, she was told, hungry-looking young men in floppy bow ties and bright shirts, who stood on the edges of the throng and looked furtively to right and left, as if uncertain why they were there. But there was no obvious royalty in sight.

Mama did not seem to mind. She swept around the room, greeting people who she may or may not have known, introducing Jacqueline, trailing a glass of champagne from her left hand and an empty cigarette holder from her right. It was all very exciting, and Jacqueline, who lacked the advantages of a cigarette holder, found that she had finished her first glass and taken another from a passing tray before she had even caught her breath, and was half way through this one as well. So much for wit and riposte, she thought, as her mind went completely blank, and she had to rely upon her smile and the second look people took at her bosom to make sure it was flesh-coloured material and not actually flesh.

'So you are the famous Mademoiselle Dumesca,' the woman murmured.

Jacqueline realised that she had lost Mama, and was now standing next to a very tall, statuesque woman, not at all elegantly dressed or pretty to look at, but with an immensely strong face, and a manner to match it in confidence.

Now the face smiled. 'Do not look so terrified, my dear. I am sure your mother would be disappointed. I am Draga Karaklaic.'

Obviously she expected Jacqueline to know who she was, but Jacqueline had no idea. Draga Karaklaic gave another smile. 'I am an old friend of your mother's,' she said. 'I am sure we shall see a lot more of each other, now that you are living in Paris. Why, Your Highness.'

Jacqueline realised that in addition to Mama, she had lost the immediate company of all the men who had been clustering round. But she was not alone; apart from Madame Karaklaic, Prince Carol was standing beside her, and holding out another glass of champagne, while removing her empty one from her fingers.

And now Madame Karaklaic, who had suddenly become a necessary friend, was also moving away, still smiling at her, leaving her totally exposed, and undoubtedly being watched by everyone in the room.

'Jacqueline Dumesca,' Prince Carol said. 'Do you know, Anna never told me before that she had a sister?'

'I . . .' Jacqueline tried desperately to collect her thoughts, and made the mistake of taking another sip of champagne. 'I think she has always been rather ashamed of me.'

'Ashamed of you?' inquired the Prince. 'Envious of you, more likely.'

Jacqueline discovered that they were strolling, apparently without direction, across the room, and that people were hastily ceasing conversation and parting to let them through. Where, oh where, was Mama?

'I meant because I have never been any good at tennis,' she explained. 'Or any games, really.'

'None at all?' asked the Prince, and she realised that they had been following a direction, and had now arrived before a pair of double doors, which were being opened for them by a manservant. 'I find that hard to believe.'

Presumably there was a continuation of the party in here. But as Jacqueline stepped through, she discovered that this room was entirely empty of human beings. It was almost as large as the other, but fitted out as a studio, with a grand piano as well as an elaborate desk against the far wall, and a divan draped with leopardskin rugs in the centre. She turned in alarm, but the doors had already

34

closed behind the Prince, who continued to smile at her. 'My den,' he said, with a wave of his hand.

'It is magnificent,' she said. 'But . . . don't you think . . .?'

He took her elbow and walked her towards the piano. 'I wish to hear about these games you play so badly,' he said. 'I wish to learn all about you.'

'About me, Your Highness?'

It had slipped out, and for a moment he was taken aback. His smile faded, and then returned quickly enough. 'Monsieur, my dear girl. Or rather, Charlie. You may call me Charlie. Anna has been indiscreet. But . . . I shall forgive her.' He took the still half full glass of champagne from her fingers, set it on an occasional table, turned her towards him, and held her waist. Before she could protest, he had lifted her from the floor and set her upon the piano. She gave a sigh of relief, having momentarily misunderstood his intentions, and then a gasp of consternation, for instead of releasing her, his fingers slid down her dress to caress her thighs and her knees.

July – September 1927

I owe a duty, where I cannot love.

Aphra Behn, *The Moor's Revenge*

JACQUELINE DID not really remember leaving the private room. She slapped his hand and ran through the doorway back to the party. She moved from conversational group to conversational group, smiling and talking, drinking far more champagne than was good for her, feeling the room begin to spin about her head, feeling too the Prince's eyes on her, and watching him smile at her across the crowded floor. She could not understand it. Surely he was angry? Yet he looked almost pleased. But no doubt princes were trained to look pleased no matter how angry they might be.

'I think you have made quite a conquest with Monsieur Caraiman,' remarked Madame Karaklaic.

Jacqueline's head jerked; she had not realised she was standing next to her mother's friend.

'I do assure you, madame . . .'

'It is nothing to be embarrassed about, my dear,' Madame Karaklaic said. 'He is an attractive man. I wish I could be as fortunate. But . . .' she shrugged. 'Instead, I will wish you every good fortune. I see a great future opening in front of you.'

'A great future?' She related the conversation to Mama as they were driven home. 'I just cannot imagine what she was talking about.'

'To be a personal friend of a prince is to be famous,' Anna explained.

36

'Oh.'

'Everyone knows who he really is. Of course they do. He calls himself Monsieur Caraiman to avoid all the embarrassment it would cause the French government were he to live here openly as Prince Carol. But Draga Karaklaic is quite right. You have made a considerable impression on him. So much so that he has invited you to dinner with him. Tomorrow night.'

'Dinner? With the Prince?' The car was slowing to enter their courtyard and she had to keep quiet until they gained the privacy of the apartment. Then she could protest. 'That is quite impossible.'

Anna raised her eyebrows.

'You don't understand, Mama. He doesn't really like me at all. He took me into his private room tonight . . .'

'I saw,' Anna said. 'Everyone saw. I was so proud of you.'

'Proud of me?' Jacqueline cried. 'My God! Mama, he was . . . well, stroking me. My legs and arms.'

Anna shrugged. 'Men, even princes, are like that, Carol more than most. Very demonstrative. But only to people he likes.'

'Well, I don't like him when he does things like that,' Jacqueline declared. 'Anyway, I managed to get away from him.'

Anna frowned. 'That was silly of you. I keep forgetting that you are only a child.' She sighed. 'You must remember, my dear, that princes are not like ordinary people. They have to be humoured. Just keep telling yourself that a prince, especially your prince, can do no wrong, and you will go very far. Oh, very far indeed. Anyway, no harm appears to have been done. He has invited you to dinner.'

'I'm sure he's just being polite,' Jacqueline said. 'I think I will let you go alone, Mama, as I am sure that is what he really wants. I shall have a headache.'

'But, my dear girl,' Anna said, quietly and with a happy smile. 'He has not invited me at all.'

In silence Jacqueline allowed the possible implications to sink into her brain.

She wanted to refuse, but that would mean a quarrel with Mama, and she wanted that even less. Mama clearly supposed that a great romance was about to spring up between an ex-prince and her own daughter, and counted this as the most important thing in the world – which was incredible if she had once thought of marrying him herself. Certainly Mama must know what kind of a man he really was, and yet she had virtually told her to accept his advances, to let him caress her . . . perhaps even more.

The situation made it even more difficult to explain about Jean-Paul. If only he would come to visit her. Once Mama met him and got to know him, things would be much easier, though perhaps she would suppose he was just an excuse.

As for Prince Carol, well, he at the least could be told that she was already betrothed. She had only to make up her mind how much she could trust him; or even better, not to be drawn into a private room with him at all. That, of course, would depend upon who else was at dinner with them. But she felt sure she could handle any situation that might arise.

'Mademoiselle Dumesca! Jacqueline!' The Prince himself came from the drawing room to take her hands. 'How lovely you look.'

'Monsieur.' She let him kiss her hands, taking her whole arm into his fingers as he did so, and moving his lips from her knuckles to her wrist. 'It is a pleasure to be here.'

The Prince straightened and smiled at her. 'I had feared you would not come. My behaviour was unforgiveable on that evening. I was impatient, overcome with delight at meeting so ravishing a creature.' He tucked her arm under his and escorted her into the drawing room.

'I am sure there was nothing to forgive,' she murmured, but halted at the doorway to the dining room in consternation; there was no one else present, except for a footman, and the huge table was set with only two covers. 'But . . . Madame Caraiman?'

'Has gone to visit friends in the country.' He urged her forward, past the doorway. 'We shall have a tête-à-tête, you and I. Because I wish to get to know you. I want to make up for all the years that have passed, *without* my knowing you.' He squeezed her hand.

They were now in the drawing room and the doors were closed behind them. She was alone with the exiled Crown Prince of Rumania. She was also alone with a lecher. Jacqueline felt a tremendous urge to run to the window, throw it open and scream for help.

The Prince had released her, was himself pouring two cocktails, one of which he now held out for her.

'Is it strong?' she asked. 'I have never drunk anything stronger than champagne.'

'Ha ha,' he laughed. 'Champagne. But this is a champagne cocktail, my dear Jacqueline. It has a little brandy added, and some bitters. Just to give it a little flavour. There is no need to fear it.'

And indeed it had a very pleasant taste. It occurred to her that it might be best to get drunk as rapidly as possible so as to put him off her. She drained the glass.

'I see you do like it.' He had hardly sipped his. Now he refilled her glass. 'But no more after this one. We don't want you to faint!' He winked at her. 'I do not like my women numb.'

Jacqueline realised that he was assuming the evening was already his. And wasn't he right, because she was alone with him? He had taken her hand again, to lead her to one of the sofas against the far wall. 'I was sure you would forgive me for last night,' he said. 'And when I knew you would come again tonight . . . oh, my dear, dear Jacqueline.' He kissed her hands once more, again slid his fingers up her arm, pushing them under her sleeves just to touch her armpit. It gave her a most uncanny feeling, a sudden understanding accompanied by a hurting rush of fear, of how much he would want from her.

And would not have. She attempted to move, and instead fell backwards. Before she could recover herself, he was lying on her, crushing the breath from her body. 'Do you know,' he smiled, 'I was going to seduce you with lobster and champagne? But we will have that later, eh?' He was trying to kiss her mouth, but she moved her head to and fro trying to free herself. He followed, holding her lips with his own, pushing his tongue into her mouth, massaging her breasts. 'You are heaven,' he said, at last withdrawing to breathe. 'You are a delight. You are a dream come true. You are . . . you must not be shy with me, Jacqueline. There is no need for shyness. I wish to see you, oh, how I wish to see you.' He pushed himself away from her. 'Show me. Show me everything.'

Jacqueline could only stare at him. The assault, for it had been nothing less than that, had happened so suddenly that all of her carefully prepared defences had been swept aside. She felt paralysed with fear. She needed time to think, but she knew she was not going to be given that chance. The only alternative was to get up and run from the room. Yet again? She had no idea what Mama would say to that. But if she stayed . . .

'I will show you first,' he said. 'I will show you what you have done to me.'

To her horror he began to undress, but only from the waist down, getting up to remove his trousers and underpants. There was something utterly ludicrous about a distinctly plump, moustachioed and carefully coiffured man, wearing dinner jacket and dress shirt, socks, suspenders and shoes, but lacking anything in between, especially when he had spindly legs. But there was nothing ludicrous about the enormity which was pointing at her. 'The Eiffel Tower,' he said, proudly. 'That is what they call it. The Eiffel Tower. And it is all yours, my darling girl.'

Jacqueline pushed herself upright, and he knelt before her, parting her legs with his hands. 'I will help you,' he said. 'I will be your lady's maid, eh?' His hands came up roughly under her skirt to grasp her buttocks and lift her from the sofa, and then moved down again, fingers locked in her knickers. She gasped and tried to turn, but was held

40

by his grip, now fastened on her thighs, leaving her as exposed as he was. She watched his head coming forward. He meant to kiss her, there. But that was impossible. She just could not imagine . . . she pushed down, and back at the same time, and slid along the couch, but fell over again as he would not let her go. 'You are so shy,' the Prince told her, abandoning his original plan and bringing his hands up her body, carrying her skirt to the waist. 'I like that. I like my women to be shy. But you, you are a treasure. You are so virginal, so pure . . .'

At last, her tumbling mind thought. An escape. 'No!' she shouted. 'You are mistaken.' His body descended on to hers with a thump. 'I am not a virgin.' But it was too late. He was crashing down on her and forcing himself into her again and again and again, before suddenly collapsing with even greater force than before. She could only lie and pant, and wait for him to move, which he did very soon. He pushed himself up, and scowled at her. '*What* did you say?'

Tears were trickling from her eyes. She felt hurt, humiliated, utterly ravished. There had been no love, no respect in what had happened. She was the victim of nothing but lust. And that lust was now spent. Well, she would obtain a little revenge. She dried her eyes on her sleeve and glared at him. 'You are not the first, monsieur.'

He left the sofa, picking up his trousers to put them on. 'You . . . that sister of yours . . .'

'She is my mother, monsieur.'

'Your *mother*? My God, I should have known. That whore, palming off her whorish daughter . . .'

Jacqueline got up herself, all her fear overcome by a towering rage. 'Monsieur! That is an insult. My mother . . .'

'Is a whore,' he shouted. 'As she has made her daughter into a whore. I have been tricked. I have been betrayed,' he flung out his arm. 'Get out! Get out, slut. Get out, or I will have you thrown out!'

Jacqueline's arm rose to hit him, but seeing his

dangerous anger, she thought better of it and ran from the room.

'*What* did you say happened?' Anna Dumesca shouted. 'You mean you ran out on him, again? You ran out on Prince Carol, twice?'

'You don't understand,' Jacqueline protested. 'He . . . he hardly got me through the door, but he threw me on a settee, and . . . and *raped* me, Mama. That's what he did. I've been raped.' She had not truly realised it on the drive home. Then she had refused even to think of what had happened. But now she was aware of being wildly angry. 'I should go to the police. I will go to the police.'

'Oh, don't be ridiculous,' Anna snapped. 'How can anyone accuse a Crown Prince of rape? But you mean . . .' her tone softened. 'He actually entered you?'

'He did, Mama,' Jacqueline said. 'It was quite horrible.'

'Oh, bah. The first time is always horrible. You will get used to it. But if he entered you . . . he will forgive you again. Oh, indeed, he will forgive you again. But really, my dear child . . .'

'He will not forgive me again, Mama,' Jacqueline said.

Anna turned to look at her. 'You didn't . . . knee him, or something like that?'

'No, I didn't,' Jacqueline said, somewhat to her own surprise. Oh, why hadn't she kneed the beast, right in his Eiffel Tower? She just hadn't thought of it. 'But he turned me out.'

'Prince Carol turned you out? After making love to you? I don't understand. Why should he do that?'

'Well . . .' Jacqueline drew a long breath. But it had to come out now. 'When he learned that I wasn't . . . well, that he wasn't the first, he became very angry.'

Slowly Anna lowered herself into a chair, staring at her daughter.

'And then he became very abusive,' Jacqueline told her. 'About you. He called you, well, he was very rude. I'm afraid I told him that I was your daughter instead of your sister. Then he threw me out.'

Anna was breathing heavily. 'Not the first?'

'Mama . . .'

Anna got up again. 'Not the first?' she screamed. 'You mean you . . . and some servant?'

'Of course not, Mama.'

'Then who was it?'

'Well, it was someone I met.'

'In Bucharest? At the Sacred Heart? I cannot believe that.'

'It was at Pitesti, in the hills. Oh, Mama, you'll adore him. He is a French boy. Well, a man, really. So kind, and gentle, and . . .'

'A Frenchman? Some . . . some tourist? And you let him . . . oh, my God! What a catastrophe. Little brute. I should beat you until the blood runs. You have ruined me. You have ruined us all, you silly slut. You . . .' She reached for her daughter, but Jacqueline had already flinched away.

'Mama,' she said. 'I know you're angry. I was going to tell you, but somehow there wasn't ever time. And anyway, after what happened tonight, my God, I have been violated. What will Jean-Paul say?' The words just slipped out. She hadn't considered Jean-Paul until now. What would happen when he found out? What would he do? Challenge the Prince to a duel? That seemed the only possibility, and that would be a catastrophe.

'Violated,' Anna breathed. 'Violated. Yes, if it can be put about that this French scoundrel violated you . . .'

'Mama!' Jacqueline protested.

'Be quiet, girl, and let me think.' Anna swung to face the door as it opened to admit her butler. 'Oh, get out, Gaston. We are not to be interrupted.'

'I apologise, madame,' he said. 'But there is a visitor who insists upon seeing you.'

He was almost pushed to one side, as Madame Karaklaic entered the room.

* * *

43

'Draga!' Anna exclaimed, instinctively patting her hair into place and attempting a somewhat uncertain smile. 'The course of true love never did run smooth.'

'Love?' Draga Karaklaic demanded, and gazed at Jacqueline. 'We have made a mistake. Her Majesty will be very angry.'

'Now, really, my dear Draga,' Anna protested. 'There is no need to assume the worst. When I tell you exactly what happened . . .'

'I already know exactly what happened,' Madame Karaklaic announced.

Jacqueline sat down. The entire room seemed to be spinning around her head, and she had no idea what was going on.

Anna was frowning. 'Indeed?'

'Do you not suppose I have someone inside the Prince's establishment?' Madame Karaklaic demanded. 'I find out about his every move.'

'Ah,' Anna said, clearly disturbed. 'Yes.'

'May I ask, madame,' Madame Karaklaic went on, her tone icy. 'What you expected to gain by this subterfuge? One is inclined to agree with the Prince, that the girl is a slut.' Again a glance at Jacqueline, who wanted to protest, but did not dare open her mouth.

'I did not know,' Anna wailed. 'Believe me, Draga, I did not know.'

Madame Karaklaic's expression softened a fraction. 'Then you are just unfortunate,' she said. 'To have such a daughter. But, there we are, the damage is done.'

'It can't be irretrievable,' Anna protested. 'He entered her. He was momentarily put out, of course, but he will get over it. She is still beautiful, and . . .'

'And by now His Highness is beginning to think,' Madame Karaklaic said, again coldly. 'And with reason. He will be asking himself how the penniless Madame Dumesca managed to set herself up in Paris in such style. He will be asking himself why one of his old mistresses should be pushing her daughter in front of him. He will

44

be coming up with answers, madame. And he will be angry. As he is already angry at having this . . . this wanton inveigled into his bed!'

Jacqueline stood up. This was too much. 'Madame,' she said. 'I must protest. I . . .'

'Be quiet, girl,' Anna snapped. 'We shall have to mend our fences. It can be done. I shall . . .'

'You will pack your bags and leave Paris immediately,' Madame Karaklaic said. 'Her Majesty will want a full account of what has happened, and your best chance lies in throwing yourself upon her mercy. I am sending a report back myself by courier in the morning.' She gave a sardonic smile. 'You will not wish to arrive too long behind him.'

'You . . .' even Anna was getting angry. 'You think you can order me about? What if I refuse to leave? What if I continue to live here?'

Madame Karaklaic shrugged. 'That is up to you, my dear Anna. But the rental of this apartment is being terminated, as of tomorrow. The car is being returned, as of tomorrow. The horses go back, tomorrow. Your bank credit is ended, as of tomorrow.'

'You cannot do this,' Anna whispered. 'You have no right.'

'I have the right to do whatever I please,' said Madame Karaklaic. 'Her Majesty put me in complete control of this affair. She told me that under no circumstances should there be any mistakes. Well, there has not been a mistake, there has been a disaster, and it is a disaster compounded by circumstances. You will not have heard the news, I suppose?'

'The news?'

'King Ferdinand is dead. The news came over the wireless not an hour ago. He died while his heir was cavorting on a sofa with this, this daughter of yours. How do you suppose Prince Carol will feel about that?'

'Oh, my God,' Anna sat down heavily.

'Exactly,' Madame Karaklaic agreed. 'I do not think the business would have been successful even had Jacqueline been everything we had hoped. Well, it is no use crying now.'

'What am I to do?' Anna wailed. 'What *am* I to do?'

'You will do what I tell you to do,' Madame Karaklaic said. 'Pack your things and go to the Gare du Lyons first thing tomorrow morning. One of my people will meet you there with tickets for yourself and your daughter, Paris–Bucharest. He will also provide you with travelling expenses. When you get to Bucharest, endeavour to see the Queen. That is your only hope, not that I see much chance for you. You know how superstitious she is. She will almost certainly link the two disasters.' Again her tone softened. 'But she can only send you back to Pitesti. For the rest of your life.'

Anna screamed in rage, but Jacqueline continued to sit in cold misery.

Angry voices. Shouting. Weeping. Big wooden trunks open on the floor, clothes torn from closets and thrown across beds and chairs. No sleep, just misery, anger and confusion.

Jacqueline felt like a little child again, listening to Mama speaking with strange people, conversations she could not understand, being pushed into the car, and then on to the train.

They sat in silence in opposite corners of the compartment. Too quickly the mists began to clear from her mind. Unwanted answers to her unspoken questions were bringing fresh tears. That Mama could betray the love and friendship and trust which had grown between them in the past two years. Perhaps, when the anger had subsided, she would explain. But then, what explanations could there be to justify sending her to Prince Carol to be raped? The horror of it made Jacqueline shudder again. And it had happened while the King lay dying, almost like some divine retribution. Draga Karaklaic had suggested that Queen Marie would think like that. But would she not be right? The rumble of the train wheels added their own misery.

Away from Jean-Paul. Away from Jean-Paul. Where is Jean-Paul? Away from Jean-Paul.

Her chest heaved with a long, shuddering sob.

'Well?' Anna demanded at last. 'Haven't you got anything to say for yourself?'

'Oh, Mama, I thought we were friends. I thought we loved each other . . .'

'Of course I love you. I want the very best for you. Why do you suppose I went to so much trouble to set all this up? And don't believe for one moment Draga's silly notion about Carol linking you with his father's death. If he had, it would have been to your advantage. He hated the King, probably because he was terrified of him. But he hated him. Had you behaved yourself properly, he would have fallen madly in love with you. You would have replaced the Lupesca. As Carol's mistress, we would . . . I mean, you could have had the world at your feet. You'd have been set up for life.'

'Mama, how dare you?' Jacqueline was furious. 'How dare you suggest that I would ever sell myself to anyone, to be "set up for life"? Especially to that revolting beast. I am not a whore. You may be, but I am not. I . . .' Her head was banged against the carriage door frame by a stinging forehand drive from her mother. Jacqueline recoiled in pain and fury.

'You bitch, you bitch, you beastly selfish bitch,' she screamed, tugged open the door to the corridor, and ran.

Even now, nearly a month after their return to Pitesti, Jacqueline wondered where she had found the courage, if that was the right word, to shout at her mother like that. Nevertheless she still felt entirely justified about it. After spending half an hour in the tiny swaying toilet, she had composed herself sufficiently to return to their compartment. Her mother had continued to stare out of the window, and had ignored her completely. But on their arrival at the chateau, orders had been given that she should be locked in her room. Meals were brought to her on a tray and she was accompanied into the grounds each day to walk for one hour.

The note Anna had sent to her room the day after their return lay ignored on her writing bureau: 'When you come to your senses and apologise for your outrageous conduct, we may start to discuss the future. Until then, you will remain confined to your room.' Following which Mama had apparently taken herself off to Bucharest, no doubt to throw herself on the mercy of the Queen as Madame Karaklaic had recommended. Although what she could expect from Her Majesty, who would surely be as angry as Jacqueline herself at what her mother had done, remained a mystery to her.

Mama's departure had made no difference to her imprisonment – Anton the butler was too faithful a family retainer, and the other servants were too afraid of him, to wish to help her in any way. Even her maid Calliope kept her distance – she had in any event only been appointed after their return from Paris – Jacqueline had only known her previously as one of the kitchen girls. Now she was clearly over-awed by her promotion, and gazed at her new mistress with enormous eyes, invariably replying to any question with: 'Oh, I don't know about that, miss.'

But, lonely and hurt as she was, Jacqueline was determined that she would never apologise, although with every day it became increasingly difficult to maintain her mental resolution. Repeatedly her tray was sent back untouched to the kitchen, she just felt too nauseated to eat. She supposed it was all the bitterness and anger with which she still seethed. Perhaps it *was* partly her own fault. Perhaps her mother was justified in waiting for an apology. Was she just making herself sick through sheer obstinacy?

The sound of the key turning brought her to her feet; she swayed and clutched the chair. Blackness. Arms supporting her to her bed. It was over in a moment, then her eyes opened. Anna was sitting beside her, but her face was more relaxed than it had been at any time since that dreadful night in Paris. 'I presume you realise you are pregnant?' she asked.

Jacqueline blinked.

'We have suspected it for some time, Calliope and I. So now we must quickly make some plans, if we are going to salvage anything from this mess. However, I think we have at last had a stroke of fortune.'

'Pregnant?' Jacqueline clutched her mother's hand. The possibility had never occurred to her. But if she was . . . a delicious sense of wellbeing spread through her system. Mama would have to help her now. 'We must find Jean-Paul,' she said. 'Oh, he will be so proud. I don't have his address, but I know we can find him. His name is Busonniere. De Busonniere,' she added, as Anna stared at her. 'He must be told,' she finished, quietly.

'Do you really suppose that a young man who has enjoyed a girl while on holiday wishes to be told that she is pregnant?' Anna demanded. 'My God, what innocence.' She patted Jacqueline's hand. 'Anyway, it is obviously not his child.'

'Not his child?'

'You may be sure it is his,' Anna said. 'I may even suspect that you are right. But it cannot be this Frenchman's child. Do you understand me?'

'No,' Jacqueline said. 'No, Mama, I do not understand you. If Jean-Paul is not the father, then . . .?' she paused, her mouth still open.

Anna smiled. 'Exactly. You are carrying a prince of Rumania. It may interest you to know that, after Carol, who has renounced his rights, there is only one Prince of Rumania, and that is his brother Nicholas. Apart from King Michael, of course, poor little soul. Your son could be a very important person indeed.'

'But Mama, that is quite impossible. Everyone will know it is quite impossible.'

'Indeed? Carol entered you. Draga Karaklaic knows that.'

'But she also knows that I was not a virgin.'

'Ah, but she does not know how long ago your encounter with this person de-whatever-his-name-is took place. How long have you known him?'

'Well, I met him at Easter. We used to ride together every day.' She flushed. 'But nothing happened then.'

'So when did it happen?' Anna frowned at her. 'You don't mean on that one day you spent here in June?'

Jacqueline's head moved up and down slowly.

'Goodness!' Anna was no longer angry, that was obvious, merely intrigued. 'But that is better and better. Your liaison with this youth was last Easter, and you did not see him at all this summer. Do you understand me?'

'But Mama . . .'

'Therefore, you cannot be pregnant by him, or you would be very advanced by now. It has to be Carol.'

'Mama, I don't want to think of Carol as the father of my child.'

'You don't want,' Anna sneered. 'I think you had just better listen to some home truths, girl. How do you think we managed to go to Paris at all? Who do you think paid for it?'

'Your inheritance?'

'Inheritance? Nonsense, I have no inheritance. We were sent by Queen Marie.'

'Queen Marie?' Jacqueline's brain was in a complete fog.

'Do you suppose Her Majesty meant to let Rumania just sink without trace? It could happen, you know. It has only been a kingdom for fifty years, after centuries of struggle. King Ferdinand was ill for some time, his son ran off and renounced the throne. What will happen now that King Ferdinand is dead and his successor is a mere child? There is to be a regency, headed by Prince Nicholas; regencies mean plots and heaven knows what else. Queen Marie foresaw all of this and was determined it should not happen. She was determined that Carol must return to rule. But how to get him away from the Lupesca? She thought of me. *Me*, do you hear? I was Carol's mistress, once. We quarrelled, or the Lupesca made us quarrel, I suppose, and we parted. But then there was you. When I took you to tea at the palace at Easter, Her Majesty was entranced. She knows that Carol has a certain weakness for young girls, however much he lets himself be bullied by the Lupesca. So we made our plans, Her Majesty and I.'

'To make the Prince fall in love with me?' Jacqueline was aghast.

'It would have worked, but for your wilful stupidity,' Anna said. 'So now I am in disgrace too. Queen Marie was furious. She is still furious with the very name of Dumesca. We have made matters worse, she insists, because Carol will certainly work out what actually happened.'

'Oh, Mama, I am so sorry,' Jacqueline said sarcastically. 'If you had only told me.' She wouldn't have gone near the lout. As for pretending he was the father of her child . . .

'I don't suppose I can blame you entirely,' Anna said, with sudden magnanimity. 'Your background – your behaviour almost made me think of your Uncle Herman. But of course . . .'

'Uncle Herman?' Jacqueline's brow furrowed in curiosity. She had never heard the name before. 'Who is Uncle Herman?'

'Um . . .' Anna shot her an arch glance. 'No one at all.'

'Mother?'

'Oh,' Anna said, sulkily. 'Your grandfather was a lecherous beast. And Herman was the result.'

'Do you mean you have a brother?'

'A half brother.'

'And you never told me?'

'He does not really exist. I assure you he has no claims on this estate. Papa saw what a nuisance he was going to be early on and sent him off.'

'Where?'

'Oh, really, child, what does it matter? Germany.

Munich, I think. He sends me a card every birthday, believe it or not, so he cannot actually have starved. But why are we wasting our time talking about him? I should never have mentioned his name. He was as bourgeois as you could possibly imagine. Just as you were, over the Prince.' Anna got up and roamed the room, straightening pictures and fidgeting in her excitement. 'However, you are carrying Her Majesty's grandchild. A direct descendant of Queen Victoria, no less.'

'Mother . . .'

'You *are*. I will have no more argument on the matter. Queen Marie will be delighted and forgive us everything. What is more important, she will have to see to the child's future. Come on, girl, get up, get up. You and I are going to Bucharest. Your condition is worth a decent pension at the very least.'

Jacqueline knew that she had to be practical. Her first instinct was to run away at the earliest opportunity and scour France for Jean-Paul. But how? She had no money and no means of obtaining any – save through Mama and her plans. Anyway, Mama held her passport. To refuse to cooperate with her mother's wild dreams would only create yet more antagonism and achieve nothing. Also, she knew, there had been a certain amount of truth in what Mama said. For Jean-Paul, still in his teens and just starting his military career, a pregnant wife would be fatal to his ambitions. This mess was entirely her own fault and she must face the consequences without also ruining him. Yes, she thought; she would cooperate, but only as long as it suited her to do so. However, she would never trust her mother again, never cease to hate her. The dear, loving, friendly Mama she had known for two brief years was gone.

Thus mentally fortified, she continued to wait in the Royal ante-chamber, alone except for two ladies-in-waiting, who soon gave up their attempts at conversation when she replied to their questions in monosyllables. Presumably the pension her mother was seeking would be granted for life. But for the present her life would be Mama's to control, though once she was twenty-one . . . plans, intrigues of her own. And when she was twenty-one, Jean-Paul would still only be twenty-three.

Of course, she told herself confidently, she would have contacted him by then. They would have laid their plans together and her life would be mapped out. Her business was to be patient, apparently willing, while never forgetting her own objectives for a moment. Her immediate duty was to have her baby, to make sure the child was strong and healthy. She also had to make sure that she remained strong and healthy as well.

The door opened, the ladies stood up. Jacqueline also stood and joined them in a curtsy as Queen Marie entered, as usual glittering with ill-matched jewellery, her greying hair unswept as ever, a lorgnette draped across her ample bosom, the whole ensemble hardly affected by her black mourning gown.

'Leave us,' she said.

The ladies-in-waiting exchanged glances and then left the room. Mama remained standing at the Queen's shoulder.

'Stand straight, Jacqueline,' the Queen said.

Jacqueline straightened and Marie came closer. She stood immediately in front of the girl, peering at her. 'Yes,' she said. 'She has the look. But I will require a medical report, Madame.'

'Of course, Your Majesty.'

'She will be examined by my own physician,' Marie said. 'As this matter must be kept utterly secret. You have told no one?'

'No, Your Majesty. But . . . the child's maid knows of it.'

'Then she must continue to be her maid. You will see that she is well paid for her discretion.'

'Of course, Your Majesty.'

'A pretty child,' Marie remarked, almost as if she was

not really there, Jacqueline thought. 'Even more than that, perhaps, with time. Yes. I think it would be unwise, Madame Dumesca, for her to remain at Pitesti all by herself.'

'Oh, indeed, Your Majesty.' Anna glowed. 'I was thinking the very same thing. Perhaps a town house . . .'

'Or anywhere, all by herself,' the Queen continued. 'There is also the matter of the child. It must have a legitimate father. I think, Count Tyroler.'

'Count Tyroler?' Anna cried. 'But, Your Majesty . . .'

'I know there are rumours about him, but he will be happy to obey me, especially if I pay his debts and settle an income on him. Do not fret, Madame, I will make it obligatory for him to support you as well. He will care for you as well as your daughter, and he will give the child a respectable, a famous old name.'

Jacqueline stared at the Queen in horror, only just realising what was being proposed.

'But, Your Majesty,' Anna was still protesting. 'Count Tyroler, well, he is older than I am.'

'Considerably, I would presume,' Queen Marie said, somewhat coldly. 'Tyroler is fifty-one years old, three times Jacqueline's age, is it not? I think that is an ideal arrangement, for a young girl who obviously needs care and discipline. They will be married immediately.'

September 1927 – June 1930

Resolve to be thyself; and know, that he
Who finds himself, loses his misery.

Matthew Arnold, *Self-Dependence*

'No!' JACQUELINE shouted. 'No, no, no.'

Queen Marie gazed at her in astonishment.

'You cannot just marry me off,' Jacqueline cried. 'I am
. . .' she looked at her mother. Anna was glaring at her to
be silent.

The Queen's face softened. 'I know, my dear child, you
are in love.' She sighed. 'He has that quality, that son of
mine. Sometimes I find it difficult to appreciate, because
I am his mother. But women have always fallen in love
with him. My dear girl . . .' she came closer and put her
arm round Jacqueline's shoulders. 'Prince Carol is already
married, to a lovely princess whom he has shamefully
deserted for an upstart Jewess.' She almost spat the word.
'One had hoped, of course, that your youth, your innocence, might wean him away from the adventuress, back
to his duty and his family. Alas, you have made that
impossible.' She held up a finger when Jacqueline tried to
speak. 'Do not be afraid. Your mother has explained it all
to me. I do not know that you can be forgiven, except . . .'
she glanced at Anna. 'Perhaps these things are hereditary.
But the past is the past and one must look to the future.
If you have failed to accomplish what I had hoped, you
have yet accomplished, or have been granted, perhaps, a
great responsibility. You carry a royal prince in your

womb. This must remain an absolute secret between us. I shall have to tell Count Tyroler, of course, but he can be trusted, in view of the honour I am bestowing upon him. I do not know whether the secret can ever be made public. Nonetheless, your future son is a royal prince. He must receive the very best education possible, be cared for and nurtured, for in this uncertain world who can tell what the future will bring? Above all else, he must have respectable parents, to love him and to care for him. I am sure you wish to do all of those things, Jacqueline. But you are just a child yourself, ignorant of the many evils that abound in this world. Count Tyroler is a man of great experience, he will smooth your path. And believe me, he will demand little of you. You have a duty and you must face up to that duty.'

'Let me speak with her, Your Majesty,' Anna said. 'She is merely confused.'

Queen Marie nodded. 'Bring her to see me the day after tomorrow. The Count will be here.'

'It is quite impossible, Mother,' Jacqueline said. 'You must see that. You can't just marry someone because he's there. I don't even know what he looks like.'

She was speaking as reasonably and logically as she could, but immediately behind the self-control lay screaming hysteria. This could not be happening to her.

Yet it was, because her mother was not losing her temper either. She stood in the centre of the drawing room of the Chateau Dumescu, and pointed at her daughter. 'I think you had better listen to me very carefully, young woman. In the first place, you are not yet seventeen years old. I have every right to marry you off to whomever I choose. In the second place, you are pregnant. I had to support the burden of a fatherless child, and it was not easy. I doubt you have the resolution or strength to do it. In the third place, you are no longer an irresponsible schoolgirl. For better or for worse, you have been launched into the world. Into history,' Anna surrendered to the dramatic.

56

'You have been with a famous personage. The world considers that now you bear his child . . .'

'The world, Mother? Now, really . . .'

'As far as you and I are concerned, Queen Marie is the world. And one day the world will know of it. You may be sure of that. These things will out. Whether you like it or not, you are now striding through the corridors of history, and you should endeavour to live your life accordingly. Fourthly,' Anna went on, keeping track of her arguments, 'you have absolutely no choice in the matter. Pause to consider the alternatives, if you dare. You suppose yourself to be in love with this French lout. But I can tell you that he is not at all in love with you.'

'Mother! You don't know anything about him.'

'I know men. You will allow me that,' Anna said sarcastically. 'I do know men. He has had sex with you. Oh, how wonderful. You tell him that you are pregnant because of it, and he will run a mile. You tell him that you are a bastard yourself, and he will run another mile. And even, let us suppose the incredible, if he decided to make an honest woman of you, do you have any idea what would happen next? What did you tell me his father was? Some itinerant jeweller?'

'Mother, Monsieur de Busonniere sells diamonds and precious gems all over Europe, even in Bucharest.'

'He is still a tradesman,' Anna's voice was heavy with contempt. 'And that means he has a tradesman's instincts. And so will his son. Tradesmen worry about money – they never have enough. You will be virtually penniless all of your life.'

Jacqueline wanted to interrupt, to remind her mother that she had lately been doing quite a lot of worrying about money, but Anna would not even pause for breath.

'Tradesmen also worry about morals. You would be a forced bride and they would never let you forget it. Your life would be a misery. My life would be a misery. And Her Majesty would never forgive you. But what is the alternative we are offering you? Wealth, a place in society,

57

a title. You will be the Countess Tyroler. Who could ask for anything more?'

'And be forced to sleep with some old ogre,' Jacqueline shouted. But she knew in her heart that her mother was right. Also, if he was that old, Count Tyroler might be expected to drop dead at any moment. She would still be the Countess Tyroler. Jean-Paul would find that hard to resist. And she would be wealthy. Oh, goodness, she thought, you are thinking like a whore. No, she reminded herself, you are thinking like a courtesan. As Mama had said, courtesans walk the pages of history.

'I can assure you that Count Tyroler is very far from being an ogre,' Anna said, her mouth twisted. 'I doubt that he will make many demands on you.'

Presumably, Jacqueline thought, because men of fifty-one didn't feel like sex very often. She knew she was trapped. But it was somehow exciting, to feel that some-one, sometime, in perhaps fifty or a hundred years' time, might come across her name in a book: *'amongst the beauties of the Rumanian Court in the nineteen twenties, there was the Countess Tyroler, lovely and spirited, and mother, so it was rumoured, of a prince of the royal house.'* However, it would all be a lie. According to Sister Veronica, most recorded history was a lie, or at least, very exaggerated.

Count Tyroler was in fact a very pleasant surprise. He was not tall, hardly taller than herself, indeed, slightly built, but with handsome, aquiline features and black hair only greying at the temples. Everything about him was neat and dapper, from the line of his clean-shaven jaw, past the carnation in his buttonhole, to the flawless white of his spats; he might have stepped straight out of the pages of a fashion magazine.

Nor were his manners inferior to his appearance. Jacqueline didn't really know what to do when she was introduced to him. Having curtsied to Queen Marie, who stood beside him, she decided the best thing was to curtsy again, and did so. Count Tyroler took both her hands to raise her. 'Her Majesty has asked me to do her a favour,' he declared, 'and indeed, the state a favour. But, Mademoiselle, it is Her Majesty and the state, as it is your own beautiful self, who are all together doing me a favour. I am enchanted.'

In the circumstances, and much to Anna's regret, it had to be a very small wedding. To wait until the official court mourning period was over would have meant waiting until Jacqueline's condition was obvious, and this neither Anna nor Queen Marie were prepared to do.

Jacqueline was more relieved than disappointed that the marriage would take place virtually in secret. She refused to regard it as more than a temporary step. In any event, she did not want Jean-Paul to read about it in some society column. She was reduced to tears when Count Tyroler – Ion – bought her an engagement ring on the day after their meeting. As he fitted the magnificent sapphire, set between two diamonds, on her finger, he said with some pride, 'I bought it from a gem merchant who has a salon by the river. A Frenchman, name of de Busonniere. He has some very good quality stones.'

Her tears brought a bewildered look from him, as he had of course been told nothing of Jean-Paul. Cautiously, he kissed her on the cheek. Apart from her hand this was the first part of her body he had touched. And now, only a fortnight later, she stood in Queen Marie's private chapel, accompanied by her mother and two ladies-in-waiting, and a handsome young man who was apparently Count Tyroler's secretary, listening to the Monseigneur pronouncing the fatal words. She had been allowed to wear a proper wedding dress, but it had been very hastily run up by the royal seamstresses and didn't fit her very well. The whole thing was a ghastly charade, and she almost burst into tears again when the Monseigneur announced, 'Those whom God hath joined together, let no man put asunder.'

Then she was being kissed by everyone present,

including her husband, and handed a glass of champagne before being whisked off to a waiting motor car. Queen Marie accompanied them to the private staircase leading down to the courtyard, and there gave Jacqueline her wedding present, a rather plain gold signet ring. 'It bears the royal crest,' she said. 'It will remind you of where your duty lies, my dear. And who knows, one day it may even smooth your path. Now, Count Tyroler,' she turned. 'I think it would be best if you honeymooned for several months. Do you understand me?'

'As Your Majesty wishes,' the Count agreed.

'I know it will be a dreadful bore for you,' the Queen went on. 'But I am sure you will have lots to do, getting to know your young bride.'

'I am anticipating that with the keenest pleasure.'

'Where are we going?' Jacqueline asked, suddenly realising that they might well be about to travel the world, which put an entirely different complexion upon matters.

'Why, to Pitesti,' the Count said. 'Your mother has very generously leased the Chateau Dumescu to me.'

'Chateau Dumescu?' Jacqueline cried, looking at her mother. 'But . . .'

'You must spend the next seven months where no one who does not already know the secret can possibly discover it,' Anna whispered in her ear. 'Do not worry. I will be out with you in, well, in a week or so. As soon as you have had time to get to know each other. And Jacqueline . . .' she squeezed her daughter's hand. 'You are now a Countess. Isn't that exciting?'

Jacqueline supposed she must be right, but she felt a terrific sense of anti-climax as she sat in the first class compartment and watched the night rushing by. She had made this journey so often before. To honeymoon at the Chateau Dumescu . . . the strange thing was, she knew, that had it been Jean-Paul sitting opposite her and smiling at her, she would have preferred to do it this way, to take him where everything was so familiar. She would have shown him all the places which had a special interest or memories for her, would bring him into her girlhood. How could she do that with a man who had been over thirty before she had been born?

Even now they were not alone, for they were accompanied by the good-looking young secretary, Bruno Balanel. Presumably counts were always attended by secretaries. Certainly the Count did not seem to have any ready money, or any idea of their travel arrangements. It was Bruno who had the tickets, who saw that they were escorted to their reserved compartment, who tipped the porters. And it was Bruno who now sat beside her, at the far end of the seat. In fact she was definitely glad of the Count's presence; Bruno was certainly a handsome fellow, but he also had the somewhat thick lips and sidelong glances which Jacqueline interpreted to mean the lecher.

Suddenly she was deathly afraid, realising for the first time that she was utterly alone with two total strangers – who were obviously very well known to each other. She felt as if she were the victim of a Gothic plot, about to be swept away to Bluebeard's castle, there to be murdered. But the marriage had been arranged by the Queen herself, except that now she did not even trust the Queen. Surely it was at least equally possible that she might wish to get rid of both child and mother, such potential nuisances, as that she might wish to care for them in case they ever became useful. As for Mama agreeing to it . . . but she now knew that Mama would agree to practically anything for money or position or acceptance into Society.

Even the signet ring Queen Marie had given to her did not really amount to anything. It could easily be taken from her dead body and returned.

She was alone in the world.

'I think,' said Count Tyroler, 'that we will have a glass of champagne, Bruno.'

'Of course, sir.' Bruno pulled the hamper out from beneath the seat, and efficiently popped the cork.

The Count himself handed a glass to Jacqueline, raised

his own. 'I would like to drink a toast to the Countess Tyroler,' he said. 'Quite the most beautiful ever to possess the name, certainly for as long as I can remember.' He drank while Jacqueline stared at him in fascinated fear. Then he leaned forward and patted her on the knee. 'There is no need to be afraid of me, my dear. Your condition means that we do not have to consummate our marriage for at least a year.'

'Perhaps we should drink a toast to that, too,' Bruno remarked.

Jacqueline was quite tipsy by the time they reached the chateau, and could not really remember going to bed. But she did remember thinking to herself how absurd she had been on the train: Bluebeard's Castle indeed. This was her castle, and she was surrounded by her servants. It was the Count and the aloof Bruno who were the strangers here.

She was confused to discover that she had slept alone. The fact was that her feelings were entirely ambivalent. She did not really want the Count to make love to her, and she could understand that perhaps he was utterly bored by the whole idea of having even to flirt with a girl young enough to be his daughter – but she was disturbed to think that he did not appear even to wish to look at her. Prince Carol had thought she was beautiful; Queen Marie and Draga Karaklaic had said so; Jean-Paul had certainly found her very attractive. Her husband did not even wish to admire her – and there was nothing wrong with her figure, yet. No doubt, she thought sadly, he had known so many women over the years that they all looked alike to him now.

They took breakfast together on the terrace the next morning, the Count in a mauve dressing gown, admiring the view. 'Ah, the Carpathians,' he said. 'The most beautiful part of Rumania, I have been told. And do you know, I have never been here before? You must take me riding in those hills. When you are able to, of course.'

'Oh, but . . .' she had been going to say that she was

perfectly able to ride now. But she supposed she shouldn't, in her condition. 'What would you like to do today?' she asked.

'I am afraid, my dear, that I am a very boring person. My routine never changes if I can help it. But then, it suits me, and keeps me fit. So I shall take the train into Bucharest, go to my club, lunch there, and this afternoon I shall play a round of golf. Then I shall take the train back out here this evening. Do not wait with supper for me.' He patted her hand. 'It will, as Her Majesty said, be a terrible bore, spending several hours a day in a train, but do not worry, I shall not leave you alone overnight.'

But we're honeymooning, she wanted to say, and the Queen said that you should stay here. 'I wondered if you would like me to show you the estate,' she said. 'Explain things.'

'Good heavens, why should I want you to do that? I am sure that the estate can manage very well without my knowing how it is done. Anyway, you must be very careful about how much you do, Jacqueline. You must not get overtired or anything like that. No harm must come to your child. I think you should spend the day reading a good book. I have one here which I heartily recommend to you.'

She picked it up. It was written in French by someone called André Gide, called *Les Faux-Monnayeurs*. 'What's it about?' she asked.

'About?' He gave a little shrug. 'It is about men and women, their feelings and desires. It explores the world of the senses. I am sure you will find much to interest you in it. But do not let it out of your sight,' he went on, lowering his voice to a whisper. 'It is, how shall I say, a trifle *risqué*? It has been banned by the Church.'

'Oh,' she said, becoming quite interested. But when she came to read it she found it utterly boring. She had hoped for a sizzling romance such as she had found in *The Sheikh*, another book of which the Church did not approve, but which had been circulated with great glee amongst the girls

63

at the convent. André Gide's book had none of that, but instead hinted at a world where men loved men, an utterly incomprehensible concept for Jacqueline. She obeyed her husband, however, as it was her duty, and read it through to the end, becoming more disgusted with every chapter. Of course she kept it hidden and did not even mention it to her mother when she finally arrived to join them, some three weeks after the wedding. However, she did feel entitled to have a little grumble. 'He has never even entered my bedroom,' she told Anna. 'Heaven knows, I never wanted to marry him in the first place, and I certainly don't want him to make love to me. But even in a sham marriage I'd have expected at least some degree of companionship. We breakfast together every morning, and that is the last I see of him all day. He never gets back from town until nearly midnight. You would suppose he was a lodger here rather than my husband.'

'You just said you didn't want him to make love to you,' Anna remarked.

'That's not what I mean. I only think it would be pleasant if occasionally he told me how nice I look, sought my company, or even shared a little affection like holding my arm when we walk along a corridor together.'

'Well, my dear, the whole thing was rather sprung on him,' Anna observed.

Sprung on him? Jacqueline thought.

'The Count is a bachelor, has been one all of his life. He never supposed he would marry,' Anna went on. 'Thus he is now very set in his ways. He needs time to get to know you. And, of course, you are pregnant with a royal child. He is afraid of harming the baby in any way. Things will be better after the birth.'

With her mother on the estate life was indeed far less boring. It was almost like old times, and Jacqueline could not have been more assiduously cared for. She almost felt herself forgiving Mama for all that had happened. Yet, when at the weekends she sat at dinner between the Count and Anna, she could not escape the feeling that they were the husband and wife, and she the daughter. In a strange way this was almost comforting – she had never known the reassurance of having a man permanently in the home.

By November she was very definitely showing, and saw even less of the Count. Whether he found her condition distasteful, or frightening, or too much of a reminder of his position, he even gave up breakfasting with her, and often did not come in at night at all. Yet he remained quite astonishingly lavish in his presents. At Christmas he gave her a sapphire-and-diamond pendant, which, added to her engagement ring and his wedding gift of a set of ruby-and-diamond necklet, ear-rings and bracelet, left her staring into her jewellery case for hours on end wondering when she would ever have the opportunity to wear them all.

Of course, she reflected, he was really spending her own money, because he would not have it at all were she not supposedly pregnant with a royal baby. This did not seem to bother the Count, but she thought it bothered Bruno, who regarded the extravagant presents with distaste – but then Bruno regarded everything about her with distaste. It was a strange feeling, to be disliked by a servant, and she was determined to do something about it as soon as she had had the baby. But for now it was simply a matter of sitting out the remaining four months, reclining on the terrace well wrapped up in rugs and shawls, and looking at the mountains where the snow and mist clouded the distant peaks. From here she could imagine the pond where she and Jean-Paul had swum together on that never-to-be-forgotten day, now frozen over and desolate. But to think of Jean-Paul was to leave her equally desolate. What must he be thinking? He would have gone to Paris, as he had promised to do, and inquired for Madame Dumesca and her daughter. He would have been told that they were here for a month before they left again. But he would have been told that they had returned to Rumania. That always made her heart quicken; she imagined him following her, suddenly appearing at the chateau. Then her heart slowed again with fear, because that would ruin everything. Nothing must happen until after the birth and she was herself again. Then she could . . . she did not really know what she could do. But she was the Countess Tyroler and surely she was entitled to travel, to go to Paris for her shopping, to live her own life as Count Tyroler was obviously determined to live his.

The mountains were still thick with snow when she felt the first cramps; it was early March and close to her own birthday. 'Clearly the babe is premature,' Mama said firmly and loudly, and immediately despatched the prescribed cypher message to Bucharest. Queen Marie's own physician, the benevolent old English gentleman who had examined Jacqueline in the previous September, came out with two nurses and seemed to take over the entire chateau. Count Tyroler declared the situation was too much for him and took himself and Bruno off to Bucharest.

This time Jacqueline did not blame him. She was put to bed and watched continuously by one of the nurses as the cramps grew more severe. Having led a life remarkably free of illness, she could not believe there was so much pain in the world, and was bitterly resentful that such a misfortune could overtake her; she even managed to feel a momentary dislike for Jean-Paul for having caused all of this misery.

And then, almost before she was truly prepared for it, the pain ceased and the room was filled with admiring faces – she was a mother.

'Jean-Jacques?' Anna Dumesca exclaimed. 'How absurd. He will be called Frederick. And,' she added, because Jacqueline was clearly about to argue, 'the name was chosen by Queen Marie herself.'

So there was really nothing to be done about that, except that Jacqueline was determined that he would be known as Jean-Jacques, no matter what anyone else wanted.

The christening was a much grander affair than the wedding. The group was still small, but the period of mourning for King Ferdinand was over and they were able to wear bright spring dresses. Queen Marie attended, as well as Draga Karaklaic, who, to Jacqueline's annoyance, had been appointed Godmother to the little boy. Count Tyroler beamed – to Jacqueline's increased chagrin, *he* received many more congratulations than she. Well, she reasoned, to become a father for the first time at fifty-two, and with such rapidity, as they had only been married six months, was presumably quite a feat. She did not enjoy herself at all; she could not still the feeling that everyone present was laughing. Of course they would all have been able to work out that the Count must have got her pregnant before the wedding. But she felt there was an extra edge to the laughter, a suggestion that everyone present knew something she did not. And Mama? Anna appeared to be having the time of her life.

Something she obviously intended to continue doing. Count Tyroler possessed a town house, and now they started spending part of their time in Bucharest, or at least Anna and the Count did. Jacqueline was feeding Jean-Jacques, which she found a delight when she was actually doing it, but rather a nuisance the rest of the time, because she was still not to be allowed into proper society. She was, however, reassured by the speed with which she regained her figure, especially as she now possessed a fuller bust – and was then depressed once more because the Count still never attempted to come into her bedroom, or to spend any time with her at all, although he always remained scrupulously polite. 'It's not that I really want him to sleep with me,' she explained to her mother, 'but I think *he* should want to, don't you? I mean, Mama, we're not properly married, are we? Until it's consummated.'

Anna shot her a very sharp glance. 'You could never prove it,' she snapped. 'You are now a mother.'

'I could prove that I was pregnant before the first time I ever met Ion,' Jacqueline snapped back. 'Isn't that what you want me to be able to do, when the time comes?'

'Now you listen to me. You are the Countess Tyroler,

67

and you are going to go on being the Countess Tyroler. Your son is Frederick Tyroler. There are lots of marriages where the happy couple, well . . . they choose to have a reasonably chaste relationship.'

'Reasonably?' Jacqueline shouted. 'He has never done more than kiss my cheek.'

'Reasonably,' Anna said with that firmness which indicated that she was not prepared to argue. 'The important thing is that he is your husband and you are his wife, and will behave as a wife. When you have finished nursing the baby we will take you to Bucharest and have some parties. You will enjoy those. But . . . no flirting with anybody. Do you understand me?'

It occurred to Jacqueline that her mother was planning again. Certainly, like almost everyone in Rumania, she had a lot on her mind. The Regency was not working well. Prince Nicholas did not get on with the other members of the council, being apparently of a dictatorial mind. If he was anything like his elder brother Carol, Jacqueline could well understand that he might be difficult to get on with. But, as her mother was always saying, Rumania needed to be ruled. The country was not yet a nation, but remained a confused mixture of separate states; the original Wallachia, to which had been added the Dobrudja, taken from Russia, Transylvania, and parts of Hungary and Bulgaria, all trophies from the peace treaties in 1921, and all filled with people who had been born to other nationalities. It was going to take time to weld them into a real nationality, but Prince Nicholas was obviously not the man to do it.

Since King Michael was still only seven years old, it was difficult to see who was going to do it. Jacqueline wondered what Prince Carol thought of it all. But he apparently had problems of his own, as he was now engaged in the ultimate denigration of his position as a supposedly Catholic Prince. Now that his father was dead, he had instituted divorce proceedings against Princess Helen of Greece. It was rumoured that he then intended to marry the Lupesca. Rumanian society was shocked.

Despite her harsh words, Anna had taken Jacqueline's worries to heart, and had a chat with the Count. The next morning, to Jacqueline's utter surprise, instead of taking the early train to Bucharest, Ion invited her to go riding with him. She was delighted and scrambled into her best habit. She walked her horse beside him over that so well-remembered trail.

'I fear I have been neglecting you,' he said.

'I am sure you have excellent reasons for everything you do.'

'Well . . . you must understand, the whole business was very sudden. I think you are very beautiful, Jacqueline, but it is difficult to think of you as mine, if you follow me.'

'Of course I do,' she replied, her heart warming to him.

'And then, of course, the child . . . but that is all behind us now, is it not?'

'Oh, yes. I shall have finished feeding in another month or so. My milk is all but dry.' For the moment she had quite forgotten that it was her intention to try and regain contact with Jean-Paul, a course which would entail an eventual annulment of her marriage on the grounds of non-consummation.

The Count looked embarrassed. 'Yes,' he said, less certainly than earlier. 'Well, perhaps in a month's time . . .' He had slowed his horse almost to a walk and was clearly contemplating returning to the chateau.

'Don't let's go back yet,' she said. Even if she had embarrassed him she still felt she should strike while the iron was hot. Why, she didn't know. She liked the Count, he was a likeable man. But she could never love him, did not really want to make love to him. Yet he was her husband. She was married, but not married, until they had lain in each other's arms. However, that would spoil everything. And yet . . . she somehow wanted him to want her. To love her, in fact. She wanted her husband to love her. Surely that was not so terribly wrong, however confused it left her own emotions. 'There really are some lovely rides further up,' she told him, wondering if she dared take him to the pool, and if she dared go swimming in front of him. The crisp spring air was making her feel more alive than she had for a long time.

'Are there?' he asked, nudging his horse with his heel. 'Well, then.' But once again he drew rein and Jacqueline gazed in dismay at Bruno walking his horse towards them. He was approaching from the side rather than from behind them, and she realised that he must have been keeping pace with them all the time, watching them.

He did not appear in the least abashed, either by her glare or by the Count's flush. 'You'll not forget the appointment you have in town, sir,' he said.

'The appointment?' For a moment the Count looked confused, then he gave a quick nod. 'Of course, I had forgotten, do you know? Thank you, Bruno, for reminding me. I really must get back, my dear. Perhaps you will be able to show me these lovely trails another time.' He rode off in great haste, Bruno at his heels. Jacqueline was left to follow by herself, which she did more slowly. She had never felt so hurt in her life, not even with her mother when she had realised how she was being manipulated. She was seething, but wanted to get over it by the time she reached the chateau. She found Bruno waiting by the car to drive the Count to the station; Ion had not yet finished changing his riding clothes. Her fury returned with force.

'I am very angry with you, Bruno,' she said. 'Count Tyroler and I have too little time to ourselves as it is. And to have you interrupting us . . .'

'I apologise, madame,' he said, refusing to lower his eyes. 'This is an important appointment.'

'Nonsense.' She dismounted, threw her reins to a waiting groom. 'I do not believe there is an appointment at all. You just made it up. Well, let me tell you, if you ever interrupt Count Tyroler and myself again when we are alone together, I am going to have you dismissed.'

'You won't do that, madame,' he said. 'I work for the

Count, not for you. And he would sooner dismiss you than me.'

She gazed at him in total stupefaction, that he could have dared to be so rude. She wanted to slap his face, thought better of it and turned away only to see the Count hurrying through the outer doorway.

'Jacqueline, my dear,' he said. 'I shall probably see you at supper. Now I must hurry.'

'Ion,' she said, holding his arm. 'Bruno has just been very rude to me, I really do not think he can stay.'

'Bruno? Rude?' He raised his eyebrows and glanced at the secretary, who waited patiently, still showing no sign of concern. 'I cannot believe that, my dear,' he patted her hand. 'You are exhausted from our ride. We shall discuss it later, when you have rested.'

'But I want to discuss it now,' she cried, stamping her foot.

Count Tyroler's eyebrows rose even higher. 'And I am in a hurry,' he said coldly. 'I will have Bruno tell me exactly what has happened on the journey into Bucharest, then we will talk about it when I return. I am sure you will realise by then that you have been behaving rather childishly. Goodbye, my dear.'

She was left staring in disbelief after him with her mouth open, while Bruno gave her a brief smile as he closed the car door behind them both. She stamped indoors and went searching for her mother, who was in her boudoir which overlooked the drive.

'I really hope,' Anna said, as Jacqueline entered the room, 'that you are not going to quarrel with your husband as well as everyone else.'

'I . . .' Jacqueline took a deep breath. 'Mother, I have just been terribly insulted. Ion trusts Bruno more than he trusts me. He has virtually told me so, and in front of that lout.'

'Mm,' Anna said, resuming her needlework. 'Well, I suppose he does.'

'What did you say?'

'Jacqueline, I think you should sit down and listen to me. I am afraid that your education, so complete in many ways, has rather been neglected in others. For that I must blame myself.'

'But . . .'

'There are men, a great many men, more men in the upper classes than in the lower, who, perhaps by education or perhaps by some form of mental inversion, well, prefer the company of other men to that of women.'

Jacqueline frowned at her, unsure of what she was being told.

'That preference,' Anna went on, cheeks pink with embarrassment, 'even extends to things like . . . like love, and sex. I'm afraid that Ion Tyroler is such a man.'

Jacqueline slowly sat down. She supposed she had to be dreaming.

'The situation does have certain advantages,' Anna spoke rather quickly. 'Quite apart from the obvious ones: wealth and position and title, with which Ion has been able to provide you. It means that he will never impose upon you, that you will be able to live your own lives, at least up to a point, and best of all, since you are parents, no one will ever even be able to point the finger of scandal at you.'

'You knew all this when I was married?' Jacqueline asked.

'Well, naturally, Her Majesty and I . . .'

'Her Majesty knew of it too?' Goodness, she thought, all Bucharest knew about it. Probably all Rumania, with one horrifying exception: herself. She had supposed all the guests at the wedding and the christening had been laughing at her. Laughing? They must have been bursting their sides. 'You have married me to a . . . a . . .' She didn't know the correct word.

'The Count is a man of homosexual tastes,' Anna said.

Jacqueline sat in stunned silence, her brain churning. She had been duped, forced into marriage with, well, certainly with a man who was not normal. Maybe it was

72

not the Count's fault that he was different. Perhaps he couldn't help being that way. But he had agreed to their marriage. She wondered if he loved some other man?

Gazing across at the little round table by the window, she pictured it laid with breakfast dishes and thought of the strained and stilted conversations they had there each morning, from which Ion always withdrew as soon as she had finished her coffee, to hurry away in the car with Bruno.

Bruno? Could he be the man Ion loved? Surely not! He was horrible. But she remembered their intimate chats together, the gestures, the secret smiles. And suddenly she realised why Ion had brought Bruno into their household. This creature he preferred to herself. She was furious, stood up.

'Mother, how dare you! You, the Queen and Ion. It was bad enough making me marry a man who doesn't . . . like women, but for him to bring that beastly Bruno into our married home, that's . . .' She clenched her fists. 'That is unforgiveable. Either Bruno leaves here immediately, or I want a divorce. I won't share my husband with that, that . . .'

'Now do not be absurd,' Anna said. 'How can you be divorced? I suppose Carol can get away with it, but the Church would never grant you one.'

'An annulment, then,' Jacqueline shouted. 'Bruno must leave this house or I want an annulment.'

'Jacqueline, it really does disturb me when you revert so readily to being an hysterical little girl. And also, which is worse, to being utterly bourgeois. I think you should remember that this is not your house. It is my house. And that little Frederick is not even entirely your son. He is a child of the Rumanian royal house, and,' she said, raising her voice slightly because Jacqueline was showing signs of exploding, 'it is only when so regarded that he entitles us to the very splendid income Her Majesty has settled upon us.'

'On us? On the Count, you mean.'

'On us,' Anna said firmly. 'Through the Count. He is well aware of his responsibilities. Has he not already been remarkably generous to you? Do you go short of anything?'

'Of anything?' Jacqueline cried.

'Well . . .' Anna made a moue. 'You seem to have had sufficient of that for the time being, for a girl of your age. My darling, you have been given the best of all possible worlds. You are married and bear one of the most famous names in the land. You are rich and will continue to be rich. And you have a husband, in name only. I had not meant to have this discussion with you so soon. You are still too young to appreciate such a situation. But you will, if you will only let yourself be guided by me. Believe me.'

'Guided by you?' Jacqueline cried. 'To someone else's bed, you mean, for our advancement? To have a child by some other prince? You don't even think I'm human, Mother. You think I'm a thing. I will never be guided by you again. Or by him.' She pointed. 'You say I must remain married to him. All right. If I must, I must. But I will not have that Bruno in this house. I will not, you understand. I will *not*!'

Anna hesitated, then made another moue. 'I suppose, as you feel so strongly about it, I could speak with the Count,' she agreed.

The Count stood in the doorway of Jacqueline's bedroom, the first time he had ever appeared there. 'May I come in?' he asked.

'Yes,' she said, getting up and standing in front of the bed. Left alone for several hours, her nervousness had threatened to overtake her anger, but that could not be allowed to happen. The Count might be three times her age, but now he was at her mercy. She had to remember this, because she knew that what advantages she failed to gain now she would never gain at all. This was her last chance to salvage even a little self-respect from the mess that was being made of her life.

The Count entered hesitantly. It occurred to Jacqueline

that he looked exactly like a rabbit, a very frightened rabbit.

'You may sit down if you wish,' she said, determined to maintain the initiative.

'Thank you.' He sat down, crossed his knees, flopped his white kid gloves on to his lap, picked them up again, and flopped them again. 'I have been speaking with your mother,' he said.

Jacqueline waited. She had no intention of helping him.

'I understand, of course,' he went on after a further hesitation, 'that a young girl like you, innocent of the world, may find some of the habits of that world a little strange.'

'Strange, Ion?' she asked. 'Am I that innocent? If I stood in the main square in Bucharest tomorrow and shouted that my husband was a homosexual, do you suppose they would think me strange for being unhappy?'

'My dear girl . . .' He took a silk handkerchief from his pocket and patted his forehead. 'The things you say. Have I ever ill-treated you in any way? Neglected you?' He flushed.

'You have never behaved like a husband to me,' she pointed out.

'Yes. Well, I am sure, having known Prince Carol, that you would find me a very poor substitute.'

'You mean you don't even like me enough to spend a moment more time in my company than you have to,' she snapped. 'You would rather be with . . . with Bruno.'

The Count coughed. 'I do not expect you to understand how it is possible for two men to . . . well . . .'

'I do *not* understand,' Jacqueline said. 'And I doubt if I ever will understand it. However, my mother has begged me not to ask for an annulment, in view of your name and your position in the community. This I will agree to, on certain conditions.'

'I see,' he said.

'Please listen to what I have to say, Monsieur. I do *not*

want Bruno to live under the same roof as myself. I am not asking you to sack him, if he means so much to you. But wherever I am, he must be somewhere else.'

'Yes,' the Count said, greatly relieved. 'I . . .'

'I also want an allowance,' Jacqueline went on, 'paid into my own bank account, starting tomorrow. An ample allowance, Monsieur, so that I need never ask you for money. And I also wish the use of your town house, as and when I require it. I propose to entertain,' she said, as his eyebrows raised.

'Men?' he asked in alarm.

'Anyone I choose.'

'Well . . .'

'Those are my terms. Otherwise I will make our exact relationship public.'

'Her Majesty would never forgive you,' he said.

'I am quite prepared to face Her Majesty's anger,' Jacqueline replied. 'Are you, Count Tyroler?'

She was amazed and delighted at how simple it had been. Not only had she demolished the Count, she had also gained a signal victory over her mother. Anna had not expected quite such a show of determined anger from her daughter. For the first time Jacqueline felt she was being respected, and her mother was obviously just as terrified as the Count that she might make the state of her marriage public, and so annoy the Queen that she would stop their pension.

But the victory was only a stepping stone on the way to freedom. She laid her plans with complete simplicity, as a direct approach certainly seemed the best. In a month or so, she would leave for Paris on a shopping trip. As Jean-Jacques was so very small, he would of course have to go with her, and she decided she would also take Cally, who in her silent way was trustworthy. Once safely in France, she would find Jean-Paul. She determined she would look no further ahead than that. She would find Jean-Paul and tell him the whole story, then do whatever

76

he wished her to do. Surely he would want an annulment of her marriage so that he could marry her himself? Deep in her heart she was sure of that. And if that left Mother and Ion to face the angry Queen Marie with probably little or no income above their own private pittances, it was no more than they deserved.

No matter what happened, she would see Jean-Paul again to show him his own son – and enjoy at least one more magnificent hour. There could be no sin in that. Whatever her mother's machinations, she was married to him, before God. She was certainly not married to anyone else.

But when she informed the Count that she was going, while he agreed that he could not stop her, he merely presented her with a written order from the Queen that Frederick Tyroler was under no circumstances to leave the country.

'This is ridiculous,' she stormed at her mother. 'Why am I not allowed to take my own son with me when I go on vacation?'

'I wish you would learn to understand that young Frederick is less your son than a Prince of Rumania,' Anna pointed out. 'Don't you suppose that Carol knows all about him, knows that it has to be his? Don't interrupt. If it wasn't his, Her Majesty would not be supporting us. And don't you also know that things are not going well here, what with Prince Nicholas quite unable to control the magnates? The Regency's sole claim to govern is because they possess King Michael. Suppose Carol, or some outside group, were to gain possession of Prince Frederick? And you talk about taking him to Paris?'

Jacqueline felt her mother was wildly exaggerating the position; clearly they suspected what she might have in mind, so there was no point in getting too upset about it. She had no doubt at all that she would eventually win the invisible chess game that was being played, because she had the greater will to do so. Obviously the Queen and Mother must have discussed the situation – with the Count as well, probably – and had worked out what she was likely to do. She would just have to be patient and change her tactics to less obvious ones. She accepted the decision with a smile and said, 'Oh well, it's not urgent. I still have good clothes to wear. And if there really could be some danger to Freddie . . . you must be right.'

Her next step was to throw herself into the social life of Bucharest. At first people were a little uncertain about being invited to soirées by an eighteen-year-old countess whose husband was very seldom seen at her side. But they came, and were lavishly entertained – she was careful to spend the Count's money and not her allowance on such things. Indeed, she became a perfect miser, hoarding her own funds for the day when she would need them. Cally was shocked, as she knew nothing of Jacqueline's plans. She could not understand why, when the stitching on a glove burst, Jacqueline had her mend it instead of merely discarding it and buying a new pair, why she had her shoes resoled again and again, and why she made so many of her own clothes. She came to the conclusion that it was the Count who was the miser, keeping his wife short of funds; Jacqueline did not attempt to change that impression.

Even so, accumulating sufficient money to bribe her way out of Rumania when the time came, and to support herself until she could feel the strong arms of Jean-Paul around her, was a terribly slow and sometimes frustrating business.

But, meanwhile, there was Jean-Paul himself. Her mother and the Count, for all their apparent determination to imprison her within Rumania, had forgotten about the Busonniere salon by the river. Jacqueline strolled down there one day to look at some gems, and remarked casually to the manager, 'Does Monsieur de Busonniere ever come to Bucharest?'

'Oh, indeed, Countess. Usually twice in every year.'

'How interesting,' she said. 'I have never met monsieur, but I did once meet his son, I think. Jean-Paul? Would that be his name?'

'Oh, indeed, Countess. Monsieur de Busonniere has a son named Jean-Paul.'

'Does he have anything to do with the business?'

'Well, I imagine he will, in due course, Countess. Right now he is in the army. He is serving with *Le Cadre Noir* of the French cavalry, you understand.'

'How splendid for him. Well, Monsieur, you must give Monsieur de Busonniere my regards and ask him to pass them on to his son. And ask him also, when next he is in Bucharest, to call. I should be delighted to see him. Now let me see, these garnets . . .'

After that it was simply a matter of waiting, but when the weeks became months and still de Busonniere had not called, she returned to the salon. 'He has not come, this year,' the manager explained.

But he would come. Meanwhile, Jean-Jacques was growing into a sturdy toddler, and therefore much more able to undertake the upheaval which would soon be upon him. Jacqueline estimated that another year would give her enough money in her savings account at least to escape and to support herself for a while – she already had more than half that much – and with that she would be quite a wealthy woman, at least for a time. If she added her jewellery, assuming that she would be able to take it with her, then she would be very wealthy indeed.

The future thus seemed to be becoming more rosy and certain with every day. Nor was the waiting in Bucharest at all unpleasant, and even if she had made no real friends out of her receptions and her supper parties, this was because she did not wish to do so. There was no future with these people, and she had no desire to begin an affair with any of the handsome young men who made eyes at her; now that two years had passed since her experience with Prince Carol, she felt almost virginal again – and wished to remain that way until she reached Jean-Paul. She knew that she had soon gained the reputation of being cold, and was content that this should be so.

A few days before her nineteenth birthday, catastrophe

struck. She was sitting in her boudoir in the town house, preparing herself for a dinner party, when the door suddenly opened and the Count entered. She turned, angrily, but was stopped by the sight of his ashen face. 'Ion? Whatever is the matter? You are not well?'

'My income has been cut in half,' he gasped. 'The Queen has ordered it. The crash on the stock market in New York . . . she had invested on Wall Street. Now her private funds are exhausted. Our income has been cut in half!'

Jacqueline immediately suspected that he was up to some scheme; she was not even aware that there had been a financial disaster in New York. But when she read the latest newspapers, she realised that things might be as serious as the Count had said. American business was reeling and American banks were calling in loans from every direction. Quite a few of those loans, the biggest ones, were to European institutions, governments, and also European heads of state. The papers were filled with the most dire prognostications concerning the world economy.

It turned out that the Count's income had been halved; he showed her his bank statement, and then suggested that she help him by returning some of her allowance. 'You cannot possibly have spent it all,' he said with a smile.

She gazed into his eyes. 'I'm afraid I have, Ion.' She certainly was not surrendering her nest egg.

'You are lying,' he snapped.

She slapped his face and left the room in discomfort. But she did not doubt that he had sufficient influence to obtain a look at her account. She hurried down to her bank that same afternoon and withdrew the entire balance.

'This is a strange procedure, Countess,' remarked the manager as he placed the large sum of money on the desk in front of her. 'In cash. It is risky, too.'

'I am going to travel,' she explained. 'I will need funds.'

'Ah . . . you do realise that the Government has forbidden the export of Rumanian currency?'

'No,' she said. 'How can they do that?'

He shrugged. 'Governments can do anything they like nowadays. If you attempt to take that amount of currency out of the country without permission, you will become liable to a long gaol sentence. But of course, I am sure the Countess Tyroler will have no difficulty in obtaining such permission. I will arrange it myself.' He reached for his telephone.

'No,' she said, stuffing the notes into the valise she had brought for the purpose. 'I will do it. There is no need for you to trouble yourself.'

He gazed at her. 'Countess,' he said. 'I think you should know that after our conversation, I feel it is my duty to inform the Minister of Finance of the withdrawal you have made here today.'

She would not lower her eyes despite the panic which was clawing at her mind. 'I am sure I have no wish to interfere with your "duty", Monsieur.'

'But will you not consider again, and re-deposit the funds?'

'No, Monsieur,' she said. 'I will not do that.'

She was trapped. The Minister of Finance was a friend of Ion's so even if she deposited the money somewhere else, he would find out about it. She went home in a panic . . . and found Monsieur de Busonniere waiting for her.

'Countess,' he said. 'I arrived in Bucharest this morning, and came round immediately. I had no idea that you had ever met my son. He will be delighted to know that I have seen you.'

She thought, and hoped, that Jean-Paul would look just like his father in thirty years' time: slim and distinguished, quietly acute in manner. 'I met Jean-Paul, oh, two summers ago, when riding in the hills behind Pitesti. My home, you know. We talked about Dracula.'

'Ah, yes,' said de Busonniere with a smile. 'Dracula. Always one of Jean-Paul's favourite subjects. Well, I will tell him that you asked after him. As I said, he will be delighted. Now, please forgive me, but I must leave. I called, not only because of your friendship with my son, you understand, Countess, but because my manager tells me you have been one of our best customers in the past. Alas, I must inform you that I am here to close the salon.'

'Close the salon?' she cried in alarm. 'But why, Monsieur?'

He shrugged. 'The financial situation. Like so many people, I require a certain amount of credit to continue my business because so much of my capital is tied up in gemstones. And at this moment credit is virtually unobtainable, which also means that customers are not buying. So I must, how do they say, pull in my horns? At least for a while. But if you are in search of a bargain, Countess, why, now is the time. I am offering large discounts on my stock here in Bucharest.'

Which was clearly why he had bothered to call at all, she supposed; he could look at what she was wearing and tell *she* was both able and prepared to buy good pieces. But might he not have a point? Jewellery! Then she would be telling the truth when she claimed she had spent all her allowance.

But Ion might force her to sell her jewellery. Did he have that right? She thought he might. Therefore he must never know, and therefore, also, she must acquire readily saleable items for use when she left the country and wished to turn them back into cash. Monsieur de Busonniere would know about things like that – and he would be returning to France in the near future, so he could not even be questioned.

'I might take you up on that offer, Monsieur,' she said. 'I have some money which I have considered spending on jewellery, purely as an investment, of course.'

'I could recommend nothing more certain, Countess. Currency exchange rates may rise and fall, but good stones never fail to rise in value. However, they must be unset stones, you understand. Settings are fashionable and what is popular today may be regarded as old-fashioned tomorrow.'

Stones, she thought. Of course. Good diamonds, which no one could possibly know she possessed, but which could be exchanged for currency anywhere in the world.

De Busonniere was studying her. 'I think I have just the stones you are looking for, Countess,' he said. 'And the transaction would be in the strictest confidence, of course.'

Monsieur de Busonniere was as good as his word. She accompanied him back to the salon, and that very afternoon, in exchange for all her savings Jacqueline was able to buy a packet of one-carat diamonds, as well as some smaller ones, each flawless, at least to her eyes, and all small enough to be carried in a tiny leather pouch which could be concealed in a recess of her purse. Indeed, Monsieur de Busonniere was so helpful that she felt a tremendous temptation to tell him everything, to ask him to help her escape too. But she decided against it for the moment. It was just too risky until she had regained contact with Jean-Paul. 'That is very satisfactory, Monsieur,' she said. 'I am delighted. Now you know, I really would like to drop Jean-Paul a line and tell him we have met. You have his address?'

'Well, Countess . . .' de Busonniere looked doubtful. She understood; she was a married woman.

'I do so hate to lose touch with old friends, Monsieur,' she said.

'You can certainly reach him at Saumur, Countess,' the jeweller said. 'It is the headquarters of *Le Cadre Noir*, you know. Any letter sent there will be delivered to him.'

'Why, thank you, Monsieur,' she smiled, and went home to face Ion.

'Where is the money you withdrew from the bank?' he demanded.

'In a safe place.'

'You . . . that is my money. And I need it.'

'No, it is my money, Ion. Every penny you have received for the past two years has been my money.'

'You . . .' He looked so angry she thought he might strike her, and prepared herself to dodge the blow. But of course, he didn't.

'Kindly leave my room,' she said. 'I am giving a dinner party tonight and I must dress. You can come to dinner, if you wish, Ion, since you are in town.'

'I have cancelled your dinner party,' he said.

'You have done what?'

'There is no money for things like dinner parties any more,' he declared. 'I have had Bruno telephone all your guests and inform them of this. And instead of standing there looking as if you would like to spit, I suggest you pack your things for an immediate return to Pitesti. I am putting this house on the market. Not,' he added gloomily, 'that I anticipate finding a buyer. But I certainly can no longer afford to maintain two establishments.'

Jacqueline only kept her temper with an effort. 'I did not really wish to have a dinner party anyway. I find them intensely boring events, and with you present it would have been more boring than ever. If you will leave my room now, I will pack.'

Because, when she thought about it, it really did not matter. Bucharest, Rumania, all was so very nearly behind her. As soon as the Count had left she sat down and wrote to Jean-Paul. There was no time now for hints and allusions, declarations of love could follow at a later date, and after they had been reciprocated, so could a detailed explanation of her position. She told him that she had been forced into marriage with Count Tyroler, that she still loved him and would always love him, and that she wished only to bring his son to him. 'Just tell me where we can meet,' she wrote. 'Reply with but a single word, the name of the town, and I will be there within a month. I love you, *mon chéri*, how I love you.'

She posted the letter herself because she was not sure that Cally could be trusted that far, and then accompanied Ion back to Pitesti that evening. She knew that the next few weeks were going to be difficult.

And indeed they were. Her mother had always considered money to be of greater value than blood, and she was easily enlisted on Ion's side. 'My dear Jacqueline,' she said. 'You are being quite unreasonable. Ion is your husband. I am your mother. We are all in the same boat. Ion tells me that you have withdrawn some four thousand *lei* from your bank. Quite apart from the dishonesty, the indecency, of withholding such a sum from your family, think of the risk? Four thousand *lei*, just lying around the place, waiting to be stolen!'

'I have taken steps to ensure that it will not be stolen, Mother,' Jacqueline said. 'And we have enough to live on without using it. Her Majesty would never let us starve.'

'You haven't spent it?' Anna was aghast.

Jacqueline smiled at her. 'No, I haven't spent it, Mother.' She wanted to keep them off that line of thought; they could tell she hadn't spent it on clothes, and they knew she hadn't spent it on entertaining, so they might well work out the truth. But, she felt perfectly safe, although she made sure the little pouch never left her purse and at night she slept with it under her pillow. Ion dared not even ask her to sell the jewellery he had given to her because of the scandal it would cause – although he did remove it from her to place it in 'safekeeping'. She suspected that he might have pawned it, and did not care. Just as she no longer cared about being trapped in Pitesti, at being unable to go shopping as and when she chose. In fact, Bucharest was an unpleasant place to live that winter as unemployment soared and tempers became frayed. Outside Pitesti there was still peace, she could ride into the mountains whenever the weather permitted, read on the terrace, and shut out what was going on around her. She had established a reputation for determined anger when crossed so her mother and Ion both chose to ignore her as much as possible. Often she felt lonely and betrayed, but kept to her vigil. It was only a matter of waiting for a reply from Jean-Paul.

Even when the winter ended in a late spring, she was

not unduly worried. Jean-Paul was a soldier and would have a soldier's duties and abrupt changes of station. Her letter might have taken longer than she had anticipated to reach him, and of course he could not reply until he had been able to arrange somewhere for them to meet. Or his letter might have been delayed somewhere en route. She refused to despair, and reflected that there was nothing more she could do until the weather improved. May came with the first warm sun and bright flowers before she began to make some actual plans. Obviously her letter had gone astray. She wrote to him again, this time saying that if she did not hear from him by the end of June she was coming to Saumur anyway. It would be nothing less than a gaol-break, of course. She would just have to make sure they did not catch her.

Now the days passed very quickly, as she decided what belongings she would take. Obviously she would have to travel very lightly – there would be Jean-Jacques' things as well – and just how would she leave the chateau, where she would join the train to give herself the maximum time to get across the border before she was discovered? She would need Rumanian cash for the ticket; she began hoarding again whenever she could: small amounts, but a rail ticket from Pitesti to the Hungarian border was not expensive. She would travel second class to avoid being recognised.

Planning her escape proved enormous fun. She found herself going over every possible occurrence in her mind, sitting for hours on the terrace looking at the snow-covered mountains, utterly content that at last it was going to happen. She was abruptly awoken from such a reverie one morning by a great deal of noise all about her; Anna's high heels were clicking rapidly over the tiled terrace floor towards her. 'Jacqueline!' she was shouting. 'Jacqueline!'

'Mama? Whatever is the matter?'

'Prince Carol . . . what am I saying. *King* Carol . . .'

'King Carol?'

'There has been a *coup d'état*,' Anna shouted. 'Carol

86

has returned, by aeroplane, would you believe it? Only three days ago. He has taken over the government, as King. Michael has been deposed. Carol has renounced his renunciation, and is *King*. And, Jacqueline, we have just received a message from Bucharest. The King has summoned you to see him. With your son.'

June 1930

Fly, fly betimes, for fear you give
Occasion for your fate.

Sir George Etherege, *The Man of Mode*

JACQUELINE SAT down, light-headed with shock.

'Isn't it marvellous?' Anna cried.

'Marvellous?' Jacqueline frowned at her.

'Well, obviously he is going to install you as a royal mistress, and bring up Freddie as a royal prince. Think of it, oh, think of it. Royal apartments, jewellery, motor cars, receptions, balls . . .' Anna's eyes gleamed. 'I have always dreamed of living like that.'

Jacqueline was still trying to bring her thoughts under control. 'Do you think the country will accept Carol back as King? After everything that has happened?'

Anna laughed. 'The country would accept Lucifer himself, I should think, if he would just solve the economic problems.'

'And Carol says he can do that?'

'Of course. He can hardly do worse than the Regency. They were too soft. This country needs iron at the helm. Carol can be quite a hard man when he wishes. He'll teach these people a thing or two.'

'What about Madame Lupesca?'

Anna's mouth twisted. 'I have no idea, but does it matter? The important thing is that you are going to be raised to the heights. There can be no other reason for such a summons. Carol knows about Tyroler, of course.

He will be pensioned off and need never bother you again. While you . . . you are going to the bed of a king.'

Jacqueline gazed at her. That aspect of the situation had not immediately occurred to her. But once again they were threatening to take over her life, to set her up for ruination and misery. Apart from destroying her plans for escaping to Jean-Paul, to have to spend the rest of her youth being pawed and savaged by that lout . . . and of course she would lose Jean-Jacques, her own child. She would lose everything. Every single thing.

So what more could she lose by fighting them?

'Of course, I understand that you are rather over-whelmed by all this, perhaps a little afraid,' Anna said. 'But there really is nothing for you to be afraid of. We now know that Carol fell for you, and if he was angry with you once, well . . . he would not have sent for you if he had not decided to forgive you. Being the mother of a man's son has a powerful effect upon his feelings. And I can tell you this: the Lupesca has never had a child for him.'

'Yes, I see,' Jacqueline said. She felt calm; her decision was taken. After all, it had already been made months ago. Perhaps she had always needed a catastrophe like this to make her act. Now it was merely a question of detail. 'When am I to go to the palace?'

'Tomorrow, for lunch. We shall leave on the second train at eight-thirty.'

'Tomorrow,' Jacqueline said, and stood up. 'Well then, Mother, you must excuse me. I shall have to pack.'

She felt happier than at any moment for the past three years. At last she was doing something for herself. And that something was a shaking-off of the intolerable burdens which had been heaped upon her throughout that time.

She knew she was taking an enormous risk. She had not originally intended to make her break for freedom until her twenty-first birthday, when legally she would be free – but that was still nearly eighteen months off. She realised now that her proposed escape at the end of this month had been a good deal too risky. She had to run away from a king, and with his child, as he supposed. She was almost tempted to go to Carol, as commanded, and tell him the whole story to prove to him that Jean-Jacques could not be his. But she doubted that he would believe her even after she had given him the relevant dates. Even if he did, he might still want to keep her. That was a risk she could not accept.

Thinking intently, she had to make absolutely sure that she and Jean-Jacques could not be caught and brought back. It was remarkable how, now that the decision to leave was finally taken, her mind became crystal clear, evaluating every aspect of the new challenge. She did not doubt she could get out of Rumania before anyone knew she had left, but afterwards they would know immediately where she had gone. Carol was now a king, he would be able to make the French government find her and deport her back to Bucharest. So France was not possible, at least until the hunt for her had died down. She had to go somewhere no one would think of looking for her, or if they did, no one would be able to find her. Somewhere she, and more importantly, Jean-Jacques, would be secure, until she could make contact with Jean-Paul. And where, if possible, she would not immediately have to dip into her precious store of diamonds. There was only one chance, because she knew she could not hope to carry out her plan entirely by herself. Once Carol started hunting, every unattached woman in Europe with a small son beside her would be suspect. It would have to be someone she could trust completely.

There was only one such person she could think of. Would he wish to help a half niece he had never seen? Would he send her packing back home? Somehow, she felt he would not do that. Besides, Germany . . . Germany was renowned throughout Europe as the home of freedom, of liberalism, of *laissez faire*. Having been regimented by their kaisers for centuries, the German people had determined to create a society in which no one need fear the discipline or censure of authority. Everyone said so. Even if Uncle Herman could not help her, there was no way even King Carol would be able to get her back from Germany.

She had Cally help her pack; after all, she was going to Bucharest to be with the King. But she had already decided that she could not risk taking the maid with her – Cally might be trustworthy when it came to fleeing a husband, but not when it came to fleeing a king. The girl was wildly excited at the prospect, as she saw it, and bitterly disappointed at Jacqueline's decision to take one single valise. 'But I shall only be away a day or two,' Jacqueline reminded her. 'If I am going to be any longer, then I shall have to send for my other things, eh? Now, off you go and pack for yourself, and mind you are ready to leave the chateau at eight sharp.'

She saw the maid out of the room, turned to get Jean-Jacques' clothes out of his bureau, and froze as she saw the Count standing in the doorway. 'Well?' she demanded.

He flushed, and held out a leather case. 'Anna says I should return these to you.'

She hesitated, then slowly stretched out her hands to take the case, opened the lid, gazed at her rings and bracelets and brooches. She could not believe her eyes. Fate was on her side, at last.

She raised her head. 'Thank you, Ion. Yes, I should look my best, should I not?'

His eyes filled with tears. 'I do not think I shall see much of you in the future.'

'I shall think of you whenever I can,' she promised, and kissed him on the forehead. For a moment she thought he was going to hold her close, then he turned and hurried down the corridor, now definitely weeping. It could hardly be love, she reminded herself. Rather the thought of losing possession of something so valuable – and of course he would still be counting on receiving his pension. She wondered if he would, after her disappearance?

91

But she would think of him whenever she thought of Bucharest, of that she had no doubt. If he ever had to go out and earn himself a living, it would do him a world of good. But for now, her wealth had been quadrupled in a single moment. She had to be careful; the attaché case too obviously contained articles of value. She concealed the various pieces all over her body, pinned brooches to her underwear, looped necklaces round her thighs and secured them with her suspenders, put rings on her toes, and even then had to wear far too many on her fingers. But her gloves would conceal most of those. Certainly she was not going to leave a single one behind.

She packed another valise for Jean-Jacques. She was going to have to carry a tremendous amount, but there was nothing else for it. Then it was just a matter of waiting until the chateau was quiet.

It really was the simplest thing in the world, she supposed, for all that her heart kept thumping so loudly she was sure everyone within a hundred yards could hear it.

But she had thought it all out very carefully, made considerable modifications to her original plan. If she was going to succeed, she had to outwit those who would chase after her. She had to accept that there was no hope of leaving from Pitesti Station without being recognised, and then she would almost certainly be arrested long before she could leave the country. Pitesti was the terminus of the main line from Bucharest into the mountains, and to go further west the railway made a tremendous loop from a junction some way up the line, down round the bottom of the high ground, to run by the Danube for a while before entering Yugoslavia, several hours away. Therefore she had to make her title and position work for her for as long as possible.

She wore her new cream woollen suit, a full-length sable coat, a matching felt cloche hat, with black shoes and gloves, and over it, a mink fur edged with sable. The outfit would be hot, but also conspicuous. She carried a cheap cloth coat she wore for walking in the hills over her arm, folded back to show the lining but not the coat itself. Then she picked up the two valises and the sleeping Jean-Jacques, and simply walked out of the castle; everyone was sound asleep, not even the dogs barked. She was seized by an urge to go to the stables and at least say goodbye to the horses, but that was far too risky. Time enough to see them again in the future, when she reached that future. As for Mama – she had no doubt she would see her again, but hopefully not for a long time.

Her principal enemy was fatigue. It was a walk of three miles from the chateau into the town, and within ten minutes her arms were burning from the weight of the suitcases and the little boy; at two years old Jean-Jacques was a sturdy fellow. She tried changing arms, but gained little relief, and soon she had to stop for a rest, feeling now too the weight of the jewellery she had concealed about her. She looked at her watch. It was half past two. She had plenty of time, the early train did not leave until six. She paced herself, walking in fifteen minute bursts – counting every second – and then sat by the wayside for ten minutes, thanking the heavens that the country outside Pitesti was so empty. But of course the stars were entirely on her side, or she would not have regained possession of her jewellery.

She reached the station at half past five, found it already quite crowded. 'Countess Tyroler?' asked the station-master, peering past her to find the servants and the car. 'You look exhausted.' He summoned a porter to take her bags.

'Thank you, monsieur,' she said. 'Would you believe it? The car has broken down half way here. My heavy bags will have to travel later. But now I simply must get to Bucharest. It is a matter of national importance.'

'Of course, Countess. Of course.' He swelled with importance; Jacqueline did not doubt that he, along with everyone else in Pitesti, knew she had been summoned to the palace. 'The early train leaves in thirty minutes. A first class compartment, of course . . .'

She handed over too large a proportion of her precious *leis*, and was installed in a compartment of her own. Jean-Jacques, who had awakened and commenced to whimper in the noise and bustle of the station, was again fast asleep on the seat beside her. 'Don't forget to send on my luggage,' she told the stationmaster.

He assumed an owlish expression, was clearly prepared to cooperate to the limit. Then the train was pulling out of the station. Of course, he might telephone ahead to Bucharest Central, but that was not relevant; the train would not get in until ten, and by then . . . she called the conductor.

'Countess Tyroler,' he said. 'Monsieur Ceanescu told me to look out for you. If there is anything you need, anything at all . . .'

'Dear Monsieur Ceanescu,' she said. 'I asked him for a ticket to Belgrade, and he has given me one for Bucharest. Out of habit, I suppose. I never checked.'

'Belgrade?' He scratched his head.

'I can catch the train to Belgrade, surely? Without going all the way into Bucharest?'

'Well, of course, Countess. You can change trains just down the line, at Topoleveni Junction.' He looked at his watch. 'We should get there in time. But Belgrade . . .'

'Just give me a new ticket,' she said. 'I will pay the difference.'

Still he hesitated. But it was not his business to decide what the Countess Tyroler might be doing going to Belgrade in the early hours of the morning with her child. He did not know that she had appeared at Pitesti Station without any servants, clearly having walked. Also, not being a local, he knew nothing of any summons to the palace either. He sighed and made out a new ticket. By eight o'clock Jacqueline and Jean-Jacques were on their way, rumbling south-west through Slatina to Craiova, then curving north-west to join the Danube at the famous Iron

Gate, the gap through the mountains where so many armies, beginning with the Romans led by the Emperor Trajan, had marched, with Yugoslavia just across the river. But the train remained in Rumanian territory, arcing away again to the north-west, until it reached the junction town of Tumsoara, with the border crossing at the village of Jimbolia only a few miles further on.

It was a long way. Jean-Jacques had been bright, happy and easily entertained for the first few hours, but the milk and biscuits she had taken from the larder on her way out through the chateau kitchens were soon finished. Unable to interpret his whimpered pleas – even feeding had always been Nanny's province since he had been weaned – Jacqueline was about to give him the slices of cold chicken she had brought for herself when suddenly a strong and very unpleasant smell made her realise her mistake. Twenty minutes later her son smelled sweet again; clean clothes from his valise had replaced those jettisoned into the passing forest and his tiny milk teeth were digging eagerly into the chicken. Watching him, Jacqueline felt a rush of guilt. She had only ever half-listened to Nanny's proud tales of his young achievements. Now she had been forcibly reminded of the story of his potty training; of course she couldn't possibly have added that heavy porcelain pot to her luggage even if she had thought of it. But she had not thought of it. She had had no idea of his appetite, either. She had played with him in his bath, walked him in the gardens, rocked him on his rocking-horse. But Nanny had always coped with the less pleasant duties, answered his distress calls in the middle of the night, sat with him through his baby ailments and given him his medicine. What a remote and selfish mother she was, just like her own mother had been to her. Did she only love this dark-haired, sunny child as a lever to restore her lover to her? Was she like her own mother who had given a little attention and affection to her only to restore her own place in society and obtain the necessary wealth for lavish living? And what about poor Nanny? She would be distraught by now, having found Jean-Jacques' cot empty, knowing he had been carried away by a mother totally inexperienced in looking after him. A surge of love flooded her as she gazed at him. All available food and drink consumed, he had fallen asleep. Occasionally his lips sucked gently on the beloved thumb as his forefinger stroked his nose.

But I am doing this for you as much as for me, my darling, she thought, and woke with a start as the train jerked and shuddered to a stop. It was eleven o'clock and they were at the border.

Now her heart really began to jump. There had been ample time for someone to have telephoned here from Bucharest, and certainly Pitesti would have been in a frenzy for hours following the discovery of her departure. She pinned her hopes on the fact that Monsieur Ceanescu would have insisted she was going to Bucharest, that the conductor of the Bucharest train would not report her change of plans before being asked, and that before anything happened everyone would suppose that she had gone straight to the palace by herself. Mother would hope it would be to throw herself on Carol's mercy, but all that was irrelevant, just as long as they dithered for one precious hour. Yet she nearly jumped out of her skin when the Customs Officer appeared in the doorway of the compartment. 'Passports?' He inspected hers with a frown. 'Your son, Countess?' He pointed at Jean-Jacques who was just waking up.

'Of course.'

'He is not on the passport.'

For a moment she stared at him while her mind went into a whirl; her first obvious mistake. 'Isn't he?' she asked. 'Oh, that is annoying. I told Ion . . . you know Count Tyroler, of course?'

'I have heard the name, Countess,' the man said cautiously.

'He knew I was making this journey. And he has forgotten to put young Frederick on the passport. Oh, I shall

96

have something to say to him, I promise you that. Well, you will just have to let us through anyway.'

He shook his head. 'I cannot, Countess, without a passport. And even if I did, you would be stopped time and again over the border.'

That hadn't occurred to her before. Panic began to lap at her mind, but having come this far she was not going to surrender to a single oversight. 'Oh,' she said. 'Well, I suggest you give me a piece of paper, signed by you under your official stamp, informing everyone that my son is allowed to travel with me, even though he is not on the passport.'

'I could not do that, Countess. I should be in trouble. I am afraid you will have to leave the train and wait while I telephone.'

'And I must be in Belgrade by lunchtime,' she said, refusing to lower her gaze, although her stomach was turning cartwheels. But she still had an ace up her sleeve. She slipped Queen Marie's wedding gift from her finger. 'Do you recognise that?'

He peered at it. 'It is the Royal Crest,' he muttered.

'It belongs to Her Majesty Queen Marie,' Jacqueline explained. 'And she has given it to me because I am travelling on confidential business, for her. Now, really, monsieur, I must insist that you give me that paper. After all, I have a valid passport. What, do you suppose a two-year-old boy is guilty of some crime?' She could see he was weakening, but not entirely convinced, so she played her trump. 'And, in exchange, so that you need not get into any trouble, I will give you this ring. Only until I return, of course. Is that not fair?'

It seemed to take an eternity for him to write out the required note, which he then had to take back to his office to stamp. By now the new guard, a Hungarian – the train did no more than dip into Yugoslavia and out again – was getting impatient, and the engine was snorting and puffing. Jacqueline kept her fur on despite the heat – she did not want the Customs Officer to be able to describe her dress

– and clearly he was thoroughly fed up with eccentric aristocrats.

At last the Customs Officer returned. 'This is all most irregular,' he said. 'But . . .'

'I am sure the ring will convince your superiors you have done the right thing,' Jacqueline said, wondering if he would ever show it to anyone, or just sell it. 'And you may be sure of my gratitude. I shall most certainly tell Her Majesty of your cooperation.'

Another man had appeared in the corridor. 'There is a telephone call for you, Anton,' he said. 'From Bucharest. They say it is urgent.'

'I shall come at once,' he agreed, and kissed Jacqueline's hand; she wondered if he noticed how it had suddenly begun to sweat. 'Perhaps you should hold the train,' he suggested to the guard. 'Until I see what is the matter.'

'We have already waited long enough,' the Hungarian growled in French, and a few moments later the station was receding behind them. They were in Yugoslavia.

Now it was necessary to explain to the already disgruntled guard that although she had asked for a ticket to Budapest, they had stupidly given her one to Belgrade. Sighing, the man made out the new one and she paid the difference in Rumanian money. He did not seem to mind, it was an international train, but it left her very short of ready cash.

Only an hour later they crossed the border into Hungary, where the Customs officials hardly bothered to look at her passport at all; if the call had concerned her they were obviously looking for her in Belgrade. But it was two o'clock before they reached Szeged, and by then Jacqueline had no doubt the telephone lines were buzzing in every direction. She had the compartment door open even before the train had stopped. 'Porter!' she shouted. 'Quick. I need a taxi.'

She waved a note at him which he pocketed without realising it was Rumanian currency – her last – then she was out of the train, clutching Jean-Jacques in one arm, her valises in the other.

'Countess,' shouted the guard. 'You have a ticket to Budapest.'

'I have changed my mind,' she retorted, and hurried from the station. 'I wish to go to a pawnshop,' she told the taxi driver. He raised his eyebrows, looked at her coat and rings, shrugged, then obliged. She sold one of her bracelets for a tenth of its value, she supposed, but it gave her sufficient money for immediate purposes. The taxi had waited, and now they were driven to a cheap restaurant for lunch. Jacqueline's stomach had groaned with hunger for hours, but when a strange looking plate of food was placed in front of her, having been ordered by a combination of sign language and pointing at another diner's plate, her appetite disappeared. The nervous tension which had spurred on her planning and daring since her mother's announcement of Carol's return, plus her physical weariness, made every mouthful difficult to swallow. It would be difficult to digest, too, but she knew she must force herself. Fortunately, she had no problems at all with Jean-Jacques. He worked away enthusiastically with his spoon through a man-sized helping and, with a large portion still on his face, smiled up at his mother and demanded, 'More!'

Afterwards she asked for the toilet and was directed across the back yard to a disgustingly smelly shed. The facilities did little to help her querulous insides and she had difficulty changing the child into worn, nondescript clothes without them becoming soiled on the floor. Having bundled her sable up roughly into a cot sheet provided for the purpose, together with a few essential items for them both, she abandoned the two expensive valises behind an old tea-chest in a corner. Then she put on the cheap coat she had carried all day, changed her hat for a scarf, hid her gloves – which meant she had to put all her rings into her pockets – and emerged looking very much one of the world's workers. She then walked back to the railway station, Jean-Jacques in her arms.

'Ma?' he asked, still at the monosyllabic stage of learning to speak. 'Where An-na?'

His way of inquiring why they were not comfortably at home.

'We'll soon be home,' she told him gently, not specifying which home.

At the station she was subjected to a hard stare by one of the many policemen to be seen, but there could be no possible connection between this shabby young woman with her obviously overtired, grubby-faced and cheaply dressed son, and the elegant creature in the sable coat and with monogrammed valises who had fled the train some hours before.

She bought a third class ticket to Budapest and sat down in a corner of the crowded compartment on uncushioned seats, Jean-Jacques on her knee. Soon he fell asleep again, and she managed to dose herself with medicine to ease her fluttering stomach. In Budapest they changed to a train bound for Vienna, although she had actually bought a ticket for Paris. In Vienna she repeated the pattern, again leaving the express and boarding the next one several hours later in the late evening, requesting a ticket for Amsterdam. They spent the time between trains sitting in various waiting rooms, existing on a diet of wieners and blackbread and milk. Jean-Jacques fretted, but most of the time he was too tired to understand what was happening and just how uncomfortable he was. The next major station after Vienna was Munich.

They arrived at half past nine in the morning. It seemed incredible that she had left Pitesti two days before, that in all that time she had not bathed or cleaned her teeth, or had more than two hours of consecutive sleep. But she was here.

She pushed her way through the crowds of people arriving in the city for work, found a telephone in a post office, and thumbed through the book, with sleeping Jean-Jacques draped over her shoulder. Her fingers trembled.

What if he had changed his name? Suppose . . . **Dumescu & Son**. The street name meant nothing to her. But underneath was a smaller entry, **Dumescu, H.**, and a different address. His home number. It had to be Uncle Herman.

She wanted to burst into tears, had to bite her lip. This was what it would be like for someone who had crawled across an entire desert to gain the safety of an oasis. But despite her exhaustion, the feeling that she would give everything she possessed for a hot bath, she knew she must still proceed with caution.

She went outside, allowing herself for the first time a look at the mountains looming south of the town, at the wide boulevards and busy streets. Munich was a great, thriving city that made even Bucharest look like a provincial town.

She waved to a taxi. The car stopped, but the driver did not look convinced that she could possibly be able to afford his services.

'Dumescu and Son,' she said.

He looked even less convinced, and said something in German.

'I have business there,' she replied in French, which he seemed to understand, for he gave a brief laugh and then looked at the rings she was replacing on her fingers, including her engagement ring. He shrugged and opened the back door for her. Five minutes later they drew up again before a disappointingly small and somewhat grubby façade. 'Dumescu and Son.'

Jacqueline opened the door and got out, rocking Jean-Jacques gently, he was beginning to wake up, and gazed at the shop front, the sign above her head. Her uncle was a pawnbroker!

Well, she thought, then I have certainly come to the right place. The taxi driver was pointing at his meter, and speaking again.

'Come inside,' she said, opening the door to the accompaniment of a jangling bell. She looked left and

101

right at the accumulation of goods, some quite valuable, but most of them utter junk, which filled the shop.

A young man appeared from the inner room and her heart leapt. He was somewhat darker than she or her mother, with black rather than pale hair, but his features were very definitely Dumescu. 'Ja?' he asked, looking from Jacqueline to Jean-Jacques, and then to the taxi driver who had followed them into the shop.

The taxi driver explained, somewhat dubiously, that the young lady wished to pawn something, at the very least to pay the fare.

'Do you speak French?' Jacqueline asked, in that language.

'Oui, madame,' the young man said.

'Then I wonder if you recognise me? I am your cousin Jacqueline.'

He frowned at her. 'My cousin?'

'Jacqueline Dumesca, from Rumania.'

The frown deepened. 'Jacqueline Dumesca? But we had heard . . .'

'Oh, yes,' she said. 'I am also the Countess Tyroler. Is your father here?'

At that moment Herman Dumescu emerged from the back of the shop, and his son spoke rapidly in German, interrupted from time to time by the taxi driver who was getting impatient.

'Jacqueline?' Herman Dumescu asked, but clearly he could recognise her face. 'My dear, dear girl.' He came out from behind the counter to kiss her hand and then embrace her. 'And this is your son? My, my.'

'It is all a very long story,' she said. 'But I need your help, Uncle Herman, most desperately. Will you help me?'

He glanced at his son. 'Of course, my dear. Of course. You are my niece. Just tell me . . .'

'If you could pay the driver,' she said.

'Of course,' he agreed. 'Of course.' He gave the necessary instructions to his son, who opened the till. 'But you . . .' he peered at her. 'You look so tired. And so . . .'

'Dirty,' she agreed. 'I have been travelling constantly for two days and have not changed my clothes in that time.'

'My dear girl, whatever can have happened?'

'Do you think I could have a bath, and change poor Jean-Jacques? He really is the most sticky mess. Then I will tell you everything.'

'Yes,' he nodded. 'Jacob, you mind the store. I will take Jacqueline home to Mutti, and we will make her comfortable. Say hello to your cousin Jacqueline, Jacob. You'll excuse me for one moment, my dear.' He bustled into the back of the shop.

'Hello,' Jacob said. 'It is good to see you.'

'It is good to be here,' Jacqueline replied, watching her uncle return wearing a wide-brimmed black felt hat on his head. Suddenly she was aware of a most peculiar feeling, a feeling . . . she was quite sure of the warmth of their welcome . . . yet there was something slightly strange about the two men. They seemed to show an abnormal degree of care and respect, not only for her, given she had only walked in on them a few minutes before, but also towards each other.

It was as Uncle Herman reached along the counter to pick up the black leather-bound book embossed with a golden Star of David that her heart gave a curious jump. Of course, she realised; her Munich relatives, so cold-shouldered by her mother, were Jews.

As if it mattered, she told herself. It might be fashionable in Rumanian society to despise Jews, and of course Queen Marie hated them because the Lupesca was a Jewess, but she had never found any cause to dislike them. Not that she knew any, save the Lupesca herself, she reflected. But Herman Dumescu, sitting beside her in the taxi, chucking Jean-Jacques under the chin and pointing out the sights of Munich, including the famous street where seven years before there had been an attempted revolution, stirred up by some political group known as the National Socialists of whom Jacqueline had never heard, was so obviously kind and disposed to be generous.

She frowned out of the window. If Uncle Herman was a Jew, then Mother . . . she could not understand it at all. But she was too tired to think clearly, and a few minutes later she was overwhelmed by the greeting she was receiving from her aunt Hannah, and her other cousin, a plump, dark-haired girl named Ruth. The boy, Jacob – both her cousins were younger than she, which made sense, as Uncle Herman was a few years younger than Mother – had clearly telephoned the moment they had left the shop, and everything was ready for her: a bath already drawn, a bed made up for Jean-Jacques, a dressing gown waiting for her to put on.

'I don't know what to say,' she confessed. 'I have to explain.'

'After you have bathed and rested,' Uncle Herman said very firmly. 'But Jacqueline . . . is there anything I should do? Anyone I should inform that you are here?'

'No!' she cried. 'Oh please, no. I can explain. I will, really. But no one must know that I am here.'

'As you wish, my dear,' he said. 'As you wish. Now you run along with Ruth, and calm yourself. No harm will come to you here.'

She believed him utterly. The Dumescu household was like a vast nest, a cavern of security. Their home was set back from the street with a pleasant and flourishing garden in front and an apple orchard at the back. Its ceilings were high and the rooms spacious, despite the enormous amount of furniture crammed into them. Aunt Hannah liked huge, overstuffed chairs, and every table-top was a mass of photographs in silver frames, while thick Persian rugs covered the floors. Uncle Herman might only be a pawn-broker, but clearly he was extraordinarily successful.

Later he admitted, with a wry smile, that his affluence was of recent origin. 'Business has been good lately,' he said. 'Since the crash. Everybody needs money now.' Although he maintained the same shabby premises in which he had first begun business, and displayed the same worthless stock that he had accumulated in his early days, his safe was apparently crammed with jewels and precious stones, surrendered by the wealthy of Bavaria in an attempt to maintain their pre-1929 standard of living.

Jacqueline bathed, changed, and rested, though after an enormous lunch she was ready for bed again. But it was necessary to explain first. By now she had come to a decision: these people were absolutely genuine and trustworthy. She would tell them everything. Which she did, talking for more than an hour. Ruth had gone out, and Hannah and Herman listened in silence until she had finished. Then Hannah said, 'You poor girl. You poor, poor girl.'

Herman got up, filled a pipe. 'There has been no word yet,' he said. 'Nothing on any of the radio programmes . . . but then, they would hardly make your disappearance public, in the circumstances. As you say, they will look for you first in France. At least until they are convinced you are not there. Then . . .' he glanced at her. 'They will certainly make inquiries here.'

'Will you help me, Uncle Herman?' she begged. 'Will you? I have money. I have a great deal of jewellery that you could sell for me.' She resisted the temptation to tell him about her pouch of diamonds as well; she felt they might not quite approve of the way she had deceitfully manipulated Ion to obtain them.

Herman Dumescu smiled and patted her hand. 'You are our guest, Jacqueline. What, sell your jewellery? We wouldn't think of it.'

'But what will you do?' she asked. 'When Mother sends to find out if you have heard from me?'

Herman looked at his wife. 'Anna has never deigned to write to me or to reply to any of my cards and letters. I do not think she can expect a great deal of cooperation from us, do you, my dear?'

'None at all,' Hannah declared.

'But she will probably employ private detectives to trace

you,' Herman went on. 'However, if you really did buy a ticket to Amsterdam, and left the train wearing a different coat . . . it is going to take her some time even to trace you as far as Vienna, in view of all your subterfuge.' He smiled at her. 'You should have been a spy. I think you will be safe here. We will make it known that you are one of Hannah's nieces who has come to visit. Not that anyone pays much attention to us, socially. I'm afraid the Jews aren't all that popular in Munich right now. This city is a Nazi stronghold.'

'Nazi?' she asked, not really interested. She was still trying to comprehend her good fortune, that she had made such a good choice in deciding to come here. It was stupid of her to doubt that any more. All she had to do was build on it.

'National Socialists. I told you of them, remember? They have a habit of recruiting their members from among the young unemployed thugs, of whom there are far too many, and whom the police seem quite unable to control.'

'Because most of the police are Nazis themselves,' Hannah remarked bitterly.

'Ah, but we don't want to upset Jacqueline on her first day here,' Herman said. 'I would just suggest that you do not go walking by yourself, especially after dark. Always have either Ruth or Jacob with you. Of course you do not look like a Jew, so I suppose . . .'

'But I am not a Jew,' Jacqueline said without thinking.

Herman Dumescu exchanged glances with his wife. 'Of course not, my dear.'

'Am I?' she questioned. 'How can I be?'

'We have just agreed that you are not. Still, one cannot be too careful these days. Now, you are utterly exhausted. May I suggest that you return to bed for a really good rest?'

'Uncle Herman,' she begged. 'Please tell me.'

'Tell you what, my dear?'

'About . . . well, what am I?'

'A very lovely, but a very exhausted, young woman,' Herman said in a kindly voice.

'Please,' she begged.

He sighed and looked at his wife again. 'It all depends whether you are referring to race or religion, my dear child. Usually, the two are the same thing with our people. But in certain cases, such as yours . . . your grandfather, you see, Anna's father, and mine of course, was of an orthodox Jewish family. Oh, he was a rich man, an important one too, but none the less . . .'

'Grandpapa was a Jew?' She was aghast. And yet, suddenly, she knew that it was true. And that was why Mama hardly ever spoke of him. It also explained so many other things. But not enough. 'But . . .'

'Father married outside the faith, a Roman Catholic,' Herman explained. 'I do not know all the details. Those were confused times in the Balkans, the 1880s. But I do know that Father abandoned his religion to marry a gentile, who was of course the mother of my sister Anna, your mother. She was brought up in her mother's faith, as you have been.'

'And then Grandpapa . . .?'

Herman Dumescu's smile was sad. 'I do not think my father's marriage was a happy one. He could not divorce his wife, by the laws of her religion. So he sought his solace elsewhere, with a woman of his own people. I am the result of that.'

'Oh, Uncle Herman,' she said. 'I am so sorry.'

'Sorry for what?'

'Well . . .'

'I am perfectly happy. I would say I have been happier than Anna ever has been. And I am happiest of all now that you have come to stay with us. I would hope, of course, that a reconciliation between Anna and yourself may be possible . . .' he faltered at her expression. 'One day, perhaps. Now off you go and lie down. No, just a moment, this young man of yours . . . would you like me to see if I can establish contact with him?'

'Would you, Uncle Herman? Could you?' She held both his hands. 'I was going to write to him again.'

He shook his head. 'I don't think that would be a very good idea. The letter might go astray or be opened by the wrong person, and you don't want anyone to know where you are, do you?'

'No, of course not,' she agreed. 'That would be disastrous. They'd make me go back to Rumania.'

'Quite. I think you should leave the matter with me,' Herman said.

'But how can you find him?'

'The easiest thing in the world. I happen to know Monsieur de Busonniere.'

'You *know* him?' Jacqueline could not believe her ears.

'We have done a great deal of business together, he and I.' He winked at her. 'I have good stones to sell, now and then, and Monsieur de Busonniere is always on the lookout for good stones. You leave it to me. I will get a message to your Jean-Paul and try to arrange a meeting between you.' He patted her hand again. 'Just leave it to me.'

Did he and Hannah believe anything she had told them? Well, they knew she was the Countess Tyroler; they could see that in her passport. And they seemed determined to help her. She lay awake for over an hour, despite her exhaustion, wondering if they were not just pretending, perhaps were already sending wires to Pitesti? Oh no, they couldn't be. They were too obviously delighted to have her with them. And why should they do anything to help Anna, who had never wanted to contact them?

Of course, she thought drowsily, they were probably considering possible advantages to themselves. If what she had told them was true, she was very well connected, which might one day prove useful. And sleeping under their roof was a boy who might one day be very important, too. Could it be that they hoped to convert her to Judaism, she wondered, and Jean-Jacques as well? In fact, she did not think that would be a very bad thing; they were so nice.

But to be a Jew! She nearly woke up. No matter what her upbringing and religion, she was Jewish. Did it matter? Had Queen Marie known? She thought that might be so. King Carol had shown a weakness for a Jewess – so send another, younger, prettier Jewess to get him back. Then, Mother was a Jewess too, for all her strident dislike of them. Oh, what a dreadful hypocrite Mother was.

She fell asleep, and all her apprehensions for what plans her uncle and aunt might have for her and for Jean-Jacques disappeared over the next few days beneath the avalanche of kindness under which she was submerged. The next morning Aunt Hannah and Ruth took her shopping to get her a complete new wardrobe, as well as outfitting Jean-Jacques. She begged to be allowed to sell some of her jewellery to pay for it, but they absolutely refused. 'You may regard it as a long-term loan, if you wish,' Hannah told her.

In the same way they introduced her to their life in Munich, which was very much a domestic one. They seemed to have few friends, apart from one or two other Jewish families, and their social life was spent within the home, listening to gramophone records and constantly debating. They were great talkers, on history, on religion, literature, and above all, politics. In the evenings Uncle Herman would read to them from the day's newspaper, editorials or articles concerning modern Germany, and then they would all discuss them, even Jacqueline, as she grew more accustomed to her new home. It was the first time she had ever become involved in politics, a subject she had always found boring in the past. But here in Germany it was a very serious matter indeed. She did not suppose that the Germans were any more hard-hit by the depression than the Rumanians, but the Germans seemed to feel it more because they were an industrial rather than a farming community, and because even the poorest German working man was used to a higher standard of living than the average Rumanian.

'Of course we shall pull through,' Uncle Herman insisted. 'But it is distressing to see the youth of the country standing around on street corners with nothing to do, their brains at the mercy of any rabble-rouser. A lot of them are Communists, you know, without any idea of what Communism really means.'

'And the other half are Nazis, which is worse,' Jacob Dumescu said.

'I'm not sure about that,' his father argued. 'The Nazis are at least against the Communists, which must be a good thing.'

Living in their quiet home in Munich, Jacqueline saw little of either faction; they were mainly only in evidence at mass meetings in the city centre, where the opposing sides, according to Uncle Herman, would often encounter each other and hurl bottles and fight with their fists until broken up by the police. She had no desire to become involved in politics to that extent, although she was relieved that her new relations were at least against Communism, which was the only 'ism' ever to have really concerned either Mother or Ion. But, she reminded herself, she was only passing through Munich, indeed, all of Germany; their fears and their troubles did not really affect her. Soon Uncle Herman would have made contact with Jean-Paul and she would go away to that life of which she had always dreamed.

Though somehow, deep down in her heart, she had always known that it was only a dream. She felt nothing except a dull lump in her stomach on the afternoon, only ten days after her arrival, when Uncle Herman asked her to sit down with him in the parlour. He gave her a copy of a French newspaper; neatly listed under the Marriages column was the name of Jean-Paul de Busonniere, to Mademoiselle Veronique Confert, at the Cathedral of the Sacred Heart, Paris. The newspaper was dated June 1928.

June 1930 – July 1930

'But cloud instead, and ever-during dark
Surrounds the cheerful ways of men
Cut off,'

John Milton, *Paradise Lost*

TWO YEARS ago. Two years. Why, Jacqueline reflected, he
had already been married when she had first met Monsieur
de Busonniere, and suggested writing to him. No wonder
the jeweller had been rather taken aback.

Had Jean-Paul received her letters? Had he even opened
them?

But to have married, without a word to her. Mother
had been right about him, after all. But of course she
wasn't right about him, she couldn't be. It was all so
easy to explain: a ghastly chapter of mistakes on her
part. Clearly Jean-Paul had learned of her marriage
to Ion Tyroler. And of course he had not known that
she was carrying his child; no one had ever told him.
Oh, if only she had followed her instincts, written to
him right away, ignored Mother's lectures . . . but now
. . . she raised her head, found her uncle watching her
anxiously.

'Did you . . .?'

He shook his head. 'It was quite simple to discover,
without telling anyone why I was inquiring, Jacqueline. I
am most terribly sorry.'

She gazed at him. To her surprise, she was not crying.
The tears were there, but they were not yet ready to

111

flow. That would come later, when the fact of what had happened had sunk in.

'Is there anything you want me to do?' Herman Dumescu asked gently. 'Anything you would like me to arrange for you?'

She knew what he meant. 'I do not want to go home, Uncle Herman,' she said. 'I can't.'

He sighed. 'Of course, my dear.'

'Have you heard from my mother?'

'Not yet. I imagine they are still trying to trace all your movements. And as you said, they will begin by seeking you in France. But they will certainly come to me, eventually.'

'Then I must leave,' she said. 'I cannot involve you in my problems. And . . .'

'Leave and go where? Do what?'

'Well, I . . .' She had no idea.

'You came to me for help,' Herman said. 'And I propose to help you. You have had a great shock, but now you must get over that shock. Then you must consider what you wish to do with your life. Believe me, I understand, and I am very pleased that you do not want to spend your life as a royal mistress. But you must give yourself time to think. The best place to do that is here, with us. On the other hand . . .' he stroked his chin, while she waited. It was so comforting to be able to place herself entirely in the hands of someone so trustworthy, so willing to help her. 'I think it would be a good idea for you to go away for a time. To Berlin.'

'Berlin?' she cried.

'Yes. Hannah's family live in Berlin, her mother and father as well as her brother and sisters. I think if you and Ruth went with her on a long visit to Berlin, with Jean-Jacques of course, then you will not even be here when Anna sends after you. That would be the safest way. Once she realises that you are not here, then you may return in perfect safety.' He took her hand. 'You will love Berlin, my dear girl. It is the finest city in Europe.

Theatres, art galleries, museums, everything you can think of. It will be good for you.' He winked. 'Perhaps in Berlin you might even meet another Jean-Paul, eh?'

She knew he was only trying to be kind and encouraging, but his suggestion did at last bring the tears. She ran from the room, hesitated in the hall, could hear Ruth and Aunt Hannah talking in the kitchen. She could not face them now.

She tiptoed out of the front door and very gently closed it behind her. It was a splendidly warm June evening, not in the least chilly; there was no necessity for a coat. Only a quarter of a mile from the Dumescu residence there was a park, a place of shady trees and quiet streams, somewhere she and Ruth had often walked together, and where she knew she would find peace, and above all, solitude.

To weep her heart out? Somehow she knew she was not going to do that. Uncle Herman had merely upset her, for all his kindness. Meet another Jean-Paul? She certainly had no wish to do that. Now, she was not at all sure of her feelings towards him, because even if it was mainly her fault, he had married someone else. That hardly suggested that he had spent much time in pining for her.

She sat on a bench near a quiet bridlepath, away from even the occasional pair of lovers strolling through the park; she had no desire to look at any lovers tonight. Jean-Paul had made love to her and then left her, perhaps to marry someone else he had recorded in his diary. What did men write in their diaries when they had made love to a girl? Suppose someone else read the diary? Suppose he showed it to his new wife?

Oh, Mother would have a field day when she found out how she had been proved right. As if it mattered. They would never meet again. What she had to do now was to consider her own future. Because at this moment she did not have one, as Uncle Herman was no doubt very well aware. She had run away from her husband and from the society which had established her. Everything that went with being the Countess Tyroler was lost to her; she could not even use the name any more. She had a certain amount of wealth in her jewellery and diamonds which was so far untouched and might be worth as much as ten thousand English pounds. Properly invested, that should secure her an income of about one thousand pounds a year, which presumably was sufficient for Jean-Jacques and herself to live on. And she had no doubt that Uncle Herman would look after her investment for her.

But what then? And where? Did she want to stay in Germany? She knew nothing of it, was in fact quite excited at the prospect of the visit to Berlin. And if not Germany, where?

She suddenly remembered that she was half American, if what Mother had told her about her father was true. It was difficult to be sure that anything Mother said was true. But, America? Having become an avid reader of the financial columns, she knew that ten thousand English pounds were worth something approaching fifty thousand American dollars. That sounded like an awful amount of money.

But America was so far away, seemed such an irrevocable step. However, it was something to be discussed with Uncle Herman. It was at least a plan, from which other plans might stem. It was . . . suddenly she became aware that there were five young men standing before her bench, talking among themselves, but talking about her. She raised her head to look at them and found them distinctly unattractive, mostly blond with curly hair, big chins and aggressive eyes. When they saw her looking at them, one of them addressed her directly, grinning.

She had no idea what he was saying. 'I am sorry,' she said in French. 'I do not speak German.'

Apparently they did not understand French. Now another spoke to her, then another, and she suspected they were abusing her, although they continued to grin. She decided the best thing she could do was leave, and stood up. The young men continued to talk at her, now one of them put his hand on his hip and minced to and fro, nose stuck in the air.

Jacqueline turned away, but now another of the young men pointed at her, and she heard the word, '*Juden*'. Her head turned sharply to identify him, and she realised that they were arguing about her. But the one who had called her a Jew was insisting, and she also heard the word 'Dumescu'. Obviously he must have seen her leaving Uncle Herman's house. Now the boy who had first spoken stood in front of her and addressed her again, apparently asking her a question which also included the word '*Juden*'.

'I am not a Jew,' she said, speaking as slowly and clearly as she could, this time using English. 'I happen to be staying with some friends who are Jews. Now kindly let me pass.'

It never occurred to her that he wouldn't, but the lout refused to move, while now they all shouted '*Juden*' at her. Her previous distress now turned to agitation and anger at this pestering when she so needed to be alone. To be so verbally assaulted . . . verbally? Suddenly one of them grasped her arm. She struck out at him wildly, swinging her open hand to slap his face. To her consternation he caught her wrist and pulled her forward so that she cannoned into him with a force that left her breathless. While she gasped he spat in her face.

Her head jerked back and she tried to free herself, but now she was held from behind; they all seemed to be grabbing parts of her body or her dress, pulling her this way and that, all the while laughing and shouting to each other. She was aware more of anger than fear, for the moment; she had no experience of anything like this. She could still feel the spittle dribbling down her cheek, and she was afraid that they would tear her new clothes.

'Let me go,' she shouted. 'Let me go, you beasts.'

She was being carried forward, away from the bench and across the grass towards a copse which lay some thirty yards away. For the first time, she realised she was in danger of being raped, and she again attempted to fight them, then gasped in horror as one of the young men released her to run in front of them, pointing and laughing. She saw the ants' nest.

They couldn't be serious. It was all somehow so juvenile . . . but so violent and horrible as well. 'Let me go!' she shouted. 'Let me go.'

She was forced to her knees only a few feet from the nest, her arms held by two of the boys, while the others poked the nest with sticks to bring the little red ants swarming angrily to the surface. The boys turned back towards her, laughing, again pointing, and the two holding her gave shouts of agreement; a moment later she found herself lying on her back while they threw up her skirt.

'Let me go,' she screamed. 'Let me go. I am not a Jew!' She felt ashamed for saying it, ashamed even to be conceding in her mind that if it were a Jewish girl lying here, they would be within their rights to maltreat her. But she was too afraid of what was going to happen to her now as she felt their hands on her thighs and pulling at her clothes, watching their ugly, grinning faces. 'Don't touch me,' she shouted. 'You . . . I am the Countess Tyroler. You cannot. You . . .'

She heard the crack of a whip and one of the boys gave a yelp of pain and anger. He swung around to face the horseman who sat above them, his chestnut mount pawing at the ground. No one had noticed his approach, so busy had they been with their sport, but now the whip snaked out again, flicking the upraised hand of another of the boys and bringing a howl of pain, while the man with the whip was obviously lashing at them with his tongue as well. The boys attempted to argue, but the whip struck another of them, they turned and ran across the park, still shouting and yelling, but no longer laughing.

The horseman dismounted while Jacqueline sat up shakily, hastily pulling down her dress.

'They are louts,' the man said in English.

Jacqueline half-turned her head, then look away again.

She felt so embarrassed, humiliated, dirty. Her heart still pounded in her throat; she was overwhelmed with a combination of fear, outrage, shame and anger . . . driving thoughts of Jean-Paul from her conscious mind but bringing a painful pressure of fear behind her eyes, dragging down the corners of her mouth. She had been shamed enough in front of this stranger; she could not add to it the shame of uncontrolled emotion as well.

'I can only apologise for them, Countess,' he said. 'May I assist you?'

His hand was outstretched. She did owe him a great deal. She allowed him to raise her to her feet, for the first time looked into his face. It was a handsome face, she thought, perhaps a shade too full at cheek and jaw, but saved from any suggestion of roundness by the prominent chin and flat lips. And above all by the glittering eyes which seemed to be able to look past her own face into her very brain. She did not think he was very old, probably about thirty, and his clothes were beautifully tailored, only matched by the splendidly groomed horse.

He smiled at her. 'You did describe yourself as a Countess? Countess . . . Tyroler?'

'Believe me,' she said. 'I am most grateful to you for coming to my rescue. Those . . .'

'They thought you were a Jewess, when anyone could tell at a glance that you are not. Equally, you are not German. And not even, I think, English, although you speak the language very well. Perhaps you would be good enough to enlighten me?' He clicked his heels and kissed her hand. 'At least, after I have introduced myself. I am Heinrich von Reinikker.'

'*Von* Reinikker?'

He shrugged. 'One's family accumulates nobility in the course of centuries. But I am more interested in your family, Countess.'

'I am French, monsieur.'

'On a visit to Munich, and set upon by a band of louts? I am horrified. Believe me, I shall find those scoundrels and make them pay for what they have done. But first, I must see you back to your hotel. We shall find a taxi over there.' He pointed to the nearest gate and she walked beside him while he led his horse. 'Which hotel?'

'I'm staying with friends,' she said.

'But that is better and better. Perhaps they are also friends of mine. Would you tell me their name?'

'Ah . . .' but he would insist on taking her home, anyway, and she rather wanted him to. He was no Jean-Paul. She was not sure that he was the sort of man she could ever even like . . . but he had saved her from a terrible humiliation, and he was clearly an aristocrat. 'I am staying with Herr Dumescu,' she said. 'The . . . jeweller.'

He frowned at her, seemed about to speak, then snapped his fingers. Instantly a groom appeared – he might have been there all the time for all that Jacqueline had noticed – to take the horse's bridle and also to summon a taxi.

Heinrich von Reinikker gave the address and the taxi driver glanced at him, eyebrows raised, before he tripped his meter and engaged a gear. Oh dear, she thought; they know all about Uncle Herman.

'I think you should try telling me the truth, Fräulein,' Reinikker said.

'The truth? But I do not make a habit of lying, monsieur.'

Once again the long frown. 'You claim to be a French countess, but you are staying with a Jewish pawnbroker, Fräulein. Did you know that?'

'Of course I know that,' she snapped. 'In my country a person's religion is quite irrelevant.'

'I did not know such places existed,' he remarked. 'Especially in France. And calling yourself "countess".'

'Would you like to see my passport?' she asked. Not that she had any intention of showing him and revealing her true nationality.

In reply he picked up her left hand, studied the wedding ring, then the sparkling engagement ring beside it. 'You are certainly intriguing,' he said. 'That is a magnificent stone. I wonder if you have any idea of its value?'

'Yes,' she snapped, trying to control her rising anger, remembering that Ion had paid the equivalent of two-and-a-half thousand English pounds for it.

'And your husband is still . . . ah . . . around?'

'I do not wish to quarrel with you, monsieur,' she said, eyes blazing. 'You have just saved me from a most unpleasant experience, but again the sort of thing we do not have to endure in my country. I am forever in your debt. But I will not sit here and allow you to question me as if I were a criminal. It is insulting. Over there is my . . . is Herr Dumescu's house. I will get out here.'

'It is only another few yards,' he pointed out, and the car glided on to a halt. 'Dear, mysterious stranger.' His tone had changed. 'To whom I have been able to render some small service, may I perhaps offer you dinner?'

She looked him up and down. She was still quite breathless. Dinner? What brazen effrontery.

'I need some time to apologise properly,' he went on. 'And to learn more about you. Someone as lovely as you, Countess, and as cloaked in mystery, cannot just flit by and disappear into memory. Perhaps I may telephone you tomorrow, when you have recovered from your ordeal.'

'Well, I . . . I suppose you may telephone me, Herr Reinikker, if you wish. I will give you my answer then.' She decided not to smile or look at him as she spoke.

'Tomorrow,' he promised and kissed her hand, then got back into the taxi. She was left standing on the pavement, feeling as if she had only just awakened from a deep sleep – and a horrible nightmare.

'Jacqueline!' Uncle Herman cried. 'Where have you been? What has happened to you?'

She looked into the hall mirror, only then realising that she was extremely dishevelled, her hair in a tangled mess, grass stains on her skirt and both stockings laddered beyond repair. 'I . . . I went for a walk in the park,' she explained.

'And were assaulted?' Aunt Hannah cried, running from the parlour. 'Oh, you poor child.'

'Nothing too awful happened to me, Aunt Hannah,' Jacqueline insisted. 'I was attacked by a gang of louts, but a Herr von Reinikker rescued me, most gallantly.'

'Reinikker?' Uncle Herman asked. 'Did you say Reinikker?'

'Yes, he said his name was Heinrich von Reinikker.'

'And you let him bring you back here?'

'Well, yes. Actually, he insisted on bringing me home. Uncle Herman, do you think those boys were Nazis? I couldn't understand what they were saying, but they kept saying Jew, I am sure.'

'Then very probably they were Nazis.' Uncle Herman put his arm round her shoulder and escorted her into the parlour. 'I think a brandy is what you need.' He always kept some drink in the house for his guests, although he did not drink himself. 'But they are unimportant, really, though I hope in future you will take my advice and not go walking by yourself. You know, those bully boys only do what they are told by their Nazi bosses.'

She took a long drink, felt the alcohol seeping through her system, reminded herself that she was once again in safety. And that she had had an adventure. If she forgot the horrid part, it became quite exciting with the appearance of Heinrich.

'So I think the sooner we get you out of Munich, the better for us all,' Uncle Herman was saying. 'Hannah, don't bother to write to your mother, it will take too long for a reply. You and the girls just go, tomorrow.'

'Oh, but . . . Herr von Reinikker is going to call me tomorrow,' Jacqueline said. 'He can't make up his mind whether or not to believe what I told him about myself.'

'I'm sure he can't,' Uncle Herman said drily. 'Jacqueline, Heinrich von Reinikker is Gauleiter for Munich. That means he is the boss of the local Nazi Party. He tells the party rank and file, people like those thugs who assaulted you, what to do. And believe me, he hates Jews.'

Jacqueline stared at her uncle with her mouth open.

'He regards us with contempt,' Uncle Herman went on. 'So I doubt his intentions towards you are in the least honourable.'

But I am not Jewish, she mentally protested, and he can see that. Once again she felt ashamed for the speed with which she was prepared to distance herself from these relatives who had been so kind to her.

'Jacqueline, I'm sure you'll agree that the best course would be to avoid this man until his attention is taken elsewhere. And that means not being here when he calls.'

Jacqueline bit her lip. Von Reinikker had been attractive and charming, and above all, interesting. Even if she were to believe her uncle that he was a hard and ruthless man – she had seen evidence of that in the way he had chased those boys, and in the way he had questioned her – as well as a prejudiced one, that made him even more interesting. Nor did she have any doubts that she could take care of herself; she had, after all, even coped with the wrath of a king.

On the other hand, if seeing the man again would distress Uncle Herman . . . and besides, apart from a sort of gratitude, she was only suffering a reaction from the news about Jean-Paul; she had really thought from the first that Reinikker was not a man she could ever like.

'Of course you are right, Uncle Herman,' she said. 'I can hardly wait to see Berlin.'

And, in fact, it was thrilling to take the train the length of Germany, away from the Alps and to the north, through such famous cities as Nuremberg and Bamberg, Erfurt and then, descending to the North German Plain, Leipzig. Little Jean-Jacques was quite a seasoned traveller by now. He played happily in turn with his mother and his two new devotees and ate ravenously from the wicker hamper, hastily but lavishly filled in the Dumescus' kitchen. Jacqueline smiled as she compared the comforts of this journey with the misery and fear of the last.

They spent the night at an hotel in Leipzig, but had no

121

time to visit any of the museums of which Herman and Hannah had spoken so enthusiastically, before travelling on again the next morning to Wittenburg and then Potsdam, and finally entering Berlin itself. This was the most exciting city of all, even more exciting, she thought, than Paris, although not so beautiful. Yet it seemed to have more personality, there was a certain tension in the air. 'It is all these political crises,' Aunt Hannah explained, as they took a taxi from the Annhalter Bahnhof past the Tiergarten to Wedding, where her family lived. 'The government doesn't know how to deal with the unemployment situation.'

'Except for the Nazis,' Ruth giggled.

'Oh, yes,' Hannah Dumescu agreed, sarcastically. 'Their solution is to put everyone who hasn't got a job to making roads and building houses. Who pays for it all, of course, is something they haven't bothered to work out.'

Certainly there seemed to be hundreds of young men just loafing on the street corners. 'But something will have to be done,' Jacqueline remarked.

'Or there will be another revolution.' Hannah gave a grim smile. 'I remember the last one, in 1919. The Communists very nearly succeeded in seizing power, then. But I think nowadays everyone knows what a catastrophe that would be. What we really need is a restoration. Not the Kaiser himself, maybe; I don't suppose the French would ever stand for it, but there are enough imperial princes about to provide an emperor. I'm sure that would be the answer.'

Jacqueline, thinking of the Rumanian problems, and the way the whim of a prince or a king had so affected her own life, could not agree with her, but she decided against saying so. A few minutes later they arrived at the Lasker's house and the rest of the day, indeed the week, was given over to happy celebrations. Their arrival had not of course been expected because Uncle Herman had not wanted to telephone even the briefest warning – he was convinced all the people in the telephone exchanges were Nazis who recounted every conversation to their bosses – and the household was thrown into a tremendous uproar which everyone clearly enjoyed enormously. The Laskers, Jacqueline quickly realised, were in a very much higher social bracket than Herman Dumescu – indeed, as Johann Lasker was apparently the director and chief shareholder of a chain of department stores, he was the sort of merchant even her mother might have been prepared to entertain. He was a perfect gentleman, dignified and charming, his household was maintained with a strict eye to the social niceties so important in Anna's life. Their home was large and luxuriously appointed, filled with servants, chauffeurs for the two Mercedes Benz cars, grooms and lads in the riding stables, and even a permanent crew on the yacht at Swinemünde on the Baltic coast north of the city.

Jacqueline quickly realised that there had been some tensions when his youngest daughter had announced her intention to marry a penniless Rumanian immigrant – but all that was in the past, and all was clearly forgiven, the more so as Herman Dumescu had at last started to make a great deal of money. Certainly neither Johann Lasker nor his wife could have been kinder to their unexpected guest. She had no idea what Hannah had told them about her. They never addressed her by her surname at all, but called her Jacqueline from the start. There were three other Lasker children, two more daughters and a son, who worked in his father's business, but these were all married and had homes of their own, and so, while the old family nursemaid was delegated to look after the baby, her host and hostess, as well as Hannah and Ruth, took Jacqueline riding in the park and sightseeing to the Unter den Linden.

Their overwhelming kindness was a blessing. Frau Lasker had been surrounded by books of wallpapers, material samples and paint charts when they arrived, and noting Jacqueline's interest, had immediately asked her opinion on colours and decorations for the rooms she was refurbishing. It was a subject Jacqueline had always adored and she threw herself into the selections and problems with such enthusiasm that her host invited her to visit his newly opened 'Interior Design Centre'. This new professional approach intrigued her, and she begged permission to sit and study the designers at work whenever it was convenient. It took her mind off Jean-Paul and helped to heal the wounds of her previous life. At the same time, she made no progress towards deciding what her next move should be, but that had suddenly become less important as the present was so enjoyable.

Then, one morning just after breakfast, she was informed by one of the housemaids that a Herr Heinrich von Reinikker was waiting to see her in the downstairs salon.

'Oh,' she said. 'Oh.' She wondered if the housemaid had told the Laskers or Aunt Hannah. She hoped she hadn't. She did feel rather badly about the way she had run away, and to suppose he had followed her, several hundred miles . . . she had to pause outside the door to straighten her dress and control her breathing.

'I feel like Sherlock Holmes,' he said, rising to take both her hands and kiss them.

'You . . .' Once again she was breathless. 'You have been looking for me?'

'Of course. Without any help at all from that stupid uncle of yours. But he did let it slip that you had gone to Berlin. Well, from then on it was only a matter of making inquiries.'

'You know he is my uncle?' Jacqueline was aghast.

Heinrich sat down, holding out his gold cigarette case. When she shook her head he took a cigarette for himself – without asking permission. The Laskers did not smoke and she hastily had to find an ornamental dish for him to use as an ashtray. 'I don't blame you for being ashamed of it,' he said. 'But I am sure the relationship is not as close as he made out.'

She sat down also. 'He is my mother's half brother,' she said, without specifying where the Jewish blood came from. Again she felt utterly ashamed, but she didn't want to be regarded with contempt by this man; suddenly she felt it was very important to meet him on equal terms.

'I knew it,' he said. 'Are you really a countess?'

'I married a count,' she said. 'But . . . they are two-a-penny, in France.'

'Of course,' he agreed. 'And is the fortunate fellow alive?'

'We are separated.' She paused. 'Why is my background so interesting to you?'

'You are interesting to me, Countess. Do you know, every man dreams of one day rescuing a beautiful woman in distress, but very few of us ever have that dream come true. And still I do not even know your first name.'

She raised her head in surprise. That had not occurred to her, nor could she believe he would not have found it out while tracing her. 'My name is Jacqueline.'

'Very lovely, and very French,' he said, as if to reassure himself that at least a part of what she had told him was true. He blew a thin stream of smoke at the ceiling, leaned back to smile at her. 'These people are your "uncle's" in-laws? Are you comfortable here? This is the first time I have ever been inside a Jewish home. They appear to live very well.'

She watched his face very closely as he spoke, looking for the sneer she suspected lay beneath the charm. 'Uncle Johann is a wealthy man,' she said.

'Yes,' he commented drily. 'Jews do have a habit of accumulating money. And you?'

'I am very comfortable here, thank you.' She was beginning to get annoyed with him; it was not a difficult thing to do.

'Of course you are. But still, as you are here, and I am here, you must let me show you something of Berlin. Certain parts of the city, aspects of life here which I am sure Herr Lasker does not even know exist.'

'Well, I . . .'

'We shall go to the Zoo,' he announced. 'Everyone goes

to the Zoo, then a boat on the river. But to start with, tomorrow night, there is the Ball.'

'The Ball?'

'I thought you might not have heard of it. Oh, indeed, there is to be a ball tomorrow night, for charity, at the Hotel Albert. Most of the interesting Berliners will be there. And, if you will come, all the best people will be there.'

A ball, she thought. What an intriguing enigma this man is. So courteous, correct, formal in many respects, yet so forward and arrogant in his questioning. Then to invite her to a formal party when they hardly knew each other, certainly not socially; it was impolite. But . . . how she would adore going to a ball, she had not been to one in nearly a year. Of course, she had left all her good gowns behind. And yet, surely, something could be sorted out.

Heinrich leaned forward, picked up her hand and kissed it again. 'I shall call for you tomorrow evening at nine o'clock.'

'Of course you must go,' Johann Lasker declared. 'It will be a great occasion.'

'With a man like Reinikker?' Aunt Hannah demanded. 'I am sure Herman would advise against it.'

'Then he would be wrong,' replied Johann. 'Whether you hate the Nazis or just feel contempt for them, they are here, Hannah, and they are going to be here for a long time. Do you know there is even talk of them forming a government?'

'Herr Hitler for Chancellor,' Sadie Lasker said with a smile. 'I cannot believe the Field Marshal would ever agree to that.'

'Hindenburg is an old man,' her husband pointed out. 'Heaven knows, these Nazis may get some order back into the country, some profit back into business.'

'They hate us,' Hannah said with a shiver. 'They hate all Jews.'

'That is just political claptrap, my dear,' her father

explained. 'All political parties have to work up a hate against somebody or nobody would vote for them. My point is that we have got to learn to live with them, and if Reinikker is interested in Jacqueline, why, that is a good thing. It is always a mistake to let politics spill over into personal relationships, anyway.' He squeezed Jacqueline's hand.

Just as if I were a child, she thought, and they are debating whether or not to let me go to my first dance.

'Anyway, she has nothing to wear,' Aunt Hannah said, decisively.

'Stuff and nonsense,' her father declared. 'Do we not have the widest range of ball gowns in Berlin? We will make her look like a queen.'

She thought she had never liked anyone quite so much. And why not, she thought, look like a queen? From her jewel box she took the ruby and diamond set Ion had given to her as a wedding present. Johann Lasker had been as good as his word and found her a white satin evening gown, a silver lamé handbag and silver kid shoes; the gown itself was high-bodiced but bare-backed, and there were bows at neck and hip. She thought it was exquisite. 'But I could never afford it,' she explained.

'It is a gift,' he said. 'From an old man to a young woman who has to take her place in the world. Wear it, my dear, and dazzle them.' He winked. '*All* the Nazis.'

She certainly dazzled Heinrich von Reinikker. When he was admitted to the drawing room where she was waiting for him, he lost his normal aplomb and simply stared until he was engaged in conversation by Johann Lasker, and absently drinking his brandy. 'I must say,' he remarked, when at last they were in the back of his Mercedes, 'you are introducing me to aspects of life I had never considered before. That is quite a pleasant old fellow, for a Jew.'

'Now why do you have to spoil it by adding that?' she asked. She had also taken a glass of brandy and was feeling on top of the world; certainly she had dismissed all her earlier embarrassment at being with him. 'If you would only overcome your unfounded prejudices, you could be quite a nice person.'

His head turned sharply.

She smiled at him. After all, he was taking her to the Ball. 'I should have said, an even nicer person than you are already.'

She had taken the initiative. He took her hand to kiss the knuckles. 'Perhaps I shall try to do that,' he said, 'if you are the sort of reward I can look forward to. Do you know that you are one of the most magnificent creatures I have ever seen?'

'I have always supposed I was a woman,' she said. 'Strange how one can be mistaken about things like that.'

Again his head jerked as he stared at her, then he gave a delighted smile. Clearly she was measuring up to his hopes of sophisticated repartee. 'I was embracing the entire animal kingdom,' he said. 'And believe me, dear Countess Tyroler, I meant it as a compliment.'

She wondered if he valued her or her title the more – and wondered too if it would occur to him to try to find out if it was real. But dreaded thoughts like that were ended by their arrival at the Hotel, where her very happiest hopes were immediately realised. They entered through enormous swing doors into a glittering vestibule, where a score of uniformed attendants waited to take her sable – how pleased she was that she had not abandoned it in the train as she should have done – and Heinrich's coat. Several other couples had also just arrived and were being attended to; it was a delight to watch their heads turning to give her a surreptitious inspection, and Heinrich obviously knew a number of them, for he allowed them stiff and enormously proud nods before taking her arm to escort her up the carpeted staircase to the first floor. The orchestra was playing and a few couples already dancing. Here they waited with the other new arrivals for the music to stop, so that they could be announced, time well used in observing the other guests. Jacqueline decided that she had nothing to fear from comparison with any of the women, either in looks or dress. I can compete with any of them, she thought. I feel like the belle of the ball.

But the music had stopped and the major-domo was looking at the card Heinrich had given him. 'His Excellency Herr Heinrich von Reinikker,' he announced. 'And the Countess Tyroler.'

A moment later they were surrounded by Heinrich's friends and acquaintances, the women looking hard at Jacqueline, making no attempt to conceal their curiosity. The men, young and old, were anxious to be introduced and then to fill her card. 'I really don't know,' she protested, feeling for the first time uncertain because her German was still a long way from being fluent. 'I really must . . .' she wondered what Heinrich would make of it. But he seemed more pleased than ever that she was making such an impression, took his place at her side with a most proprietorial air and smiled at his rivals.

'I think we can spare every other dance, Countess,' he said. 'I shall have the odd numbers. And, of course, they may only have one each.'

'Then I shall have number two,' said one young man.

'And I number four!' cried another.

'Number six . . .'

'Number eight . . .'

She watched the names being scrawled, one after the other, people whom she had never met. But would she meet them again? She could see an entire new life opening before her, here in Berlin, of flirtations and balls, of rides in the country and picnics in the park . . . and perhaps, even, of meeting someone who would rip the memory of Jean-Paul forever from her heart and allow her to begin her life all over again.

She would owe it all to Heinrich. She was so grateful she gave him her brightest smile and gently squeezed his hand as they took the floor for the first waltz. They went spinning through the throng, attracting attention wherever they moved. Jacqueline danced exquisitely, thanks to strict

Rumanian instructors in her childhood, and could see his amazement growing as his face glistened with perspiration; he had indeed rescued a princess in distress. Clearly he could hardly believe his fortune.

'Champagne,' he said as they left the floor. He signalled to a waiter who hurried towards them with a laden tray. 'And then . . .'

'Heinrich, my dear boy,' someone said nearby. 'Will you not introduce me? To the "Countess", is it not?'

Heinrich turned, as did Jacqueline. The voice had been quiet though utterly confident, speaking German with a strange and interesting accent. But Jacqueline was disappointed. The man was tall and slim and extremely distinguished in appearance, with handsome features and the most exquisitely cut dinner suit – but he was at least twice her age, she decided, looking at the grey wings of his neatly brushed dark hair. She associated all men of over forty with Ion Tyroler, and immediately dismissed them from any further consideration.

'Why, of course, my dear Count,' Heinrich said, although without his recent cordiality. 'Count Marco-Gregorio Luzzi di Calitri, the Countess Jacqueline Tyroler.'

'Tyroler?'

'The Countess is French,' Heinrich explained. 'And is more at home in that language, Marco.'

Marco Luzzi took her hand and raised it to his lips. 'Why, Countess,' he said, in French. 'So am I. German is for barbarians, n'est-ce pas?'

Jacqueline gave Heinrich an anxious glance, but he continued to smile even if the amusement did not reach his eyes.

'I shall be forever honoured if you will dance with me, Countess,' Luzzi continued.

'Oh, I . . .' Jacqueline looked at Heinrich again.

'Jacqueline's card is full, my dear Marco,' Heinrich said, using the possessive Christian name with great deliberateness.

'But you cannot entirely possess so dazzling a beauty, Heinrich,' Luzzi said, his voice faintly mocking.

'I do not, I assure you. I only have every other dance.'

'Far too many,' the Count asserted. 'You must allow me one of those, Heinrich. No, two.'

Jacqueline gazed from one to the other. She had never actually been, well, she supposed, fought over would be as good a term as any, and she found it quite exciting. In any event, surely Heinrich would now slap this insolent Italian down. But to her surprise, after a brief hesitation, Heinrich merely nodded. 'Very well, Marco,' he agreed. 'Two.'

The Count inspected Jacqueline's card. 'I will have numbers five and nine,' he decided. He returned the card, kissed her hand again. 'I am enchanted, Countess, and hope to be again, before the evening is over.'

'I really would have preferred to be asked if I want to dance with someone,' Jacqueline said. She was not really annoyed, after all, what had happened was rather flattering, but she felt it was necessary to appear annoyed.

'We must humour the fellow,' Heinrich explained. 'He is a great friend of the Italian ambassador and is stinking rich into the bargain. He has extensive business interests in Germany, and owns some kind of a castle down in southern Italy. But keep your eye open for his little tricks, he's a lady's man. You know, his marriage turned out badly, but he can't get a divorce because he's a Roman Catholic – so he thinks that gives him licence to make love to every woman who takes his fancy.'

But it may be that his marital situation is only the same as mine, she thought. Even so, she had mentally to brace herself before allowing herself into his arms. But he did not attempt to caress her, as so many of the Germans had done while dancing; his left hand, once placed on her back, never moved, and he held her fingers lightly but firmly. His dancing was superb; he moved with far more ease and grace than Heinrich, who had been stiff and angular by comparison.

He said little until just before the end of their second dance, then he observed, gazing at her as he had done throughout. 'It is strange, but do you know, the only Tyrolers I know of are Rumanians. And I had heard . . .' he watched her mouth open in dismay. Of all the unutterable catastrophes.

The Count smiled. 'I was going to say, Countess, that I had heard that Ion Tyroler had married a girl half his age. And found it difficult to believe. But obviously it cannot be you. You are far too lovely to be the wife of someone like Ion Tyroler.' The music had stopped and he kissed her knuckles. 'That was enchanting. I give you my word, Countess, that I shall entirely forget your name the moment I leave here tonight. I have a terrible memory for names, but your face will remain engraved upon my heart forever. I give you my word on that, too.'

He bowed and walked away, leaving her for a moment incapable of movement. Because it wasn't bad luck. It was sheer stupidity, her own fault for taking such an absurd risk by coming to a place like this at all. She should have kept to herself, as she had planned to do.

'Was he rude to you?' Heinrich asked.

'Rude? Oh, no,' she said. 'He was charming. Heinrich . . . could you take me home?'

'My dear Jacqueline, it is hardly midnight.'

'I am very tired,' she said. 'This place, the noise . . .'

'He was rude to you,' Heinrich said. 'By God, I'll . . .'

'Please, Heinrich.'

'Of course,' he agreed. 'If that is what you want.' He escorted her down the stairs, and they had gone before any of the young men still waiting their turn to dance with her were aware of their departure. She had been a little apprehensive all evening that Heinrich might want some tangible reward for having taken her out – she had already formed a quite definite opinion that he was not truly a gentleman, however many 'vons' his family might have accumulated, but he contented himself with kissing her hands. 'Tomorrow,' he said. 'I will call for you at eleven.'

At last she was alone in bed, able to think and to consider her next move. She was not sure that Count Luzzi could be trusted, especially if he knew anything about Ion. Once it became public knowledge that she was the one who had stolen away from Rumania with King Carol's child . . . but could that ever become public knowledge? Surely Carol had enough on his hands getting to grips with Rumania's economic problems to risk becoming involved in yet another scandal. She had simply been shocked at even the slightest recognition, that was all. But how she wished Heinrich hadn't learned her real name. Still, she had shouted it without thinking at the louts attacking her, and he had heard it. After that she hadn't really had any choice. So now she just had to face it out.

And what about Heinrich? He was a very difficult man to assess. There was a coldness about him . . . perhaps because he only smiled with his mouth, leaving his ice-blue eyes expressionless. But he was, nevertheless, an attractive man.

'Well,' Johann Lasker said at breakfast. 'You must have had a good time last night; there are flowers for you.'

'Red roses,' said Sadie in an arch whisper.

'Oh, let me see.' Jacqueline ran down the room to the huge bouquet waiting on the table by the window. 'They are quite beautiful.' She felt tremendously excited. Maybe this was Heinrich's first warm gesture.

'And very expensive,' Hannah pointed out. She had already appropriated the card. 'From Count Marco-Gregorio Luzzi di Calitri. He sounds awfully wealthy. And he has only signed himself as Marco.'

'Oh.' Jacqueline too wondered at his confident familiarity.

'Is he very wealthy?' Hannah persisted.

'Yes,' Jacqueline said. 'I believe he is.' The count seemed even more of a lady-killer than Heinrich had intimated – he had promised to forget her name immedi-

133

ately. 'If you would like them, Aunt Hannah, you are welcome to them. I'm afraid I am not going to accept any flowers from Count Luzzi.' She listened to the telephone ringing. 'Please, if that is him, I am out.'

Johann Lasker was shouting down the mouthpiece. Now he raised his head. 'It is Herman, from Munich. He wants to speak with you, Jacqueline.'

'Oh!' She took the receiver. 'Uncle Herman? Whatever has happened?'

'Nothing to be alarmed about,' he said, his voice remarkably clear given the distance over which they were speaking. 'But there have been men here, asking for you. They have finally decided that you must have left the train here.'

'Oh, my God,' she said. 'What did you tell them?'

'The truth, my dear. That you did come here, that I said I could not help you, and that you left again, immediately. I thought that was enough and I said I had no idea where you had gone.'

'Uncle Herman,' she said. 'Thank you.'

'It's not quite as easy as it sounds. I don't think they believed me. In fact, I have the distinct feeling that I am under surveillance, just in case you come back. So I would suggest you do not come back for a while, Jacqueline. If you stay on in Berlin for another couple of weeks, they will get tired and go away. Yes, I think that is what you should do. Stay in Berlin for another week or two.'

Jacqueline was actually delighted to have a reason for remaining in Berlin. The Lasker household was the happiest she had ever been in, utterly relaxed, content to let her pursue her own amusements. For the first time in her life she was allowed to do whatever she wished, and she found in Uncle Johann's Interior Design Centre a treasure trove of ideas to stimulate her imagination – she had nursed an interest in interior design ever since she had helped Mother to redecorate the chateau. To her enormous pleasure the people there seemed perfectly willing to accept some of her suggestions.

Then Uncle Herman telephoned his father-in-law again and suggested that Hannah and Ruth should now return to Munich as their continued absence might give a lead to Jacqueline's whereabouts, but asked that the hospitality shown to his niece be extended; apparently there were still men watching his house.

Now she very much wanted to make some attempt to repay all the kindess she was receiving. 'I really am overwhelmed by your generosity,' she explained, 'but you must see that I cannot continue to accept your charity indefinitely. Surely if I were to sell my jewellery and the diamonds, I could realise sufficient funds to provide me with an income?'

Johann Lasker smiled at her understandingly. 'We all know how you must feel, Jacqueline, but before you decide to part with all your valuables, would you care to consider an alternative idea of mine?' He drew some papers from his pocket and continued. 'I have here two letters from clients of the Design Centre. Both refer to projects of theirs in which you have been involved, and request that you, personally, should work on further such projects for them. One is for the furnishing and decorating of a small block of luxury apartments overlooking the park, and the other for a modernised banking house. Now, I know that you may not feel you wish to be in a position of employment . . .'

'Oh, Uncle Johann, on the contrary. I should be delighted . . . but do you really think I have learned sufficient about the work?' Jacqueline bounced up and down on the sofa in her excitement.

'My dear girl, I have known designers who have studied for years, but who will never have your natural flair for it. You really are gifted, you know. Besides, you will be working with staff who can aid your ideas with their experience. Your remuneration would be a percentage of the cost of each project on which you work. You would not be required to give too many hours per week, so that you will still have plenty of time to spend with

135

your little fellow. Now, tell me, how does that sound to you?'

Jacqueline's answer was to rush across the room and throw her arms around his neck, much to his delight.

Life quickly settled down to a very pleasant routine. Most mornings were spent either at the Design Centre or 'on site'. In the afternoons she played with Jean-Jacques or took him for walks, laughing at his multi-lingual baby-talk, but grieving that he might never know the father he grew more and more like every day. Heinrich von Rein-ikker invited her out several times. He either sent polite little notes by hand, or telephoned. She had not altogether enjoyed their visit to the Tiergarten the day after the Charity Ball. The zoo itself had been impressive, but Heinrich had seemed utterly disinterested in the animals and had instead spent the time watching her closely. Every time she turned her head his eyes were on her face, he was half smiling, half . . . she still could not make up her mind.

However, she accepted his invitation to the Berlin State Opera, where the lavish production of Wagner's *Tannhäuser* left her in an ecstatic daze. On another evening she accompanied him to a formal dinner party at which all the men were wearing military dress uniforms, many speeches were delivered, received with great enthusiasm, and the diners frequently called to their feet for toasts. Although Jacqueline had swiftly acquired a good deal of conversational German, she found it impossible to follow most of the speeches and had to rely on Heinrich to supply her with whispered translations. Afterwards he apologised.

'I had forgotten that you do not yet know much German. Never mind, let me make it up to you. I have in mind another dinner party. Maybe I could telephone you about it tomorrow?'

On the next afternoon, instead of a phone call, Jacqueline received a bouquet accompanied by a note requesting the pleasure of her company for dinner the following evening. She would be collected as usual unless she notified him otherwise. He was a strange man, she thought, while she arranged the flowers in the garden room, so different from any other she had ever known. Sophisticated, immaculate in dress and manners, and apart from his suspicious attitude when they first met, which was perhaps understandable, he had always been the perfect escort. And when she felt the hard muscles in his arms and thighs as they danced or sat close in the car . . . yes, he certainly aroused in her a desire for something more. So what was it then that held her back from giving him a little encouragement? The coldness of his blue eyes? Some illogical feeling that she could not like him, no matter how attractive he might be?

The doorbell rang promptly at eight. Their journey lasted barely five minutes and ended in a quiet square where a manservant opened the door of a tall, terraced house. It was some minutes before she realised that this was to be an evening *à deux* . . . but silently assured herself that this should not alarm her. The same manservant served cocktails on a silver salver, then withdrew.

'This is my family's *pied-à-terre*, but the others seldom use it,' Heinrich told her. 'They prefer the estate outside Munich. I find it very convenient when I am visiting Berlin.'

He was as charming as ever, but his eyes never seemed to leave her. Only when the meal was finished was she able to overcome her tension and relax, enjoy the coffee and liqueurs. Her host's conversation at last turned from politics to frivolities, and when he put a record on the gramophone she willingly rose to dance. She did not object when his arms tightened round her and his lips pressed hard against her forehead.

The record stopped.

'Perhaps you would like to go upstairs?' Heinrich asked as he lifted the needle and returned the arm to its rest.

Jacqueline glanced in the mirror. 'Yes, I suppose I should. Where do I go?'

'I will show you.'

Collecting her evening bag, she followed him up the stairs, through a dimly lit but obviously sumptuous bedroom, from where he directed her to the boudoir and bathroom beyond.

She did not see him when she returned to the bedroom until his arms slid around her. She looked up into those pale blue eyes as his mouth crushed down on hers, and, half thrilled and half frightened, unsure what she wanted to happen even though she had known all evening that something must, she neither responded nor drew back until she felt the zip on the back of her dress slide down. She realised that his jacket and tie had been discarded, and suddenly knew that she did not want anything to happen, anything at all, between them.

'No, Heinrich!' she said as she tried to free her mouth. She dropped her hands to push his body away from her, but the dress slipped from her shoulders, pinning her arms and giving him time to undo her brassiere with practised ease.

Not even Carol had handled her with such casual certainty. 'Heinrich, how dare you?' she demanded. 'Let me go.'

'My darling Jacqueline, my beautiful Countess. Have I not waited very patiently for this moment?' he murmured, and before she could free her hands she was picked up and placed in the middle of the bed.

She wanted to fight, but against his weight and muscle she could not move – and a deep instinct warned her that he would not hesitate to hurt her if he became angry. She thought of screaming for help, but obviously the manservant would not dream of interfering. She wanted to weep. Dear God, how she wanted to weep. At her own naïvety for thinking that a man like this could be turned away by a simple refusal? So what could she do?

Gather up her courage and make him feel that he was nothing more than a clumsy cad.

'You appear to be having a problem with my suspender belt. Here, let me help you before you break it.' She sat up and he looked at her in surprise while she finished undressing. She coolly lay down again. 'There you are.

Would you please hurry up and get it over with?' She kept her eyes fixed on the ceiling, her legs slightly apart and her arms folded across her chest.

She heard him gasp with annoyance. 'You stiff-necked little Jew,' he exclaimed. 'We will have to see if we cannot show you how to love, and be loved.'

His hands wandered over her body. She did not appear to notice. He tried to kiss her. She turned her face away, pretending to yawn. Angrily he pushed himself on to her, and she felt him, hard, probing, thrusting until he entered her. She lay limp and motionless, urging herself to give him no hint of the pain of his assault. Suddenly, just as he was working himself up to boiling point she willed an urgent desire to laugh. And she did. The laughter was very nearly hysterical, perilously close to tears, but the effect on Heinrich was perfect.

His body went limp and he rolled on to his elbow. 'You damned bitch!' he exclaimed.

'Oh, poor Heinrich,' she could laugh properly now. 'Couldn't you manage it? Well, thank goodness for that. Now tell me, am I free to go yet, or do you intend holding me prisoner until you can eventually prove your manhood?' She started to pick up her clothes.

'Shut up, you little Jewish bitch,' he screamed, grabbing her arm. In wild anger her free hand flashed out and caught him across the face. A trickle of blood ran down his cheek, but her arm was twisted up her back until she cried out.

'That's right, scream. Go on, scream. My God, you are going to pay for this. Go on. Go home, now.' He thrust her away from him. 'Crawl back and whine to your Jew family. But just wait, you will see. Oh yes, you will see how you will pay for this one day!'

July 1930 – February 1933

'And all is well, tho' faith and form
Be sunder'd in the night of fear.'

Alfred, Lord Tennyson, *In Memoriam*

SURPRISINGLY, SHE was not surprised at what had happened. It was as if she had always known something like this would happen with a man like Heinrich. She supposed she had been incredibly blind to have let it go on as long as it had. But it had been so nice, to attend the parties and the dances and the dinners, to be escorted by a handsome and wealthy young man . . . on the other hand, he had introduced her to many other handsome and wealthy young men. She did not suppose she would be left without an escort for very long. Certainly she did not in the least regret his departure from her life.

More important, she thought the next morning as she considered the matter, was the question of what would happen next. Because now that her association with Heinrich was most definitely over, she was forced to admit to herself that she had only been using him as a distraction. She could not forget Jean-Paul; she had no wish ever to forget Jean-Paul – how could she, when he was the father of her son? She therefore could not bring herself to make the vital decision of facing the future without him. But that decision would have to be taken sooner or later. He was married, no doubt happily. He would probably have children of his own by now and she would only ever be an embarrassment to him. But the decision to erase him from her mind forever would necessarily entail another: just what was she going to do with the rest of her life? It would have been so simple if she had been able to meet someone to replace him, not just dashing and handsome, but much more important, gentle, loving and kind. Obviously Heinrich had not been and never could be any of those things, but while in his company she could hope to meet someone like that. Although, she said to herself, none of his Nazi friends had even remotely suggested the paragon for whom she was searching. She wondered if she should tell Uncle Johann; by now she could not think of Johann Lasker as anything less than an uncle, about what had happened. Not about the assault and the rape, of course, that would cause endless trouble, and it wasn't as if she had been an innocent young girl. But Heinrich's threats . . . oh, they had been absurd in this day and age. Uncle Johann would undoubtedly laugh at them. Besides, if she mentioned the threats, the reason for the threats might easily come out. Far better to forget Heinrich altogether and get on with her life. If only she could decide what that should be.

Of one thing was she absolutely sure. She liked Berlin more than any city she had ever known, and she wanted to stay here. She raised the matter with the Laskers, asking them if they could find her a flat somewhere, and predictably, they refused, insisted that she remain with them – and only very reluctantly agreed to her insistence that she pay at least some board for herself and Jean-Jacques. Then she could throw herself heart and soul into her work: that at least was progressing very well. It seemed that she really did have a flair for combining colours and fabrics, for highlighting rooms and disguising blemishes. 'Madame Jacqueline,' said Herr Holzhausen who managed the Centre, 'you are the best thing that has happened to us in a long time. Quite apart from your talents, you are beautiful and charming . . . you would be surprised at the number of people who telephone for our services and ask for you by name.'

Praise from customers was intensely gratifying and added to the enormous interest of visiting house after house and flat after flat. By now they had completed the remodelling of Johann Lasker's main store, which attracted a great deal of attention. The days, then the weeks and months, flew by, and before she knew it Jean-Jacques was old enough to attend nursery school. She surged past her twenty-first birthday hardly realising it, desperately trying to convince herself that she was utterly happy. Only when she lay awake in the small hours of the morning did she ever question what she was doing, whether or not she was still marking time, wasting perhaps the best years of her life.

Socially, she was a great success. Hostesses were delighted to seat her amongst the numerous elegant young men at their tables. All attractive, élite and unattached young women were in demand, but especially the beautiful Countess. Occasionally she met Count Luzzi; once she was seated next to him at dinner, another time at a musical soirée. He was always charming and flattering, but made no attempt to pursue their acquaintance, for which she was thankful. At all costs she was determined to avoid ever again becoming involved in a relationship which might end in yet another sexual battle. Since that awful episode with Heinrich, even the memory of Jean-Paul's lovemaking made her start to tremble. That treasured event in her life, remembered a hundred times to re-awaken the sweet response Jean-Paul had first roused, had lost its magic power, and left her icy-cold and shivering.

In all this time she had heard nothing from Rumania. She did not actually want to hear a word from Rumania, not even from her mother. Still, it was disconcerting, after all that she had gone through to get away, to feel that her departure had been so easily accepted. She went back to Munich from time to time to visit the Dumescus – the watchers had long been withdrawn. But she had no desire to return there to live; Munich was Heinrich's town, she was happier in Berlin.

She considered applying for German citizenship, but apart from the investigation of her background, and the possible references to Bucharest, something else held her back. She was determined not to tell Uncle Johann, or indeed anyone, about Heinrich's threats. Yet the fact was that that very September, only just after their quarrel, the Nazis had gained over a hundred seats in the General Election for the Reichstag. This left them still a relatively small party, but there could be no doubt of their growing importance. Their followers were becoming bolder than ever, roaming the streets in great gangs, seeking Communists in the main, but not above baiting Jews whenever they could. And when, the following summer, the failure of a bank in Austria brought a whole rash of banking collapses, followed inevitably by business failures as well, and unemployment soared from its already high level, she could almost see the Nazi support growing. She could certainly feel the tension developing around her. Throughout the following year one political crisis followed another, Chancellor followed Chancellor: Brüning, von Papen, von Schleicher, while the old President, Field Marshal von Hindenburg, resolutely refused to call Herr Hitler, the Nazi leader, to the Chancellorship. It was becoming clear that with his solid block of more than a hundred votes, Adolf Hitler was the only man who could conceivably create a working majority in the Reichstag.

That he would have to be called, eventually, was obvious, as the country slid perilously towards bankruptcy. It made no difference that most other countries in Europe seemed to be in the same boat – what conditions must be like in Rumania now did not bear thinking about – and even the United States, the richest nation on earth, apparently had breadlines and soup kitchens to cope with their unemployed. But none of them were equally menaced by the Brownshirt mobs which roamed the streets of every German town, avoided where possible by the police who were as aware as everyone else that these same noisy and aggressive young men might one day soon be their political masters. Did she really wish to belong to a nation with such an uncertain future?

Opinions as to what was likely to happen next varied from those who openly embraced the Nazi cause, if only because it would mean the extinction of Communism – to those who felt it would mean total financial and social disaster for the nation. But the majority were like Uncle Johann who trusted absolutely in the parliamentary process, and the German's innate respect for the law. 'Oh, I know the fellow tried to lead a revolution once,' he would say. 'But that was ten years ago. We all do foolish things in our youth. He has done nothing wrong since then, has he? No one can deny his popularity. Look at the election results.'

'You'll be telling us next you voted for him,' his wife would snort.

When Jacqueline asked what he really thought would happen, he would shrug. 'Who knows, my dear girl. But one thing is certain: governments come and go, financial crises come and go, but the people, you and me, go on forever. The days when governments could really change the lives of the people are history. And a very good thing too.'

She did not doubt he was right, because the most surprising aspect of the situation was that there still seemed to be as many parties and balls as ever; the Tiergarten was still crowded every fine afternoon, as were the cafés and the street bars – and work at the Design Centre only increased. There might be several million men on the breadline, but there were also quite a lot with money to spend, with enough confidence in the future to spend it on both their business and private properties.

The only actual word of advice and warning that she received came from a most unexpected quarter, when one day in the early autumn of 1932 Count Luzzi walked into the Centre. As always, he was elegantly dressed, from his grey fedora to his spats, his gloves to his silver hilted cane. He had obviously come for only one reason, and stood in

144

the centre of the floor looking about him until he spotted her. 'My dear Countess,' he said, raising his hat. 'I heard you were here, and could not believe my ears. You, working in a . . . well, a shop?'

'I enjoy working, Count Luzzi,' she said. 'And this work I enjoy more than any other.' She was tempted to ask why he thought it was his business, but decided against it.

'Hardly the place for a countess,' he remarked. 'But I am a firm believer in everyone living their own life. Believe me, my dear, I did not come to criticise. I came to ask you to dine with me.'

'Dine?' she cried, before she could stop herself.

He raised his eyebrows. 'Am I that much of an ogre?'

You are a friend of Heinrich's, she thought, and in his opinion, far worse than him.

She smiled at him. 'Of course not, Count Luzzi. But I have a very full diary.'

'For every night this week?'

'For every night this week,' she said, looking him straight in the eye.

He gave her a little bow. 'Alas, I am returning to Rome on Friday, but I shall be in Berlin again. Happily, now I know where to find you, instead of having to rely on chance encounters.' His smile died. 'Although I would hope to meet you somewhere else.'

She frowned, mystified. 'Count?'

'May I speak frankly?'

'Of course,' she said, not having any idea of what was coming.

'You cannot doubt that from the occasion of our first meeting I found you one of the most charming young women I have ever met.'

Oh dear, she thought, he is going to proposition me.

'And,' he went on, 'although I well understand that you have no such interest in me, you will at least believe that I have kept you much in mind, wondered about you, and worried for you, a lovely woman entirely alone in such a turbulent society.'

'You are too kind,' she murmured.

'A society which can only deteriorate. Countess, this place is not for you. Berlin is not for you. Germany is not for you. If you will not dine with me, at least take my advice. Seek your future somewhere else.' He leaned across the counter. 'Do it soon.' He placed a card before her. 'Believe that I am ever at your service.'

A very odd man, she thought. But really his behaviour was not so very odd. Clearly he had decided that she would only accept him as an older friend, who could take her away from all this. He could not accept that she was perfectly happy here – and that she had no desire whatever to become somebody's mistress.

In any event, she soon had reason to forget all about the Count. Shortly after Christmas, an occasion celebrated in the Lasker household only for the benefit of herself and Jean-Jacques, there was a telephone call from Uncle Herman in Munich. 'Jacqueline,' he said. 'I don't quite know how to put this, but . . . could you come down to see us? Your mother is here. She is, er . . . not very well,' Uncle Herman added by way of explanation, because Jacqueline did not immediately reply. 'Jacqueline . . . I think she does need you.'

A thousand possible disasters tumbled through her mind; uppermost was the thought that it was a trap. Into which Uncle Herman had fallen? She could not believe that.

'I think you should go,' Uncle Johann said, when she discussed it with him. 'After all, she is your mother. But we shall take no risks, eh? Why not leave Jean-Jacques here with us? That is the best thing to do.'

Of course it was. No one was ever going to get their hands on Jean-Jacques, of that she was determined. As for what other reasons Mother might have for appearing in Munich of all places . . . they were pointless even to consider.

She sat in the train, gazing out of the window at the

snow-covered countryside whizzing by, trying unsuccessfully to keep her mind empty of fear or speculation. How
had Mother found out where to look? Heinrich? He might
have pursued his vendetta against her to the point of
tracing her background, but if he had done that, why would
it have taken him three years?

Well, then, Count Luzzi? She sat up straight. He had
never threatened her, but he had indicated that he knew
who she was. Had he informed Ion, with whom he was
obviously acquainted? And then warned her to flee Germany? That did not make much sense, either.

Uncle Herman was waiting for her at the railway station.
'Now, Jacqueline,' he said. 'Anna does not know you are
coming today. She does not even know you are in Germany. You must be very kind to her.'

'But, you mean she hasn't tracked me down?'

'No,' Herman said. 'She is not well. I told you this on
the telephone.'

Then I needn't have come, she thought. I am going to
give myself away for no reason at all.

Herman could read the expression on her face. 'You
have nothing to be afraid of, Jacqueline,' he said. 'Believe
me, she needs you.'

Her mother had never needed anyone, she thought
angrily, but she received an enormous shock when she
entered the Dumescus' living room and gazed at the white-
haired woman who sat there. Without make-up and wearing a shabby dress, a greater contrast to the elegant creature of the Bucharest salons she would not have thought
possible. 'Mother?' she whispered.

Anna Dumesca stared at her daughter. 'Jacqueline?' she
asked. 'Oh, Jacqueline!'

They were in each other's arms, while Herman and
Hannah beamed at them, and then they were gazing at
each other again. 'You look so well,' Anna said. 'These
clothes . . .' she touched the sleeve of Jacqueline's heavy
silk blouse.

'I have managed to survive, Mother.'

'To survive,' Anna muttered. 'Yes, you would always survive. You survived!' she suddenly shouted. 'While I . . . I have also *survived*.'

Jacqueline looked at Herman who raised his eyebrows.

'Perhaps you should tell me,' Jacqueline said.

Anna sat down and Herman hastily gave her a glass of brandy. Not her first today, Jacqueline estimated.

'Survived,' Anna repeated. She raised her head. 'Did you realise the position you placed me in, running away like that? And with a royal prince?'

'He is not a royal prince, Mother, as you well know,' Jacqueline was determined to keep her temper. 'Did you ever, in your life, stop to consider the position you placed me in?'

'Ungrateful child. I have always thought only of your advancement. But you . . . do you know that I was accused of treason?'

'Treason?' Jacqueline also sat down. Apparently Herman and Hannah had already heard the story.

'Carol would not accept that I did not have a hand in it. He knew only that you had absconded with his son. I have never known him so angry.'

'My God!' Jacqueline was concerned, despite herself. She had not properly considered such a development. 'So what did you do?'

'What could I do?' Anna cried. 'He might have had me shot. I confessed the truth.'

'About Jean-Paul?'

'Of course. I told him everything about that French scoundrel, about Queen Marie's plans, everything. I convinced him that the child could not be his.'

'Well, then,' Jacqueline said. 'If only you had told me you would do that . . .'

'And I was sent to prison,' Anna said, as if she had not spoken.

'To . . . to prison? But why?'

'If Jean-Jacques was not Carol's son, then I, you, we, and Ion, of course, had committed fraud and accepted a pension from the Queen without any justification. King Carol demanded that every penny be repaid. How were we to do that? I put the chateau on the market, but there were no buyers. So we were sent to gaol.'

'Ion went to gaol, too?'

'Yes, of course.'

Jacqueline felt a stab of conscience. She had deliberately set out to acquire as much of that money as possible so that she could run away to Jean-Paul, leaving Ion and her mother to face the music. She felt very little sympathy for her mother because of the selfish attitude she still maintained, but Ion, like herself, had really only been a pawn in the game which Queen Marie and Anna had been playing. She really couldn't think of him as a bad man.

'You have no idea,' Anna continued, shivering. 'Two years, I spent in that prison. Two *years*, because of you. Then I was released and told to leave the country. My country! To leave, and never to return. All because of you.'

'Has Ion also been released?'

'I do not know. I don't think so. The pension was paid to him and Carol would not believe he was not the ringleader of the entire plot.'

Herman stood beside his sister. 'I have told your mother that she is welcome to stay with us for as long as she wishes,' he said. 'But . . .'

'It is a daughter's duty to care for her mother,' Anna said. 'You have done well, Jacqueline, that is obvious. You are well off, but then, you have always been well off. You have the mark of success in you. Are you living in Berlin itself?'

'No,' Jacqueline said, then looked at Herman and realised that wouldn't work. 'Yes, but with friends. I shall have to think about things. You must stay here for the time being.'

'You ungrateful girl,' Anna shouted. 'After everything I have done for you.'

'Yes, Mother,' Jacqueline said. 'After everything you

149

have done for me, I am not going to let you ruin my life all over again, I can promise you that.'

'You . . . you . . .'

'So I think you had better accept Uncle Herman's kind invitation and remain here for a week or two while I attempt to sort something out.' What, she had no idea. She was earning good fees for her design work, but they were certainly not sufficient to keep Anna Dumesca in the style to which she was accustomed. And just now she was not in the mood for filial thoughts. She had never been so angry in her life. She had been enjoying herself, feeling secure, for the very first time in years. And now . . . this.

'I am sure Jacqueline is right,' Herman said, loyally. 'There are big decisions to be made, and they must be carefully thought out. Now, I suggest that we all have some coffee, and . . .' he turned to the door as it flew open to admit Jacob, looking very hot and frightened. 'Jacob?' his father demanded. 'Who is at the shop?'

'I have closed the shop,' Jacob said. 'I have put barricades on the windows and barred the door. Father, it has just come through on the wireless: Adolf Hitler has been made Chancellor of Germany.'

Surprisingly, Jacqueline was awake as usual by seven o'clock, because throughout the long, tedious journey back to Berlin – a journey punctuated at every station by bands of deliriously happy young men wearing swastika arm bands and singing triumphant songs – her mind had been plagued with indecision. She was torn between what some might call a daughter's duty, and others a misguided loyalty. Instinct swayed her towards the miserable, suffering Anna one minute, recoiled the next from the picture of her mother's influence in a possible future joint household. 'Honour Thy Father and Thy Mother.' What father? Her mother had tried hard to achieve for her what she had judged to be the best possible future. Could the fact that that judgement had been an appallingly ill-conceived mistake justify abandoning her? Yet Anna admitted to no mistake. In Munich she had only blamed Jacqueline for her term of imprisonment and seemed determined that she, Jacqueline, should 'atone' for her sins by feeding, housing, clothing her, and doubtless paying for lavish entertaining as well. Could that possibly be fair? How would the Laskers and Dumescus answer her problem? How would God?

And then there was the Dumescus' consternation about Herr Hitler becoming Chancellor. This she couldn't understand at all; everyone knew that it had to happen sooner or later. Like Uncle Johann, she was almost inclined to think that it might be a good thing if it improved the economy or took the Brownshirts off the streets.

The quiet of the morning was disturbed by the ringing of a telephone. The household was just stirring as Jacqueline swung her feet on to the floor and carried her unsolved problems across to the bathroom mirror. She was about to step into the bath when she heard a rapping on her door and a maid calling, 'Countess, Countess, an urgent telephone call . . .'

It was Jacob, his voice high and cracking with fear and emotion. 'Jacqueline,' he gasped. 'Jacqueline . . .'

'Jacob? Whatever is the matter? Is my mother all right?'

'They came, last night,' Jacob panted. 'They broke down the front door, and came into the house. They hit Papa. They knocked him down.'

'Who?' she shouted.

'Brownshirts. Sent by Reinikker. They tore the place apart. Looking for enemies of the state, they said. But, Jacqueline . . . they were looking for you!'

'Me?' Her voice rose an octave.

'I heard them say so. They knew you had come to Munich, but not that you had left again. Jacqueline, you must hide.'

'But what about you? What about your father? What about Mother?'

He gave a sort of gulp. 'The house is a mess. Mama has taken Papa to hospital. She thinks his jaw is broken.'

'And Mother?'

'She lies on the bed and screams. But Jacqueline . . . you . . .'

The telephone went dead.

'What has happened?' Johann Lasker called from the breakfast room.

Jacqueline told him.

'My God,' he said. 'But . . .'

'I always said that Reinikker was no good,' Aunt Sadie remarked.

'Yes, anyway, one thing is certain: no one is going to trouble you here.'

'But what about Mama?' Jacqueline asked. 'And Uncle Herman, and . . .'

There was a sudden spate of banging and shouting from the entrance hall, then the breakfast-room door was flung open with a crash and four brown-shirted young men armed with sticks ran into the room. Johann Lasker pushed back his chair and started to rise.

'Sit,' one of the intruders commanded in a high, squeaky voice. He seemed the youngest of the lot, not one of them was over twenty-one, Jacqueline estimated; but he was obviously their leader.

'Do not move until you are told to,' he went on. 'Obey, and no one will be hurt. Attempt to resist and you will be sorry.'

'Resist?' Herr Lasker was enraged. Rising again he demanded, 'Resist what? How dare you break into my house like this, you damned young thug?'

In two strides the boy crossed the room and swung his stick at the old man's face whilst his companions shoved theirs into his ribs. Sadie screamed and Jean-Jacques howled in terror. Jacqueline, her mind spinning with the thought of Uncle Herman's injury, seized Johann's arm to help him back to his seat.

'Any more insolence and you will cause yourself considerable pain and trouble,' said the Brownshirt leader. 'Just sit still until we finish searching for weapons.' He

152

strode up and down the room, thwacking his stick against his boots.

Jacqueline sat down numbly beside Johann Lasker. The impossible had happened. They had been so sure that the horrors of the Dumescu household could not be repeated here, but it seemed that these thugs were everywhere. Could they be the same young men who only last night were singing so happily?

Jean-Jacques continued to cry noisily.

'If you don't silence that brat, I will.' The leader banged his stick on the table. Fortunately more of the gang now appeared, distracting his attention from the child's fresh screams.

'There do not appear to be any weapons in the house. No resistance was offered to our search.' One of the newcomers clicked his heels and saluted.

'Good. I wish I could say the same for this old fool,' his leader sneered.

There was another disturbance and more raised voices in the hallway. The leader turned and frowned as Marco Luzzi strode into the room.

'What in heaven's name do you think you are doing, you young idiot?' the Count demanded, totally ignoring the batons being brandished around him.

'Be very careful, stranger,' the young man threatened. 'Do not get yourself involved in something which does not concern you. However, before we throw you out you will state your name and business here.'

'Most certainly, you young fool. Here is my card. You will see that I am the Count Marco-Gregorio Luzzi di Calitri. As for my business here, I have come at the special request of my good friend Gauleiter Herr Heinrich von Reinikker.'

The young man blinked. 'Why should he want you here? He has ordered me to come and hold these people under house arrest until his own arrival.' He was trying to maintain his authority, but his voice dropped with uncertainty.

'He asked me to ensure that you carried out his orders

correctly. Being so young, he was not sure you would be able to handle the situation with the dignity required of a troop leader.' The Count gazed slowly around the room as he spoke. 'I see,' he continued, 'that the Gauleiter was sadly correct in doubting your ability.'

'I am carrying out my orders as instructed.' The lieutenant was almost whining now.

'Rubbish,' the Count snarled at him. 'Herr von Reinikker did not order you to come here and assault Herr Lasker.'

'But he was trying to resist arrest.'

'What, with a knife and fork against a troop of Brownshirts? Get out of here, you stupid young idiot. Put a couple of men on duty in the front hall and take the rest away with you. I will remain in charge until the Gauleiter arrives.'

'But . . .'

'No buts,' roared the Count. 'I have seen and heard enough. Any insubordination and you will be in serious trouble when the Gauleiter hears my report.'

Under this threat the young man, face red, clicked his heels and called his men to follow him out. As the door closed everyone got up and started to talk at once.

'Ssssh!' Luzzi held his finger to his lips. He crossed to the door, swung it open . . . then closed it again, gently. 'We must be very quick,' he whispered. 'There is very little time. Von Reinikker is coming for the Countess. If she is still here when he arrives she will be in great danger.'

'Eh? What is this?' Herr Lasker looked totally baffled. 'You just said you were going to hold us . . .'

'Yes, I know. But that was just to get those young hooligans out of the house. Believe me, I am no friend of Reinikker's, nor he of me.'

'But what could he do?' the old man queried. 'He surely cannot harm law-abiding citizens in their own homes here in Berlin? He would be thrown into prison. I shall call the police, now.'

'Do you not understand, Mein Herr, that now Hitler

and his Nazis are in power, there is no law other than that they will administer to suit themselves? Von Reinikker is not going to arrest himself.'

'I cannot believe what you say. I am sure you are grossly exaggerating the situation.' Johann shook his head. 'What possible reason can von Reinikker have to harm Jacqueline?'

'I do not know his motive, but perhaps the Countess herself knows of something?' He looked at her quizzically, but continued when she did not reply. 'We have no time to debate the matter. I can only tell you that Reinikker left Munich . . .' Luzzi consulted his watch, '. . . six and a half hours ago, and intends to come directly to this house. Of that I have no doubt.'

'The journey takes more than a day,' Aunt Sadie said.

'By train, Frau Lasker. He is travelling by motor car, fast. If the Countess is still here when he arrives I will be powerless to help her. Therefore she must leave immediately.'

Jacqueline had been trying to follow all that was said while attempting to comfort Jean-Jacques who was still crying noisily. She still found it difficult to believe that all this was really happening, and that Luzzi should be here, apparently trying to help them. She looked from him to Herr Lasker and back again, tried to speak reasonably. 'But where do I go? If it is not safe here, where will it be safe? Surely no one can just take me away without a warrant? I have committed no crime.'

'Quite, quite, my dear child,' Johann Lasker assured her. 'I am sure you will be safe here. In fact, until these political disturbances settle down I think we shall just keep the outer doors locked and check carefully on all callers before they are admitted. We don't want any more of these bully boys, or even Herr von Reinikker, in here.'

'With the greatest respect, Mein Herr, I must disagree with you,' Luzzi said. 'I am very much involved in politics and in recent developments within the ruling party in this country. The men to whom Herr Hitler has given authority are hard and ruthless. They will stop at nothing to achieve their ambitions, both for their Party and for themselves. Locked doors will not prevent a man like Reinikker from entering this house and removing the Countess. Why, I do not know, but . . .' he turned to Jacqueline. 'Maybe it has something to do with the abrupt termination of your friendship with him.'

Jacqueline gasped and bit her lip. Her face turned scarlet as she recalled Heinrich's parting words: She would pay. And what of Jacob's warning on the telephone? But it was too absurd to be true, that someone could just come in here, and take her away . . .

Luzzi seemed able to read her thoughts. 'He will trump up some charge that you are a subversive. You know, you are not a German citizen, Countess. Oh, no doubt Herr Lasker and myself would be able to go to a lawyer and have you free soon enough, but for several hours you would have been held by Reinikker and his people. Can you imagine what could happen to you in that time?'

Despite her attempts to think logically, she could not suppress waves of fear, the pounding in her chest. She did not want to imagine what it might be like to be entirely in Reinikker's power, even for a few minutes. And she was equally frightened for Jean-Jacques. She tried to speak, but not a sound came out.

Luzzi took her hand. 'Countess, I can take you where Reinikker can never touch you for as long as you live.'

You? she thought. A man I hardly know. What little I do know hardly reassuring. But what was she to do? She looked at Johann Lasker, who was now nodding.

'Yes, well, my dear, perhaps it would be better for you to leave with the Count. It is not worth taking the risk. I don't know where he intends to take you, but . . . maybe it is better that way.'

'But what about you and Aunt Sadie?' Certainly she couldn't go off alone with Luzzi.

'Reinikker has nothing against us. We will be perfectly safe here. Besides, where on earth would we go?' He smiled at her. 'Now, why don't you quickly pack a bag. Jean-Jacques can stay here with us until everything settles down.'

'No!' Jacqueline shouted. 'No, he must come with me.'

'Jean-Jacques? Who is he?' Luzzi asked.

'This is Jean-Jacques. My son.'

Luzzi stared at mother and child in amazement. 'Your son? Tyroler had a son?'

'Yes . . . er, well, no. Oh, it is too long a story to explain now. But he must come with me.'

'But of course he must come with you. He cannot remain here. I am sorry to have sounded so surprised. I just did not realise.' For once the Count looked flustered.

Sadie went upstairs with Jacqueline.

'I have two suitcases in my room. I will fetch them.' She had remembered her houseguest's arrival with her clothes tied in a bundle. Quickly she put Jean-Jacques' clothes into one case, while Jacqueline filled the other. Her mind had become a blank; she couldn't think what to take and what to leave, realised she hadn't included any shoes, and returning to the wardrobe, suddenly remembered her jewellery and stock of diamonds.

When she opened her door again, Luzzi was standing outside. 'I think it might be wise,' he whispered, 'if we were to use the servants' staircase; we don't want to be delayed by any arguments in the hall.'

'Where are we going, Mummy?' Jean-Jacques piped up.

'Hush, my darling. We are going to play a game of hide-and-seek. We must be very, very quiet or we will be found, won't we?' Jacqueline tried to make it sound like a game, but her heart was pounding and her mouth was dry.

'But who is going to look for us?' he continued in a loud stage whisper.

'Never mind. I'll tell you in a minute.' He was firmly led away, down the landing and through the servants' quarters.

The Laskers were waiting for them, hugged them both, wished them 'God Speed', then walked slowly into the drawing room, past the watching Brownshirts, who looked expectantly up the stairs, shrugged at each other, and said nothing.

Meanwhile, Luzzi, peering out of a back window, had received a signal from his chauffeur, and the three hurriedly crossed the cobbled yard to a waiting car. A moment later they were speeding through the Berlin streets, and Luzzi leaned forward to open the glass behind the driver.

'Careful, not too fast here, we don't want to attract attention. It is not far to the aerodrome.'

'Aerodrome?' Jacqueline exclaimed. 'Where on earth are we going?'

'To Italy, of course. Where else?'

March 1933 – October 1934

Down on your knees,
And thank heaven, fasting, for a good man's love.

William Shakespeare, *As You Like It*

THE VILLA was quiet. Jean-Jacques fell asleep before
Jacqueline finished reading his bedtime story, and now,
having bathed and changed into a turquoise silk dress, she
sat on the terrace outside the open drawing room windows
to watch the evening sun over the distant Mediterranean.
She smiled as the chair rocked her gently to and fro. It
was only mid-March, but the weather was so much warmer
here than in Berlin she felt no chill. The midday breeze
had dropped away and now not a leaf stirred in the garden.

The Count had telephoned two days ago to invite himself
to dinner tonight, but he would not be arriving for nearly
an hour. Apart from his two previous visits, she had seen
no one except the servants since her arrival here a month
ago. It would be pleasant to spend an evening in his
company again.

During their drive to the aerodrome outside Berlin,
Luzzi had explained that Jacqueline and her son could
remain safely beyond Heinrich's reach in Italy. She could
stay at an old holiday villa belonging to his family in the
hills north of Rome, until she had had time to consider
her next move. He would attend to all the passport arrangements, and even try to have Jean-Jacques added to hers.

It had been impossible to speak during the flight because
of the noise of the engines and the nervous excitement –

159

she had never been in an aeroplane before, and this was an Italian government machine which the Count had apparently been able to requisition – but while driving to the villa he had told her how the house was never used by the family nowadays and should indeed have been sold years ago, save that they had not had the heart to dismiss the old couple who had worked there all their lives. Darkness had fallen by the time they had arrived, and the rooms, shrouded in dustcovers, had seemed damp and eerie. But with the winter sunshine brightening the house next day, Jacqueline had worked with Rosita, airing all the rooms, cleaning and polishing the few they would use. After settling in at the house she had waited nervously to see what Luzzi's next move might be. But he had only remained long enough to give Rosita and Giuseppe a few instructions in Italian before bidding her good night and promising to visit her as soon as possible to see that she had all she required.

His first visit had been unexpected, one morning two weeks later. During lunch he had asked if she and her son were well, did they have everything they needed – the question of money had not arisen because apparently he had given Rosita sufficient to buy additional provisions. Indeed she had not known how to raise the subject of paying for her board. He had then told her he intended to return to Berlin in a few days and wondered if she would like him to take letters to the Laskers and her family. Was there anything she had left behind in Berlin that she would like him to bring back, if possible? She was grateful because she suspected that the post was being intercepted, not having received any replies to her letters. Most of her books had been abandoned in her haste to leave. So when the Count had returned ten days later with a trunk and two boxes loaded with her possessions, plus letters and news, she had been delighted.

Anna had gone with Herman and Hannah and their two children to a holiday chalet belonging to friends of the Dumescus in Switzerland. Herman had left a letter for her addressed to the Count at the Italian Embassy in Basle. He said they were quite well – his jaw had apparently not been broken after all – but the house and shop had been wrecked and they had decided to remain at the chalet until things settled down. It seemed that many Jewish homes and shops had been attacked by the Nazis in the euphoria of taking power; things had now quietened down considerably, and since Anna was in a very depressed state, Uncle Herman hinted that he hoped Jacqueline would be able to join them. He had no doubt that he would be able to re-start his business in Munich, and even that she now had little to fear from Reinikker.

Johann only had time to write a brief note while Sadie had the grooms fetch the trunk and boxes from their hiding place. He had told Luzzi of Reinikker's arrival at the Lasker house within a couple of hours of their departure. He had been enraged to find only two Brownshirts in the house and Jacqueline gone, and had taken over Johann's study to make a number of telephone calls. Meanwhile, Sadie had assembled the maids hastily to pack all Jacqueline's and Jean-Jacques' things . . . just in time. As the grooms carried the boxes out through the back door more Brownshirts had arrived, and with them, Reinikker had ransacked every room hunting for anything belonging to the Tyrolers. Sadie had felt very pleased with herself, Luzzi reported. Fortunately, little damage had been done in the search, and afterwards Reinikker had left with his boys and not returned.

Well, Jacqueline had thought, Uncle Herman might think there was nothing more to fear, but she had no intention of ever setting foot in Germany again.

After he had told all his news and Jacqueline had read her letters, she had asked the Count if he would care to stay to dinner. He had been delighted to accept, and, because it was not yet five o'clock, had offered to show her and Jean-Jacques a pretty walk up through the hills behind the house. From there the panorama was magnificent and he pointed out the features of interest across the wide flat plains to the coast in the west, the ridged summits of the Apennines to the east, and in the distant south, the hills circling Rome itself.

'One day I hope you will allow me to show you our beautiful capital,' he said. 'It has a certain magic, you know. It will captivate you. And you will captivate it.' Luzzi had smiled as he spoke, in a way she had never seen anyone smile before. His eyes lit up, crows' feet appearing at their corners, and his mouth stretched wide, showing his big, white, even teeth.

He had insisted on being present for Jean-Jacques' tea and asked if he might be permitted to read the bedtime story. He adored children, he explained, and had none of his own. Jean-Jacques was delighted with the arrangement and had stayed awake right to the end of the story that night.

Rosita had lit a fire as the evening was cold, so Jacqueline and her guest could sit on either side of the wide grate sipping martinis until dinner was ready. The meal had been somewhat formal, they sat facing each other from opposite ends of the long dining table being waited on by Giuseppe, who also doubled as gardener, messenger, and handyman. They returned to the fireside for coffee and Luzzi had started to talk about his childhood on the Calitri estates in Southern Italy. Mellowed and relaxed, Jacqueline had listened with interest, mentioning in turn the Carpathians and the Chateau Dumescu. She had hardly noticed as the Count led her on to speak of her own childhood: Mama, Paris, and . . . suddenly she stammered and was silent.

'You say Monsieur Caraiman was one of your friends?'

'Well . . .' she hesitated. 'Actually, he was an old friend of my mother's.' She blushed, looking at the floor as she spoke.

'You did not like him?'

'No!' She shuddered. 'No, he was horrible. Beastly.'

Luzzi had nodded. 'Now I understand, I think. I could not believe that Tyroler was a father. So Jean-Jacques is really the son of King Carol of Rumania?'

That he could have known the true identity of Caraiman had not crossed her mind, but she could not allow him to make that mistake. So that evening, hesitantly at first, but encouraged by his gentleness, Jacqueline had told him everything. About Mama, Jean-Paul, Carol, her marriage to Tyroler, the flight from Rumania to Munich, Heinrich . . . well, almost everything.

He had not interrupted. His mouth closed to a thin, hard line, a frown between his brows; he had sat rigid in his chair, his nostrils dilating at the effort to control his anger. When she had finished he lit a cigarette, inhaled deeply, eyes closed, head shaking, slowly.

'Oh, Jacqueline! Caro mio. Poor little Jacqueline.'

It was the first time he had ever used her Christian name.

The sun finally dipped into the sea, leaving a few clouds on the horizon etched in gold. A faint breeze rustled the hem of her dress. Nothing more had been said that evening, she recalled. Certainly nothing of significance. She smiled to herself, remembering how tense she had become after her revelations, fearing Marco might take her into his arms, try to make love to her on the pretext of comforting her. But he hadn't touched her, just gave another of his long, warm smiles as he hunched into his driving coat.

'Please believe me, Jacqueline, you will have nothing to fear as long as you remain here. You will receive no unwanted visitors and no unwanted attention. I promise you.'

Without warning her eyes had filled with tears and her throat had tightened. 'Oh, Marco, thank you.' Her hand had touched his sleeve. 'Thank you for being so understanding. I am very grateful to you.'

His gloved hand had patted hers gently, then he had let himself out into the night.

'So there you are, sitting outside in the cold and the dark, brooding. Is there something wrong?'

'Marco, how good to see you!' Jacqueline sprang up to greet him. 'No, of course not, everything here is marvellous. Actually, I was just thinking how wonderfully kind and generous you have been.'

'It was not for nothing that I kidnapped a professional decorator and imprisoned her in my old villa. Nor was it too dark when I arrived to see how well my clever idea is paying off. The gate pillar repaired, the gates rehung and painted; the driveway raked and weeded, trees trimmed and now even the house is being painted. And all in a month?'

'Poor Giuseppe,' Jacqueline laughed. 'He finds me a terrible slave-driver, I'm sure. I hope you won't mind, but I let him bring his nephew up from the village to help. The poor man is out of work and has seven children to feed.'

'Of course I don't mind. But how do you communicate? I thought you couldn't speak any Italian?'

'I found a French–Italian dictionary in your library, and I ask Rosita to sit with me for at least an hour a day, teaching me. Let's go inside. It is quite cold now that the sun has gone down.' She led him into the drawing room and they stood together at the chiffonier while he poured their martinis.

'Ciao!' She raised her glass.

'Ciao!' He laughed. 'Shall we speak in Italian tonight?'

'No, no. It will be a long time before I am proficient enough for that. Now come and sit down, I want to talk seriously with you.'

They settled into the same chairs as on his previous visit. Leaning back against the red velvet, she crossed her legs, took a deep breath, and began.

'Marco, I do appreciate your generosity and your understanding. Jean-Jacques and I have fallen in love with this villa. Rosita and Giuseppe are darlings, but we cannot stay here indefinitely.'

A shadow crossed his face.

'I feel I must find a place, somewhere in the world where I can live and work, where Jean-Jacques can go to school, and where I can make friends again. Not only do Jean-Jacques and I need people around us, but, please forgive

164

me if I say this, but to stay here puts me in a very compromising position. Daily I become more indebted to you than I can ever repay. I cannot continue to impose on our friendship.'

'No,' he sighed. 'No, I can see that. So, have you any idea where you wish to go, what you want to do?'

'Well, Uncle Herman would obviously like me to join them in Munich, principally because of my mother. He says things have settled down again, although there are all sorts of rumours, especially since that fire at the Reichstag. But I don't want to go back to Germany again . . .' She paused, but there was no need to explain. 'Also, if I am going to help Mother, I would rather she came to me.' Another pause, accompanied by an understanding nod.

'I've been thinking,' Jacqueline continued. 'There is only one type of work I know anything about: Interior Design. The work I was doing in Berlin. I can sell my diamonds and my jewellery and maybe realise enough to open my own salon. But I don't know where. I thought you might be able to make some suggestions.'

'Why not Rome?'

'I'd hoped you'd say that. Do you think it's feasible?'

Marco swept a hand over his black hair. 'I don't know what demand there might be for your work at the moment. We have our economic problems here in Italy just as much as anywhere else. On the other hand, there are even greater economic problems in Germany and you were able to secure plenty of commissions in Berlin. I will be in Rome in a day or two, and I will happily look into it for you. Perhaps you would tell me exactly what you have in mind, and I will see what can be done. What would you call it?'

She hadn't even considered that. 'Perhaps . . . Salon Tyroler?'

'I'm not sure that would be a good idea. We don't want to announce to your "friends", either in Germany or Rumania, just where you are.'

'Then Dumesca would be impossible as well,' she mused.

'Yes. Have you considered using Stevenson?'

She stared at him, eyes wide.

'It is your father's name,' he pointed out. 'And yet is known to you alone. From what you have told me, even your Mother would hardly connect it with you. I shall tell you something: Americans are very popular in Italy just now. And British, for that matter.' He raised his glass. 'I give you a toast: the Salon Stevenson.'

The salon was crowded and noisy, people weaving among each other to view the display stands. Part of an executive office was screened from a section of ultra-modern dining room and beyond that a corner of a *Louis XV* bedroom. Island displays of textures, fabrics, wood finishes and carpeting, willingly loaned by manufacturers hit hard by the depressed economic situation, were set off by plants in clay pots, wicker baskets and Chinese painted bowls.

Through the doorway of her office, Jacqueline happily surveyed the reception. The months of investigation and work, tension and worry, had so far borne excellent results. Marco had produced a suggested invitation list for the opening which had read like an Italian *Who's Who*, and she knew that without the influence of his family's giant industrial interests with merchant and commercial banking houses, there would not have been more than a fraction of the acceptances. He had stayed at her side as the guests arrived, making the introductions, encouraging everyone to take an interest in the salon and its purpose, rather than in the mysterious young Countess herself. Señor Alto had declared the salon officially open for business.

She saw Marco send a waiter to refill her glass, smothered a laugh as he winked at her over the mauve coiffure of his voluble companion, and moved back into the throng.

People were starting to leave, seeking her out to express their thanks and interest . . . polite, but in the main, meaningless remarks. With luck some would be genuine and the projects would follow; she mustn't be greedy, and she had had three serious prospective customers here this evening to add to the two who had not waited until the opening to give her commissions. As always, the first guests to leave started a mass exodus. Marco stayed with her until the last of the hangers-on had repeated their goodbyes. The waiters were collecting glasses and ashtrays, clearing away the serving trays and the uneaten canapés.

'I'll leave you to supervise the tidying and locking up while I return to the office,' he said. 'I'll collect you in about fifteen minutes. There's a table waiting for us at the Hassler.'

Dear Marco, she thought, tilting her chair back behind her desk, what a very good friend he has proved. Of course he had been quite right; she was completely captivated by Rome. On her first visit she had been taken through the Vatican City and St Peter's Basilica, peered at modern Rome from the arches of the Coliseum, wandered around the memorial to Victor Emmanuel and, by the time they had climbed the Spanish Steps, been only too glad to sit sipping iced drinks in the beautiful Hassler Hotel at Villa Medici.

'Everyone must see the tourist sights first,' Marco had explained. 'Now you can get to know the real, modern Rome and the people who live and work here.'

Impressive as those sights were, it was the ordinary buildings which fascinated her. Most of them seemed so dull and dilapidated on the outside, yet, like the Hassler, enter and you were in another world. The extensive use of coloured marble for pillars, walls and floors, the lovely Persian rugs, Venetian mirrors and chandeliers, gave an exciting new dimension to her own ideas on décor.

Marco had helped and encouraged her to speak his native tongue. She had a good ear and aptitude for languages, and her now conversational Italian had been a great asset in the last few months.

They had had no difficulty in finding premises. Many businesses had fallen victim to the depression, leaving shops and offices empty. The place she selected, just off the Piazza Barberini, had been occupied by a firm of manufacturers' agents, and rather than let it stand empty, the landlord had agreed to a short-term lease at a low rent. Jacqueline had the whole of the first floor: a large room for the salon itself, where the reception had been held and which occupied the entire front of the building, while behind was the design room and storeroom with two small offices for Jacqueline and her assistant. Despite the low rent, expenses had been higher than she had anticipated. The diamonds did not sell for anything like the figure she had hoped, so she had had to sell most of her jewellery as well. She and Marco had nearly quarrelled over that. Only when she assured him that she would never wear any of it again because it reminded her of so much unhappiness, did he agree to arrange the sale. Dear, dear Marco, always looking after her, always so wonderfully attentive, nothing like her previous concept of the bold, lecherous, Italian male. She had been very aware, this evening, how tall, handsome and charming he was, and, despite the grey wings of hair at his temples, how sexually attractive. All the women present, from the young and glamorous, the elegant and sophisticated, to the stout and stately, had vied to engage him in conversation, to laugh and flirt with him. He had responded gallantly, but few could have failed to note the way his eyes constantly sought her out, or the smiles they exchanged across the room. She supposed everyone had assumed she was Marco's mistress . . . but did that matter? Now that the organising and planning was over and she could start work, she supposed she would seldom see him. She sucked in her breath sharply at the thought. She was going to miss him dreadfully, but she must start to be independent, to stand on her own feet. Marco had given her so much of his time in the past months, despite the demands of his own business and political life. And, of course, he was married. He and his wife apparently lived very separate lives, but surely he must spend some time with her?

Jean-Jacques was going to miss him too, Jacqueline

sighed. A pity their friendship should virtually come to an end. But need it? Of course it must. She could not expect him to continue visiting her at the villa, escorting her in Rome, spending so much time with her, knowing that their friendship could never become love. As long as he was cast in the role of knight errant, rescuing a damsel in distress, while he was helping her start a new life, she had been able to accept his friendship without embarrassment. Now she could accept it no longer, knowing she could offer nothing more. Would she want to offer more, if she could? She knew she was very fond of him; perhaps she did love him in a way. There had been occasions when a look or an accidental touch had stirred feelings deep in her stomach, feelings which brought tremors of fear to her. She had had to drive such feelings away lest they soured their friendship.

She looked at her watch and hastily wrote a cheque for the waiters, as a motor car hooter sounded in the street below.

'You have been very quiet,' Marco remarked when they finished dinner. 'I expect you are tired.'

'Have I? I'm sorry. No, I'm not really tired.' Jacqueline brought a bright smile to her face.

'Well, then, why so pensive?'

'Nothing. Really,' she insisted. 'Are you sure you don't mind driving me all the way out to the villa tonight?' She changed the subject.

He shook his head. 'Perhaps you would like to leave coffee until we get there?'

'Good idea.'

Concentrating on traffic and pedestrians in the still busy streets, he drove in silence until they reached the open road.

'Jacqueline,' his voice sounded serious. 'I thought you shared all your problems with me now. Why will you not tell me what is on your mind?'

How she wished she could. She longed to explain her

distorted and conflicting emotions. Let him know that she had not been born cold and frigid; that she longed to seek the comfort of a man's arms. But it could never be. She did not think Jean-Paul could now overcome the horror implanted by Heinrich and King Carol.

'I have told you, it is nothing. Perhaps I am more tired than I knew.'

But later, standing in front of the fireplace, he gazed down into her face, waiting. For an explanation, she understood. He would not be fobbed off; he knew her too well.

'It was only when the reception was over and I was waiting for you to come with the car that I realised all our work together is finished,' she tried to explain.

'Yes?' He waited for her to continue.

'I mean, it will seem strange without you. Jean-Jacques is very fond of you . . .'

'And you? Will you miss me?'

'Of course. Dreadfully, dear Marco.' Suddenly her arms were round his neck and he was stroking her hair, holding her against him, kissing her eyes. Almost immediately she pushed away from him.

'I'm sorry, I didn't mean to do that. I do apologise.' She fought back tears. 'I'm afraid I cannot explain.'

'You don't have to explain, my darling. Do you think I have not understood all these months, ever since the evening you told me about yourself? Do you think I don't know how much a man's touch could terrify you?' She did not resist this time as he gently slipped his arms around her. 'Why do you think I have never tried to kiss you or even hold your hand? It has been very hard for me, because I love you, my darling. I love you so very much.'

Tears slid silently down her cheeks and Marco dabbed at her face with his handkerchief. He continued to hold her, but he did not crush her to him or press his body against hers.

'My little love, you have been raped and abused. You have experienced three so-called lovers, but no man has ever really made love to you.'

'But with Jean-Paul . . .'

'Jean-Paul was just a boy, an inexperienced boy. That was not lovemaking, only experimenting. Jacqueline . . .' He held her away from him and looked into her red-rimmed eyes. 'I know you can never enjoy a man's touch again until you allow a man you love and who really loves you, truly to make love to you, with caresses which express his love for you, not just his desire to possess your body.'

She was trembling all over. 'Yes. Yes, I know you are right. Dear Marco.' She gazed up at him for a moment, took a deep breath, and asked, 'Please. Please, Marco, will you come upstairs with me now, before I lose my courage?'

He lay sleeping at her side in the big, canopied bed, his hand, long and smooth-skinned like his body, still unconsciously holding her arm. She smiled into the darkness. A gentle hand. A gentle man, loving and patient. He had agreed to her plea for darkness without question; so at least he had not seen her constant tears as she lay naked under the sheet waiting for him, nerves taut, schooling herself not to flinch when he touched her. But he hadn't, not for a long time. Instead he had lain at a distance, talking, telling her of his first love when he was only fourteen, and his grand passion for a Spanish beauty, the daughter of a visiting diplomat. He spoke of his wife, chosen for him by his family, the alliance agreed between their elders before they ever met. He admitted his search for love, his many mistresses.

'Now, at last, I have found love, dearest Jacqueline.'

His hand had reached out and touched her face, traced her features one by one like a blind man, in the darkness.

'I knew from the first time I saw you at the Grand Charity Ball in Berlin that you were the woman of my dreams.' The tips of his fingers played around her ears and the nape of her neck. She could feel his breath against her cheek.

'You were breathtakingly beautiful that night. Exquisite. You always do look beautiful, but that first night I saw

171

something special. I saw the woman I knew I was destined to love for the rest of my life.' His words so relaxed her she was hardly aware of his hand on her breast, softly caressing, until she felt the deep response within her . . . wanting more. His face touched hers. Almost without knowing it, she turned to seek his mouth, opening to let their tongues meet and gently circle. His hand moved slowly down her flat belly to brush over the silken hair of her sex . . . and on to stroke outside her thigh, returned to brush again, and again away. His leg was pressed against her, his foot rubbing gently on her own.

'Marco. My dear, darling, patient Marco. I do love you,' she had whispered, parting her thighs for his hand to slip between. His fingertips continued their arousal until he could no longer resist the urgent invitation of her arms.

Unlike the three previous occasions in her life, there was no pain. He took her in a continuous caress, stroking her, building her passion. She surged to meet him again and again, their bodies melding from breast to toe. Eagerly she returned his kisses, completing the circuit of their loving.

Afterwards, Marco had repeated his love for her, caressing, nibbling her ear, whispering his happiness. And, lying back in the darkness, her heart still pounding, she knew she loved him too, this dear, kind, older man, exactly twenty years her senior. True she had not felt the fierce, passionate need which had consumed her seven years ago in the Carpathians with Jean-Paul, and, as with Jean-Paul, was again left with the feeling that it was all over too quickly, that maybe there could be more. But perhaps that had to be just her naïvety. This must surely be the very best of lovemaking, and if she and Marco could repeat this joy together for the rest of their lives, what more could she want? Life would be filled with happiness and contentment, forever.

So her plan to move with Jean-Jacques from the villa to a Rome apartment never came about. Marco offered her *carte blanche* to redecorate and refurbish the shabby, old-fashioned interior of the villa, to which she gave priority, so that before Christmas the work was finished and Marco had moved in with many of his belongings. To Jean-Jacques' delight his adopted Papa came to spend two or three evenings a week with them, and the trio went driving and sight-seeing together on occasional weekends. The boy had been enrolled at a school quite close to the salon and Jacqueline drove him into Rome each day in her Alfa Romeo, Marco's first gift. Jean-Jacques sat in the passenger seat, immensely proud in his new black uniform, pleased that he had to dress like a miniature soldier and belong to something called the Ballila. Military drilling and weapon handling was a regular part of the school curriculum, a point that aroused fears in Jacqueline, but Marco was as ever gently reassuring.

'It is part of Il Duce's attempt to introduce some discipline, some sense of purpose, into the lazy Italians,' he explained. 'Believe me, it has no sinister or warlike purpose.'

The initial rush of commissions at the Stevenson Salon had produced more work than she and her assistant could handle, so extra staff had been engaged. She was worried that the additional salaries could not be paid if business slackened the following year, but by Christmas she was very glad of the competence they displayed in their work. Because a new factor had arisen.

Marco was able to spend Christmas Eve at the villa, and would not be leaving until after Christmas Day lunch. When Jean-Jacques finally fell asleep with a large stocking hanging from the foot of his bed for Santa Claus to fill, the Count and Jacqueline sat on either side of the fire as usual, sipping aperitifs before dinner.

'I don't know if you are going to be pleased with one of your Christmas presents, darling,' Jacqueline announced. 'So I think I had better tell you what it is now, while we are alone.'

'Could I fail to love anything you choose for me?' Marco grinned.

'I haven't exactly chosen it, although I know I will love it. Dearest Marco, you are going to be a father.'

'What? Are you sure?' He crossed the hearth and knelt before her, his arms round her waist. 'My darling, darling girl!' She raised his head from her lap and to her consternation saw tears streaming down his face. 'Don't worry,' he laughed. 'I weep for joy. It is so wonderful.' He sat back on his heels, suddenly frowning. 'But you do realise, don't you, that there is no divorce here in Italy. Our child will be illegitimate.'

'You forget that I was too. Better an honest bastard than a dishonest name like Frederick Tyroler, in my opinion. Poor Jean-Jacques, there will be so much to explain to him one day.'

It had become increasingly obvious from Uncle Herman's letters that he felt Jacqueline should take some step towards making things up with Anna. Marco agreed with her that she should not risk returning to Germany, but although he felt she owed Anna nothing, he did not object to her inviting her mother to stay at the villa for a few weeks before the baby was born.

Anna did not reply to the invitation, she arrived. She was laden with a great deal of luggage, appearing almost exactly a year after Jacqueline's own arrival in Italy. She walked into the salon just as Jacqueline was preparing to leave for the weekend. They gazed at each other in amazement.

'Mother! What are you doing here?'

'Jacqueline! You are pregnant again.'

Jacqueline eyed the stack of luggage in the lobby with misgivings; it looked as though Anna intended to stay for a long time. They drove out to the villa, with Jean-Jacques on his grandmother's knee, and as many of the suitcases as the Alfa Romeo would hold piled behind them. Anna looked very well; she had dyed her hair – red. She was charming and friendly, obviously impressed by her daughter's salon – she did not comment on the choice of name

174

– and by her motor car. Her only *faux-pas* was in repeatedly calling Jean-Jacques 'Frederick', despite frequent corrections from the boy himself, while Jacqueline pretended not to notice. She admired the villa, loved her bedroom, but failed to comprehend why her daughter should want to live so far out of Rome, so cut off from society.

Marco had not yet arrived when they came down to the drawing room, having changed for dinner.

'This room is quite charming, darling.' Anna wandered about examining the pictures and *objets d'art*. 'Somewhat old-fashioned for my taste, but charming. Now, I think this will be my chair from now on.'

'Sorry, Mother, but that is Marco's chair. Why don't you take this one between us?'

'But I don't . . . oh, very well.' Anna submitted, pursing her lips.

Jacqueline realised that it would be up to herself to make all the effort to maintain a friendly atmosphere with a mother who seemed determined to treat her as a mere child who must acquiesce to her parent's wishes in all things. Now six months pregnant, she felt healthier than ever before and continued to drive into Rome three or four times a week. Anna was still in bed when she departed each morning, but when she returned her mother never failed to voice her disapproval. Jacqueline knew she was bored, left alone at the villa all day.

'Would you care to come in to Rome with me sometimes for a day's shopping; we could lunch together,' she suggested.

'Shopping? What with? I haven't any money,' Anna whined.

'Mother!' Jacqueline exclaimed. 'That's not true. Why, I wrote you another sizeable cheque only a few days ago.'

'Yes, dear, very good of you, I'm sure. But of course it wasn't enough to buy a decent blouse, let alone to spend a whole day shopping.'

Jacqueline wanted to point out that in the circumstances her mother could no longer expect to dress at the top couturiers, but instead just said, 'Very well,' and dropped the subject.

However, she felt obliged to take action two weeks later when, on arriving home from the salon, she took the fruit she had purchased through to the kitchen and discovered Rosita in tears, being comforted by an angry Giuseppe.

'I am sorry, Signora, but it is Signora Dumesca. Every day she finds something wrong. Always she is criticising Rosita and me. Today she says that Rosita has not pressed her clothes properly, not cooked her luncheon properly, is no good at her job. She says if she does no better next week we will be dismissed. Signora . . .' he threw his arms wide. 'We have worked here for the Count and his family for thirty years. Always we have done our very best to please. Never,' he banged his fist on the table, 'never have we been so criticised. It is finished,' he shouted. 'We will go now, immediately. My Rosita will not stay here to be insulted, any more.' And to the amazement of all three, Jacqueline burst into tears, Rosita comforted her, she comforted Rosita, and, between repeated pleas for Santa Maria to come to his aid, Giuseppe tried to comfort the two weeping women.

Later, having recovered her composure, Jacqueline found Anna in the garden. 'Mother, I know Rosita and Giuseppe are perhaps not the most expert servants we have had, but they are very sweet and obliging. They really do their very best to please.'

'Best? Don't be ridiculous, darling, they are hopeless. I can't imagine why you have tolerated them for so long.' Anna held out her long cigarette holder to flick ash on to the path. 'They simply have to go.'

'That is impossible. They have been here . . .'

'For thirty years. I know. I have been told that several times. But it only proves that they never learn.'

'Mother!' Jacqueline could feel her temper rising. 'I told you . . .'

'Nonsense, darling, you are just too young to have the confidence to deal with servants. Now, I will dismiss them for you and find someone more competent.'

'Mother!' She was shouting this time. 'Will you stop it.

This is my home and they are my servants. If you don't like Rosita's pressing, do it yourself. And if you don't like her cooking you had better cook your own meals, too. But for the last time, THEY STAY!' She stalked back to the house, leaving Anna speechless with fury.

Knowing that Marco already disapproved of Anna and tried to avoid her company, Jacqueline told him nothing of the incident. Instead she decided to go to the salon only once a week until after the baby was born, taking Anna with her, 'shopping for the baby', and on other various pretexts, in order not to leave her alone at the villa. Despite his misgivings, Marco had been very thoughtful, trying to arrange something to entertain Anna each week. Usually she showed little appreciation, but one of his ideas bore unexpected fruit. Some six weeks after her arrival, Marco had to entertain a party of French industrialists, important business associates of one of his companies, on holiday in Rome. Three men and two wives, they were hard-drinking, noisy and very rich. He did not enjoy their company, he admitted later to Jacqueline, but thought he might 'kill two birds with one stone' by inviting them to dine at the villa with Anna. Anna was seated next to the unpartnered visitor, the loudest, fattest and apparently wealthiest of the group, and the two of them proceeded to flirt outrageously.

She drank almost as much as he did, and, much to Jacqueline's embarrassment, before the meal was over there was obviously considerable activity between them under cover of the tablecloth.

Three times during the following week Anna requested transport into Rome, twice returning late in the evening, flushed and jubilant. On the third occasion she did not come home until the following day, only to announce that she had invited 'dear Claude' to stay. Jacqueline was incensed.

'Really, Mother, it is too bad of you. You should at least have spoken to me first. We both find Claude thoroughly objectionable; I cannot let you inflict him on Marco.'

'How dare you speak to me like that about one of my

friends?' Anna flared. 'You are quite the most ungrateful child any woman could have had the misfortune to bear.'

'Me? Ungrateful?'

'Yes. That's what I said. Ungrateful. Here I am, shut away from the world, bored to tears, purely to keep you company and look after you while you await your second "love-child".' Her lip curled as she spoke. 'And what thanks do I get?'

'Thanks?' Jacqueline cried. 'You are joking, I hope. You have done nothing but make trouble and solicit money from me since you arrived here. Why don't you face facts? You have been a useless parasite all your life. You have never done a day's work or earned an honest penny. You have lied, cheated and prostituted yourself . . . and me. I have tried hard to forget the past and be friends with you again during your visit, but I have had enough. You will have to go. Why don't you ask your precious Claude to take you back to France?'

Which Anna did. It appeared that Claude was very taken with the elegant socialite, a friend of royalty, and eagerly bore her away like a trophy to show to his friends in Rouen.

Jacqueline, Marco, Giuseppe and Rosita waved the happy couple goodbye from the steps of the villa a few days later, breathing profound sighs of relief.

The last month of Jacqueline's pregnancy was peaceful and happy. Marco had employed a chauffeur to take Jean-Jacques to school each day, and to drive her whenever she wanted to go out. A leading gynaecologist came out from Rome each week to attend her, and as her time drew near, a nurse was installed in the villa.

Though a few days late, the arrival of Marco's son caused little trouble or discomfort. At ten minutes old, his father held him in his arms weeping for joy, smothering his contented mother with kisses and gifts. Francisco Luigi Marco-Gregorio was a model baby; he ate and slept well, and was adored by his parents and stepbrother. Jacqueline and Marco were careful to give Jean-Jacques as much attention as they lavished on the baby, and the small boy happily posed for the photographer, holding Francisco in his arms.

That summer the villa contained an idyllically happy household. The Count spent as much time as he could with his mistress and baby son, frequently requesting that the child should be in the garden with them, or sitting out on the verandah where he could peep at him from time to time and roll the pram to and fro. He loved to be present at feeding time to watch Francisco suckling at his mother's breast.

Jacqueline watched father and son admiring each other one evening during their 'playtime hour' before the baby and Jean-Jacques were put to bed. Busy with his toy truck Jean-Jacques was oblivious to all else, and didn't notice his mother kneel on the floor beside Marco and kiss the top of his bent head. The Count turned to meet her eyes, saw her love and happiness.

'Darling Marco,' she murmured. 'You are as dear and wonderful a father as you are a lover.'

He smiled. 'I'm surprised that you can remember. It's been a long time.'

'Too long,' she replied.

Together they rose, and with little Francisco kicking and chortling on the carpet at their feet, they kissed, gently at first, but with building desire.

There was a knock on the door and they sprang apart as the nurse came in to fetch Jean-Jacques and the baby.

'We will come and kiss you goodnight when you are in bed, darling,' Jacqueline promised, and the little boy followed the nurse out of the room, clutching his truck.

Marco put an arm round Jacqueline's shoulders and drew her outside on to the terrace where they stood close together, silently watching thin streaks of cloud drift across the setting sun.

After going to the children, by unspoken agreement they drifted towards their bedroom.

179

'Changing for dinner tonight, my love?' Marco asked playfully.

Jacqueline started to unbutton her day dress. 'Yes,' she answered, smiling across at him. 'I think I will. How about you?'

They laughed together in happy anticipation.

Marco was nervous and gentle, and it was Jacqueline herself who encouraged him, drew him over her, arms tightly clasped round him, body lifting to receive him.

They went down to dinner laughing like schoolchildren, toasted each other across the table, eyes glowing with the special happiness they shared.

Jacqueline sighed with contentment. I wonder, she thought, if I could ever have been so happy with anyone else, even Jean-Paul?

The only shadow in their life was the regret that there could be no marriage, that Francisco would bear the stigma of illegitimacy. But even to that problem Marco offered a solution; he broached the subject one evening as they sat together on the terrace.

'You are aware, my darling, that Francisco is legally yours; I have no right to him at all, so you must think very carefully about the suggestion I am going to make. I would like to adopt the little one so that he may bear my name.' He waited while Jacqueline thought for some moments.

'But then I would have no legal rights to him. Your wife could demand custody of him, couldn't she?'

'You know that Camilla has only one interest in her life . . . horses. She lives for dressages and show-jumping. However, it is an expensive hobby and for some time she has been asking me for a very large sum of money to modernise and extend her stables and buy more horses.' He paused to light a cigarette, pressing it carefully into a gold holder. 'I think I can strike a bargain with her. I will agree to give her all the money she requires if she will agree to the adoption and . . . to a legal separation, giving me custody of the child. Of course it still means that you lose legal custody. You only have my word that he will always remain in your care.'

Jacqueline laughed. 'Oh! I see. I will have to think about that, won't I? But seriously, do you think that Camilla might agree?'

'I feel sure she will. She is really quite a nice woman, in a horsey sort of way. We have honestly never had any interest in each other, and she is quite devoid of sexual or maternal instincts. But she is pleasant and intelligent, can even be quite good company at times, if one can bear the use of horse liniment in place of perfume.'

'Marco! You brute.' Jacqueline suppressed a giggle. 'I believe she never should have married, poor girl.'

'You are absolutely right. She viewed our marriage as the major catastrophe in her life, right from the start.'

As Marco had prophesied, Camilla happily agreed to his proposals and lawyers were briefed to start the legal machinations.

Francisco was weaned at three months and Jacqueline was able to return to the salon. She was satisfied with the way business had continued in her absence, but realised a growing demand for contemporary design. She wanted to attend the European Fair for Art and Design in Paris that autumn. Marco was too busy to accompany her, but he was quite happy for her to go without him, leaving the children in the care of Nanny for five days. He saw her off on the Rome–Paris Express, with Maria, her personal maid, and a minimum of luggage. He had reserved sleeping accommodation for her on the train and a suite at the Hotel Georges V, just off the Champs-Elysées. It was her first visit to the hotel and she was overwhelmed by its vast, stately rooms filled with beautiful carpets, paintings and giant wall tapestries, similar to the Hassler at Villa Medici, but on a far grander scale.

She enjoyed her first visit to the Fair, not least for the attention she received as one of the few business women present. Most of the other women were simply accompanying their husbands. This was definitely a man's world. Not that the attention was always of a nature she desired; too few of the men could accept that the beautiful young countess was seriously concerned with business. They made fatuous remarks about her charm and her clothes, one eulogised on the colour of her eyes and was somewhat put out when those eyes turned cold as she suggested that they discuss business as her time was limited. But generally she found the Fair interesting, stimulating, and she thoroughly enjoyed the day. Despite her previous decision to the contrary, she decided to accept the invitation to a reception being given by a group of textile manufacturers. She was feeling far too exhilarated to spend the evening alone.

Maria dressed her hair and helped her into a moss-green, long-sleeved dress with squared shoulders, plunging neckline and a skirt which fitted closely over her hips, flaring from the knees. Her diamond pendant and ear-rings, set in yellow gold, were a gift from Marco after the birth of their son, as was the golden fox fur which hung from her shoulders.

She was greeted warmly at the reception, accepted a glass of champagne from a waiter and was quickly surrounded by admirers who seemed interested in anything but business. The excessive flattery bored her somewhat, and with the advantage of her high heels she allowed her gaze to wander over the shoulders of her entourage, seeking a familiar intelligent face, anyone who might prove interesting.

Suddenly her glass slipped from her hand and shattered on the floor. People bent to pick up the shards and dab with handkerchiefs at her dress, but Jacqueline was unaware of anything, anyone – save the man who was shouldering his way across the room towards her. She was gazing into the deep, dark eyes of Jean-Paul.

October 1934 – November 1935

You have ravished me away by a power I cannot
resist; and yet I could resist till I saw you; and
even since I have seen you I have endeavoured
often 'to reason against the reason of my love'.

John Keats, *Letters* (No 160,
to Fanny Brawne, 13 October 1819)

JACQUELINE COULD not remember leaving the reception.
Her only memory was of trembling all over, her dry mouth
speaking meaningless platitudes. 'How nice to see you
again. Are you still in *Le Cadre Noir*?' While all the time
her mind and body were tensed and crying – no, this cannot
be true. I cannot feel like this after eight years. They had
so much to tell each other, they politely agreed. Where
could they talk?

First he took her where all Frenchmen in Paris seem
naturally to gravitate – the Champs-Elysées. They had
drifted into a pavement café to sip coffee and cognac, to
ask and answer questions.

'No, I am no longer in *Le Cadre Noir*,' Jean-Paul had
told her. 'I completed my six years this summer. I enjoyed
the dressage, but not the army, so I am now in business
with my father. He continues to specialise in gems, and I
specialise in antiques, particularly clocks and *objets d'art*,
which was why I was at the reception. And what of yourself?'

Their conversation had remained light, impersonal, both
wanting to delve deeper but reluctant to do so in such a

public place. So eventually he had accompanied her back to her sitting room at the Georges V, where, much to her surprise, Maria was dismissed for the remainder of the evening.

Jacqueline closed the door and leaned against it, looking at him. 'You never came back to see me.'

'I came as soon as I could, but you had already left.'

'I met your father in Rumania.'

'Yes. He told me he had met the Countess Tyroler. You married very . . . young.'

'My mother and Queen Marie insisted. I felt I had no choice . . .'

'Queen Marie? What on earth had she to do with your marriage?'

'My mother told her that the baby I was expecting was Prince Carol's.'

'Prince Carol's?' Jean-Paul shook his head in disbelief. 'I don't understand. You say you were expecting a baby?'

'Yes.'

'And Prince Carol was the father?'

She shook her head. 'No.' Her voice dropped to a whisper. 'Jean-Jacques is your son.'

'My . . . then why did you not contact me? You knew where I was, at Saumur.'

'I did write to you, but . . .'

'I never received anything from you. Was it addressed to Saumur?'

'Yes.'

'I must have been away on a special training course; I had several. They never did forward post properly. Why didn't you try again?' he asked.

'I began to think it would ruin your army career before it had even started, to be burdened with a wife and child so young. I thought you would hate me.'

'Didn't you hate me?'

'No! I . . .' she could not finish. Without thinking they moved over the carpet and met in the centre of the room, hesitating only a moment before they were in each other's arms. As they clung together, Jacqueline knew that Jean-Paul was trembling too, knew that the lava which spread from her belly, down her thighs, up through her breasts, was matched in him. Soft, tentative kisses quickly became fierce and passionate. Still embracing, they moved to the bedroom. Eyes and mouths locked, their fingers fumbled urgently with each other's clothes which were trodden into a heap on the floor. Jacqueline gasped and swayed, faint with the intensity of sensation as Jean-Paul's hands caressed her body, slid down her back, clutched her buttocks to hold her tight against him, releasing her to cup her breast, stroking his thumb over the hard nipple, then bending low to kiss her. She buried her face in the nape of his neck, caressing skin and curls with her lips. Falling back on to the bed she pulled him over her, frantically aroused as never before, desperate for his entry. And when it came she had to fight the delicious waves of faintness, determined to enjoy total awareness of the enormous fire which burned through her body. Her hands and feet tingled, numbed as her blood flowed to the centre of her being.

They reached the summit together, their joint climax seeming to last forever. Then, as it faded, they laughed with joy, kissed, clung and laughed again. It had all happened too quickly for exhaustion, but not too quickly for Jacqueline to reach a height she had never known before. This was the mountain she had tried to climb so many times with Marco, and with Jean-Paul too that very first time, without success, without ever knowing there could be such an ultimate joy.

'I am hungry,' she announced.

'So am I. Shall we eat here or go out?'

'Out. I want to see Paris, the city of love, with you tonight. Show me, then let us return and make love again.'

They ate, danced, gazed into each other's eyes throughout a spectacular floor show.

They made love again that night, feeling far too exhilarated for sleep. Passers-by watched the happy couple wandering hand in hand, kissing and laughing, through the Tuileries Gardens and along the banks of the Seine. They took a boat trip on the river round Notre Dame; a climb to the top of the Arc de Triomphe; coffee at pavement cafés on the Champs-Elysées.

Reality hit them hard on the third morning. Jean-Paul lay on the bed watching her pack. 'How long before we meet again, chérie?'

She shook her head. 'Never, my darling.' Tears welled up as she looked at him.

'Never!?'

'I cannot. This . . . this was an accident. We did not plan it. It just happened. Even so, I feel very guilty. But to plan to deceive Marco – no, I cannot do it. I could not lie in his arms, accepting his love and trust, only living for our next meeting, my love.'

'But Jacqueline, he would never know,' Jean-Paul pleaded.

'But I would. Perhaps it is different for a woman. Certainly it is for me, because Marco has been so good, so kind and patient. You know, after those vile incidents with Carol and Heinrich, I never wanted another man to touch me, ever again. But for Marco . . .' Again she shook her head. 'Don't tempt me, Jean-Paul. For pity's sake don't tempt me.'

She turned from him to pack, weeping.

'You are right, I suppose. I admit I have not been faithful to Veronique, but she would not expect it of me. We grew up together. Our families are friendly and it was always agreed between them that we would marry. We liked each other well enough, but after you and I met in Rumania – well, I never wanted to marry anyone but you. I came to Paris from Saumur that year, full of ideas for our future to discuss with you. But you were not here and the next thing I heard was that you were married. Veronique is a wonderful wife and mother. In fact she is very beautiful, and in a way I do love her. But not like . . . this.' He sighed. 'I suppose if we continued to meet we would be endangering the happiness of too many people; your two sons, my two daughters, as well as Marco and Veronique. But, Jacqueline, I do so want to meet my son.'

'That would only bring confusion and heartache to you both..It would be cruel to introduce him to his father only immediately to say goodbye. Marco would then know that we have met again, and he would never rest happy about that. We cannot live our lives on fantasies, on dreams of what might have been, or the misery of others.'

'I know. It was stupid of me. But my mind and my body will cry out for you for the rest of my life.' He sat on the side of the bed, head in his hands.

'Mine too, dearest, forever.'

'Have you enjoyed your visit to Paris, Maria?'

'Signora, it was beautiful. And you were kind to let me have so much time and money to spend on enjoying it. I went right up the Eiffel Tower and saw all of Paris from the top, but I felt sick when I looked straight down.'

Jacqueline forced a laugh. She was trying very hard to appear normal, talking to Maria about the Paris Fair as though she had spent all of every day there. She had limited the girl's duties to the laundering and tidying of her clothes and toiletries, barely two hours' work each morning, leaving the remainder of each day free. So she doubted if Maria would suspect anything. The most difficult period of subterfuge was now, while she fought the lead weight in her stomach, the burning behind her eyes. Her breathing came quick and shallow, followed by long, deep gasps. Jean-Paul's face was permanently mirrored in her mind; laughing, talking, head tilted sideways as he emphasised some point, thrown back in ecstasy, reflecting her misery as he stood on the platform at the Gare du Lyons, receding from her sight.

'Signora does not like it?' Maria was holding up a coloured print of the Church of the Sacré Coeur for her approval.

'Oh, yes, Maria, it is splendid. And you say it is for your

mother? She will love it. Now, will you go to the restaurant car and bring me some coffee?'

Alone, she could abandon the pretence.

Eight years ago she had made this journey, weeping as the wheels beat out their rhythmic reminder: 'Away from Jean-Paul', 'Goodbye, Jean-Paul'. He was her lover; they were meant for each other. The excitement, the delirious joy they experienced together should have been theirs for life. But fate had only allowed them three stolen days, shadowed by guilt. Because she did feel guilty towards that dear, gentle, understanding man who had helped to transform her life from disaster to success, given her a happiness for which she had never dared hope. How hurt he would be if he ever learned what had happened. He would understand, no doubt, but oh, how miserable it would make him. He must never find out.

Another tiny station flashed past her window. Tears fell intermittently as waves of bitterness, self-pity and anger against fate, swept over her. History had repeated itself.

Suddenly a new thought struck her. Perhaps her mother had fallen just as deeply in love with her father as she had with Jean-Paul. Wimbledon fortnight: a two-week whirlwind love affair, the consummation of which had destroyed her tennis career, left her alone and pregnant, a social outcast. Until she had met Prince Carol? Had he ever been her Marco? No. It was impossible to imagine that vile, lascivious brute ever being kind or restrained. No, there had never been a Marco for her mother, which explained so much. Little wonder that she was hard and bitter, determined to take out of life all she could in payment for the bad hand she had been dealt by fate. And she, Jacqueline, was a major part of that bad hand. It was not surprising that her mother had shown her so little love, understanding, or sympathy. What sort of mother might she have been if she had had someone like Marco?

'Your coffee, Signora.' Maria arranged the tray on the seat beside her.

* * *

Jacqueline dreaded meeting Marco, fearing that he would read the guilt in her eyes immediately. He was waiting for her on the station platform, but, although his welcome was warm and loving, there was obviously something on his mind.

Surely he could not have learned about Jean-Paul already, Jacqueline thought. Is it possible that someone recognised us and hurried back from Paris with the news? Or telephoned?

He said little as he escorted her to the waiting car, leaving Maria and the chauffeur to deal with the luggage.

'You are very quiet, darling,' she remarked, heart beginning to pound.

'I am afraid I have heard some very sad news, sweetheart. I will tell you about it on the way home.'

He does know, oh God, what am I to say to him? Deny everything? He would know she was lying. No, she would have to confess everything.

Separated from Maria and Claudio by the glass partition, Marco turned to Jacqueline and took her hands. 'My darling, there is very bad news from Germany.'

'Germany?' She frowned at him, wondering what on earth could have happened there.

'Herr Lasker and his wife have gone to Switzerland. They were allowed to leave the country provided that they took nothing with them. No money, no possessions. They are not destitute, however. Lasker has some foreign investments he can realise, but they are desperately worried about the Dumescus. They believe all four have been imprisoned and their home and business premises gutted by fire.'

It took Jacqueline a few moments to assimilate the unexpected, dreadful news.

'But why? Why? What had they done?'

'They had not done anything, but they are Jews.'

'I know they are Jews. Is that a crime?'

'It is, in the eyes of the German Nazi Party.'

She frowned as a new thought struck her. 'What about

189

Il Duce and his government? They are Fascists, too. Do they persecute Jews as well? You do realise, don't you, that I am partly Jewish?'

'Of course I do,' he laughed briefly. 'But you don't have to worry about that at all. Nobody in Italy has anything against Jews, I promise you, only respect and perhaps a little jealousy for their ability to make a profit from any business they deal in, even during a depression.'

'I wonder what the Laskers will do now?'

'A businessman like Herr Lasker will no doubt have investments in other countries. They have lost a great deal, but I don't imagine they will be destitute. The main worry is the Dumescus. They do not know where they have been taken or what will happen to them. Johann plans to try to obtain their release. I will keep in contact with him and get information for you. I'm afraid there is a very unpleasant faction within the Nazi Party. We are all aware of it here in Italy. Herr Hitler would like us to have a close alliance with him, but we do not want anything to do with the brutalities which we believe are being carried out by the Nazis in their drive to gain absolute control in Germany.'

'What do you think will happen to Herman and Hannah, and Ruth and Jacob?'

'It is difficult to say. Perhaps Herman will be able to buy their freedom, but I must warn you that there have been many mysterious disappearances recently in Germany. One day, people who are active and respected members of their community, are just not there the next. They simply cease to exist. Furthermore, unpleasant things happen to those who inquire about them too persistently.'

'Are you telling me we cannot try to find out what has happened to them?' All thought of Jean-Paul and the events of the past few days were swept away by her horrified concern for the Dumescus.

'I can make inquiries in diplomatic circles, but I doubt if there will be any satisfactory answers. However, in strictest secrecy, I will tell you that I do have a number of unofficial sources of information in Germany, and we can hope that through one of these we may obtain news of your family.'

Jacqueline need not have worried that Marco would find out or even suspect that she had met Jean-Paul in Paris. That first night after her return, when he made love to her, she had to steel herself not to weep for her lost love – and for shame in her duplicity. Not until she thought he was sleeping did she allow a few tears to come, and then could not stem the flood. Aware of her sobbing, Marco turned to comfort her, believing she wept for the Dumescus, which did nothing to ease her guilt.

Guilt which flared anew a few weeks later when she realised she was again pregnant, with no idea which of the two dear men in her life was the father.

The third pregnancy was very easy. Jacqueline continued with her business life, as usual, organising and training staff to fulfil the ever increasing demand for her services. The economic depression had hit the workers very hard, but the property speculators and the very wealthy who used the Mediterranean as their playground were relatively unaffected. During the past year Jacqueline had been commissioned to handle the re-designing, decorating and re-furnishing of a large office block in Milan, a Venetian palace, several luxury holiday homes on both the west and Adriatic coasts and – her favourite assignment – the interior designing and complete furnishing of a brand new luxury motor yacht, the latest toy of a Greek shipping millionaire. There were also numerous lesser projects. Her flair and originality in blending colours, her dramatic use of black and white, subtle mixing of textures, wood and stone finishes, brought her recognition, fame . . . and clients. To have one's decor designed by the lovely young Countess became *de rigueur* for the rich and famous.

Jacqueline thanked her Jewish ancestry for her business acumen. Instinctively she knew the correct decisions to make in building up supply and demand, turnover and profit margins. Although the lire was reasonably stable, she felt reluctant to invest all her steadily increasing capital in one country, so she invited foreign clients to pay her in Swiss francs or English pounds whenever possible, offering discounts for their cooperation, and opening accounts in both Geneva and London. Marco would arrive home in the evenings to find her engrossed in three- or four-day-old copies of London's *Financial Times* and New York's *Wall Street Journal*, planning her investments. He was not too happy about this, worried that she was breaking Mussolini's strict exchange control laws, but he had to smile when she demonstrated to him that there was no way any irregular payments could be proved against her. He was rather proud of his clever, canny, businesslike mistress.

Despite their unorthodox domestic arrangements, Marco and Jacqueline were soon in demand socially, both in Marco's political circles and with Jacqueline's clients and business associates. The tall, dark, attractive Count Luzzi di Calitri, personal friend of Mussolini, and his beautiful, talented, honey-blonde 'companion', the Countess Tyroler, were popular with everyone. Their charm and lively personalities brought them invitations from the more liberal hostesses in Rome and from the wealthy immigrant sun-seekers who fled the Northern winters. In addition to the dinners, balls, parties and receptions, they were often invited to join weekend house parties on the coast or in the country. But Jacqueline made it a rule from the beginning that they would only accept these when the children were invited, so that the family could be together as often as possible.

Since the birth of Francisco, Jacqueline's figure had not returned to its previous very slim, boyish look. Her hips remained smoothly curved and her breasts full. She was proud of her five feet seven inches, walked tall and gracefully. Declining the latest fashion for permanent waving, she allowed her hair to grow long. Thick and glossy, with a slight natural wave, she wore it loose on her shoulders during the day, pinning it up into a sleek chignon in the evenings. Marco adored her hair, he loved to stroke it when she sat at her dressing table, or twine it through his fingers as he kissed her. She chose her clothes with care, designing and making some of them herself: dresses and suits in varying shades of cream and brown for day wear and business, black, white or emerald green to set off her hair and eyes at night. For a woman still in her early twenties, she had exceptional poise and self assurance.

All thanks to Marco. Cocooned in his love and encouragement, her fears and uncertainties, though not wholly forgotten, were well under control.

Thoughts of Jean-Paul were seldom far beneath the surface. Alone in a room without risk of interruption, where guilty thoughts could not be read, she would sometimes allow herself to dream. She wondered if, in a settled, domestic life, she and Jean-Paul would have achieved the same accord that she shared with Marco? Certainly the wild, passionate loving of their brief affair in Paris could not last a lifetime; even after a few weeks that pleasure would surely be exhausted. And what would be left? The same happiness and contentment she had now? She no doubt loved both men. She admired and respected Marco . . . in a million ways; ways which could not apply to Jean-Paul. She didn't know Jean-Paul well enough, only sufficiently to feel that the sight of him across a room, a street, would set every nerve in her body on fire.

Camilla's new stables grew rapidly on the Calitri estate. Marco visited her once or twice a month and discussed matters concerning the family property with the resident steward. He was pleased that his wife was so happy with her horses and horsey friends, happy that she was not bothered because he now lived permanently with his mistress.

Jean-Jacques and his mother were delighted to have Marco with them throughout the Christmas holiday. On Christmas morning they drove to the village church together and, despite not being able to take communion as they were 'living in sin', Jacqueline and Marco smiled happily as they sang the Christmas hymns. Jean-Jacques' treble piped up between them, and they gave thanks for their blessings and good fortune. After the service the priest shook their hands warmly, effortlessly overlooking their transgressions. They were much loved by the villagers, many of whom had profited from the recent work and trade at the villa.

Naturally, the couple had to be careful not publicly to offend the Vatican. Their social life was restricted to unpublicised and non-church events; they were ever mindful that in Italy adultery was, officially, against the law – a law which could be implemented if broken too flagrantly.

Marco's plans to adopt Francisco were progressing, but since Jacqueline was pregnant again, he delayed the legal separation so that he could also adopt the new baby.

During the spring, Marco gave instructions to install a swimming pool at the villa. It was to be built on a natural terrace in the hillside, some forty yards from the northwest corner of the house, half shaded by tall pines. Blue, pink and white hydrangeas would form a hedge to the north, and changing-rooms would be built into the steep hillside at the east end. The west would remain open, allowing bathers a clear view over the distant Mediterranean. Jean-Jacques was delighted at the idea. Several of his friends had pools and already he was an enthusiastic swimmer.

Jacqueline found that her third baby dragged heavily on her by the sixth month, causing discomfort and backache. By early May she could drive into Rome only once a week, content to allow her assistants to proceed with minimal supervision. Her work on the yacht was finished; she and Marco had accepted an invitation to join the three-day inaugural cruise at Easter, and in spite of being tossed vigorously by a Mistral wind on the second day, they enjoyed themselves enormously.

Jacqueline schooled herself not to worry too much about the business. When she was at the salon she worked hard, giving all her attention to every aspect, feeling at the end

194

of the day that the best possible had been done, the best decisions made. She expected equally the maximum efficiency from her staff, and left them in no doubt about this. She paid them well, took a personal interest in their private as well as their working lives, always anxious that they should not be distracted by unnecessary problems. But no one was given the opportunity to make more than two mistakes. The first brought a quiet warning, the second an even quieter request to leave. It had only happened once; but they all knew.

So she enjoyed her temporary retirement, relaxing with the children and supervising the finishing touches to the pool. She loved to watch Jean-Jacques playing with Francisco. They adored each other, the baby chortling gurgled replies to his big brother's endless chatter. They crawled after each other in games of chase, and hid behind chairs, squeaking with delight when found. If she continued to worry that so much of Jean-Jacques' schooling was of a military nature, that he seemed uncertain of himself unless he was wearing his black uniform, and that he stood to attention whenever she spoke to him sharply, it did not seem to be having an adverse effect on his character. It was Jean-Jacques who insisted that his brother should have a first birthday party, and he asked to be driven into Rome one Saturday morning to select a present for the baby. Inevitably the guests were mostly of Jean-Jacques' age, and failed to share his enthusiasm for baby games, but they all enjoyed themselves and shouted 'Happy Birthday' while Jean-Jacques stood beside the high chair at the head of the table, to assist Francisco to blow out his one candle.

Early in July, Jacqueline's pains started. She telephoned the doctor herself as they swiftly progressed to four-minute intervals, sent Giuseppe to find the midwife who had gone shopping in the village, and with Rosita's help, settled herself into the room she had prepared for the delivery. The doctor and midwife arrived together, just in time to witness the birth of her daughter.

Arriving home that evening, Marco was met at the front door by Rosita. 'Signor, the Signora says please will you come upstairs, there is something she wishes to discuss with you.' He failed to notice the suppressed giggle, so was quite staggered on entering the room to see Jacqueline sitting up in bed holding the baby girl.

'And now, my darling, you have a daughter,' she said, determined that it should be so.

Marco had asked if the baby might be named after his mother. Jacqueline had been feeling more sympathetic to her own mother in the past few months, but she had no desire to name her daughter Anna. However, both the Laskers and Dumescus were very much in her mind, so the child was eventually christened Katarina Ruth.

When the baby was two months old, Jacqueline started working at the salon again, on four mornings a week. One morning she was seated at her desk, checking through the accounts ledger when Teresa, the receptionist, knocked on her door.

'Signora, there is a gentleman in the salon who wishes to see you. He came here several times asking for you while you were away. He wanted to know where you lived, but I didn't think you would want me to tell him.'

'Quite right. What does he want? Do you think he might be a prospective client?'

'He won't give his name, just says he wishes to speak with you, personally. But . . .' the girl shrugged her shoulders. 'I don't think he has much money. He is a foreigner, looks a little . . . artistic. Perhaps he wants to work here. Do you want to see him?'

'No, but I suppose I had better come out.' It would be easier to get rid of him from the salon than if he sat himself in her office.

He stood with his back to her, looking out of the window. The pale blue suit was cheap and flashy, his blond hair too long. She realised that she had seen the suit and the hair at least twice before, in the street outside. Had he been watching her movements?

'Good morning. You wish to see me, I believe?'

When he turned, she saw that his hair was dyed, black roots showing through the parting. He wore a navy shirt and a white tie with a gaudy pin. He minced across the room towards her.

'Jacqueline! It is good to see you at last. It has been so difficult to find out where you have been hiding.'

She frowned, quickly dropping the limp, wet hand he proffered.

'I see you don't recognise me. Well, thanks to you fate has not been very kind to us in the past few years. However . . .' he gazed round the room. 'It seems she has been very good to you.'

There was something familiar about his insolent manner.

'What is your business with me?'

'I think we should have some privacy while we discuss that.' He cupped the straggly blond hair neatly over his collar, as he stared directly at Teresa. 'Have you a private office we might use?'

'We will stay here. Teresa, would you leave us please, until I ring?'

'Let's sit down,' the visitor said, heading for a display chair.

Jacqueline was irritated. 'That won't be necessary. I doubt your "business" will take long.'

'I'm sure it won't, provided that you are prepared to cooperate . . . with your husband.' He smirked at her.

'My . . . Bruno!' At last she realised who he was, and her anger mounted. 'Bruno, how dare you come here? Get out immediately.' She strode across to the bell on the reception desk.

But he was there first, standing between her and the desk.

'You would be wise to listen. I am speaking on behalf of your legal husband, the father and legal guardian of young Frederick.' The menace in his voice was obvious,

197

setting bells of fear jangling in her. She had no choice but to hear him out, yet she mustn't let him even suspect that she was afraid of him.

'Tyroler has never been my husband. The marriage was never consummated, as you well know.'

'You'd be surprised what he could father if he wanted to. If you'd seen what I've seen . . .' he was laughing in her face.

'Don't be disgusting. Just tell me why you are here.'

He strolled back to the chair, lounged with his legs crossed and lit a cigarette, dropping the match into a Chinese vase.

'Poor Ion,' he said. 'He is nearly sixty now, you know. His health has not been good since he was imprisoned. All because of you!' he suddenly snarled at her.

She ignored his tone and sat with one hip on the desk, her fingers drumming lightly beside the bell.

'He is penniless,' he continued. 'He cannot afford any of life's comforts.' Jacqueline knew what was coming. 'Now, it is obvious that you could well afford to help him.'

'I see no reason why I should.'

'Otherwise, of course, he could still be paid a comfortable pension were he to return to Rumania with young Frederick. King Carol has promised him. He is still not convinced the boy is not really his.'

'That is nonsense,' she declared, struggling to keep the terror out of her voice. 'I would never let him take my child away.'

'Ion does not need your permission,' he sneered. 'Frederick is legally Ion's son. We can prove that the child was illegally abducted from the Chateau Dumescu, and the Italian authorities would have no choice but to assist in his return.'

Jacqueline felt quite faint. Was this true? Could they really take Jean-Jacques away from her? No doubt they could. In fact she had always been aware of how doubtful her rights to the boy might prove if challenged. She must give herself time to see Marco before committing herself.

'Blackmail is also illegal, don't you forget that.' She hoped he would not see her hands trembling. 'Anyway, what princely sum did you hope to extort from me?'

'Enough for us to buy a nice little villa here in Italy, and a motor car for us to come and collect our "pension" every month. We don't have expensive tastes, you know. We would only require enough to keep a couple of servants and purchase a few little luxuries occasionally.'

'That is quite ridiculous. I don't have that sort of money,' she lied. 'But even if I did, I don't really know that Ion is still alive and I certainly wouldn't take your word for it.'

'I will take you to him right now, since you don't believe me,' he countered.

'I wouldn't dream of going anywhere with you. No, you may bring him here to me in . . . let me think, in four days' time. He can plead his destitution to me himself.' She pressed the bell and stood up. 'Show the gentleman out, please, Teresa.' Praying that her knees would not give way, she strode back to her office, closed the door and lifted the telephone.

Marco arrived within fifteen minutes. Jacqueline stood trembling in his arms, dry-eyed but incoherent. After a few minutes he sat her in a chair and left the room, returning with two glasses and a bottle of good Frascati normally kept for clients.

He waited, grim-faced, until she had finished her story, and then stood up.

'Leave this to me, my darling. I promise you, you need have no fear. I will see that they do not bother you again, nor get near Jean-Jacques. Now, do you have any idea where Bruno and Tyroler might be staying?'

'No. He didn't say. But what can you do?'

'Get rid of the pair of them. We will try to find them, but if we cannot, we will have a reception here ready for them when they come on Friday. Sweetheart, you look exhausted. Leave your car here overnight. I will send Claudio to fetch you in the Lancia and take you home.'

'Thank you. I do not really feel like driving myself at the moment.'

'Just relax, and remember that you have nothing to fear. Those two will be out of your way by the end of the week.' He blew her a kiss from the door and was gone.

Despite his assurances she remained nervous for the next few days, jumping whenever anyone entered the room or the telephone rang. She had not wanted to allow Jean-Jacques to attend school, fearing he might be kidnapped, until Marco told her the boy would be guarded. When Marco returned home on Thursday evening Bruno and Ion had still not been found.

'But it doesn't matter,' he said. 'We will pick them up at the salon in the morning.'

'Pick them up? I don't understand.' She looked puzzled.

'Arrest them. You need not be there. Stay at home tomorrow and I will tell you all about it in the evening.'

'But I can't, Marco. I must be there. It would not be fair to leave my staff to cope with such problems. Please tell me what you plan to do.'

'Well, if you are determined to come . . . you and I will wait in your office for the visitors. We will have men with us who will make the arrest and escort the pair of them to the Italian border and see them out of the country.'

'Are you the Chief of Police or something, that you can authorise arrests?' She was amazed.

'Good heavens, no! We don't want to involve the Carabinieri in this. These men will be Fascisti! Far more useful for our purpose.'

'But . . . if you just take them to the frontier, won't they come back? Or make trouble in some other way?'

Marco smiled, and for the first time Jacqueline realised that he had a singularly strong face which could look almost frightening in its intensity. 'No, my darling,' he said. 'I promise you they will neither return nor make trouble after they have had a chat with my Fascisti.'

Jacqueline had never thought to question Marco about either his work or his political status. From his occasional references to ambassadors and embassies she presumed he was some kind of diplomat, apart from his business connections. She knew he had unofficial as well as official contacts in other European countries, but she had had no idea that he could wield this degree of authority.

'You must be in an important position, then. Tell me . . .' a new thought struck her. 'Do you work with Il Duce?'

'All the time.'

'Really! Then tell me about him. What sort of man is he? I hear people talk about him and I read about him in the newspapers, but one cannot believe all one reads and hears. What is he really like?'

'That's not an easy question to answer. From a political viewpoint he is a remarkable man: enormous energy, determination and courage. A man of vision. He is devoted to his country and its people. An ideologist, perhaps, but with his feet firmly planted in reality. Socially . . . well, you have to remember he is of very humble origin. His father was a blacksmith, you know. His manners are not what you are used to. He has never bothered to acquire the social graces, he doesn't dress well or change his clothes often enough. But there is some strange charisma about him. Women seem to fall at his feet.' He laughed. 'We are very lucky to have such a man. In the twelve years since Victor Emmanuel made him Prime Minister he has done a great deal for Italy.'

'I should love to meet him, one day.'

'Why not? I will see that you are invited to one of his receptions.'

'Oh, splendid. I look forward to falling at his feet.' She laughed and took his arm as they headed for the dining room. 'My darling knight, rescuing me again.'

They were waiting in her office with two Fascisti as planned when Teresa announced the arrival of her visitors. Jacqueline took a deep breath and walked out into the salon with a large, black-shirted man on either side of her.

Bruno looked startled. 'What is this?' he demanded. 'Who are these men?'

'These men' ignored him, but one turned to the Countess and asked, 'Are these the men, Signora, who are attempting to blackmail you?'

'Yes.' She looked Ion straight in the eye while she spoke. As Bruno had suggested, the Count had not aged well. The immaculate bearing had gone, and with shabby and threadbare clothes he looked more like what he actually was – one of life's failures, who happened to have inherited a title.

She could not help feeling sorry for the pathetic shambling figure, but he was attempting to take Jean-Jacques away from her. 'Yes, these are the men.'

The Fascisti moved forward. 'You are under arrest . . .' Bruno bolted for the door, flung it open and stopped short. Two more black-shirts were waiting for him.

'Bruno!' Tyroler exclaimed at the attempted desertion, then turned to the Fascisti. 'It is not we who should be arrested. She is the crim . . .' A handcuff was snapped on to the pointing arm.

'You are a blackmailer, and therefore a criminal yourself. We do not tolerate criminals in Italy. You will accompany us, please.' And the indignant Rumanian count was given an unceremonious shove towards the door.

Jacqueline watched from the window as a big black car pulled away from the curb. She gave a huge sigh of relief.

October. As Marco entered the front door wind gusted through the villa, rattling the ancient windows and shutters. Jacqueline looked up from her newspaper as the living room door opened. He was not alone.

'Jacob!' She sprang up from her chair and ran to embrace her cousin. 'Oh, Jacob! How good it is to see you. We have been so worried.' She could feel sharp shoulder blades through his jacket, stood back to look at him. She had never seen anyone so thin; he was like a skeleton.

His hair was sparse and wispy, red-rimmed eyes sunk into dark hollows, dull and staring. His hands were like claws.

'What has happened to you?' she cried. 'Have you been ill?'

He shook his head.

'And what about your parents, and Ruth? Are they here with you?'

Jacob shook his head again, slightly, looking at her yet hardly appearing to see her.

'Dead,' he murmured, lips barely moving. 'All dead.' He swayed on his feet and Marco put a supporting arm around him.

'Ring for Giuseppe, my love; we must get him to bed.' The Count gently steered the boy out of the room.

Jacob was nursed back to health at the villa. He was put in the nursery bedroom, and attended by the local doctor and a nurse until nearly November. Then he was moved to a large, airy room with a south-facing balcony where, on fine days, he could sit in a big rocking-chair, wrapped in rugs.

Mentally, he was perhaps scarred for ever. Even when he seemed physically recovered he looked at least ten years older than his twenty-three years. He made a great effort, trying to smile, to look bright, and play with Jean-Jacques. But the haunted look was always in his eyes, a legacy of the mental and physical agony he had endured.

Gradually in quiet conversations with Jacqueline, the horrifying story emerged. The four Dumescus had been put into a huge, old-fashioned mental hospital now being used by the Nazis for interning so-called political prisoners. It was cold and filthy, the food disgusting and inadequate. Every week the gaol was visited by officials, men in civilian clothes, but obviously bearing some rank in the Party. Prisoners were questioned over and over as to the whereabouts of their hidden property, who their friends were, asked to name other Jewish families. Favours and promises of early release were offered for cooperation. And every week more families arrived, good, God fearing, law abiding citizens, all terrified for their lives.

Hannah had fallen on some steps one day, tearing the skin of both shins. Instead of healing properly, the sores became ulcers which grew and spread until she could hardly stand up for the pain. They were living in a big, overcrowded ward, and a fellow prisoner, an ex-nurse, told the Dumescus what treatment she should have – but it was refused. Months later several hundred prisoners were herded into a cattle train, the Dumescus amongst them. Without food, water or sanitation, they travelled for two whole days before being unloaded and marched to a prison camp. They all felt weak and ill, but poor Hannah, semi-conscious for much of the time, had to be half carried, half dragged by Herman and Jacob. At the camp the men and women were segregated, allotted to primitive bunkhouses, and fed. Herman was distraught with worry and paced the wire which divided the camp, desperate for a glimpse of his wife and daughter.

It was a labour camp. The men were loaded into trucks each day and driven to a vast building site to mix and carry endless buckets of cement. The women were also taken each morning by truck to work in the fields of vegetables, planting, weeding and digging. The food, watery soup and dirty bread, served at dawn and dusk, made the mess they had eaten at their previous prison seem luxurious. Though often weak with starvation, if they paused in their work they were flogged.

The truck on which Herman and Jacob were travelling one morning broke down, and one of the guards had had to walk some distance back to camp to fetch a replacement. The women had all been at work for two or three hours when the men eventually passed a field where they saw Ruth and Hannah labouring quite near the road. They were digging up potatoes, but Hannah kept stumbling, obviously too weak to lift the soil, and, just as the truck drew level, she fell. Immediately two guards ran up, one to kick her legs, the other to beat her shoulders with his rifle butt. Hearing her screams the truck driver slowed to watch and in a flash Herman was over the side, scrambling down the bank into the field. He never reached his wife. Bullets ripped through his clothes, jerking his frail body this way and that like a rag doll on a string.

Jacob had described the scene vividly, searching his mind for every detail as though, in the telling, he might sweep away the horror from his memory. He had watched, a machine gun muzzle pressed into his ribs, as the body of his father was dragged back to the truck and dumped in a corner, a pathetic little pile of rags and bones. He learned later that his mother had never walked again. Her ulcerated legs became infected, probably by dirt from the guard's boots, and within three weeks she too had died.

The young Dumescus never knew what happened to their parents' bodies.

Jacob had known nothing of the escape plan until the night it was due to take place. A young man from the same bunkhouse had shaken him awake, hissing in his ear for silence. One word had been whispered:

'Out?'

He had understood and followed his friend, with others, away from their hut. Groups joined them from other huts and when they reached the unguarded dividing wire they cut through and slithered on their stomachs across the open ground to the women's bunkhouses. Several groups of young women were waiting, Ruth among them. The idea was apparently to get over the women's bath-block which formed part of the boundary. Women were not regarded as potential escapees, so fewer guards were on duty around their side of the compound. A mass break-out had been planned, knowing that some would die, some be recaptured, but giving some a chance of freedom. Those who remained much longer in the camp would probably die anyway, so they had little to lose. Jacob and Ruth had stuck together, landing on the grass behind the bath-block, running hand in hand as fast as their depleted leg muscles could carry them towards the distant trees. Ruth had fallen painfully, slowing them down so that they were still within range when the guards opened fire. They were just entering the wood when the bullet struck her. Jacob had dragged her into the cover of the trees and for a while she was able to walk with his help before suddenly collapsing. He tried to revive her, but she was dead. Covering her with leaves he pressed on. He saw neither guards nor other escapees again. In an old cabin beside a disused railway he found a tattered map of the area, from which he had been able to link up with the route they had taken years before into Switzerland.

Marco insisted that Jacob should stay with them indefinitely at the villa. Jacqueline begged him to assist her at the Salon Stevenson. Both invitations were gratefully accepted.

November 1935 – June 1936

The purest treasure mortal times afford
Is spotless reputation; that away,
Men are not gilded loam or painted clay.

William Shakespeare, *Richard II*

JACQUELINE HAD never looked more beautiful. Marco felt a surge of love and pride as he watched her descend the stairs in a dress of her own design. It was made of white crêpe-de-chine, the skirt fitting closely in a band decorated with rhinestones at her knees, from which two gathered tiers of material fell, the lower to touch the tops of her white kid shoes. The bodice fitted snugly from waist to bust and a swathe of material lay in graceful folds across her breasts, gathered on the shoulders and swaying down her back to the hip like a slashed cape. Her hair, swept up and back from her face into a wide chignon on the crown of her head, was encircled with a light diamond tiara. She wore emerald and diamond ear-rings and a matching bracelet over her white elbow-length kid gloves. The ensemble was completed by a stiff emerald green taffeta cloak lined in white velvet.

Marco himself looked magnificent. Although Jacqueline was wearing high heels, he stood taller by three or four inches, his height accentuated by the tails of his dress-suit and the black, calf-length cloak which was held across his chest by large silver lion's-head clasps joined by a silver chain. He carried white gloves and a silver knopped malacca cane topped with a gleaming amethyst. Jacqueline looked up at him and smiled to herself. No one looking at the classic Roman bones of his face, would ever guess how loving, gentle and caring a lover and father lay behind the stern façade.

Claudio, in dark green uniform, held the car door while Maria assisted with Jacqueline's dress and cloak, and Jacob stood on the steps to wave them goodbye. As they sped towards the glow of the city lights in the south Jacqueline watched their dim reflections created by the pale interior light in the car windows. They were so fortunate . . . had so much. Three lovely children, a beautiful home, business, social and political status, security and almost limitless wealth. Why, she wondered, why should some people be so lucky while others, like her Dumescu cousins, were robbed, bullied, tortured, starved and murdered? She thought that this would probably have been her own fate if Marco had not snatched her away before Heinrich got to her in Berlin. Yes, she had not only survived several nasty situations in the past eight or nine years, she had come through it all with everything any woman could wish for . . . or nearly, but now was not the time to think about him. How had fate selected Marco and herself to be two of life's winners when so many others were such unfortunate losers? Was it perhaps because they were both determined to win, to turn every event in their lives to their advantages, or, seeing the losers, should they go down on their knees and say, 'There but for the Grace of God go I'? Years ago, she had believed that good fortune was God's reward to the good, and bad luck His form of punishment. But how could that be? Unrepentant she daily broke one of the Commandments. She had stood by and watched the husband she had married in a church of God arrested and thrown out of the country when he had found her again. She had abducted Jean-Jacques, abandoned her mother and her country. Surely she was the one who should be punished, not the sweet, gentle Dumescus. She couldn't imagine them breaking a law, certainly never a Commandment. They had returned to Munich to rebuild their shattered lives, loyal to their adopted country, only to be cruelly punished, while she, the stateless, runaway adulteress was driven in luxury to a dazzling reception at the Italian Prime Minister's official residence, the Palazzo Venezia.

'A penny for those deep, dark thoughts.' Marco's voice startled her.

'Oh! I have been in a brown study, haven't I? I was just pondering on why we should be so lucky when there are so many less fortunate people in the world.' She smiled and twined her fingers in his.

'It is not luck.' He feigned offence. 'Just good management. I checked the list of coming receptions and decided this was the one you would most enjoy. Then I added your name to the guest list.' He had quite mistaken the luck to which she had referred, but she didn't try to correct him. Indeed she was very pleased he had chosen this reception. Il Duce loved official functions, delivering speeches, showing off Italy's strength and policies. They were his policies, although she was sure such events could often be boring. However, this particular reception was being held in honour of visiting VIPs from other countries, and she looked forward to meeting interesting foreigners.

'His Excellency the Count Marco-Gregorio Luzzi di Calitri and Her Excellency the Countess Tyroler!'

'Marco!' The huge, black-uniformed man turned from the group with whom he was conversing, hands out-stretched. 'At last you bring your beautiful mistress out of hiding. Ha! I don't blame you for trying to keep her to yourself – she is magnificent.' Benito Mussolini ignored his friend's hand and instead grasped Jacqueline's, holding it for several seconds while he stared straight into her eyes. She didn't flinch, however astonished she was at the blue-black stubble of beard which marked his chin – in contrast to the nearly shaven scalp above – and at the unwashed odour which emanated from his uniform.

'Yes, Duce, this is my Jacqueline,' Marco grinned. 'But please, not too much of the famous Duce charm. I don't want to lose her, even to you.'

The Prime Minister chuckled. 'I must greet my guests as they arrive, Jacqueline, but I look forward to flirting with you later.'

He was quite intriguingly uncouth, she thought as they moved on through the throng, men in a variety of uniforms as well as evening dress and insignia, women afire with gems.

Jacqueline had met some of the Italian guests before and politely answered and returned their inquiries about health, children and business. It was the type of cocktail chatter which bored them both and Marco quickly steered her towards the foreign visitors. She joined in a brief discussion on world economics with the French Minister of Finance, listened to a boring discourse on Lippizaners by a Spanish cavalry officer, and a fascinating discussion between two bankers, one Swiss, one Swedish, on their respective countries' neutrality in the light of Hitler's re-arming of Germany. Sir Percy Loraine, the British Ambassador, was charming. Knowing her interest he explained in some detail the redecoration of various embassies in Europe and Washington. The reception was in full swing when her host firmly grasped her elbow and drew her aside.

'Now, my beautiful Jacqueline, I wish to know more about you. I believe you run your own business here in Rome. Tell me about it,' he ordered.

She explained, briefly, the nature of her work and answered his questions, though never quite sure that he was listening. After a few moments he interrupted the verbal list of clients he had demanded.

'So you designed the interior of Stavros' yacht, eh? What is the name of your business? I may call for your services one day.'

'Casa Stevenson, Centre di Disegno.'

'Stevenson? Why Stevenson?'

'It was my maiden name.' Not strictly true, but that did not matter.

'Well, that is a coincidence. Have you met the Admiral?'

'No, I don't think so.' She tried to remember an admiral among the introductions.

'Then come, I will introduce you myself.' Il Duce grasped her wrist firmly and dragged her unceremoniously through the crowd. 'Here he is, my dear, may I present Admiral William Stevenson of the United States Navy.' The Admiral had turned as they approached and took her hand in greeting as their host continued, 'and this, signor, is my dear friend Her Excellency the Countess Jacqueline Tyroler. By coincidence her maiden name is the same as yours.'

'Really?' the Admiral responded. 'Tell me, were your family Scandinavian, English, or American?'

'American, but I spent my childhood in Rumania with my mother.'

Mussolini drifted away as Stevenson remarked, 'Rumania? Well, now, I have never been there, but I once knew a beautiful Rumanian girl, who looked rather like you, as a matter of fact. Met her in England at the 1910 Wimbledon Championships. Fell in love with her at first sight and I've never forgotten her. A marvellous tennis player, she was, named Anna Dumesca. Ever heard of her? Say . . .' he suddenly realised that the face of the young countess was scarlet, her mouth hanging open, eyes as big as saucers, while her champagne poured down her dress. 'Say . . . are you okay? Come and sit down over here and give me your glass.'

He led her to a group of chairs, sat her down and wiped her dress. 'I'll go and get you another drink.'

Her mind was racing. What do I do? What do I say? Admit that Anna is my mother, that he . . . oh, my God, that he is my father? But why not? Apart from some embarrassment . . .

'Here you are, this should make you feel a bit better. Tell me, what happened just now? Did you feel faint?'

She accepted the glass and sipped for a few moments, then looked up at the Admiral with a smile. 'No. I didn't feel faint at all, it was just a shock. You see . . .' she took a deep breath. 'Anna Dumesca is my mother.' She lowered her voice. 'I don't know if it is at all relevant, but I was born in March 1911.'

It was William Stevenson's turn to look thunderstruck. 'You mean . . . that I . . .'

'My mother fell madly in love with a young ensign in the American Navy while she was playing in the 1910 Wimbledon Championships. She was still travelling around the European tournaments when she realised she was pregnant. When she returned to Rumania the following year she claimed she had married and had had a daughter. I was told as a child that my father died before I was born.'

'So I did have a daughter after all.'

At that moment Jacqueline saw Marco approaching. She beckoned him to her side. 'Darling, there is someone I wish you to meet. Admiral, this is my dear Marco, the Count Luzzi di Calitri. Marco, this is Admiral William Stevenson, my father!'

Before either man could speak loudspeakers crackled into life and a voice asked for silence. Mussolini was going to make a speech.

'Friends! Italians! Fascisti!' Mussolini advanced into the centre of the huge room, hands on hips, blue-jowled chin thrust forward. His voice was harsh but resonant, his eyes glittered magnetically as they stared from face to face. 'I speak to you tonight on a sombre occasion. Because tonight the eyes of the world are upon us, here in our beautiful country. The world chooses to condemn us. Fifty nations led by one! What, do they suppose we are children?'

He strutted in front of his silent audience, like a cock before hens. 'We are condemned, my friends, for defending what is ours. Ethiopia was agreed to be in the Italian sphere of influence in Africa at more than one conference during the last century. No one has ever said otherwise. It was the Italian government of those days which did not proceed. Those were weak governments, my friends. But they were not *Fascisti!*' He gave a shout of laughter, which was immediately taken up by the other black-shirted guests.

'They chose to forget,' Mussolini said, 'that an Italian army was defeated. At Adowa, my friends, the military reputation of this great nation was laid in ruins. 1 March, 1896, will always be the blackest day in modern Italian history. We must go back to the days of Rome, to the Caudine Forks, for a parallel. Twenty thousand men, my friends, were destroyed. Destroyed! The survivors castrated, reduced to pitiful hulks. And our government did nothing about it. For forty years that open sore has rankled in Italian breasts. It would have rankled in French breasts and in German breasts, and most of all in British breasts. Fifty nations led by one. But, my friends, Great Britain has a habit of remembering only what she chooses to remember.'

He paused for breath, continuing to stare from face to face. Jacqueline's knees felt weak. She realised she was listening to a declaration of war, or at least of defiance, against the entire world.

'It needed the coming of the Fascisti to raise Italian heads again,' Mussolini was speaking more quietly. 'To remind the world that we are a great people, not to be trampled on with impunity. To remind the world that we are Romans!' he shouted, his voice reverberating. And then it dropped again. 'I did not seek to destroy this Haile Selassie, believe that. I sought only to deal with him, man to man, to trade with him, to utilise the supremacy granted to us by the colour of our skins, by the fact of our being, and by the decision of the Powers in 1888. But he would not deal with me, my friends. He defied me, his tribesmen fired upon Italian soldiers. Well, we have taught these tribesmen a lesson. Now they scream that they are being struck down by falling bombs and machine-gun bullets. My friends, that is the face of modern war. That is the inescapable violence of one great power imposing its will upon a lesser. The Abyssinians should have considered these terrible consequences before defying us. And now they whine, and call for help. They appeal to the League of Nations, and the League of Nations has chosen to condemn us as the aggressor. The League of Nations! Of whom is this league composed, my friends? Which nations dominate it? Great Britain and France. Look at a map of Africa. Where you do not see the red of the British occupied territory, you will see blue, standing for French. Between them they have all Africa, save for one or two tiny corners. They threaten sanctions against us. Fifty nations led by one! Well, let them come. Let the entire British fleet steam up the Tyrrhenian Sea, and let them throw their shells on the eternal city itself. We shall still defy them. We are Romans. We are Italians. We are Fascisti! We will have our place in the world, or we will know how to die.'

The following morning, Jacqueline and Marco waited in the drawing room with the children for Bill Stevenson to arrive. He had been invited at eleven-thirty to give him time to meet his grandchildren before lunch. The surprise meeting with her father gave rise to a number of questions and decisions. Before parting after the reception they had unanimously agreed that the newly discovered relationship should remain a secret; telling their respective families could only create innumerable upsets and complications and achieve nothing. Certainly, after the initial shock to them both, they found the situation more humorous than dramatic. In fact, Jacqueline felt almost guilty at the lack of emotional impact on her, but maybe that would come later when he ceased to be a comparative stranger. Obviously Anna should not be told of Bill's reappearance, and fortunately, though curious to hear news of her, he showed no inclination to meet her again. It was a relief because

Jacqueline suspected her mother might not be above making capital out of the circumstances.

At first Jean-Jacques was quite overawed by the huge American with the booming voice, but was soon enchanted by the exciting sea-stories his grandfather had to tell.

'Do you drive a warship, Uncle Bill?'

'No, J.J., I used to do that, but now I have some other guys do it for me.' Bill shortened nearly everyone's name.

'Is the warship your very own?'

'No again. It belongs to the people of the United States of America.'

'Do you have to wear a uniform?' Bill had arrived in a blazer and flannels.

'Yep. Gotta look smart on board ship; be a smart sailor.'

'I have to wear a uniform at my school. Gotta be a smart soldier,' he mimicked the American accent.

Marco poured drinks and the three adults sat by the window to talk as Nanny wheeled Katarina away, leading Francisco by the hand. Jean-Jacques followed, but reappeared five minutes later in his Ballila uniform.

'Look at me, Uncle Bill,' he called from the doorway, and marched towards them, calling his own drill orders with perfect military precision.

'Say, do you want a job, J.J.? You can come and drill my marine squad any time. You do it a darn sight better than they do.'

The miniature soldier dropped his mock rifle and ran to his grandfather's side. 'Do you mean I can come on your warship? Oh, yes, please, I've never been on a warship.' And he turned pleading eyes on Marco and his mother.

Bill raised a quizzical eyebrow towards them, and received nods.

'Well, boy, I reckon that if you were to report for duty, in uniform, mind, tomorrow morning at ten-thirty, we could show you how we "drive the boat", and mind you show the boys how to drill. Is that a date?'

'Yes, sir!' The little chap clicked his heels and saluted and they all grinned as he did an about-face and marched out of the room. But Bill was frowning as he turned to face Jacqueline and Marco.

'Where the hell did he learn to drill like that? I've never seen a kid that size drilling so accurately. I'm serious, he really is better than my marine squad.'

'It's all part of government policy,' Marco replied, and went on to explain the Italian system of forcing young men to a military career after leaving school.

'But Italy already has a massive army; does Il Duce mean to go on enlarging it? You know, Count, despite what he said in his speech last night, trying to justify your invasion of Ethiopia last month, you must all have realised from the League of Nations' immediate condemnation of your action that other nations would get more than angry about it. It is pretty obvious that your armaments are way above your requirements in Abyssinia.'

'I can understand your concern,' Marco nodded. 'But I think you are inclined to forget our history. We have had centuries of problems with our neighbours to the north, as well as in our colonies. All we want to do now is establish the same security and stability that you have in the United States and that Britain has at home and in her colonies.'

Jacqueline sensed that her father would have liked to continue the discussion, but obviously felt that this was not the occasion. Instead he changed the subject.

'A different matter of interest. Jacki, what nationality are you?'

'Rumanian. I have wondered if I should try to change it. If I ever ran into any problems with the authorities here, I would hate to be sent back to Bucharest; in fact, it would be disastrous. But as long as I have Marco looking after me there is no chance of that.' She smiled affectionately at the Count.

'Marco may not always be around. What will you do if the silly fellow walks under a bus?' her father quipped.

'I just won't let him near any buses,' she replied.

'Well, if you ever want to become an American citizen, just let me know and I'll try to help you, though I doubt

216

if there'd be any difficulty. Not if I recognise you as my daughter.'

'But wouldn't that . . . well, upset your wife?'

'You know, I don't think it would. Let me work on that. And you think about it.'

'Yes, thank you, I will. Now, let's go in to lunch.'

It was a happy meal, all three lightheartedly recounting their life stories, Jacqueline deliberately avoiding mention of the unhappy problems she had had with her mother. Bill Stevenson made life in America sound very attractive and he insisted they should cross the Atlantic for a holiday.

'We certainly will, one day,' Marco promised.

Jean-Jacques stood between Marco and his mother on the dockside at Naples, still waving vigorously as the warship diminished into the distance. He had had a wonderful day, first driving in Marco's Ferrari to Naples, then being piped aboard the vast ship. They had been taken on a brief tour of the upper decks by his grandfather and whilst the Admiral took Marco and his daughter for coffee in his quarters, he was guided down through the engine room and quarters by a willing young ensign. There had followed a very convivial lunch in the officers' wardroom which Jacqueline enjoyed enormously, surprised at the friendliness shown by the Americans, especially considering the tone of Mussolini's recent speech. She liked these open-faced young men and their good-humoured teasing, even if Marco found it difficult to reconcile a lunch served without wine or alcohol of any sort.

It had seemed quite natural, as they said their goodbyes in private, to give her father a hug.

'I'm so glad I found the courage to tell you the truth at the reception,' she said.

'So am I, Jacki. I've told you all about your two stepbrothers, but as you know, I never knew I had a daughter until three days ago! We must never lose touch again.'

*   *   *

That evening Marco raised the subject of her nationality once more.

'I quite agree with your father, darling. You should change your nationality. It could produce endless problems in the future, especially if anything were to happen to me. Why don't you let him help you to obtain American citizenship?'

'Because I'm not wholly convinced that that is what I want. I feel so much a part of you, and now, a part of Italy, that I cannot see the point in belonging to a country so far removed from you, my children, my home and business. If I am not to be an Italian, why not become French?' she countered.

'No, no, you must not consider that. The United States are neutral and despite their criticism of Italian policy right now, I am sure they will remain so. But the French . . .' he shrugged his shoulders. 'Well, they are different. For years they were our staunchest allies, but recently . . . you heard Il Duce on Thursday night saying that, along with the British, they are making the most aggressive verbal attacks and threats on us in the League of Nations. They will never be neutral, and if we were ever in conflict with them you would immediately be classified as an enemy alien.'

'Oh, dear! I'm becoming more and more confused. I don't know what to say except that I don't want to rush into a decision because I have just met my American father for the first time.'

'Well, you have a point. There is no urgency, I suppose, but you must make a decision eventually. My darling, I so wish I could marry you, then the problem would be solved.' He took her in his arms and kissed her lovingly.

Six months went by before the subject was discussed again.

Six beautiful months in which Jacqueline celebrated her twenty-fifth birthday and Jean-Jacques his eighth.

After Christmas Marco had persuaded her to let Jean-Jacques accompany them on a skiing holiday in St Moritz,

218

where the boy had excelled himself by winning a beginners' prize for his age group. He was tall for his years, hard muscled, supple – and with his straight, dark hair his mother found him agonisingly like Jean-Paul.

She herself took several tumbles on the nursery slopes before mastering her skis sufficiently to accompany the others on chair-lifts to the higher pistes, from where Jean-Jacques would confidently fly ahead to await them on the verandah of the chalet restaurant below, lemonade in hand. Only on their return from holiday did Jacqueline and the boy discover that it had all been a ruse to take them away from home. In their absence the old stables behind the villa had been renovated, and there, awaiting them, were their birthday presents . . . a dappled grey mare for Jacqueline and, especially imported from England, a 'New Forest' pony for Jean-Jacques. A third loose-box housed Marco's big black stallion, brought up from the Calitri estate.

'Papa!' the boy yelled, flinging his arms round Marco in excitement. 'Oh, Papa, are you going to teach me to ride? Can we start now?'

Jacqueline felt constant surges of love and gratitude towards Marco for the kindness and affection he showed towards Jean-Jacques. Certainly he could not have been a more loving father had the boy been his own son.

The lessons commenced immediately and within a week all three were able to start riding together up into the hills every weekend.

Jacob had become one of the family. His physical health restored, he now worked and studied hard to gain knowledge of Jacqueline's business. But there remained a dull sadness in his eyes, and on some evenings he would shut himself away in his room, fiddling with an old radio, reading, brooding.

Francisco was walking well and daily extending his vocabulary. By May, Katarina, with blonde curls and grey-green eyes already strikingly like her mother, was attempting her first faltering steps.

219

The Abyssinian war dragged on, and although in the League of Nations the criticisms had continued, nothing more threatening had developed.

Jacqueline had driven to work as usual one day, as the sun rose over the mountains to her left, silhouetting the tall cypresses and clusters of pantiled roofs. On her right the silver Mediterranean, glistening beyond the rose-tinted plains, merged without horizon into a cloudless sky . . . a May morning so perfect that even Jean-Jacques sat silent all the way to school. She felt so happy, relaxed and contented that, while going through the post on her desk, she had to read the letter from her father a second time before she could assimilate its contents . . . and then she couldn't believe it.

My dear Jacki,

I am so horrified by recent events in Abyssinia that I find it impossible to write to you without expressing my feelings.

On my return home after meeting you and hearing Mussolini's speech at the reception I was prepared to argue the Italian point of view with people here who condemned Marshal Badoglio's actions; an attitude which has left me with egg on my face since the Italian atrocities against the Ethiopians this month. There can be no possible excuse for the wanton use of poison gas against defenceless women and children. The reports and photographs in our newspapers are revolting. Whole towns and villages wiped out, women lying dead in the road still clutching the children they were trying to carry to safety. A hospital where children, already mutilated by war, lay choked to death.

How are the Italian people reacting? Surely they do not condone it. Or do they believe that because the Ethiopians are black-skinned they are somehow sub-human and therefore have no feeling?

I hope this does not offend you, but I long to hear that my dear, newly-found daughter, and equally that

Marco Luzzi, condemns Badoglio and Mussolini as much as we do here in America.

I will write to you again when I have cooled off!

Affectionately,

Bill

The beautiful day was eclipsed by anger; first towards Il Duce, then, swinging like a pendulum through doubt and on to disbelief at this vicious American propaganda, at her father for believing it. Then back again. Certainly in the past few days the newspapers and the radio had confidently forecast an imminent end to the conflict . . . but there had been no mention of poison gas. So either it had not been used or the government dared not admit it.

The hours dragged slowly by until evening when she was at last able to face Marco with the question.

'Is it true?'

Marco's face was grey with tiredness, his lips pressed together in a hard line. He drained his glass and returned to the chiffonier for another. With his back to her he answered: 'Yes.'

'Holy Mother of God!' she exploded. '*Why?*'

He swung round. 'Because this stupid war has gone on long enough,' he shouted. 'For the past seven months innumerable young Italian boys have been dying, daily, for want of a decisive end to the fighting. We didn't want to do it, but it was them or us . . . we had no choice.'

'Rubbish! Are you suggesting that the mass murder of babies is a fair military tactic?'

'No, I'm suggesting nothing of the sort.'

'Well it has happened, so tell me how any Italian who condoned such atrocities can ever hold his head up again. What about you?' she demanded, her finger aimed angrily at his chest.

He sighed and shook his head. 'It is useless to point at me. I had no hand in the decision to use gas. In fact, between ourselves, I would certainly have voted against

221

its use had I been asked, but having expressed disapproval when it was first shipped out to the colony I wasn't consulted. Believe me, I am as horrified as you are.' He certainly looked very upset.

'Why has it not been reported in the Italian newspapers? There should be a public outcry and the officials responsible at least brought to justice.'

'What would that achieve? The war is over. Those people are dead. We cannot bring them back to life. If there is a public outcry it will only lose us confidence in the government, and Duce's government has done more for Italy than any previous one since the fall of the Roman Empire.'

'I fail to see why, because of a man's achievements for his own country, he should be allowed to get away with murdering women and children in someone else's,' she persisted.

'You are being very young and naïve. Try reading more world history and you will see that it has been forever thus. And don't forget . . .' it was his turn to point at her, 'that these Ethiopians are savages. They may not be able to use poison gas, but if they could reach Italian women and children the atrocities, torture and mutilation they would enjoy performing on them before twisting spears in their stomachs are beyond your powers to conceive. Do you know we have to shoot our boys wounded in the fighting rather than let those savages get to them . . . just out of mercy.'

They sat throughout dinner in stony silence, but later, in bed, Jacqueline put her arms around him.

'I'm afraid I cannot accept your point of view, darling, but it doesn't stop me loving you.'

'Sweetheart,' he murmured into her hair. 'This has been our first real quarrel. Most couples argue like this at least once a week, you know. We are very lucky. And I do adore you.' But for the first time he was unable to make love to her.

*　　*　　*

222

A fortnight later, Jacqueline and Marco were invited to a small private dinner party at the Palazzo Venezia. There were only a dozen people present, including Mussolini's daughter Edda and her husband, Count Gian Ciano di Cortelazzo, a strikingly handsome man. He had just returned from Abyssinia where, as a pilot, he had been on operational flights against the Ethiopians. Knowing that he had also been Secretary of State for press and propaganda last year, Jacqueline could not help wondering, when they were introduced, how much he had had to do with the suppression of information concerning the use of poison gas. Though the son of a statesman himself, marrying Edda Mussolini had obviously advanced Ciano's power and position. Two other government ministers were present with their wives, two senior Fascisti officers, and two lively ladies who were introduced only by their Christian names, and Claretta Petacchi, Duce's mistress – like Marco, Mussolini preferred to live apart from his wife. Certainly Jacqueline found nothing to dislike in the pretty, dark young woman who was obviously devoted to Il Duce.

The round dining table of green marble and green upholstered dining chairs, ridiculously inadequate for Mussolini's bulk, looked magnificent against the shining white marble floor. In each corner of the room stood a green marble column surmounted by a bust of a Roman Emperor. The walls were divided into vast red panels, edged in gold, the centre of each bearing works of old Italian masters. It was an ornate but beautiful way to display to dinner guests a theme of the Italian national colours.

While waiters served soup and antipastas, the chatter was light and amusing. Il Duce flirted outrageously with the woman on his right, Jacqueline exchanged riding anecdotes with the minister on her left. Only when the waiters retired after placing vast trays of assorted seafood before them did Duce mention the war.

'Ladies and gentlemen,' he raised his glass. 'I propose a toast to Marshal Badoglio and our victorious troops.'

Everyone stood, glass in hand, repeating, 'Badoglio and

the troops!' Everyone except Jacqueline, who sat picking a lobster claw in silence.

'Countess!' Mussolini exclaimed as they all sat down again. 'You are not drinking with us?'

'No, Duce, I'm not.' She looked him straight in the eye as she spoke. Marco shuffled in his chair, looking very uncomfortable; Ciano glared at her.

'Come, come, surely you are delighted that the war is over, that our glorious army has won?' her host demanded.

'Oh, yes, I'm delighted that the fighting is finished. I will drink a toast to that. But I see nothing glorious about an army or its commanders who can only win their battles by massacring innocent women and children. I will never drink a toast to murderers!'

There followed an appalled silence broken only by Count Ciano hissing furiously through his clenched teeth.

An angry flush covered the Prime Minister's neck. He drained his glass and grabbed a decanter from the centre of the table before addressing Ciano. 'You know, I have always adored women of spirit, especially in bed.' Then, turning to Marco, 'Tell me, Luzzi, how does a mild fellow like you handle such a gorgeous creature? She really is far too good for you.'

Ciano pursed his lips; Marco flushed in humiliation, but the other diners, relieved that a storm had been averted, laughed at Duce's joke and quickly began to chatter on topics other than the war.

Jacqueline, simmering with rage at Mussolini's attitude towards herself and to women in general, looked up to glare defiantly at Marco, before resuming her attack on the lobster claws. But her hands were trembling.

She was sitting at her desk next morning when Teresa brought in a message. A secretary had telephoned to say that she was invited to lunch with Prime Minister Mussolini. Not so much an invitation, she mused, as a command.

'I thought we should continue last night's discussion in private,' he explained, and holding her firmly by the arm he led her to a small sitting room. Without asking her he pressed a large goblet of Frascati into her hand and indicated one of the two wing-backed chairs by a window, throwing his vast weight into the other.

'So, my beautiful Countess Jacqueline does not approve of the way we defend our colonies against savages, eh?'

'That is not what I said last night, Duce.'

'Oh, yes, it is, that is what it amounted to.' His head tilted back, chin jutting. 'I'm disappointed in you. You are a countess, one of the ruling classes, mistress and loving companion of a senior Fascisti nobleman. And you are a businesswoman. Therefore you must know that for a business or a colony or a country to be strong, advance socially and economically, leaders have to be strong and sometimes fierce in administering the rules. Even in disciplining one's children we know that leniency is seen to be weakness on which the child may play next time he transgresses.'

'But . . .'

'You cannot look out of this window at those pretty young women and their children on the street and consider them in the same light as Ethiopian women. They are savages. I know they are reputed to have some charm, but the fact remains that by our standards they are a cruel and ruthless people, holding human life very cheap.'

'Duce! They are still human beings,' she expostulated.

'The Germans used gas in the war,' he continued, ignoring her outburst. 'So did the British and the French. *And* the Italians.'

'I know that. But only against opposing troops, not on civilians.' As he opened his mouth to speak she raised her voice and continued. 'The towns and villages Marshal Badoglio gassed were not even on the Italian Somaliland border, they were miles away . . .'

'Not far enough. They were feeding and assisting their warriors and supplying arms . . .'

'How far is enough? Fifty, one hundred, a thousand miles? Where does the licence to massacre begin and end?'

Before he could reply the door swung open and a waiter wheeled in a service trolley, clicked up the flaps and arranged the plates and cutlery.

'Will that be all, Your Excellency?' he murmured.

'Yes, yes.' Mussolini waved him away and turned back to the discussion. 'You, my dear, are a theorist. There are two types of people in the world: Theorists and Doers. Unfortunately, instead of thinking what should be done, the Theorists only think about what the Doers should not be doing, and tell them to think more before doing anything. But if we Doers thought as much as the Theorists we would still be savages like the Ethiopians. Now, come and eat.'

She realised she would never make her point with this practised politician.

It was a simple meal to say the least, a large pile of steaming spaghetti with a thin tomato sauce and a jug of white table wine. The Prime Minister tucked his table napkin into his collar, munching and slurping, with worms of spaghetti dripping down his chin as he beamed at his guest. He obviously considered he had won the debate. Before she was halfway through her plate, he was helping himself to another huge portion from the serving dish.

Jacqueline, having accepted long ago the impossibility of talking whilst eating spaghetti successfully, chewed in silence. His second plateful demolished, Mussolini pushed back his chair and wiped his chin on the napkin.

'Right. Now that we have put the world in order, and eaten, it is time to work.'

Realising that it would be pointless to argue with him any more, Jacqueline coolly but politely thanked him for lunch and left.

June 1936 – May 1940

> . . . good lady; the bright day is done,
> And we are for the dark.

William Shakespeare, *Antony and Cleopatra*

IN RETROSPECT, Jacqueline realised Marco was right when he accused her of being naïve. It was not so much for criticising the Italians of using gas on civilians, but for openly accusing those who had authorised its use of murder. All she had done was embarrass him, make Ciano furious, and amuse Mussolini, who, after his initial amazement at her attitude had obviously decided to treat her like a silly, empty-headed female. One should have the courage of one's convictions, stand by one's beliefs, but to take a positive stand as she had done at Duce's dinner party was really risking one's neck with no hope of gaining anything. However, the whole episode had convinced her of one thing: she replied to her father's letter saying that she not only shared the American view of the Italian actions in East Africa but also asking if he had any information about acquiring US citizenship. She had definitely made up her mind that this was what she wanted for herself and Jean-Jacques.

Only a week after her lunch with Duce, Marco brought home another invitation to an official dinner at the Palazzo Venezia.

'Darling, I have said I am sorry for my behaviour at Duce's dinner, but I still don't want to go back there, at least for a while.'

'Why not? That episode is over and done with.'

'It's not that. I just don't want to be near Duce.'

She just did not wish to be any part of the present Italian political scene . . . a fact which she knew would upset Marco were she to tell him. Their quarrel was over and she had no wish to stir it up again.

So Marco attended the dinner without her.

Not long after Katarina's first birthday, Marco arrived home one evening looking very worried. 'I think I will have to start reorganising my business commitments,' he told Jacqueline. 'The government has decided to send troops to support General Franco's rebellion in Spain. As we are already maintaining a peace-keeping force in Abyssinia, we will have to enlarge the army. As a senior reserve officer I may be called up at any time, so I will start with the Milanese offices tomorrow. I'll be away for at least a week, I'm afraid.'

She was stunned. The thought of Marco being called up, away for perhaps months on end . . . and she didn't even understand what it was all about. When she thought about the upheaval in Spain, it had been to reflect how thankful she was not to live there. 'Will you have to go to Spain? In what capacity would you serve?'

'Communications. I would almost certainly remain at Rome Headquarters so you need not worry about me dashing around with a fixed bayonet. I will definitely be posted to a desk, and able to get home for some of the weekends!'

That was a relief, but then another thought occurred to her. 'How on earth can the government afford to fight another campaign?'

'They can't. Strictly between ourselves, I see no way we can carry on without heavy tax increases. We are not doing as much foreign trade as we should, either. There is far too little money coming into the country.'

'Why? I thought the trade embargo had been lifted?'

'It was. Not that it was ever really effective, anyway.

No, I think the lire is just too expensive to attract foreign trade.'

She lay awake for hours that night, staring through the open window at the big summer moon, thinking.

Was she being fair to Marco? Her rescuer, protector, guide, mentor, husband in all but legal formality. How frightened she had been at the thought of him going off to war. With his loving encouragement and advice she had become a strong and successful woman. What might have happened to her without him? She couldn't envisage life without him, yet she had used the courage he gave her to embarrass him publicly, criticise and condemn the people and policies he stood for. After all he had done for her, shouldn't she now support him and those policies against the criticisms of other nations? But she could not do it without breaking faith with her own principles. She believed he shared those principles to a degree, he had half admitted it during their quarrel. Also, why had he always discouraged her from applying for Italian citizenship, supported the idea of turning to America instead? Did he have secret doubts, fears for their future in Italy? But their lives, businesses, income, property, all were in Italy, with the exception of a few small investments abroad. If they ever left they would be virtually penniless. Even here their wealth was obviously going to be reduced; the government had to raise money somehow and, as Marco had said, it would have to be through taxation . . . of what? Capital, assets, property or just income? And that would not bring more money into the country; only devaluation of the lire would do that.

She fell asleep just before dawn, having made her plans.

'Well, what do you think of her?' Jacqueline asked, her voice high with excitement. They were standing on the deck of an eighty-five foot motor yacht, berthed in the little port of Civitavecchia.

'She looks beautiful, but isn't she rather large?' Marco was rather dubious.

'Not really. As the children get bigger they will want to bring their friends with them on holiday, and sometimes we will want to take friends cruising. Neither of us knows anything about boats or navigation, so we have to have a crew and they must have their own berths and mess.'

'But darling, how are we going to find a crew when all able-bodied men are needed in the services?'

'I understand that this is very much a family boat,' she laughed. 'The captain, who is sixty-five, doubles as engineer; his wife doubles as cook and deck hand. Their son is classified as disabled because he has a club foot, but he knows almost as much as his father about the sea and boats, and his wife will be stewardess. They have been with the boat since the owner commissioned her five years ago, in England. She was built in an English boatyard, by Camper and Nicholson, who have a first class reputation.' She had done a great deal of homework on this project. 'And isn't the name just right? *Ocean Dreamer*. I think that's ideal.'

Despite his doubts, the idea of holidays spent cruising through the Mediterranean with their family, exploring Greek islands, foreign ports, became increasingly attractive to Marco as they followed the vendor's agent through the large deckhouse saloon furnished with armchairs and fitted sofas, table-lamps and carpets. The cupboards and dining suite were all in polished mahogany. He had not thought that a yacht could be quite so comfortable when he inspected the master stateroom and guest rooms with their luxurious private showers and baths. Nor had he guessed how well fitted the galley would be with the cooker and a cooling unit built into the fitted storeboxes. The engine room housed two brand new diesel engines, recently installed to replace the original steam power. Jacqueline was very eager to invest in a yacht, though he was not sure that holidays were her only reason. She seemed to think it was also a good capital investment, but he couldn't agree there. Any time they should wish to realise the value, everyone else would be wanting to do the same thing and finding a purchaser would be difficult. Still, the price seemed very good as it was a forced sale through bankruptcy, and he could well afford the two-thirds of the cost she had asked him for. Why not, if it made her happy?

Marco left all the purchasing arrangements to Jacqueline, who was to be the new owner. He didn't know what she had in mind until she registered the boat in Panama – then he understood that she did intend it to be a capital investment, but a floating and therefore movable one, which, if it ever became necessary, she could take with her anywhere in the world, and there realise its value free of Mussolini's tax assessors. He had to disapprove, but she looked so much more relaxed and happy after completion that he was glad he had said nothing. And before he took up his army appointment they spent two glorious weeks cruising with the children around Sicily and Corsica.

Capital tax was introduced that summer, and when the government finally devalued the lire in October Jacqueline was very relieved that she had completed her plans in time.

Despite her fears, Marco remained in Rome for the next two years and their lives fell into a comfortable pattern of short, two or three-day summer cruises with Jacob and the children and one longer cruise interspersed with trekking the horses up into the hills between Mount Tolfa and Lake Bracciano. They entertained at home around the swimming pool and spent a fortnight each winter at St Moritz. Civitavecchia was only fifteen miles from the villa and when they were not cruising, Jacqueline often drove down to supervise the maintenance of the yacht.

Francisco, at four years old, was small, thin, and very wiry. His blond baby hair had darkened, but remained curly, and his grey, almost black eyes were deep-set and intense under mobile and expressive brows. He displayed all the outward signs of a gregarious and fun-loving character. He adored entertaining and noisily resented any effort to

231

curtail his participation in adult pursuits. He liked being lifted into the saddle of Jean-Jacques' pony and hated having the reins held to prevent him from charging off alone. Nanny had to keep him quiet each morning lest he awake the entire household at dawn; each night he fought off the bedtime hour. He loved everyone passionately, particularly his little sister, and happily played down to her at doll tea-parties.

Katarina looked remarkably like a photograph Jacqueline remembered at Chateau Dumescu, taken of herself at the same age. She seemed to be more of a watcher than a participator, always studying people. Although she was a happy and contented child, she was very quiet in comparison with the rest of her lively family.

Jacqueline and Jacob were both worried in August of 1938 when Il Duce introduced a 'racial programme' under which Jews could be expatriated, Jewish children banned from Italian schools, and Jewish teachers dismissed. But Marco laughed at their fears.

'Duce is only trying to impress on Adolf Hitler our government's willingness to keep in step with Nazi Germany. But I assure you the programme will never be implemented. It would cost far too much and we simply don't have the money.'

But three months later they were all shocked out of their tranquil lives. Following the assassination of a German diplomat in Paris, a Jewish pogrom started in Germany. The stories which reached them through foreign newspapers were horrific, and they thanked God that the Laskers' children and grandchildren had followed Johann and Sadie into exile in Switzerland.

Jacob shook his head sadly. 'Even if my parents and Ruth had survived, they would surely die in this present slaughter. It is hard to understand why the Nazis are such animals.'

Marco turned away, silent. Italy seemed very friendly towards England and France at the moment, but relations

232

had undoubtedly been strained by the opposition to the Abyssinian venture, and a pro-Nazi attitude in the Italian government was becoming more and more obvious. Jacqueline wondered how long it would be before Duce took another step towards identifying himself as Hitler's potential ally?

Much to her relief she was asked to call at the American Embassy where, after three months of form-filling and letters to and from her father, passports for Jean-Jacques and herself were waiting. Marco was obviously relieved too. His face often looked drawn and worried nowadays, and Jacqueline felt he knew a great deal more about the prevalent political tensions, secret pacts, and 'gentlemen's agreements' than he would admit.

'Now that you are a citizen of the United States I do think you should go there for a visit. Of course I would love to come with you, but you realise that is out of the question at present. Why don't you suggest it to your father the next time you write? He will want to organise leave well in advance so that he can introduce you to America and to his family. Why not ask if you can go next Easter?'

'What, go away and leave you and the children with no one to look after you?' she queried.

'Now that we seem to have Rosita and Giuseppe's entire family here for that very purpose, I doubt you would even be missed!' He grinned slyly at her in the mirror over the mantelpiece.

'Beast!' she exclaimed.

But she wrote to Bill Stevenson next morning.

Having made business and domestic arrangements for the period of her absence, planned Jean-Jacques' transport to and from school, and written endless lists of instructions for cook, Nanny and Jacob, Jacqueline was able to put all thoughts of her responsibilities out of her mind when late in the following March the liner left Italy. Apart from the visit to Bill's flagship, three years before, she had never been on a really large vessel and she found herself casting

233

a professional eye over the decor. Her first class stateroom, filled with flowers from Marco, was cream and chocolate brown, with light stained woodwork; pleasant and comfortable, if a trifle uninspired.

She saw little of the other passengers, probably because the seas were quite boisterous for much of the journey and they remained in their cabins. Jacqueline had never felt seasick in her life. Wrapped in a fur coat and headscarf, she walked the decks, eyes streaming from the bracing wind, all very good for a healthy appetite at the captain's table each evening. It really was amusing to see the stewards standing between the tables, huge trays on one hand over their heads, swaying and weaving like balancing acts in a circus.

There had been photographs of the Statue of Liberty and the Manhattan skyline in various Italian magazines, but Jacqueline was still unprepared for the beauty of the colossal figure, radiant in the sunshine, seeming to welcome all to America.

Admiral and Mrs William Stevenson came aboard as soon as the passenger gangway was craned into position; a privilege afforded by his uniform, no doubt. Jacqueline had expected some embarrassment at meeting Bill's wife, but Louise just caught her in a warm hug before handing her on to her father for the same treatment.

'Well,' Louise drawled, 'your mother must have been a beauty, because you never got those looks from Bill. Silly man was scared stiff to tell me about you, you know. He'd confessed his first love was a Rumanian tennis player when we started dating, but he never told me what he'd done with her.' She grinned fondly at him. 'Suppose it was naïve of me to imagine my sailor boy was so innocent!' She was a tall woman, big boned with a broad face and wide smile. Smart, but casually dressed, she epitomised the relaxed confidence Jacqueline had first noted among the American officers on Bill's ship at Naples, and also in the few Americans she had met since.

They stayed at the New York Plaza for a few days,

overlooking Central Park, the Stevensons having rightly guessed that Jacqueline would want to visit the traditional sights. She was taken up the Empire State Building, given a close-up of the Statue of Liberty, fed at the Waldorf-Astoria, and entertained to a Broadway show. Finally, Bill let the women have a day's shopping on Fifth Avenue before driving them up to their home in New England.

The countryside was low and flatter than any she had ever seen, and the people, the way of life, the standard of living, so different. She supposed there must be poor people in the United States as there were the world over – the Italian newspapers were always carrying articles on the high levels of American unemployment – but she was never aware of seeing any. Everyone seemed healthy and well dressed by European standards, and the houses stood freshly painted in trim gardens. Voices and conversations were strange. Italians always made even the friendliest discussion sound like a furious quarrel, with much waving of arms and fierce expressions. These people spoke with an easy drawl, constantly smiling. She was quite alarmed at the casual lack of respect shown the Admiral by a garage attendant when they stopped for petrol; he seemed to address Bill as an equal . . . yet Bill apparently expected it, and replied in kind, very unlike the strict European class barriers.

They arrived at the Connecticut house after turning up a slight incline through thick woods. The trees appeared to have been pushed back in every direction to make way for wide lawns sweeping down to a beautiful stretch of water . . . one of several local reservoirs, Jacqueline was told, overlooked by the white-painted clapboard homestead.

'This is so lovely!' she exclaimed. 'So peaceful.' Indeed, apart from the crunch of gravel under their feet, and the birds swooping out of the tall cedars to spiral up calling joyously to their mates, there was no noise.

The front door was opened by a manservant, introduced as Eli, who rushed to greet them with handshakes and friendly chatter, closely followed by two excited golden retrievers, both eager to help carry handbags and parcels very carefully in their mouths. Jacqueline was startled by a high-pitched shriek, and a huge black woman appeared round the side of the building.

'Miz Louisa, Master Bill, I didn't know you was come. Now where is that daughter of yours?' She stopped to appraise the new arrival. 'Man, but you are beautiful.'

'Jacki, this is Cleo.'

Jacqueline put out her hand, but it was brushed aside as two huge arms clasped her to a vast bosom.

'Man,' Cleo said. 'You're family.'

A welcome which made her arrival feel like a home-coming.

Perhaps it was the absence of terrace roofs around the house which made it seem so bright compared with Italian villas. There was one glass-enclosed porch running down the south side of the living room and dining room, but both had more unshaded windows admitting light to every corner. The use of wood, both for building and decor, was accented throughout the house. All the floors were stained and polished, and in the ground floor rooms, wood panelling on the lower half of the walls was similarly treated. Thick, brightly coloured Indian carpets and rugs and loose, floral cretonne chair covers and curtains added to the relaxed, happy atmosphere, where pets shared equal status with the family. The bedrooms had brass bedsteads with patchwork quilts, flower-painted ewers and basins stood on marble-topped washstands, frilled cotton curtains framed the windows and there were children's paintings on the white wood walls.

The porch was painted white inside and out, as was the wicker furniture. Two of the armchairs, stuffed with soft blue cushions, housed black cats. Ferns hung from the roof in wicker baskets and similar baskets held electric light fixtures. From the porch steps a paved area led across to the swimming pool, heated at this time of the year, and beyond, a path led through the trees to a gravel tennis court. On the far side of the house, white wood rails marked the paddock where horses stood under an old elm, flicking at flies with their tails.

'Oh, how pleasant,' Jacqueline remarked when she saw them. 'I didn't realise you kept a stable.'

'Can't imagine life without horses,' Louise laughed. 'I grew up with them. Do you ride? Would you like to come out tomorrow morning?'

'I'd love to, but I haven't brought any riding clothes.'

'No problem. We'll soon fix you up.'

Later, sipping her first John Collins in Bill's den, she remarked on the warmth of the house.

'We have a coal-fired boiler in the cellar and hot water is circulated to radiators throughout the house. Even when it snows we keep snug as bugs,' he explained.

Louise was as good as her word. Early next morning she brought a tray of breakfast to Jacqueline's room, and a check shirt and faded dungarees similar to her own. 'These may not be a perfect fit and they're certainly not *haute couture*, but we're not entering any dressage events this morning.'

The shoe cupboard was raided and produced suitable boots and, with a stetson tied under her chin, Jacqueline strode out to accept a leg-up from Eli. Her mount was a lively little chestnut who circled impatiently as the stirrups were adjusted, followed Bill's lead through the trees at a proud trot and finally, with a joyful kick, stretched her neck and galloped away over the open grassland, determined to keep up with the larger mounts.

Next day the Stevensons' sons arrived with their wives and children. It was a happy occasion, Bill being subjected to much good-humoured teasing.

'Boy, when I think of all the lectures he read us when we started eyeing the girls,' his younger son remarked to Jacqueline. 'He gave us the idea he'd never laid a finger on a skirt before Mom . . .'

'You have to admit, though, Dave, what he did, he did well,' his brother observed.

'Don't be vulgar, Robert,' Louise chided, laughing.

Jacqueline enjoyed the big noisy parties as well as quiet intimate chats with her new relations. She only wished her own children could have been with her, vowing to bring them on her next visit.

One evening after the family had returned to their homes, she confided to Bill and Louise the plan she had devised for getting money out of Italy, should it become necessary.

'I don't want to sound alarmist, but Hitler's massive re-arming of Germany does make me nervous. Perhaps it's because of my quarter Jewish blood and the awful mass murders of Jews in Germany. But surely Hitler wouldn't spend so much on arms if he wasn't going to use them.'

'Mass murders?' her father asked. 'What mass murders?'

'Oh, well, I suppose I was thinking of the Dumescus. They can't have been an isolated case.'

'Maybe not, but Hitler isn't guilty of half the crimes Mussolini is, through that Abyssinian business,' Bill pointed out. 'I have to say I'd rather deal with him any day than your Duce. As for a war, well . . . I know the British aren't too worried. Of course there are some notable exceptions . . . Winston Churchill, for instance. And there are some pretty varied opinions over here. Certainly, if Hitler does get pushed into war there is no way the rest of Europe can avoid getting embroiled, even the neutral countries. Mussolini may try to keep out because of his economic situation, but I reckon he'll finish up siding with the chap who waves the biggest stick.'

Jacqueline sighed. 'I have felt this all along. Marco doesn't agree with me, but then Duce is a personal friend of his. You may think he's a villain, but he has done so much for the Italians over the past fifteen years that his friends and admirers think he can do no wrong.' She hoped she didn't sound as disloyal as she felt. 'I am nervous for Jean-Jacques and Jacob as well as for myself. Marco and I are not married. If he has to go away with the army I have no standing in Italy. We three all have Jewish blood. If Italy and Germany become allies . . . you know, I still feel guilty about the yacht, but it is a comfort to know that if we did have to flee Europe I could sell the boat in America. We wouldn't have to starve and there might even be enough to start up in business again.'

Had she been right to persuade Marco to help her buy the boat? Without telling him the real reason for her wanting it? Wasn't it very unjust of her to inveigle him into a deal which was obviously intended to evade tax and enable her to take money out of the country illegally? Over the past two years, feeling safely cocooned by Marco's confidence and the peaceful luxury of their lives, she had been able to forget most of her worries and the secret plans she had made . . . except when news of yet more Nazi persecutions and Italy's growing friendship with Germany brought waves of doubt and fear to disturb her. Then she would spend long hours staring into the darkness, her brain beset with a confusion of facts and emotions. Marco must have known what she had done, and felt hurt. The guilt and regret at causing that hurt made painful knots of tension in her chest. She remembered the way he had looked at her when she told him the deal was completed. She had known he wouldn't want to know the details, even if she had dared to tell him. Despite knowing his agony of split loyalties she had gambled on his love for her . . . and won. And ever since, when a new wave of fear reminded her of that gamble, the tension of guilt and regret returned to be subdued again by the cold, defiant logic of self-preservation. She loved him, admired and respected him, joyfully weaved her life through his in almost continuously happy unison . . . except during political discussion. And he loved her. He would tell her, in the privacy of their bedroom, all the reasons why he adored her. How he admired and respected her resilience, determination and strength – the very strength which gave her the courage to stand up against all the beliefs he held so dear.

Would Jean-Paul have given her that strength? And still loved her when she used it against him? Jean-Paul. Oh, yes, she still thought about him. How old was Katarina now? She seldom pictured their lovemaking any more, and she so seldom felt the lead weight in her stomach that came with their parting. But the memory of his face smiling at her recurred too frequently, even now.

Bill and Louise took their 'Italian friend' visiting up the New England coast and entertained her at home. They flew to Washington, Bill on official business, for a week of receptions and sightseeing. From there they went on to Charleston, South Carolina, for Louise to show her the cotton plantation where she had spent her childhood.

Waiting at Charleston rail depot for a west-bound train, Jacqueline browsed among magazines on a newsstand, purchasing a few for the return journey. Their day had been a great success. A distant cousin of Louise's now owned the old house and managed the plantation. He and his wife were delighted to entertain them and show them around, though Jacqueline found it almost impossible to understand their Southern drawl. However, she did learn a lot of American history from Bill's stories of the Civil War.

That evening, rumbling back to Charleston through the darkening countryside, Jacqueline thumbed through a news weekly, peering at pictures by the dim carriage light. A photograph of Ciano suddenly caught her eye, getting into a car which flew Swastikas, and another shaking hands in a doorway: both had obviously been taken from a distance with a telephoto lens.

She read the article and silently handed it on to Bill.

'What is it?' Louise asked.

'US Intelligence information reveals that Count Ciano, our Foreign Minister, has been having secret meetings in Berlin to negotiate a pact with Germany. According to this article an agreement has been reached for a firm alliance, the talks are over, and the pact will be signed later this year,' Jacqueline explained.

'How do you feel about that?'

'Frightened. Germany is preparing for war and now, I suppose, Italy will be part of it. It's a bit like sitting

240

on dynamite and waiting for someone to strike a match.'

'Surely it's not that bad?' Louise reached out to pat her hand.

'I'm afraid it is.' Bill set the magazine aside. 'Jacqueline is right – Europe could explode at any time.'

His daughter stared through her reflection in the window. Only the train wheels spoke: You have to get back . . . you have to get back . . . you cannot stay here . . . you have to get back. Once again beating time with her unhappy thoughts, as they had on other unhappy occasions in the past.

She turned, squared her shoulders, and looked from one to the other. 'I must return home as soon as possible. I am very sad to cut short my visit, you have both been so wonderful, but I must be with Marco and the children if and when a war does start. Should things get desperate I may well come back here with the children. I can only pray that my fears are unfounded.'

Strangely enough, it seemed her prayers were answered.

Life in Italy was extraordinarily relaxed and normal. She had expected to find things changed; people, buildings, but everything was exactly as and where she had left it. So much so that the holiday, the Connecticut home, the newly found family, took on a dream-like quality, almost as if it had never happened, as though she had never been away.

Marco was able to spend quite a lot of time at home. Together they taught Francisco to swim, they cruised on the yacht, they laid a tennis court. No one ever spoke of war or even appeared to think of it.

Duce came to dinner one night at the villa, together with Claretta and a small group of mutual friends – and did not attempt to argue with Jacqueline, though he was as pompous and noisy and vulgar as ever, insisting, even at so small and private a function, on standing to propose a toast at great length. He had come to regard himself as the authority on any subject on which the conversation touched, which Jacqueline tolerated with grace.

241

It was a beautiful summer. Looking at his mistress, Marco thought that Jacqueline at twenty-eight had matured exquisitely. Whether in a bathing costume, business suit or ball gown, she always looked perfect, without apparently trying. Relaxed and laughing, entertaining with natural ease, she retained an almost regal dignity.

And that summer they loved. Stretched out on the yacht's sundeck, Jacqueline would gaze at Marco's lean, tanned, strong-boned face, half hidden by sunglasses, crisp dark hair, showing more grey at the temples now, and she knew by the response low in her stomach and her thighs how much she still loved and wanted him. When, through the dark glasses, he read her gaze, he would get up and lead her by the hand down to the privacy of their stateroom. Twice she reached the magic she had longed to share with him – only a pale shadow of the magic she had found, briefly, a thousand years ago in Paris – but still she cried with happiness.

Their friends were from the highest levels of society. With royalty and nobility, the rich and the famous, Marco and Jacqueline whirled on a carefree and glittering merry-go-round; loving and loved parents by day, glamorous and pampered socialites attending receptions, cocktail parties, dinners and balls each night.

She wore emerald green satin to the British Embassy Ball. The cut was simple and dramatic, set off by her emerald and diamond jewellery, and with a tiara holding her golden chignon. Marco, immaculate in dress uniform, led her into a waltz.

'Trying to get one dance with you in an evening takes a lot of strategic planning, my beauty,' he said with a mock expression of pain. And he looked even more pained a few minutes later when the music changed to a romp.

'Oh, no! It's one of those stupid dances the English call a Paul Jones!' They had to separate to join their respective circles, gentlemen on the outside, ladies on the inside, revolving around the ballroom in opposite directions until the music stopped and normal dancing re-commenced with whoever happened to be standing in front of one.

Jacqueline was uncertain whether the elderly gentleman in the uniform of a British Major General was about to partner her or the lady next to her, when an unseen arm was placed firmly around her waist and she was led into a foxtrot.

'I wondered how long it would be before we met again, my dear Countess.'

Her legs were paralysed. She couldn't breathe.

Deathly white she looked up into the eyes of Heinrich von Reinikker.

Colour rushed back into her face. With an enormous effort she forced herself to think logically. It was ridiculous to be terrified here in the British Embassy in Rome, by this . . . this monster. Why was he here? Why had the British dared to invite such a brute? They could have no idea of who or what he was. Presumably he was in Rome as an official guest of the Italian government.

Quickly her fear was replaced by anger. That members of the government, so-called personal friends of hers and Marco's, should associate with him, entertain him. That she should suffer the humiliation of having to dance with this animal, who had murdered her family, tried to rape her and forced her to flee Germany. It was outrageous.

She thrust him away from her violently. 'Don't you dare touch me,' she hissed.

'Come, come, Countess . . .'

'And don't address me again.' She raised her voice. 'You have no right to be here. No right to associate with civilised people.'

Couples stood around them, staring in amazement, and drew back to allow Jacqueline, flushed and furious, to stride out of the room.

One of the host diplomats hurried after her. 'I say! Is there something wrong?'

'There most certainly is,' she paused to reply. 'I'm afraid your guest list was not adequately vetted. That man there

243

'. . .' she pointed a jewelled finger at Reinikker, '. . . is a mass murderer. No decent person should have to be in the same room with him, let alone be expected to dance with him. Please inform Count Luzzi di Calitri that the Countess Tyroler is leaving.' And she stalked out, leaving the German visitor, puce with rage, to exit by another door.

Marco found her in the car, trembling and weeping. He held her close in his arms all the way home, half carried her to the bedroom and, with Maria's help, tucked her into bed. Despite the hot August night she was icy cold, so she was given warm milk laced with brandy, then a sedative, but even so it was hours before she stopped shaking. She dozed once, just before dawn, and woke screaming.

Marco sat beside her bed all the next day, stroking her hands and hair, coaxing her to eat and drink a little, and by the next evening she was able to talk, though there wasn't much to say. The British diplomat had hurriedly told Marco what had happened as he delivered Jacqueline's message. She had little to add.

'I don't understand why I am like this,' she murmured. 'It is stupid and illogical to be frightened of him. I know he cannot hurt us here in Italy.'

'I expect it is just the shock of seeing him again, especially after hearing Jacob's story. Obviously you see him in your mind as personally responsible for all the horrors we have heard and read about, being perpetrated against the German Jews over the past few years. Don't worry, my sweetheart, I don't blame you at all for reacting the way you did.'

A view not shared by everyone. He never told her of the meeting he had with Ciano a few days later.

The Foreign Minister was furious. 'It is about time you kept that mistress of yours locked up, Marco,' he snapped. 'How dare she publicly insult an official guest in our country?'

'Just a minute, my friend. Are you aware that he is personally responsible for the murder of a number of her close . . . er . . . friends in Germany?' Marco demanded.

'Jewish relatives, you mean. Oh, yes, Reinikker told us. Subversives and enemies of the régime. But don't worry . . .' seeing the alarm he had caused. 'Out of respect for our friendship, if for no other reason, no harm will come to her here . . . if you can keep that tongue of hers under control. You know, we may not like everything our friends do in their own homes, or in their own countries, but the fact remains that Germany is our friend and ally. They have assurance of our support in all they do . . .'

'Everything? Not content with annexing Austria and Czechoslovakia, they are demanding half of Poland now. Are we going to support them in that?'

'Of course. Just as they will support us when we decide to move into Albania. We have signed what Duce calls "The Pact of Steel". Only a few days ago in Berlin I personally assured Adolf Hitler that we support their claims in Poland. You may have read about it in the newspapers.'

'But Duce told me that he didn't agree with their latest demands.'

'My father-in-law is old and tired. Sometimes he gets nervous and wants "peace at any price", like the democracies. Ah!' He stood up impatiently and thumped his desk. 'We are an important country now. We must have the courage to honour our treaties and stand shoulder to shoulder with our allies against their enemies.'

Two weeks later, on 2 September, Marco vividly recalled their conversation when, following the German invasion of Poland the previous day, the Italian government proclaimed neutrality.

On 3 September, Britain and France, honouring their pact with Poland, declared war on Germany.

There was a change in the gaiety of the parties that Christmas – from calm relaxation to brittle tension. The humour was forced. There was just as much noise and laughter as ever, Jacqueline mused, but rather as though life was on a stage and everyone acting a jollity they did not feel. Perhaps because Christmas was that one, unique period of the year from which one gauged things, looked back over past Christmases for comparisons. How the children had grown, who was with us last year; who had died leaving an empty chair at the festive table. And it was a period when one would normally look forward to the new year, wondering what it would bring. But this year was not normal. She dared not think about what might happen in the coming year, lest the ball of fear she had felt in her stomach last August, face to face with Heinrich, return to spoil everything. Maybe they were all trying to mask their private fears.

Like most men, Marco was seldom out of uniform, spending long hours on duty even on Christmas Day. He arrived home in time for Christmas dinner in the evening when even Katarina was allowed to stay up late. She was not a demonstrative child, but adored her father and loved to be carried high on his shoulders, her tiny arms clasped around his head. They sat side by side at the table, pulling crackers together and arranging each other's paper hats on their heads.

'There, a crown for my little princess.' Marco tried to prevent it slipping down over her face.

'Papa, that is a hat for a sailor, not a soldier,' Jean-Jacques remarked.

Francisco shrieked with laughter. 'Mama looks like a cook in hers.'

Jacob was much brighter this Christmas. He and Teresa, Jacqueline's secretary, had fallen in love and planned to marry in the New Year. He seldom had that haunted look nowadays, his new-found happiness perhaps at last dispelling the ghastly memories.

Even Anna, still in Rouen with Claude, had planned a gay Christmas, despite France being at war. Jacqueline had gathered from her occasional letters that she had settled into a comfortable domestic routine with Claude, though they had never married, and she felt relieved that, at last, her mother seemed to have a more settled and stable life. The great love of Claude's life was apparently motor racing. He kept racing cars and a team of mechanics and drivers with whom he and Anna travelled to national rallies all over Europe. In fact Jacqueline accepted an invitation to join them for the Monaco Grand Prix next year – but if this war lasted there might not be a Grand Prix.

Jean-Jacques had entered Marco's old school last term. He had grown tall, with a serious expression and military bearing that made him look older than his years. He arrived home from his first day of the new term unusually excited. 'Mama! Mama, where are you?' He ran through the villa.

Jacqueline emerged from her room. 'I am here. What is it, Jean-Jacques?'

'Mama, I have to have a suitcase packed. Look, here is a list of things. We are moving out of Rome to the Caesaro Palazzo Military Camp in two days' time.'

'Military Camp? There must be some mistake, darling. That would only be for the older boys. You are only eleven.'

'They said all the boys who will be twelve years old this term and who are over five feet tall must go. That means me. We were all examined by a doctor today. He said a few of the boys were not strong enough for full military training, but I am.' He was very proud.

But his mother exploded. 'This is ridiculous. I cannot believe it. I know you are big and strong for your age, my darling, but you are still a child. There must be some mistake.'

She telephoned the school several times. It was always engaged. Other mothers, no doubt. Knowing that Marco would not be home until very late she tried to telephone him at his headquarters. He was at a meeting at the Palazzo Venezia.

'Mama, please stop making a fuss. I am right. I know I am right, and it will be awfully embarrassing if you start protesting to my officers. You will only make me look silly!' Jean-Jacques was dark with anger.

Jacqueline lost her temper. 'How dare you speak to me like that? I tell you someone has made a mistake. It may be deliberate, but nonetheless it is a mistake and somebody has to correct it. All the boys' parents must be horrified.' She lifted the receiver to give the operator the school number again, and replaced it with an impatient hiss.

They sat in angry silence that evening, books open on their laps. After Jean-Jacques had gone to bed she saw he had been reading *Command of the Air* by Giulio Douhet.

It was almost midnight when Marco came in.

'You should not have waited up for me, darling.' He bent to kiss the top of her head and then slumped in the opposite chair.

'I thought I should, Marco. A problem has arisen with Jean-Jacques' school. He has come home with some idea that he is going off to a military camp in two days' time. It is obviously some mistake. I have been trying all evening to get through to the school but the phone is permanently engaged. I had hoped to sort it out before he went to bed . . .' She paused as he held up his hand.

'There is no mistake. The ruling applies to all the schools. I suppose I should have warned you earlier, but I thought you knew.'

'You knew? And you approve?'

'I indulge the luxury of approving or disapproving only when given a choice. In this instance we don't have a choice. We must just accept it.'

'My God! Does this pompous, neutral country need to cower behind a row of schoolboy soldiers who have not yet reached puberty?'

Her sarcasm made him wince. 'There is no point in getting angry with me . . .'

'I wouldn't be angry with you if you would just do something instead of sitting there arguing.'

'Holy Mother of God! I am not arguing.' He passed a hand wearily over his forehead. 'I am only telling you there

248

is nothing, my darling, nothing that we or any other parents can do, short of starting a civil rebellion, perhaps.' He sighed and stood up. 'Come. I will explain it to you as we get to bed.'

She knew, of course, that she shouldn't have lost her temper, especially with Jean-Jacques and Marco. She often felt tense and irritable nowadays. She saw so little of Marco and she supposed the thought of losing Jean-Jacques as well had sparked her off. Anger was such a waste of energy unless one could harness it to solve a problem. There must be something one could do. But they could do nothing. Marco and Jean-Jacques were right – he had to go. It was a government ruling that covered the whole country, and Marco had warned her that any boys who failed to report would be rounded up by officials, punished, and their families as well. As he said, she would have to accept it.

She apologised next day to Marco, and to Jean-Jacques before he left.

'It is all right, Mama. Several of my friends had trouble with their mothers, you were not the only one.' His gracious smile and stiff farewell kiss didn't make her feel any better.

There were no new commissions for the Stevenson Salon, which was really just as well because she and Jacob were the only ones left. Jacob had been worried. The men were all in the services and the women including Teresa in the munitions factories, and, although he was a German national, he had no wish to join the Italian army to fight beside the Nazis. Marco had reassured him that as Italy was neutral the problem wouldn't arise, and he certainly would not be required to enlist; in fact, no official record existed of his being in Italy at all, and it would be best just to keep it that way.

By the beginning of April the last contracts were completed. Together, Jacob and Jacqueline chased up the last few bad debts, paid the bills, and drew up a final balance sheet.

She had decided not to clear everything out completely. This stupid, phoney war – as the Americans were calling it – would probably be settled in a few months, and then everything could return to normal. She wandered through the design room where clean sheets of papers lay waiting for the draughtsmen's pencils; the specialist workshop where neat racks of tools awaited their craftsmen. From her office door she looked across the main salon. Was it yesterday or was it a lifetime ago when she had caught Marco's eye above the guests at the opening reception? He had taken her to the Hassler for dinner and had stayed the night at the villa to make love to her for the first time.

So much had happened since . . .

Ah! It was stupid to feel this way. In a few months they would all be back at work. Business would flourish again, better than ever.

Tears fell on her hand as she turned the key.

Even when the Nazis overran Denmark and Norway, the feelings of existing in limbo persisted.

Jacqueline felt restless and paced the villa trying to find things to occupy her. There was plenty to do now that nearly all the servants had been conscripted into the army or the labour force. Maria and Nanny had both left in tears. But tending to chores and children only occupied one's hands – not one's mind. She gave Francisco reading lessons each day, he learned quickly when he was in the mood. His sister learned to count with wooden blocks. Jacob helped old Giuseppe in the garden and stables.

Summer was approaching with perfect sunshine. Jacqueline sat back on a sunbed to read the letter which had just arrived from Anna.

By the time you receive this, Claude and I will have left for Paris. Then we move on to Le Mans. The team are trying out a new modification in one of the cars on the Sarthe Road Circuit and Claude wants to be there to see how it goes. No, of course he has not been conscripted.

Claude knows all the right people, and he certainly doesn't want to have to kill anyone.

Don't worry about cancelling your visit to Monaco. Claude is quite sure all this war scare will be over soon. Not even Hitler would attempt to break through the Maginot Line, and as we are obviously not going to invade Germany, what else can the idiots do but make peace?

She was playing in the pool with the children when Marco suddenly appeared.

'Darling! What a lovely surprise. What are you doing home at this time of day?' She sat on the edge of the pool and shook her hair free from her bathing cap.

'I have to move up north for a few weeks. I can spend the rest of the day with you, but I must leave tomorrow morning.' He saw on her face the look of fear he dreaded. 'Don't be alarmed, sweetheart. I will still be at a desk and as soon as I arrive I will telephone with a number you can use to get me at any time. And I will come down to see you whenever I can. Now, I will put on my swim suit and join you all in the pool. Ugh!' He added in mock horror as he tested the temperature with his hand. 'I must be mad!'

Drying in the sun an hour later, with iced drinks, Jacqueline told him about her mother's letter.

'Yes, I've been thinking about her.' He sounded quite serious. 'I don't think she should go back to Rouen at present. Why don't you ask her to stay here for a while? You seem to be getting on a bit better with her now.'

'Here? Why? What on earth's the matter? Why shouldn't she go back?'

'Haven't you heard the news? The Germans have attacked Holland and Belgium. Rouen is now uncomfortably near the fighting.'

'No, I hadn't heard. Both the radio accumulators are dry. But how can Belgium have been attacked? And Holland? They're neutral.'

251

'But they were mobilising. I suppose Germany interpreted that as a threat.'

She frowned. 'Didn't I read somewhere that France has extended the Maginot Line along the Belgian border?' She saw his lips tighten. He had been about to make some retort – but changed his mind.

Instead he said, 'If I were you, I would try to get through to the Le Mans exchange and see if you can locate their hotel. Try and find her before she returns home.'

Jacqueline stared at him long and hard. 'You know something. What is it? Surely you can tell me?'

'I don't know anything for sure. Nobody here knows what is going to happen. All I can say is that if Hitler does decide to go into France he has the arms to do it. And I doubt if the Maginot Line will stop him.'

'Oh!' She closed her eyes and lifted her face to the sun. It scorched her skin, but failed to reach the chill in her veins. Then, as the full implications filtered through . . . oh, my God, Jean-Paul! He will be called up. Well, there was nothing she could do about that, but Anna? She would have to get out of France, and quickly.

She wrestled all afternoon and evening with telephone operators and switchboards. At last she got through to Le Mans and explained who she was trying to contact. The operator either couldn't hear her, or couldn't understand her Italian accent.

'Qu'est ce que vous voulez? 'Allo. 'Allo. Qu'est ce que c'est que ça? Qu'est que vous voulez?' And eventually they were disconnected.

Jacqueline nearly wept with frustration.

There was a letter for her next morning, postmarked Le Mans, addressed in a strange hand. It was from Claude.

. . . thought I had better let you know that your mother was involved in an accident yesterday. It is not very serious, but she was bruised and badly shaken. Her right arm is broken so she will not be able to write for a while.

252

She is still in hospital and the doctor does not think she will be well enough to make the journey home for at least ten days . . .

Marco had left. She tried telephoning Le Mans again, but with even less success than before. Her mind spun round and round in circles. Claude had told Anna the Maginot Line would hold. Marco said it wouldn't – and he would probably know more about it than Claude. But he hadn't said the Germans would definitely invade France. Did Anna still have a Rumanian passport? But even if she did, she was still half Jewish and if the Germans did get to Rouen, would she meet the same fate as her brother? It was a possibility.

But what could she, Jacqueline, do about it stuck here in Italy? Nothing, short of going to fetch her mother.

Her eyes opened wide.

She hadn't consciously considered it. They were just tired thoughts tumbling out of her brain. But slowly the thoughts took shape. It seemed quite a logical idea. She was a good driver. She had driven with Marco up to Nice and Cannes several times. This time she would just have to go further, but how much further? Maps. There were Michelin road maps in Marco's bureau.

She laid them out on the dining table, calculated distances, made notes regarding money, fuel and clothes. It was like being back in business – she had something to think about at last.

But wasn't she just playing? Wasn't this just a game to keep herself amused? Or was she serious?

The telephone rang.

That would be Marco. What would he think of the plan? She doubted if he would approve. He might even forbid her to go.

She picked up the receiver. 'Hallo?' She wouldn't mention the idea to him – then she could make up her own mind later.

But of course she had already decided to go.

253

May – June 1940

Caesar's spirit, ranging for revenge,
With Ate by his side, come hot from hell,
Shall in these confines, with a monarch's voice
Cry, 'Havoc!' and let slip the dogs of war.

William Shakespeare, *Julius Caesar*

IT TOOK hours to get to sleep that night, and consequently
Jacqueline overslept. While gulping a hurried breakfast in
the kitchen she gave Rosita and Jacob instructions for
looking after the children.

She told them she was going to stay in Rome for a couple
of days with friends and might go on with them to their
seaside home. She couldn't say exactly when she would
return. Jacob gave her a very odd look – she had never
done anything like this before – but said nothing.

The bank in Rome was full and she had to stand in two
frustrating lines, first for lire and then to buy French francs.

A hardware shop on the outskirts of the city was able
to supply her with four ten-litre fuel cans which she filled
at a nearby station and stowed in the trunk, at the same
time filling her tank to capacity.

There were numerous army vehicles on the Appian
Way, but she was still able to reach Florence in time for
lunch, then on, joining the coast road west of Pisa, to
Spetza. By now she was feeling tired, so she allowed herself
half an hour for coffee and a rather stodgy piece of cake.
She had never driven any distance alone, and her nerves
had been taut as she left Rome, wondering if she had

started something that would prove to be beyond her. But why should it be beyond her? Several of their acquaintances drove to Paris and back quite regularly. She was surprised at how refreshing the short break had been, as she headed on to Genoa.

She wanted to pass through the old port during darkness. Marco was stationed there, he had told her last night, and though the chances of him seeing her were remote, she didn't want anyone to report seeing his car. He might even telephone ahead and have her stopped at the border.

The map hadn't really conveyed how tortuously the road wound inland again to avoid the mountains which reached westward right down to the sea along this stretch of coast, and when she finally rejoined the shoreline she was entangled with heavy traffic caused by more army lorries filled with troops. They moved very slowly and it was nearly half past nine before she entered Genoa.

By now she was utterly exhausted – but dared not stop until she came to an almost deserted stretch of road which took her into Vitri, where she had planned to spend the night. The back of her neck and shoulders burned with tension and she realised she had been hunched over the wheel. She drew up outside an unlikely looking building with crumbling plaster which claimed, according to the faded sign, to be an hotel. It was. And it did have a vacant room – but no food. There was a café just across the street, they pointed out, and she reluctantly left her room for a plate of spaghetti. It was well cooked and delicious, but she should have known that it would lie in a lump on her chest all night, giving her nightmares.

There was a long, dark tunnel with headlights coming straight at her, but she couldn't stop because she was being chased – by Claude in a racing car. Then there were soldiers in a lorry calling at her, but when she looked more closely they were cows, mooing.

She woke exhausted.

In the spotty mirror she looked at the bags under her

eyes. If she was this tired already, she wouldn't get half way to Le Mans before Anna left.

Downstairs, coffee and rolls were served in a rather dirty public bar. The thick, sweet espresso helped her to shake off the tiredness and think clearly. Today she would take it more easily, pause for more short breaks and stop earlier for the night. There was no point in arriving at her destination on the point of collapse.

It would be so good to see Anna again. Judging by her letters there seemed to have been a subtle change in her since they had last met. The cold, selfish arrogance was no longer apparent. Jacqueline had been surprised that Anna had stayed with the awful Claude, but there was never a criticism of him and lots of references to 'Claude and I'. Could people really change? Was it possible for Anna to be a warm person?

And what about herself? Could she, Jacqueline, ever forgive and forget what Anna had tried unsuccessfully to do to her? Perhaps if they both made an effort to understand each other more, a warmer relationship would develop between them. One had to allow for the fact that they were not only different generations, but also of different ideas, different ways of life . . . but it would be wonderful if they could learn to love each other.

Surprisingly, the border presented no problems, and for the first time she truly appreciated the immense value of possessing an American passport in a Europe distorted by war. After a light lunch in Cannes she took the inland route into the hills, avoiding the busy streets of Marseilles, and at dusk drew up in front of the Hotel Europe in Avignon, where she took a very comfortable room.

All the aches in her muscles and joints eased as she lay soaking in a hot bath. A maid carried away her clothes to be laundered overnight. She dressed and went down to dinner and ordered the gourmet menu and an expensive bottle of burgundy.

She thought about Marco. He would be telephoning the villa again this evening, asking if they had word of her.

Might he guess what she was doing? Would he have tried to stop her?

Then she thought again about Anna. It was now seven days since Claude had written about her accident and said the doctor advised against her travelling for ten days. Pray God she didn't decide to disobey him and leave earlier. Better leave here at dawn tomorrow to have any hope of reaching Bourges by nightfall; then, by her reckoning, she should be in Le Mans on the afternoon of the ninth day.

Before getting into the car she pushed the driving seat back a couple of notches, determined to be more comfortable and relaxed. The road to Lyons was so good she decided against branching on to the more direct route through St Etienne at Andance; the mountain road would certainly be much slower. Strangely, although there was plenty of southbound traffic, the northbound carriageway was quite clear and she raced ahead. This was easy and relaxed driving. The big car responded smoothly and she enjoyed the sensation of speed.

So far there had been no problem in obtaining fuel. Indeed, she wondered if the spare cans in the trunk had been an unnecessary precaution, until she saw the first lines of vehicles outside the garages in Macon. Once on the Bourges road, she hoped to fill up at one of the smaller towns, but the needle on her fuel gauge was stationary on nought when she finally pulled into a forecourt in Paray le Monial. She hooted several times before a woman appeared, flour up to her elbows, and insisted she had no fuel. Jacqueline, in turn, insisted that she read the fuel gauge. The woman shrugged and piped in half a tank, looked Jacqueline in the eye without flinching, and charged her double the advertised price. Thereafter she coaxed a few litres here and there from whomever she could.

Then the traffic really started to amass. First there were big cars, some chauffeur driven. Then smaller and older and slower ones with fast modern models pulling out to overtake straight into her path.

The entire population of Bourges seemed to be on the

streets. Jacqueline could not help pausing to admire the beautiful old city, the site of so much exciting French history, dominated by the huge cathedral with its apron of neatly tended flowers around the War Memorial, gazing down through the centuries at the flow of people across its ancient bridge. It would be a lovely place to visit, in other circumstances.

The first two hotels she tried were full, so they said, and at the third no one was about. She rang the bell three times before a little girl in pigtails emerged from the kitchen.

'*Où est votre maman?*' Jacqueline asked.

'*Je ne sais pas, madame. Que voulez-vous?*'

'*Une chambre, s'il vous plaît.*'

'*Oui, madame.*' She stood on tiptoe to pull a key from its hook. '*Venez-vous avec moi,*' and she led the way upstairs.

The room was adequate, with heavy, old-fashioned furniture and one of those disastrous French beds constructed of wire mesh stretched from head to footboard, so that one lay U-shaped all night and rose half crippled in the morning. The probable cause, Jacqueline thought wryly, of all the elderly bent backs in France.

Downstairs the dining room was empty, and even the little girl had disappeared. Wandering out into the street Jacqueline had no difficulty in locating food; she simply followed her nose. It was a little café beside the market, filled with noisy diners. A young woman, thumbs well into the sauce on two loaded dinner plates, found her a place at a table already occupied by three men, all shouting and gesticulating.

'Messieurs?' Jacqueline paused before sitting down.

''Dame,' they nodded briefly and continued. Their dialect was difficult to follow, but she gathered they were discussing the war. One of them was quite confident that the Maginot Line would hold; his thin, dour friend seemed positive the Germans were already attacking Amiens; the third had been told that the enemy was even now entering Paris.

This was not the sort of café where one was shown a menu. One sat and waited. A carafe of wine was placed on the table, together with a jug of water. Then a tureen of delicious fresh soup, thickened with yesterday's bread, was left for one to take as many helpings as one wanted. Bread, baked within the hour, cut into thick chunks from a wheel-shaped loaf was served with a coarse terrine. Lamb chops followed with sauté potatoes. Then salad and goat's cheese. Jacqueline calculated the rate of exchange and decided she must have misunderstood the price of the meal. But she hadn't, it was amazingly cheap.

Before leaving, she asked the patron for news of the war. He too, was confident the Maginot Line would hold. 'There are a great many scaremongers about,' he said. 'Telling everyone to flee south. But why leave your home to the mercy of looters? When you return everything will be gone.' He was one of life's fat, jolly optimists. But who to believe? Him, or two of her fellow diners?

There was another noisy argument going on at the foot of the hotel stairs. She couldn't tell if the hotelier was part of it, but since they all ignored her, she climbed straight past them to her room. As she undressed she wondered if she would perhaps be a fool to go on. She desperately wanted to reach her mother, to take her beyond the reach of German pogroms, but she did have her own responsibilities to think of. She must not risk being unable to return to the children and Marco. Though what was one more day? The Nazis had swept through the Low Countries because they had met no resistance. It would be different here in France. Even if they did manage to advance against the combined French and British armies, it would have to be very slowly. She would be in Le Mans tomorrow, so next day she would be driving south again. If she drove due south she would be well ahead of any advance. Then, if it was safe, she would drive across to the Riviera and back into Italy, the way she had come. If that did not look possible, she would continue south into Spain and return by sea.

She dressed before daylight. Another early start should give her some mileage in hand before the traffic built up. There was no one about to take payment for her room – and nothing to eat. But she could always buy a baguette, pâté and wine en route.

The streets were surprisingly busy and it took nearly half an hour to cross the old bridge north over the Yevre on to the main road. Vierzon was packed with people coming south from Orleans. It took ages for the traffic from Tours to filter through, but hers was the only car going northwest – which was rather disturbing. Could all of these people really just be scaremongers? There was no doubt now that many were abandoning their homes: chairs and mattresses, pots and pans, were tied on car roofs. She even saw a pair of china dogs in the rear window of an elderly Renault. The treasures of family homes were moving slowly south, on what might have been an uproariously funny collection of conveyances had it not been for the fear and distress they represented.

After Vierzon the road was fairly clear. Lack of breakfast adding to the ache of fear inside, she stopped the car in a tiny village and ordered coffee and rolls in the local brasserie. The patron and his wife were engaged in a heated argument, ably assisted by their customers. It was the inevitable subject: Were the Boches coming or not? Was it worth leaving for the south? As the wife pushed her coffee towards her, she asked Jacqueline where she was going.

'My mother is in hospital in Le Mans,' she explained. 'I am going to fetch her.'

'But that is north, madame. You cannot go north, the road is blocked. This road is clear, but Alphonse here . . .' she indicated an elderly man leaning on the bar over a crème de menthe, '. . . he has just come from Tours and he says nobody can move.'

Alphonse joined in. 'She would do better to turn south over the Cher at Croix, then cross the big road south of Tours. The traffic will be easier there and she can stay on

260

the smaller road till Azay le Rideau.' Jacqueline hastily spread her map on the bar counter, trying to follow the place names. 'She can cross the Loire at Langeais. It is longer, but it will be quicker, *n'est pas*?' It seemed to make sense.

The village shop was next door. She purchased bread and pâté and a litre of wine. She would have preferred water, but there wasn't any bottled, and she didn't want to risk 'French tummy' by drawing from the pump. She had to join the flood of refugees for a short distance south of Tours before crossing to the eastbound road, after which it was easy – except that the road was narrow, badly cambered and full of potholes.

There might have been a glimpse of the beautiful Chateau at Azay le Rideau, had she paused to peer through the big iron gates. She remembered seeing a magnificent picture of it, pointed grey turrets reflected in the lake on which it stood.

Still avoiding the main roads, she pulled on to the grass patch in front of a farm gate for a late lunch. It had been tempting to eat whilst driving, but fear and worry about whether she would ever find Anna had added to her weariness and she decided it would be better to rest. The crisp baguette, bought five hours ago, had become leathery. She tore at it with teeth and fingers, dug pieces into the pâté which was still in the paper, and scattered crumbs all over the car. She had never drunk cheap, unlabelled wine from the neck of a litre bottle before.

Leftovers went into the dashboard glove compartment. The car duster served as a crumb brush, and she climbed over the gate to use the traditional French toilet facilities, closely scrutinised by four cows.

The narrow, winding road was painfully slow. Jacqueline repeatedly checked her watch as Le Mans drew nearer. Tomorrow would be the tenth day since Claude had written – the day Anna would leave for the north, if they hadn't already done so. Or if they hadn't joined the flight south. But if they were still there, she had only a few hours left in which to find them. But how? The map gave no indication of the size of the town. She would just have to try all the hotels, starting with the most expensive and on down the price range – if she could find a list of hotels.

A sign indicated a major road ahead, left to Nantes, right to Le Mans. Perhaps she could pick up speed on the better road. Her heart sank as she approached the human river ahead, moving at a snail's pace towards the west coast. They had spread right across the road, barring her way.

For a moment she panicked. It was impossible, solid. She would never reach Le Mans. Then anger took over. She had a right to part of that road. Nobody could prevent her from driving north on the right hand side. The heel of her hand pressed down on the horn and stayed there. Steadily the car edged out, forcing oncoming vehicles to pull away against their neighbours on the crown of the road. The hub of a farm cart scratched past her offside wing. People shouted, hooted, waved fists at her, but she ignored them, and gradually, with nearside wheels off the tarmac, she made progress. An ancient lorry had broken down in her path and, pulling out to avoid it, she collided head on with a car emerging from behind it. The pace was too slow to do more than smash a headlight and make a few dents, but the other driver jumped out of his car and wrenched open her door to shout at her.

'*Tais-toi*,' she shouted back. '*Vas-t'en*,' slammed the door shut again and locked it; reversed into the side of another car and, with horn still blaring, forced her way forward, disregarding the chaos behind.

The big signpost suddenly appeared beside the car – Le Mans. Houses, footpaths, and even more people. There was every description of vehicle imaginable, in hopeless confusion. People were shouting and weeping, trying to turn to escape the tangle. A frightened horse reared and deposited half the contents of its overloaded cart on to the bonnet of a shiny Citroën. There was no hope of moving the car another inch. She would have to walk, but how far? And could she possibly find her mother in this mêlée?

An old man was leaning with his bicycle against a lamp-post.

'*Pardon, M'sieur, je cherche le plus grand hôtel. Où-est-ce, s'il-vous-plaît?*' She hoped he was a local.

He was. '*Là.*' He pointed with the stem of his pipe.

It was only fifty yards away, a modest building with louvre shutters behind tiny wrought iron balconies. Could he possibly be right? She weaved round the stationary traffic and pushed through a swing door where the usual noise of heated discussion greeted her. The vestibule was jammed with bodies, sweating from energetic arm-waving. Trying to elbow through, she was pushed into the empty dining room -- empty save for one person. Anna was sitting beside one of the tables, her plaster cast resting among cutlery on the checkered cloth.

Claude found them clinging together, weeping.

'Jacqueline? How the devil did you get here?' He leaned against the doorpost in amazement.

'With difficulty.' She blew her nose. 'I'm starving. Is it dinner time yet?'

'They haven't served food in this place all day,' Claude growled.

'Well, let's go and raid the kitchen.' Tired as she was, she wouldn't let hunger add to her problems. 'Come on.'

Anna followed them. 'Claude went out and bought some fresh bread and saucisson for lunch.'

'We all need a good meal, then,' Jacqueline commented.

She chopped and sautéed vegetables, adding liquid from a stock-pot for soup. She hacked a plucked fowl into portions and fried them, heated a fat bath for chipped potatoes. She was almost numb with exhaustion; legs and arms moved as if made of lead. She found it hard to concentrate or to think about what she was doing. But she had arrived in time, had found Anna. That was all that mattered. Her worries were over, once they got out of the traffic jam. Then they would be home in a couple of days.

One-handed, Anna washed salad. Claude tapped the barrel of house wine. They carried their feast into the dining room, where they were soon joined by a group who sat at another table – and waited.

'Are you wanting a meal?' Claude asked.

'Yes. Where is the waitress?'

'There isn't one. Or a cook. We've been in the kitchen and made our own,' he told them proudly.

Amid much laughter the would-be diners trouped out into the kitchen, apparently to follow their example.

Claude explained that his car was stuck in the hotel garage and the yard was full of vehicles jammed against the doors. Half of the owners seemed to be missing – with their keys. There was little hope of moving the car in the near future.

'Even if I could move it, I wouldn't know which direction to take.' He shrugged, palms turned out. 'There is no doubt, now, that the Boches are in France. But I don't see the point in abandoning the factories in Rouen. I think perhaps I should accompany you girls south, at least part of the way. Then I will return home.'

Jacqueline sighed with relief. 'Please, if you would. Being the only one driving all the time is so tiring. When should we start?'

'Soon as possible, I think. People are saying our forces have retreated south of the Somme already. Ah! All that talk about the strength of the Maginot Line! We have been living in a fool's paradise for too long.' He shook his head and covered his face with his hands.

'I think we should have a few hours' sleep first,' Anna suggested. 'If we get up at about four, we can start off in Jacqueline's car by five. Agreed?'

'Good idea,' Jacqueline nodded. 'Now, I'm going back to the kitchen to "borrow" some things we will need on the journey.' She smiled. 'I'll add some extra francs to the bill when we leave.'

*   *   *

264

When Anna and Claude groped their way downstairs in the dark next morning, they discovered Jacqueline waiting for them in the kitchen, with hot coffee. She had toasted stale bread and fried eggs. She and Anna forced the food into dry mouths, but Claude's appetite seemed unaffected.

'When you come back this way after leaving us, will you collect my suitcases and take them back with you to Rouen, Claude?' There was no doubt in Anna's mind that this hiatus would soon be over and that she, too, would return.

Claude was about to argue but changed his mind. 'Yes, yes, my love, of course I will,' he assured her.

The congestion outside didn't seem to have altered during the night. They lifted their bags and the pillowcase full of Jacqueline's loot from the kitchen over bonnets and bumpers to the opposite footpath.

'I think the hotel patron must have left with his family. I haven't seen anyone who looked as though they belonged there,' Jacqueline remarked as she unlocked the boot, which now reeked of gasolene. She explained about the spare cans.

'Luckily I have only had to use one so far, and the tank is three-quarters full.'

Claude walked around the car, surveying the damage. 'Hm. I'd like to see what you did to the other blokes,' he commented. 'Now, how do we get out of here?'

Jacqueline realised that neither of them had any idea of the problems ahead. She got behind the wheel, moved forward till she touched a farm cart, shunted back to the wall of a house . . . and did it again and again until she was able to drive away, down the footpath.

'Hey, what the hell do you think you're doing?' Claude exclaimed as she smashed a shop signboard and nudged café chairs out of the way. 'Come. Let me drive.'

'If we don't do it this way we won't move at all. How do you think I got here, driving against all this?' She pressed long and hard on the hooter at a family sleeping on a mattress across her path. They got up, but didn't move the bedding, so she drove over it. That got them awake and shouting.

Claude remained silent.

Their progress only lasted the length of the footpath. When it ended they were forced to accept the fractional forward movement of the main stream. After passing the junction with the road to Nantes, the pace quickened slightly.

'Why are all these people going west?' asked Anna.

'Maybe they hope to find boats to take them to Spain or Britain,' Claude suggested. 'But only a fraction of them have a hope of getting away.'

By mid-morning they had covered barely twenty miles.

'I think we would make more progress if we changed to the minor road I came up on,' Jacqueline remarked. 'Let's take the next turning.'

But even the little road from Chateau du Loir was busy.

Claude took a turn at the wheel, his fingers drumming impatiently. 'This is a waste of gasolene,' he fumed. 'With this crowd on the road we have no hope of buying any more.'

'Do you think we could stop for a while?' Anna asked from the back seat. 'I would love to drink something.'

Jacqueline noted how the bruises and scratches on her face stood out livid against her pallor. Apparently she and Claude had climbed up on to a disused spectator stand for a better view of the racing cars out on the Le Mans circuit. Claude's weight had been too much for the rotting wood, and when it collapsed he had bounced clear of trouble, but her mother had become entangled and had been trapped for nearly two hours before Claude could get help to her.

'Yes, why not,' she agreed. 'I'm thirsty too.'

A farmyard came into view, so they drove in behind the house and parked in the shade of a barn.

'This will give the car a chance to cool off,' Claude said, stretching his legs.

Apart from a few hens there was no sign of life, so they

spread their lunch on the yard table under a tree, and settled down to eat and rest.

'I can hear a big engine – several, in fact.' Anna tilted her head towards the sound. 'I wonder what they are?'

'Sounds like aircraft to me.' Claude moved away from the tree for a better view. 'Yes, there they are, flying in formation. They're very low.'

Jacqueline joined him, watching one after the other of the planes break formation to swoop over the road they had just left. Smoke appeared on the wings followed by a loud clattering. It was several moments before she understood what was happening.

'Holy Jesus! They're shooting at the people on the road,' Claude shouted. 'Quick, take cover. They could come this way.'

The back door of the farmhouse was unlocked. They stood around the kitchen table facing each other in horror, hearts pounding and knees weak with terror.

Jacqueline tried to speak, but could not make a sound come out. Eventually words tumbled out in gasps. 'What does it mean? Are the Germans that close behind us? What can we do?'

'I shouldn't think it means they are very close.' Claude mopped at the sweat pouring down his face. 'It could have been a few bombers who had dropped their loads further north. They carry machine-guns as well . . . they were probably just emptying them before returning to base.' He paused and listened. 'They don't seem to be making a second run. We'd better wait for half an hour, though, to be sure.'

Anna slumped into a chair. 'This is going to be a long journey,' she remarked, and closed her eyes.

They listened, waited.

Eventually Claude said, 'It must just have been an isolated strike. Perhaps they realised the people on the road weren't troops, but civilians.'

Jacqueline disappeared, and after a few minutes called

267

down the stairs, 'Claude, will you help me?' She had dragged a mattress on to the landing.

'What are you doing with that?' he asked.

'Taking it out to the car. Grab that end and pull.'

'But you cannot just walk into someone's house and take things,' he remonstrated.

'This is no time to moralise,' she snapped back. 'I intend us to survive this journey. Tied on the roof of the car this just might stop bullets getting through. Come on, Mother, tuck this bolster under your good arm. We can stick it in the rear window. Now, let's find some rope.'

Claude suddenly seemed to get the message; from then on he made every effort to get them as far as possible in safety. He was full of ideas. The farm people had stripped the cupboards of food, but Claude found thirteen eggs in nests in the barn and put them on the stove to boil.

'Hope you're not superstitious,' he attempted to joke. 'But we may as well have them all.'

The air was breathless, the heat scorching as they edged back on to the road; the increased crowd made progress even slower.

Through the open car windows they noted with horror the bullet wounds and blood around them. Some people were sobbing. They wore makeshift bandages, and Jacqueline saw a young woman on a farm cart nursing a dead child, her grieving eyes staring vacantly into space.

The snail's pace allowed too much time to think. The shock and misery of their fellow refugees prompted new waves of fear. Jacqueline's determined optimism melted in the sweltering heat. For the first time she wondered if they would ever reach Italy. Would they be overtaken by the Nazis? Would she and Anna, Jews, survive? Was it possible she might never see the children again? And Marco? And . . . Jean-Paul?

Already the stench of death was everywhere, bringing swarms of flies. To move at all, the physically able had to work in groups, clearing space for their vehicles to pass. A horse lay screaming and threshing in agony. Fortunately someone was carrying a revolver and put it out of its misery, but no one dared do that for the shattered humans.

Claude had his shoulder pressed against the back of a van, pushing it towards the side of the road. He turned to call Jacqueline to drive past and saw her bending over an injured woman.

'What are you doing?' he called.

'Trying to help her, she's in agony,' she replied.

He left the van to put an arm round her shoulders and led her away. 'There is nothing we can do for these people. It would take teams of doctors and nurses with lots of medical equipment and morphine to make any impression.'

Tears ran down her face as she looked around at the tortured bodies. 'We cannot just leave them.'

'We must. Believe me, I wish there was something we could do, but there isn't. And better some of us survive, than all stay here to be killed.'

'Can we not help that old man with his wife's body? He can't just leave her there.'

'No, Jacqueline. He has to make his own choice whether to stay and be killed with her or save himself.'

He was right, of course. Still weeping, she got back into the driving seat.

Cyclists made the best progress. They weaved in and out among the wider vehicles and, when the road became impassable, dismounted, lifted their bikes over hedges or walls, and carried them through the corn and wheat until the obstacles were passed.

They had reached the top of a long hill just south of Mazieres where they had a perfect view of the Loire and Cher flowing parallel through the silt islets of willows, when they heard more aeroplanes behind them.

This time there was nowhere to run. They ducked low in the car as bullets spattered like rain over the cavalcade, followed by momentary silence. Then the shrieks and wails started as the living discovered their wounds and their dead.

269

Anna sobbed in terror. Claude and Jacqueline sat up rigid, staring at the holes in the dashboard and at the scarred windscreen. The mattress had done nothing to prevent bullets ripping through the roof. Yet they had been unbelievably lucky. Beside them a woman sprawled over the side of a lorry; the back of her head was missing. Anna retched and just got her head out of the window in time to deposit her lunch on the running board.

People were running towards buildings a hundred yards away. Claude and Jacqueline half carried Anna into a stable already packed with human misery. The stink of manure and ammonia made them choke. Claude vanished for a few minutes, then returned to lead them to a vacant pigsty. Sitting on the stone floor, Jacqueline produced a bottle of water from the now filthy pillowcase.

'Let's eat,' Claude said. Anna shuddered. 'Come on, we never finished lunch, remember? We must keep our strength up. It will be dark in a couple of hours, then we can move without fear of any more attacks.'

Jacqueline laid the food out on her lap. She had discovered the remains of yesterday's lunch in the glove pocket. The terrine helped them to swallow the dry bread. They had one of Claude's boiled eggs each. The wine was vinegary, but they managed to drink some.

Anna shivered.

'You are cold, my love, and there are all those blankets in the car. I'll fetch them.' Claude started to crawl out on his hands and knees.

'No, please don't,' Anna begged.

'It's all right. I'll be back in no time. There are no planes around now.'

He was wrong.

Minutes later they heard the roar of engines followed by the earth-shaking explosions of bombs. Anna shrieked and ran to the door. Jacqueline held her back.

They waited. But Claude did not return.

Nor did the planes. After a while Jacqueline left Anna, shivering and weeping in the sty, with orders not to move.

270

Taking a circuitous route under hedges she reached the road and saw a pall of smoke and flame rearing up over the tattered remains of the procession and from what had been their car.

There was no sign of Claude.

The grass verge was strewn with bodies, some living, some dead. She hurried along, ignoring the pleas for help, searching. He was there, alive, but only just. Blood soaked the grass around him; she couldn't tell where it came from. He still clutched the blankets.

'Claude,' she murmured.

His eyes found her face. 'Take these to your mother.' His voice was a choked whisper. 'She's cold.' His lips tried to smile. 'My fault. I was greedy. Should have left one of those eggs behind.'

Blood started to trickle out of his mouth; he gasped for breath.

'You'll be all right. There are only ten left.'

She kissed his cheek and stroked his hair, but he no longer looked at her . . . or breathed. One of the blankets was soaked in blood. She spread it over him; there was nothing else she could do. She bundled up the other two blankets . . . and paused. Dropping to her knees she removed his watch and ring and put them with the contents of his pockets into her handbag. Then she went back to Anna.

Despite the heat of the day, the night was cold. They huddled together in the blankets, Anna shaking and sobbing. There was no hope of sleep for either of them, so, after a while, they talked.

'Have you noticed how surprised you can be when someone you like does something bad . . . or vice versa?' Jacqueline asked.

'You never liked Claude very much, did you?' Anna knew what was in her mind.

'Not until today. But then I never really knew him before. I feel badly about that.'

'I don't blame you. We both behaved atrociously in Italy, but it was largely my fault.' She sat up and leaned against the back of the sty, drawing the blanket up under her chin. 'Sounds silly, but do you know, I didn't much like him then, either. I only went off with him because he seemed such a good meal ticket. I thought him loud and gauche. So I just drank like hell and pretended not to notice.'

'When did you change your mind about him?'

'The day he threw me face down on the bed and tanned my bottom with his slipper.'

Jacqueline giggled into the darkness.

'I had been on a gin binge,' Anna went on. 'We had been at a party where I was making wild passes at some of the men. Claude took me home in a rage. Said he was damned if he would have the woman he loved behaving like a drunken whore.' She sighed. 'He is the only man who really loved me in my whole life.' She started to sob again.

Jacqueline wondered whether to tell her about Bill Stevenson, but decided against it. Later, perhaps.

Anna blew her nose. 'I've been so vicious to you. Nearly ruined your life. Looking back, I feel so terrible, so guilty.'

'I suppose the whole attitude to family and social life has changed since you were a girl,' Jacqueline mused.

'Oh, it has. My parents believed that anything and everything could and should be sacrificed for the sake of family advancement, even to the extent of offering a daughter's honour to a prince or nobleman. I resented not being allowed to develop my own life so much – it is ridiculous that I should have done the same to you. When I think of the uproar in the family and the year of misery I experienced when I had you. It was hell.' Anna sighed, and fell silent.

'I think you must have held me responsible for that hell, even if you didn't realise it at the time,' Jacqueline murmured.

'Perhaps, but that doesn't excuse me, does it? God! When I think how I handed you to Carol on a plate – that dreadful, lecherous beast. And I should know. I've slept with him often enough. Tell me . . .' she suddenly sat bolt upright. 'Why on earth did you come to fetch me?'

'Because I love you. You see, something happened about four years ago, not long after your visit to Italy. It made me understand how unhappy you must have been for most of your life. After that I realised that your coldness, the way you tried to use me, were part of a determination not to care, to feel. You had built a protective shell round yourself. You seem to have changed, now. Perhaps Claude broke your shell with his slipper.' She put her arms around her mother as she began to weep again.

Anna found a wheelbarrow. It had been used for cement and had rusty holes in the bottom, the wheel squeaked badly, but it revolved. It would certainly carry their belongings. Jacqueline was convinced they would be safer south of the river. They were not able to sleep on the cold, stone floor, and a brilliant moon lit the road, so there seemed little point in staying.

Others had had the same idea. They walked in single file between the ditch and the stationary vehicles, ghostly figures drifting by. They had to ignore the groans beside them. It did seem dreadful, but without medical supplies or adequate light there was nothing even a doctor could do, for so many.

A little car lay upsidedown in a ditch, wheels to the sky. As they drew level, Jacqueline and Anna heard a thin wail; it sounded like a child. It was too hard to resist this one. They slid down the low bank to investigate. Jacqueline lay on her stomach to peer through an open window, but it was pitch black inside. She put her arm in as far as she could. Her hand met a sticky mess. She jerked back, shuddering, banging her elbow on the door-frame. The child cried again, so she tried again. Groping in the opposite direction she found it.

'Hello. Would you like to come out through the window to me?' she coaxed.

Using the roof as a floor, the child crawled towards her. 'Maman won't talk to me. I want my Maman to talk.'

'Come and let me talk to you, instead.'

A mop of platinum blonde curls caught the moonlight. Jacqueline passed her to Anna and stood up. 'I'm going to see if I can borrow a torch.'

A man returned with her, unwilling to allow his torch out of his sight. He shone it into the car and they could see an elderly couple and a young woman, lying in grotesque postures, obviously dead.

'What will we do with the little girl?' Anna asked the torch bearer.

'Take her or leave her. It's up to you,' he said over his shoulder as he walked away.

'But we don't know who she is or where to take her!' she shouted after him.

'Take her wherever you are going. She's yours now,' he shouted back.

As if they hadn't enough problems, but they couldn't just leave her; so they played a game of 'rides in the wheelbarrow', and when they asked her name she said, 'Bobo.' And that was what they called her.

Pushing the wheelbarrow for a mile was a strenuous effort. After two and a half miles Jacqueline found it almost impossible. She frequently stopped to rest aching arms and shoulders – remembering that nightmare escape from the Chateau Dumescu – and was sorely tempted to abandon it. But it not only held the two blankets, the pillowslip containing the remains of their food and drink, and the bag she had grabbed as they bolted to the pigsty. It also substituted as a pram for Bobo. Although the child was tiny – a very small two-year-old, Jacqueline guessed by her speech and movements – she was still very heavy to carry for any distance. Anna could barely keep up at all; she certainly couldn't carry anything. So she staggered on, the weight of her load increasing with every step. Even when they reached the river, they had to follow the road west along the north bank before reaching the Langeais bridge. A family passed them before they crossed. They had young children and Jacqueline told them about Bobo and asked if they would take her, but the young mother shook her head.

'I haven't enough food for ourselves. I couldn't feed her.'

So Bobo stayed.

No one crossed the bridge with them; everyone else was heading for the west coast. They trudged on to the regular squeak of the barrow wheel, alarming the river birds who were roosting for the night. Though nearly faint with exhaustion, they were reluctant to make another stop before they found shelter, because of the heavy dew. But no buildings appeared. Casting her mind back, Jacqueline could only recall a pair of gates between the village of Azay le Rideau and the Loire.

It had become pitch dark, so they were lucky to find them. Jacqueline set the barrow down gently so as not to disturb the sleeping child.

'Shall we see if the gates will open? Surely there must be some sort of building up the drive. What do you think?'

'Let's try.' Anna was swaying on her feet. 'Look, isn't this little side gate open? Yes. Come on.'

The drive wound through trees and bushes. There were no weeds and it seemed well kept, which raised their hopes. They found themselves in a courtyard surrounded by large buildings, but it was impossible to tell what they were. Jacqueline sat Anna on a stone balustrade while she explored. There was no reply when she tugged on the bell by a huge studded door. She twisted the great iron ring and heard the latch lift, but the door was bolted from inside. Eventually she found an unlocked door into what felt, in the dark, like a dairy, at the far end of which an open door led into the kitchens. With the help of the remaining matches purloined from the Le Mans hotel, she found and lit an oil lamp.

It was either a small chateau or large country house and had obviously been lived in within the past few days, judging by food in the cupboards. A large drawing room, a dining room big enough for a banquet, library, study and ladies' sitting room all led off from the vast baronial hallway, from the centre of which a wide marble staircase carried up to the bedrooms.

She went back outside. 'Come on, Mother, we are going to make ourselves at home. There is a beautiful feather bed waiting for you.' Jacqueline put an arm round Anna and supported her up the stairs, tucking her into someone else's used sheets without a second thought. She fetched Bobo and climbed into a vast, canopied bed with her. All three slept until nearly midday.

She had never milked a cow. Fortunately the animal was as eager to have her distended udder relieved as Jacqueline was to obtain fresh milk for them all. There were tins and packets of food in the cupboards, so they were able to lunch well.

They were in an old, renovated chateau; Jacqueline discovered the name engraved above an archway into the courtyard: Chateau Lavare. Compared with its neighbours, Azay le Rideau and Chinon, it was quite small. It did not open to the public; all the rooms were apparently in normal use, the bathrooms and kitchens well modernised.

Anna was still quite weak. There were black rings around her eyes and alarming spots of red in her otherwise grey-white face.

'Why don't you lie on a sofa in the drawing room where it is cool,' Jacqueline suggested. 'I am going out to search for some kind of transport.'

She had noticed some horses in a nearby field. Two were sturdy cobs and with them in mind she prowled through the stables and outhouses. She found the perfect answer – someone had loved horse-drawn vehicles, old and new; there was quite a collection. A stately glass-windowed carriage which would look superb behind a team of four matched greys, a high-perch phaeton, fast but perilous; a

276

little, brightly painted donkey cart and, at the end, a fairly modern lightweight but roomy carriage with fore and aft folding hoods like a landaulet.

Halters and loaf sugar in hand, she spent a weary hour trudging around the field before finally bringing in the animals to be fitted with equipment. The saddle room was filled with all manner of harnesses, and it took time to sort out appropriate collars and traces, bridles and reins.

Twice during that day she heard aircraft and thudding noises in the distance. In the peace of the chateau garden, it was hard to believe the German Army were approaching. She was too tired to worry about losing a day on the road; the wheelbarrow had left her aching in every muscle. The tension and the shock of Claude's death were exhausting too. She looked forward to a long soak in a hot bath, a light supper, and an early night.

Entering through the kitchen she heard Bobo crying. The little girl was alone in the drawing room. She ran through the rooms, calling, and eventually discovered Anna in a bathroom, vomiting.

Selfishly, she wanted to weep. She was at the end of her tether. Her strength gone, she just wanted to give up. Bobo tugged at her hand. Looking down she thought of Katarina and Francisco; she looked at her mother sitting on the floor holding the lavatory with her good hand, sweat running down her fevered face, too weak to move. Jacqueline slumped to her knees, clasping Bobo against her and lifted her face to heaven.

'Dear God, Holy Jesus, Sweet Mother of Christ, help me. Give me strength,' she begged.

It was impossible to move Anna the next day. Jacqueline had catnapped on a chaise longue at the foot of her mother's bed, trying to comfort her when she cried out with stomach cramps, bathing her face, helping her on and off the commode a dozen times and holding a porcelain chamber pot while she vomited. She had found a half-full bottle of kaolin and morphine with which to dose her. Eventually she was able to leave the sickroom for a couple of hours to go to her own bed.

In some respects the extra day at the chateau proved to be a blessing. She was able to rest a bit longer and assemble an excellent hamper of provisions. She loaded the carriage with such an assortment of useful items, including a huge bundle of hay and half a sack of oats, that by nightfall it looked more like a gypsy caravan than a gentleman's equipage.

The ladies of the household had departed leaving only old and worn underwear in the drawers and formal gowns in their wardrobes, but at least they were clean. Jacqueline and Anna 'borrowed' the least unsuitable items they could find, packing a change of clothes for each in a large tapestry bag. They even found some little boy's clothes to fit Bobo, with which she was delighted.

Jacqueline had hoped that by giving each cob a turn in the shafts while the other trotted behind, they might cover fifty miles a day, but she hadn't allowed for the fact that a horse-drawn vehicle is far more tiring to drive than a car. The upright bench seat was uncomfortable, and her arms and back ached before they had covered five miles. Anna was still too weak to even provide comfort when her spirits sagged. If only Claude had still been with them . . . she had worked so hard through her tiredness at the chateau to arrange this means of travel. It had seemed to be the perfect answer to fuel problems – to all their problems. But at this rate it would be impossible to cover more than ten or fifteen miles a day without fainting from exhaustion.

Then they had a stroke of luck.

A haywain lay on its side in the middle of the road, its broken rear wheel lying on the verge. A plump middle-aged woman and a young boy had unhitched their horse and were tying a few possessions to the harness. Both looked miserable at the prospect of a long walk.

Jacqueline had an idea. She pulled the carriage to a halt beside them. 'Want a lift?' she asked hopefully.

They seemed to think she had been sent from heaven. Thérèse le Bel was delighted to share the driving. Her horse took his turn in the shafts, and while she and young Jean changed horses and adjusted traces, Jacqueline and Anna laid out the food for their meals, to which Thérèse added a huge, home-cured ham. She was also heading for the east coast of Spain, where her eldest son worked in an hotel.

Keeping to the minor roads, their progress was slow but steady. Anna slowly recovered from her attack of French tummy, and Jacqueline's muscles became accustomed to handling the reins. Towards dusk each day they kept watch for likely hotels or pensions and were always able to find accommodation of some sort. Each evening Jacqueline begged the use of a telephone and tried to get through to Marco, but the operators in the small country exchanges were unable to make international calls.

Late in the afternoon of 5 June the bizarre cortège trotted through the streets of Toulouse to the Hotel de Ville. Jacqueline was relieved to find it still open and hurried inside to look for an official who could direct her to the Italian Consulate. She was desperate to contact Marco. He would certainly have realised days ago what she had done and would be distraught with worry.

She paced up and down beside the counter and read the dog-eared notices on the walls, while three officials conferred and thumbed through books. Not one of them had ever heard of an Italian Consul in Toulouse.

'Have you looked in the telephone directory?' she asked. It would be typical of an Italian to nail up a consulate sign and tell no one, least of all anyone at the Town Hall, that he was there.

They found it straight away: 'Italian Consul, Signor Bruno Cavero.' Directions to the address were very complicated and in the end one of the men agreed to join them as navigator, and sat on the driving seat with Jacqueline while his cohorts waved him out of sight, hooting with laughter.

The Consul turned out to be a prosperous garage owner, whose forecourt was full of excitable Italians seeking advice on whether or not to remain in France.

'I have told you fifty times,' he shouted at them. 'Italy is neutral. You have nothing to worry about. The French army has held the German forces on the Somme for two weeks, so perhaps now if they are hungry they will retreat. So why don't you all go home and stop panicking?' He turned and saw Jacqueline waiting to speak to him.

'Yes, Signora, what is it?' he asked impatiently.

'I wish to make a telephone call to my husband in Italy, and I need your assistance.'

'To make a phone call?' He looked annoyed.

So was she. 'I have been trying for days to get through, without success. My mother and daughter are with me. We have been travelling for over a week, and my father has been killed on the road by German aircraft. We are tired and urgently in need of your help, as our Italian Consul.'

Her autocratic style of Italian speech alerted him.

'Who is your husband, Signora, and where do we find him?'

'Colonel Count Luzzi di Calitri. He is in Genoa. I have his number here.' She opened her now dilapidated crocodile handbag, which she had hung by its strap across her chest like a school satchel.

'Signora, I apologise for my rudeness. Please, come this way.'

She left the two older women, two children, three horses and the dirty carriage beside the gasolene pumps to follow the now obsequious Consul into his house.

It took a long time. Signor Cavero kept looking at his watch between gesticulations and shouts at the unseen operators. Jacqueline wondered whether he was worrying about an appointment or his vast stomach. She went out to send Anna and Thérèse to a nearby hotel, and returned to wait. Signora Cavero brought in a meal, which they ate on the office desk.

It was nine o'clock when she finally heard Marco's voice. 'My darling, my darling, I have been so worried. Where are you?'

'Toulouse,' she shouted above the crackle.

'Oh, thank God. I was so afraid you might have gone north up to Rouen to fetch your mother. The fighting is very fierce up there today.'

She explained very briefly what she had been doing, and that she and Anna were going to rest for a couple of days in Toulouse and then travel on to Spain.

He interrupted her. 'No, no, don't do that. Just one minute.' He was obviously talking to someone beside him. 'No, you must leave France immediately. Go to Sete. There is an Italian cruiser moored there.'

'But Marco, we are so weary and we must buy some clothes. Can't we rest for a little . . .'

'No!' His voice sounded urgent. 'You must leave immediately. You must be on board by tomorrow night. I will make arrangements for them to embark you. Understand? This is most important. You *must* get to Sete by tomorrow night.'

She sighed. 'But why, darling?'

There was silence. He obviously couldn't answer.

'Oh, very well. We will go there.' She turned to Cavero. 'Are there any trains from here to Sete?' she asked. 'How far is it?'

'Yes, there are trains, Signora. It is only about two hundred and fifty kilometres. You will have to change at Narbonne and also perhaps at Beziers. I will make inquiries for you tomorrow.'

'But my husband says we must leave immediately.'

'Oh, no, Signora, there are no more trains tonight.'

They were all very relieved.

* * *

The hotel, not much more than a pension, at least had comfortable beds. Next morning, as the five sat over coffee and croissants, they discussed the parting of their ways.

'Thérèse, you and Jean must keep the carriage and horses,' Jacqueline said. 'Perhaps you can sell them in Spain.'

'Really, it is too kind of you,' Thérèse protested.

'I'm not giving them to you, they are not mine to give.' She laughed. 'Maybe when this is all over we can pay the people at the chateau for them. But they had been abandoned.'

She and Anna felt sad as they waved goodbye. It seemed incredible that they had known Thérèse and Jean for such a short time. In normal circumstances, they could never have developed the friendship and intimacy of the past few days. Thérèse would never have referred to the stately young countess and her mother by their Christian names. She had told Jacqueline that she could neither read nor write, but she had proved to be a very intelligent, kind and generous companion. And young Jean, at ten years old, had acted the man of the party, tending the horses and cutting wood for fires to heat Bobo's milk, and had bounced the little girl on his knee to make her laugh.

Jacqueline and Anna had discussed asking Thérèse to take Bobo as a foster child until she returned home, from where she would have a better chance of tracing the child's relatives. But they knew she would not accept money, and life would be difficult enough for her without the extra burden. So Bobo stood between them now, on the footpath, waving a fat little arm until the cart was out of sight.

The first train to Narbonne left at seven-thirty in the morning . . . the Consul explained, at ten. The next was at twelve noon.

They stood at the station barrier from eleven-thirty until the train came in at two o'clock. They were elbowed and trampled in the stampede for seats and the train was moving again before a place was found for them on the wooden pews. It was a slow train, stopping at every station on the way – plus for numerous other reasons known only to the driver. The train for Beziers had left Narbonne at four-thirty, half an hour before they arrived. The next was at seven o'clock. Tired and frustrated they left the station in search of food.

A modest restaurant offered three menus and they stepped inside, only to be turned away. The patron took one look at these gypsies and not even Jacqueline's withering denouncement of his attitude could weaken his resolve to be rid of them. A pavement café proved more accommodating, and a lot less expensive. Having paid for their train tickets, Jacqueline had precious few francs left, and thanked heaven she had forced herself to take Claude's wallet from his body.

Again the train was late, and eventually arrived at Beziers where they learned that the last train for Sete had left them stranded for the night without money. Once again they wandered out into the town.

A window in a grimy terrace of houses beside the station displayed a hand-written card saying 'Chambres'. Jacqueline removed her watch as she knocked on the door and offered it in exchange for beds. The woman weighed the 18-carat gold jewel in her hand, and nodded. In grubby pinafore and curlers, she led them up the narrow, linoleum-covered stairs to a tiny room, completely filled by a small double bed. Inevitably the toilet was an evil-smelling grid in the floor of a shed in the back yard, difficult enough for Jacqueline and Anna, but impossible for Bobo, who had eventually to be held screaming over a pail. The child sobbed herself to sleep between the two women, who could only doze and scratch themselves all night.

Fortunately the train deposited them within sight of the Sete docks the next morning. The Italian vessel could be seen lying at anchor outside the breakwater. Jacqueline hurried up and down the wharf trying to find someone to ferry them out.

'They use their own liberty boats,' an old fisherman

explained. 'We don't go out to them. They're taking up their boats, anyway. Seems they're leaving.' He spat a plug of tobacco into the water and walked away.

Heart pounding, she ran to a building where she could see uniformed men working. The man at the counter did not look up.

'I need to contact that Italian vessel out there, urgently.' She addressed the room at large.

Still without looking up, the nearest man said, 'Too late, m'dame, she has just notified us that she is leaving.'

'But it is not too late. We are supposed to be sailing with her,' Jacqueline insisted.

'Oh, no, you've made a mistake. Naval ships don't carry passengers.' Now at last he looked up to grin irritatingly at her.

'This one will,' she shouted desperately. 'My husband, the Count Luzzi di Calitri, has made arrangements. I know they are expecting us.'

Another man strolled up to the counter. 'There were a couple of officers from that ship in here yesterday. They were asking about some countess.' He eyed her up and down. 'But that's not you.'

She squared her shoulders, tilted back her bedraggled head. 'I am that countess,' she announced.

They all laughed uproariously.

She picked up a large inkwell and banged it down on the counter, showering papers, men and herself with ink.

'Haven't you a radio? Call them. Ask them if Colonel Count Luzzi di Calitri hasn't made arrangements for them to take us.' Her shouting hurt her throat and brought on a fit of coughing.

The men were angry, but one of them turned to a wall set and switched it on.

He returned to the counter. 'They are putting out a boat, now,' he growled, wiping ink from his face with his sleeve.

And so, at last, she was leaving France. She had only been in the country twelve days, but it felt like a lifetime.

*　　*　　*

The captain had expected a countess and her mother.

Jacqueline stepped on deck with an oversized floral cocktail dress draped about her, held together at the waist by a man's tie. The lace-trimmed hem reached just below her bare knees, leaving an excellent view of mud-caked brogues. Most of her hair was held back from her ink-stained face by a length of box-cord; the rest hung in strands over her ears.

Anna had cut her mauve taffeta ball-gown to a fashionable calf-length with blunt scissors. Her stockingless feet were encased in equally dirty lace-ups. Her cast was supported by a tasselled shawl and the bruise on her face had faded to a greenish-yellow.

Bobo would have looked resplendent in her blue satin breeches and frilled jacket – had it not been for the remains of at least four meals down the front. They were not what the captain had been expecting. In fact, he hadn't been told about the child at all.

'I understood you were to join us yesterday,' he commented stiffly. 'You are lucky. This morning we received orders to sail immediately.' He gave instructions for the passengers to be taken below, and returned to the bridge.

Their cabin allowed for only one person to dress at a time, but what did it matter? They were safe. Even so, Jacqueline found it impossible to relax. Every unexpected sound made her jump, muscles tensed. She would lie in her bunk and deliberately relax each muscle, then make herself think about the villa and the children . . . and a few minutes later she would be aware that her body was rigid again and her ears were straining, listening.

The demands of the journey had kept Anna reasonably occupied, but now she had time to brood on the fact that Claude was gone, that his body lay putrefying on a roadside; the business empire he had built up and of which he had been so proud, left to . . . what? Their home, personal treasures, photographs, mementoes . . . would she ever see any of them again? It was as though these past precious four years, the best period of her life, had been completely erased. All she had was his watch and ring, and a photo of them taken together, which Claude had carried in his wallet.

The sailors took pity on the bedraggled women and between them found shirts and trousers which would fit Jacqueline and Anna fairly well. The civilians were privileged to use the officers' mess whenever they wished, and limited areas of the deck. Jacqueline washed Anna's and Bobo's hair as well as her own, and they all enjoyed drying it in the warm breeze on deck.

They spent a hot, airless night in the tiny cabin, but Jacqueline did get some sleep. Bobo had to sleep at the foot of Anna's bunk; Jacqueline did not dare take her up on her top one. During the day she was entertained by off-duty sailors missing the company of their own children.

When she woke the ship was not moving. She hurriedly dressed and went on deck, hoping that Marco might be there to meet them. The port seemed strangely familiar. She gazed around in amazement as she realised that, far from being in Genoa as she had expected, they were at anchor off Porto Torres, in northern Sardinia – they had been here in *Ocean Dreamer*.

An officer was examining something in the foredeck gunturret.

'What are we doing here in Sardinia!' she called up to him. 'I thought we were going direct to Genoa?'

'Our orders were changed from Rome during the night. We are at present waiting here to embark senior naval personnel before proceeding to the base at Taranto.' He smiled. 'I see you have visited Porto Torres before.'

'Yes. On our own yacht, several times. But can't we at least be disembarked at Naples? Otherwise it will be days before we reach home.' Which would be so disappointing.

'I am sorry, Signora, but there is no possibility that the captain will make an unscheduled stop. I think there is something important happening, which is why we are returning to Italy at all. We had expected to be visiting foreign ports for another month.'

The Straits of Bonifacio between Corsica and Sardinia were as usual rough and windy. The Sodalti class destroyer had been built for speed, not comfort, and Anna and Bobo were both sick that night, until they passed into the Tyrrhenian Sea. However, both were well enough to come on deck and enjoy the view of the island of Stromboli, dominated by its volcano regularly erupting, every six minutes, and later carefully to scrutinise the water in the Straits of Messina, for the swirl of the Charybdis whirlpool. Finally, Jacqueline refused to allow them below until they had seen the magnificent Mount Etna, hunched threateningly ten thousand feet above Sicily's eastern shoreline.

The destroyer anchored overnight in the Mar Grande at Taranto, waiting for daylight to sail through the assembling squadrons to the entrance of the Mar Piccolo. The captain had been quite friendly after hearing of their ordeal, and came on deck to say goodbye as they left on the liberty boat for the dock. He even gave them sufficient money to visit the nearby shops before catching the train, to purchase slightly more feminine clothes.

They were on their way to Naples by mid-morning. The track wound between the Lucarno and Neapolitan ranges, twisting and turning through gorges and tunnels. Jacqueline realised that they were passing only fifteen miles south of Calitri, the nearest she had ever been to Marco's family estates.

The station at Naples seemed more crowded and noisy than ever; it was a relief to be able to sit back on the last leg of the journey to Rome. Because Rome, and its environs, was home: its own brand of noise and bustle was all familiar and Jacqueline longed for the peace and tranquillity that only loved and familiar sights and people can give. Was there any possibility that Marco would be in Rome to meet them? Just to see his face, touch his hand, would be so soothing to her frayed nerves. She looked across to Anna, dozing in her corner seat. Poor

Mama. Only time, a long, long time, would bring her any solace.

He was there. She saw him before the train stopped moving and waved frantically out of the window. He ran beside them until they halted and then wrenched open the door to sweep her into his arms.

They stood together, speechless, eyes swimming. He hugged Anna, too. His obvious pity for her in the loss of Claude made her eyes fill with tears.

Not until they were all in the car driving out to the villa did they start to talk.

'That was a sweet, crazy, heroic thing you did, my darling. I was so afraid you wouldn't reach Sete in time. I couldn't tell you on the phone, of course, but I knew that our ships were being recalled from non-neutral foreign ports on the seventh.'

'Really, I see.' She nodded. 'But why were they recalled so suddenly, if Italy is neutral?'

'Because we are no longer neutral. Italy declared war on France today.' He was no longer smiling.

June 1940 – December 1942

The angel of death has been abroad throughout the land;
you may almost hear the beating of his wings.

John Bright, *Speech, House of Commons,*
23 February 1855

MARCO HAD no idea who Bobo was. Seeing her with Jacqueline and her mother he assumed she was a relation of Claude's and had carried her to the car without question. When he learned that there was no way to trace her family, if there were any alive, until after peace was restored, he was happy for her to become part of the family. Francisco and Katarina were so delighted with her that, after a quick hug and a kiss, they ignored their truant mother for the newcomer.

Marco saw very little of his family nowadays, as he continued to be based in Genoa long after France surrendered. Both women felt sorry for him. Though he never spoke a disloyal word or even expressed a doubt, his silent refusal to discuss any aspect of the war betrayed his feelings. He never mentioned Il Duce, nor did he join in the Italians' jubilation at the news of Marshal Graziani's successful attack and advance into Egypt from Libya, in September. And when news leaked out, three months later, that the British had thrown Graziani and his troops out again, with great loss of men and materials, he pursed his lips, shrugged his shoulders . . . and remained silent.

Meanwhile, the women had settled into a comfortable domestic routine. Rosita and Giuseppe had viewed Anna's arrival with blank stares and obvious trepidation, distrusting her attempts to be friendly until the day Rosita tripped and fell heavily, breaking a big jug of milk and cutting herself on the broken china. Giuseppe walked in five minutes later to find his wife sitting at the table watching the dreaded Rumanian woman on her hands and knees mopping up milk.

'. . . and don't you move until I've bathed your hand in disinfectant and washed it,' Anna was telling her.

'I will wash the floor afterwards, Signora, you don't have to do it,' Rosita insisted.

'Nonsense. You mustn't get your hand wet until it has healed. Anyway, you have more than enough dry jobs to do.'

'But what about the dishes?'

'I'll do those, too.' Anna looked up and saw Giuseppe standing in the doorway. 'I'll get your husband to help me.'

It was the beginning of an unlikely friendship.

Food was in short supply. Jacqueline knew there was nothing they need do without if she bought on the thriving black market, but this she refused to do. Instead, she insisted they should be as self-sufficient as possible. Part of the garden was given over to a rotating programme of vegetables. The chicken coops were enlarged, piglets introduced to the paddocks and a young heifer, awaiting her first calving, would eventually provide them with milk.

Anna and Rosita were kept busy in the kitchen bottling the produce. The villa gardens yielded splendid crops of fruit; more peaches, nectarines and apricots, oranges, lemons, grapefruit and olives grew each year than they could ever use or give away, and much had always been wasted. But no longer. The old 'butler's pantry', a relic of years gone by, was turned into a storeroom and filled with bottled fruit, tomatoes and olives, and a selection of home-made jams, marmalades, chutney and pickles.

They all teased Jacqueline for being a slave driver.

'I do believe the garden is twice as productive now than

when there used to be a team of gardeners here,' Jacob pretended to complain.

'The trouble was that I used to be in Rome all day, and not available with my whip,' she would laugh.

Soon after her return from France, Jacqueline went down to Civitavecchia. Now that Italy was no longer neutral she feared that *Ocean Dreamer* might be requisitioned. This had already happened to some of the larger boats belonging to their friends and she didn't want her carefully laid plans to be spoiled.

She gazed at the yacht, its gleaming white hull and superstructure etched in freshly varnished teak, brass fittings flashing intermittently. They had had some wonderful holidays together with the children, she and Marco. Might it be worth keeping the boat here just a little longer in the hope that he would be able to take a few days' leave for a trip? The perfect summer, crystal water mirror flat for as far as the eye could see, made it very tempting. But no, it was too big a risk.

The captain's wife was alone on board. She sent a boy who was fishing from the pontoon to fetch her husband, and the two women sat together on the deck, waiting. While she was brought up to date with the latest adjustments and fittings added in the galley, Jacqueline's mind drifted to thinking about this odd couple. They were very well read and cultured. They had no desire for a conventional life; they chose to live by the sea, both physically and financially. The captain had started his working life as a schoolteacher in a small seaside town, supplementing his meagre salary by taking holidaymakers out in his little fishing boat. One day he had been offered a job crewing on a cruise yacht for the long summer vacation. Newly wed, his wife was taken on as stewardess, too. They loved it, and packed up their home, having decided this was the life they wanted until they started a family. A few months after their son was born they returned to the sea and had never had a permanent shore home since. They were a happy, relaxed pair, whose worldly goods consisted mainly of books.

Heavy steps on the pontoon broke into her thoughts.

'Signora, it is good to see you looking so well after your ordeal in France. You are a very brave woman.' The captain's brown, wrinkled hand shook hers firmly. His short-cropped grey hair and beard and darting brown eyes made him look younger than his sixty-eight years. His character was an interesting blend of vitality and cool confidence.

'Would you be prepared to take *Ocean Dreamer* to America?' Jacqueline asked him. 'We may need some re-fitting done and as we are now at war with England she will have to go to an American yard.'

'We would be prepared to do it, Signora, but the British will either take us or sink us long before we get past Gibraltar. They are giving Italian ships a hard time at the moment.'

'Only if you are flying the Italian flag. But since we are actually registered in Panama, as soon as you are outside the harbour, change flags. I have a Panamanian one in my locker. Would you be able to leave immediately? What about fuel?'

'There is enough fuel on board for us to cross the Atlantic, Signora. I have always kept the tanks topped right up, and no one has ever asked any questions, so far. But it would be unwise to attempt such a crossing before mid-November. We don't want to risk running into a hurricane when we get to the other side. However,' he went on knowingly, 'we don't want to risk being requisitioned, do we?' Jacqueline flushed. 'So I suggest we leave the Mediterranean immediately and sail down the west coast of Africa to the Cape Verde Islands. They are neutral, being Portuguese, and would be a good starting point for the Atlantic crossing. We can wait there safe and snug.'

'Will you mind being stuck there for five months?'

'My wife's cousin lives there; it will be a nice holiday to take my son and daughter-in-law to meet them. But tell

292

me, Signora, what do you want us to do when we get to America? Where must we go?'

'I suggest you berth in Miami. Then you must post this letter to Mrs William Stevenson. She is a very close friend of mine. Her husband is an admiral, you know, in the US Navy. Keep her address and contact her if you have any problems.' She handed him the letter. 'Let me know when you arrive and I will send further instructions as and when I can. There is no point in you returning with the boat before this war is over, so I would like you to remain with her. But if you prefer to come back, will you find someone really reliable to take your place? I am sure I can trust your choice.'

'I doubt that will be necessary. She is our home. But when would you want her back? As soon as the war is over?'

'I think the Count and I may come over to America for a holiday. We might bring the children and cruise in the Caribbean for a few months. Have you sailed the West Indies at all?'

'Yes, for about six months, some years ago. Beautiful, very beautiful.'

'Then hopefully we will all be together there within the next year.'

Which would be perfect if all went well. If not . . .? She wondered if this wise old sea-dog could guess why she had really bought the yacht.

They went on to discuss finance and means of communication before she collected up a few belongings and waved them goodbye.

Marco arrived home one day and immediately called Jacqueline and Jacob to the study.

'I am sure you are aware, Jacob, of being the only able-bodied man around here,' he started.

'Indeed. I find it very embarrassing. I do try to keep out of sight as much as I can,' Jacob assured him.

'Well, unfortunately, if you remain here that won't be

enough for you to avoid the next round-up, which starts in a week. I think you would be much safer at Calitri. In fact, you had better leave right away.'

'I suppose this could be for some time?' Jacqueline queried.

'Until the end of the war, certainly. Take all your things with you. My wife, Camilla, will welcome you, I am sure, if you will help her as you have done here. The estate is very short-handed now. Anyway, I will give you a letter of introduction.'

'Thank you, Marco. You have been so kind and understanding about this, and so very generous to let me share your home.'

'We hope you will come back to us afterwards, don't we, darling?' He turned to Jacqueline.

'Of course, of course. We are all going to miss you.'

Jacqueline was glad to have Anna's company. She missed Marco so much, and with Jacob gone, when work was finished and the children were in bed the hours before retiring for the night were long. The parties, dinners and balls were all things of the past. She sometimes thought about them, how she and Marco would drive off together, resplendent in their evening dress. They had made a stunning pair, and would again when this horrible war was finally resolved. She longed to see Marco relaxed and happy again, magnificently tall and good looking, his coat-tails flapping or evening cloak swinging from his shoulders, that fascinating arrogance in his bearing . . . somehow never apparent when he was in uniform. It was as though he took no pride in his army rank, as though he carried out his duties with reluctance. Was he that disillusioned with Duce's government, she wondered?

She was glad there were no longer social events to take them out on the few evenings that he was home on leave. She preferred to have him to herself. Anna would discreetly occupy herself in the kitchen or on a sewing job in her bedroom, leaving them to enjoy their drawing room alone together. They would discuss home problems, the children. She would report the progress of her miniature farm and the developing friendship between Rosita and Anna – which would make him laugh.

Jean-Jacques was granted frequent weekend passes, often arriving with a friend from Military Camp. The two boys rode off into the hills together during the day and in the evenings they tried to draw Marco into discussing the war. But Jacqueline could see that Marco was as alarmed as she was herself at the degree of indoctrination the boys displayed. They were obviously fed regular doses of patriotic propaganda, digesting it without question. Together with Jean-Jacques' increasing stiffness and disapproval of her lack of enthusiasm for his military interests, these evenings made her thoroughly uncomfortable and she always prayed that his leave passes would not coincide with Marco's.

Marco had a ten-day pre-embarkation leave at Christmas. It was lovely to have him home for so long, although Jacqueline was distressed at the thought of him leaving for Libya. Once again he tried to reassure her.

'Remember, sweetheart, I am a long way behind the lines trying to coordinate communications, organise coding, decoding and relay orders. I sit at a desk all day trying to untangle other people's mistakes. You would be amazed how one incorrectly coded word can change the meaning of an order. When we went into France a message came through . . . *B unit advise G unit of your position* . . . and it was relayed . . . *B unit advise G unit of their position* . . . resulting in a terrible row when the captain in charge of B tried to tell his counterpart in G where he should be.' He grinned at her. 'So you see, as long as I can stop our chaps from firing on each other, I am unlikely to hear much gunfire.'

Jean-Jacques had a long Christmas pass, too. He came home alone, for once and joined in the festivities with some of his old enthusiasm, lying on the floor with Francisco to demonstrate mechanical toys, while the two girls played with their new dolls and prams.

What an odd collection of people we are, Jacqueline reflected, looking round the drawing room on Christmas evening. Jacob, who had dared join them for two days, a German Jew, a refugee who had watched his family die horribly around him. Mama – strange that she thought of her as Mama, now that they were close again – yes, she too was a refugee, a Rumanian Jew who had tried so hard to make something of her life, though probably in the wrong way and certainly unsuccessfully, and was now dependent upon Marco for everything she possessed. Herself, illegitimate daughter of an American admiral and a leading amateur tennis player; ex-mistress of a Frenchman and a king, wife of a homosexual Rumanian count and now mistress of an Italian count and mother of his two children and also of the illegitimate son of her first love. Jean-Jacques, not yet thirteen, a very serious child soldier. Little Bobo, the French orphan. And Marco himself, now an army colonel, going off to Africa to fight for a cause in which he no longer believed. They all seemed so happy together, due partly, no doubt, to the bonds of problems overcome, separately or together. Perhaps, she mused, if more people suffered periodic visits to hell, as some of us have, they would fight less and settle down to appreciate how good life really is. Permanent heaven only seemed to make for selfishness and greed. She looked up to see Marco's eyes on her, smiling.

'You were miles away, darling,' he teased.

'On the contrary, I was right here, thinking what a lovely, happy family we all make, and what a gorgeous Christmas it has been.'

'Indeed. And here's to many more such happy Christmases.' He raised his Martini. 'Let's hope this war is over before the next one, and we can all be united in peace.'

11 December 1941. Nearly a year since Marco had left for Libya. And what a disastrous year for Italy. First Marshal Badoglio had resigned after the failure of his invasion of Greece. Then in February Marco had been fortunate to

escape from Beda Fomm before several Italian divisions were surrounded by the British and forced to surrender. By May Ethiopia had fallen to the British who returned Emperor Haile Selassie to the throne. Hitler had had to send German forces to Greece, which they now occupied, and to North Africa under General Rommel, who had virtually taken over from General Bastico.

All very humiliating and demoralising for the Italian people, and especially for Mussolini. Why had Duce been so power crazy? Or was he still, stupidly, trying to impress the German Dictator . . . perhaps through fear? Preferring to be a friend than an enemy?

What a mess the world was in! The Germans were now almost at the gates of Moscow, having occupied nearly all of Europe save three of the neutrals and Italy, 'their friend' – how long might that last? – and now the world was reeling with the news of the Japanese attack on Pearl Harbor.

When she had first heard of the attack and of the American declaration of war, Jacqueline had felt very uneasy. But today, with the radio announcement that Italy had declared war on America in turn, she was really alarmed.

'Do you think you will be regarded as an enemy alien?' Anna asked.

'I don't know. I wish I did. Oh dear, how I wish I could speak to Marco. Even if I write it will take months before I get a reply. I don't know what to think . . .' she pushed her fingers through her hair. 'The authorities here must surely know that I only took American citizenship for convenience. I've only been there once, briefly, so I don't imagine they will take it very seriously. That is, unless they learn of my connection with Bill Stevenson . . .' she had been thinking aloud.

'How could they possibly know that? There is no record of his name . . .' Anna stopped, seeing Jacqueline's hand over her mouth. 'What is it? How do you come to call him Bill?' she asked suspiciously.

'Mama, I know him. We met accidentally. It's a long story, so you had better sit down.'

At the end she added, 'I do hope that you aren't offended I didn't arrange for you to meet again.'

Anna smiled. 'Not at all, my dear. I understand perfectly, and I agree with your reasons. But I must say it comes as rather a shock. So my young American ensign has become an admiral. Well, Well.' She sighed. 'How different all our lives would have been if I'd married him.' She walked over to the window and stared out at the sea, Jacqueline's current problem forgotten.

In fact, Jacqueline felt quite sure that Marco's protection would still hold good even though he was not in the country at the moment. To a degree she was right. Only a week later Rosita called her in from the stables. 'Signora, you must come, there are some Fascisti to see you.'

Her heart missed a beat. 'Fascisti? What do they want, do you know?'

'No, they just asked to speak to you,' was all the maid could tell her.

They were very polite and respectful.

'Countess, I am so sorry to disturb you, but I am obliged to call on you in an official capacity. I am Capitano Callone from the Central Immigration Office, and this is one of my officers.'

'Shall we sit down,' she suggested, knees still shaking, and led the two men into the drawing room.

'Your . . . er . . . that is to say, Count Luzzi and I,' he started, 'have been in communication regarding your American citizenship . . .'

'Have you?' She was quite excited. 'Is he well? I haven't had a letter for nearly a month.'

'Yes, he is very well. Now, as I was saying, he is very anxious that you should not be interned . . .'

'Interned?' She was aghast.

'. . . and I have agreed that for the present you may remain at liberty within the bounds of house arrest.'

'But why? Have I ever been anything but a good supporter of Italy?' she demanded, hoping he couldn't read her mind.

'Countess, you may be sure of your loyalty to Italy, and so may the Count, and personally, I do not doubt it, but I am afraid the sad fact is that governments the world over intern residents who hold enemy alien passports in time of war. However, as the Count is prepared to guarantee your good behaviour, and also to pay the expenses incurred in posting an officer to your household, I am agreeing to place you under house arrest only. But . . .' he held up his hand as she started to speak, '. . . this is on a temporary basis only. If the arrangement presents no problems it is possible it may continue indefinitely. Remember, though, that I cannot foretell whether or not the overall policy of my office will become stricter.' Obviously he was warning her: so far she was being lucky, but if she tried to push it . . .

'I see. Well, I cannot imagine there will be any problems,' she assured him with a touch of jollity she did not feel. 'When will the arrangement be starting? I assume I will be allowed to go shopping in Rome under escort?'

'You are under house arrest as from now, and there is no question of you leaving the perimeter of this property at any time, even under escort. I must also ask you to relinquish your passport.'

Up to that moment she had so enjoyed her newly domesticated life at the villa, she had avoided even the drive into Rome unless it was absolutely necessary. Now, stupidly, she felt irked by the thought of the restrictions.

Ernesto Matarossi, Capitano Callone's officer, fetched his suitcase from the car before his senior drove off and immediately moved into a spare bedroom.

The adult members of the household resented his presence at first, but he was very anxious not to intrude on Jacqueline's privacy any more than was necessary. Indeed, he went to extraordinary lengths to be helpful both in the house and in the garden, playing with the children and telling them stories, so that with seasonal good spirit they invited him to join their Christmas celebrations.

'You are very kind,' he told them. 'I was not looking forward to being away from my wife and children and my little grandchildren. I can see you understand that I do not enjoy being obliged to guard you in this way.' He was a nice person. Jacqueline thought he must be nearly seventy, far too old for the army, which was presumably why he had been given this job.

They were, therefore, only one less around the dining table than last Christmas; Jacob's was the empty chair and the guard took Marco's. But what a difference – to have a dear lover, companion, guardian and mentor replaced by a gaoler, however nice the latter might be.

Jacqueline was thrilled to receive a long letter from Marco two days before Christmas. It was full of nostalgia. He missed them all so much and wished he could have got leave, but it was impossible. If they would raise their glasses at exactly one o'clock on Christmas Day he would be doing the same and they could drink at the same moment to each other's health and to all the Christmases they would share in the future.

He also mentioned having met 'Mr R' several times, and liking him very much. Jacqueline mentioned this to Jean-Jacques late one evening when they were alone.

'Who do you think Mr R can be?' she asked.

'General Rommel, of course,' he replied rather curtly. 'He is an extremely good strategist, they say. By the way, Mother, I have been meaning to tell you, I will complete my training early next year, so I may be sent abroad with an Army Unit at that time.'

'Jean-Jacques, that is not possible . . .'

'Oh Mother! Don't start that again,' he snapped.

'All right, there is no need to be rude. This time I am not being a fussy mother, I am being practical. Just who do you think you are going to fight? Americans?'

'Possibly. Why? Just because you know an American admiral doesn't mean I cannot fight them, if necessary, does it?'

'It most certainly does, for the simple reason that you are an American citizen. You have an American passport, as I have. Haven't you realised that Ernesto is here to keep me under house arrest as an enemy alien?'

He turned quite white. 'I am what?' he shouted.

'In the eyes of the Italian government, you are an enemy alien.'

He dropped into Marco's chair and stared at her in horror. 'Why have you never told me this before? You knew I was doing military training.'

'Because, my darling, I never really took it seriously. Heaven knows, Italian soldiers have been wiped off the face of virtually every battlefield they've set foot on in the past year or so . . .'

'That's not true . . .'

'It is. Forget all the lies they tell you boys to keep up your morale. So I find it hard to comprehend the mentality of anyone who imagines that replacing the grown men they have lost with boys of fourteen will improve matters. I wish you would try to understand my point,' she pleaded. 'I don't doubt that all you boys are well read in warfare, well trained in weaponry and drill, but that still does not make you strong as men. I'm sure none of you has any idea how strong a person must be to withstand days, weeks of marching, fighting, watching your friends die in agony, living in camps without proper food, sleep or sanitation, drinking only polluted water . . . you haven't, have you?'

Jean-Jacques was silent for a long time before looking up. 'Mother, who am I? What nationality was I born? You have never told me about my real father.' He spoke very quietly.

The moment Jacqueline had dreaded for so long had finally arrived. She took a deep breath. 'You were born in Rumania, and so was I. We are both Rumanian by birth.' She paused, but he didn't interrupt. 'Your father was a Frenchman . . .'

'French? But I thought Count Tyroler was Rumanian, too?'

'He is. But he was only acting as your father.'

'Why? Why did you marry him and not my real father? Who is my real father?' He looked at her suspiciously. 'Was I conceived before or after you married?'

That took her breath away.

She was about to say that he was too young to understand, trot out all the clichés about 'when he was old enough to fall in love he would realise . . .' but stopped herself. This was no time to hedge. He had to know one day – and perhaps sharing her secrets with him would bring them closer together. So she told him. About Jean-Paul and King Carol, Queen Marie and Ion Tyroler. She tried to play down Anna's part in the story, not wanting to create any ill-feeling between him and his grandmother. She told him of their flight to Germany, the Jewish element in their blood . . . did she see him flinch then? He heard about the German Fascists and the full story of Jacob's tragedy.

In the silence that followed she wondered how he would feel about the Fascist movement here in Italy, now that he knew the truth. Perhaps, now that he knew how hard she had tried to protect him, he would feel closer to her . . .

'So you don't really know who my father is, you are only guessing. I could quite well be a Rumanian prince.' He was talking as though she wasn't there.

'Nonsense. I knew perfectly well . . .'

'You had no right to kidnap me, to keep me from my father . . .'

'Kidnap you! Jean-Jacques, you have no idea what you are saying.' She couldn't believe her ears. 'Carol was not your father, I swear . . .'

'My real name isn't Jean-Jacques, is it? I can remember Grandmother calling me Frederick a long time ago, and being cross with her. Was she right? Is that my real name?'

'That is what you were christened, though against my wishes.'

'Who chose the name?'

'Queen Marie . . .'

'My other grandmother!'

'No!' She was exasperated.

'Mother, don't you think perhaps you believed what you wanted to? You thought you loved the Frenchman so you wanted to believe I was his son.' He got up and crossed to her chair. 'And I prefer to think I am King Carol's son.' His kissed her cheek. 'Goodnight, Mother.' The door closed quietly behind him.

She was trembling. She could never have guessed he would react like this. He had always seemed to be a practical child, a realist – despite the fact that he had swallowed so much Italian propaganda. But far from it . . . he was just a dreamer. Was that all his military knowledge and bearing amounted to? Dreams of glory? Still, that didn't make him so different. Look at Benito Mussolini! At least Jean-Jacques was still a child. Of course by telling him he was an American citizen and illegitimate she had destroyed all the dreams he had had until now . . . so he immediately replaced them with others – of being a royal prince denied his birthright! How little she really knew about him. Or about his father, understandably as she had shared so little time with him. But why was Jean-Jacques so distant always? Because she had followed a career and only been a part-time mother? Had he needed her more than just in the evenings and weekends? The long school holidays had probably left him too much time on his own, to dream and drift without her there to guide his thinking and share his interests.

I suppose I have only myself to blame, she thought as she turned out the lights and went up to bed.

Ernesto was on duty for four weeks at a stretch followed by a week off when his place was taken by a younger man, Sergio, whose diabetes kept him out of the army. None of the family liked him much. His manner was surly and he resented the 'favouritism' shown to Jacqueline, whom he considered should have been interned. Unlike Ernesto he took no part in their family life, just sat watching them and sniffing. He seemed to have a permanent cold or out-of-season hayfever. The only letters Jacqueline was allowed to send were to Marco, and even these Sergio insisted on reading. She mentioned this to Ernesto one day in March.

'I hoped he would not cause too much offence, Signora.' Ernesto was apologetic. 'He always was a difficult boy. Joined the Fascisti very young and had his head filled with big ideas. Agh! Where have all those big ideas got us now? Italy is in a mess. How stupid, imagining we are so big we can declare war on the United States! They could wipe us off the face of the earth – poof! – just like that. Huh! The fat one, he thinks the one with the big mouth is his friend and protector. Why does he not see that, when it suits him, that friend will walk in and take Italy as he has the rest of Europe.'

Jacqueline was staggered. She had never heard such open criticism of Mussolini before.

'Italy did win the war in Abyssinia,' she remarked, deliberately leading him on.

'Put guns and gas against bows and arrows and you can hardly lose, can you? But who wants Abyssinia, anyway? The British have thrown us out now, and immediately put Haile Selassie back on the throne. They don't want it.'

'I had no idea you felt like this.'

'I tell you, Signora, there are many, many Italians today who think Il Duce should have gone years ago. He was good once. He did much to help the Italian people and we thought he was our champion. But now he has wasted our money and our men. And for what? We will be lucky if Italy survives this war.'

''Nesto, 'Nesto, tell us a story!' The children ran into the room and hurled themselves into his arms. The subject was closed.

Anna was highly amused that she was allowed to visit Rome while Jacqueline was not. Sergio had to go with her – to prevent her contacting enemy agents with messages

304

from the alien Jacqueline, the women joked – and he also insisted on scrutinising the shopping list. So they deliberately put on it items to alarm him, such as the nutty food supplement for the pigs which they always called 'bullets'.

'Bullets!' he shouted, waving the list. 'One bag of bullets. You are not allowed to have a gun. Where is it?'

Much to his annoyance, the women laughed.

'Look,' Jacqueline showed him. 'These are the bullets. We load them into pigs, not guns.'

On another occasion he was angry to find poison on the list.

'Yes,' Anna told him. 'There are rats in the stables.'

He let that pass, but they thought he was surprisingly off his food the next week he was on duty.

Anna made capital of his company when shopping. She paraded in front of him in suits and dresses, asking his opinion which of course she ignored. Making him carry her parcels and shopping bags, she took him to a café for tea, eating rich sweet creamy cakes, which, as a diabetic, he could only look at, drooling.

'Mama! You really are a sadist.' Jacqueline collapsed laughing at Anna's description of the scene, later.

'Well, he shouldn't be such a horrible little boy.'

Listening to the fluctuating war news, Jacqueline's feelings and loyalties were hopelessly divided. She spent hours discussing it with Anna, but always remained confused and unhappy. She did not believe in the 'New European Order' which Hitler had announced last year and he and Duce had attempted to inaugurate. She was aware that she and her mother had both seen Fascism from the inside, the beastliness of its inner core. If Fascism and Nazism were to win the entire conflict, what would life be like for the people Mussolini and Hitler ruled, dominated? Those, of course, whom they didn't murder. What would happen? What was happening now, in Europe, to all the millions of people with Jewish blood? How could so many different nationalities be united under one government without tyrannical force?

Yet on the other hand, could she bear to think of Marco being defeated? Taken prisoner or even killed? Even if he wasn't hurt or imprisoned, if the English and Americans won, what would happen to Italy? And to themselves? The English fancied themselves as great colonisers, and had pompously lorded it over large tracts of the globe for generations, but would they try to colonise Italy? Lord it over the Italians? They hadn't in Ethiopia, apparently. But after the 1914–18 war the English and Americans had handed Germany back to the Germans, and then look what happened; they just re-armed and started all over again, twenty years later.

As the summer wore on and General Rommel pushed the British back into Egypt to within sixty miles of Alexandria, and the Germans checked the Russian counter-offensive and were once again advancing on the Eastern Front, it looked as though Marco would be on the winning side. He wrote regularly, but the letters would arrive only in batches, very intermittently.

One such batch arrived in November: there were three. The first two he had written in September, mainly in reply to letters of hers which had taken months to reach him. In the third, written in October, he said he hoped to be back in Italy by Christmas. He longed to be with her again and see the children. Transport was very difficult, as she might imagine, but he had put in for a flight and felt sure he would be with them in time to raise their glasses together this year. Jacqueline looked at the date on the letter. It was a miracle it had come at all. Within days of its despatch the British had launched an attack at a place in Egypt called El Alamein, and now the Germans and Italians were in full retreat across North Africa. So where was Marco now? Was there still a chance he would be back in Italy before Christmas?

He was.

Capitano Callone sent a note to inform the Countess

that Count Luzzi was in a military hospital in Taranto, and that in future her letters would be forwarded to him there.

'He doesn't say what is wrong with him, Ernesto. I don't know if he is ill or wounded. Surely the Capitano will let me visit him? Please ask him for me, will you?' It was so frustrating to think of Marco being back in Italy after nearly two years and not being able to see him.

Ernesto grimaced. 'I will try, of course, Signora, but please don't raise your hopes too high. Taranto is a long way from here.'

Callone sent another note.

. . . I regret it is impossible to grant you permission to visit Colonel Count Luzzi in hospital. He is under the best possible medical care for his wounds in his stomach and legs. As soon as he is well enough he will return home to convalesce.

I am sure I need not remind you that any unauthorised attempt to visit him would almost certainly result in loss of the privileged liberty you now enjoy . . .

She wrote to Marco daily, at first.

'I am afraid that only one letter can be sent each week, Signora.' Ernesto sadly handed several envelopes back.

'Oh, really! This lack of communication is ridiculous,' she fumed. 'Why can't I get news of his progress? Why haven't I received a medical report?' Sometimes she felt quite calm and confident, at others she paced the rooms worrying that he might be lying in agony, longing to see her; fearing that he might be permanently disabled.

A few days later a letter arrived from Taranto. Ernesto handed it to her in the drawing room where Anna had joined her for the revolting coffee substitute they now drank. Jacqueline tore eagerly at the envelope.

'At last. Now perhaps we will know how he is and when he can come home.' She scanned the two pages, a frown gathering.

Anna watched as the colour drained from her face and her fingers convulsed, crumpling the paper in her lap.

'It is written by a nurse. She says I must prepare myself for the worst.' Jacqueline's voice sounded to herself as though it came from a long way off. 'There is little hope of recovery . . .' she choked. 'He asked her to send me his love.' Tears streamed unhindered down her face.

'Marco!' she whispered. 'My darling, for God's sake don't leave me. No. No, don't go.'

'Brandy!' Anna hissed at Ernesto, and rushed to put her arms round her daughter.

After a few minutes Jacqueline's breathing was a little easier. She mopped her face with a handkerchief. The brandy warmed her but still she shivered and her whole body shuddered with gasping sobs. She handed the letter to Anna.

It had been written in the childishly rounded hand of a very young nurse, and said little that Jacqueline had not already told them.

Jacqueline got up suddenly and stood swaying in front of Ernesto. 'Well, now, presumably Capitano Callone will let me see him. Please call him.'

Ernesto went to the phone.

Capitano Callone was not in the office and no one else could help. Telephone later, was all he was told.

By late afternoon he still hadn't got through. 'I am afraid, Signora, it will have to wait until tomorrow. Sergio will come to take your lady mother shopping. If he stays here instead, I will go to see the Capitano in his office.'

'Thank you,' she sighed. She was weary from the physical effort of controlling her desire to rush out and drive to the railway station in Rome.

Marco! Marco! No, it was not possible. The girl must be mistaken. She spent the next day pacing, sobbing, starting jobs to occupy herself and then forgetting what she was doing. Last week she had started re-painting the woodwork in their bedroom . . . but he would never see it.

Sergio continued to sniff and stare.

'For Goodness' sake, what's the matter with you?' she snapped at him. 'Haven't you got a handkerchief?'

He produced an unpleasant rag from his pocket and waved it.

'Well, use it.'

He replaced it in his pocket and gave an extra long, deliberate sniff.

'Disgusting oaf!' She slammed out of the room.

Next day Ernesto reported that he had seen the Capitano, who said he would consider the Countess's request and let her know.

Three miserable, tense days passed and she heard nothing. Ernesto tried to telephone again. Callone was out.

When Sergio arrived on Monday morning to take over guard duties for the week, Ernesto and Jacqueline were waiting for him in the garden, hoping for news.

'Have you heard from the Capitano whether the Countess can go to Taranto?' the kindly officer called across the lawn.

Sergio waited until he had reached them. 'He says no, it is not possible.' He walked past them into the house.

Her nerve snapped. 'The damned fool!' she cried. 'What harm can I do? I've got to go to him. I've got to! I will telephone Callone, now. Ernesto, what is the number of his office?'

The Capitano was in his office, but he was adamant. He was sure the nurse's letter exaggerated Marco's condition. She would have to wait for a doctor's report. He would try to obtain one and contact her later.

If only she could saddle up and ride into the hills, it might relieve some of the tension and anger she felt at this ridiculous situation.

Ernesto tried to comfort her. 'Please, Signora, don't distress yourself so. If the doctors report that the Count is so gravely ill, the Capitano will surely let you visit him, but it is quite possible that the nurse was inexperienced and over-anxious when she wrote. He may yet be back here for Christmas.'

Jacqueline desperately wanted to believe him; tried to calm herself when downstairs with the family, until her agitation became too obvious and she would hasten up to the privacy of her room to pace, to think, to weep, or just sit staring at Marco's photograph on her dressing table.

On Saturday, Rosita called Sergio to the phone. Jacqueline hovered in the hall, anticipating news.

'Was it the Capitano?' she asked as he replaced the receiver. 'Has he heard from the doctors yet?'

'Yes, it was him.' Sergio's voice was unusually quiet. 'He heard from the hospital this morning. Count Luzzi died of his wounds last night.'

'Countess Tyroler does not wish to see anyone.' Anna was a magnificent and formidable woman when she chose to be: she chose now. Wearing a plain black dress, her high heels and grey-gold chignon adding extra inches to her already considerable height, she sent an icy stare down her long, Jewish nose.

'I would like the opportunity to tell her how sad I am that I was not notified of the seriousness of the Count's condition until it was too late.' Capitano Callone smiled up at her gravely.

Anna's expression did not change – except for the slight raising of one eyebrow.

'To what end?' she asked quietly. 'It might possibly make you feel better, but it certainly won't help my daughter. Your attitude during the past two weeks has been quite extraordinary. We are all aware that you have a duty to perform and we have never failed to comply with the requirements of that duty, as you well know.'

'Absolutely, Madame Dumesca,' he nodded.

'A man who is able to carry the responsibilities of his office doesn't need to assert his authority with petty, inhumane rules. Before you leave,' she went on, 'tell me, when is the funeral and who will be escorting my daughter?'

'Escorting the Countess . . .' he stammered.

'Yes. Who will be escorting her to the funeral? Ernesto Matarossi? I shall be going with her myself, of course, and the new Count, young Francisco, must be there. Were you planning to attend?'

'Er . . . yes. Er, yes, naturally.' He hadn't intended to go but now felt an urgent need to appease this awful dragon. 'The Count's body will be put on the train to Rome this evening, so the service will take place on Monday afternoon. Can you tell me at which church it will be held?'

'In the Count's own capella at Calitri, where he will be buried in the family vault.'

'Calitri? But that is much too far . . .' he stopped and nodded again. 'Yes, Madame, of course he must be buried with his family. I will use your telephone, if I may, to make the arrangements.'

'Certainly, you may use the one in the hall. If you will excuse me.' She led him out of the drawing room, heart thumping triumphantly. 'I must go to the Countess . . . and tell her that her two wishes have been granted.'

'Mama! How did you manage it?' Jacqueline exclaimed. 'I didn't think he had any intention of agreeing to either.'

'He hadn't. With my best Rumanian accent and worst Italian I did my pompous, bullying act. Beat him at his own game. Not difficult, really; he is a very little man.'

Jacqueline managed a smile. 'I wonder if Camilla will be there? Do you think she will object to me going?'

'I doubt it. She sounds rather a nice person, to me.'

The coffin stood on a catafalque in the little capella, flanked by six tall candles.

Jacqueline was thankful for the heavy black veil which concealed the misery that shook her whole body and brought tears streaming down her face as she walked down the aisle to a front pew. She held her head high and her back rigid, but only with an immense effort. Her knees felt weak and threatened to buckle at any moment. Marco's six-year-old successor to the title and estates walked beside his mother, holding her hand. They moved into the pew and she knelt down to pray, but her mind was a blank. She could not obliterate the picture of Marco lying there. They would have closed his eyes. His hands would be folded on his chest; those strong, gentle hands which had softly caressed her, roused her, restored her desire. Was it possible that he would never stand beside her again? Sit, or lie with her, envelope her with his passionate, gentle love? Why did this have to happen? But had it really happened? She found herself staring at the coffin lid, willing it to lift, willing Marco to sit up and prove it was all a mistake.

The priest's voice droned on in Latin. She had never learned the prayers used at funeral mass, so most of the words were meaningless, but she knew he was speaking of the resurrection. Was there really such a thing? It was a beautiful thought, even if it was difficult to believe. Surely the vigorous, industrious, confident mind which had inspired her for nine marvellous years could not be reduced to . . . nothing? Extinguished like a flame? No, it wasn't possible. The coffin contained only his body, a shell. His mind and spirit were free now, warm and inspiring as ever. He was here, with them, watching, knowing her grief yet proud as he ever was of her composure and dignity.

Francisco tugged at her sleeve, jolting her mind back to the living.

'Mama, how much longer does it last?'

'Not long now, darling,' she whispered, squeezing his hand.

The pall-bearers moved forward to lift the coffin and started to walk slowly towards the opening to the vault. For the first time Jacqueline was aware of the woman in the pew immediately on the other side of the aisle. She wore no veil, nor did she weep, but her heavy features were solemn. Camilla! Stepping into the aisle, Jacqueline paused to allow the other woman, the wife, to go ahead. But Camilla raised her eyes, smiled faintly and shook her head, waiting for Jacqueline and Francisco to walk immediately behind the coffin.

Suddenly Jacqueline realised that the capella was full; recognised old friends and two members of Duce's government. They were looking at the young boy Count.

The priest intoned the final prayers as the mortal remains of the Count Marco Gregorio Luzzi di Calitri were lowered into their last resting-place. Only a few deep, shuddering breaths betrayed the grief of his loving and adored mistress, the Rumanian Countess Jacqueline Tyroler. Otherwise she appeared quite composed.

Marco is gone. He'll never return. Marco is dead. Never come home.

Train wheels. Beating the rhythm of her misery yet again.

They sat together in the carriage, Anna trying to keep Francisco amused; the Capitano and Ernesto occasionally conversing, all of them hurtling north through the dark mountains, homewards. Home? Could she ever feel the same again about the villa she had turned into a home for them? Where they had lived and loved together, where she had given birth to his son and heir? The bedroom on which she had worked with paintbrush and ladder, paper and paste, to prepare for his homecoming at Christmas? Christmas! What a thought. Less than three weeks away. Presents bought and wrapped, 'To dear Papa with love from Katarina' written in big, uneven letters. The black morocco briefcase with his family insignia in the corner from herself. She took a handkerchief from her pocket.

'You dropped this, Signora.' Callone handed her a crumpled envelope.

'Thank you, but . . .' she was about to disclaim it, then changed her mind. Inside was a single, folded sheet.

Better it not be known that we communicate.

I was with him at the end. He was in a coma and felt no pain. He woke only once and asked me to send his love to you and the children.

313

Jacob regrets he is unable to attend the funeral. It is good to have him here.

Perhaps we may meet one day. I would like that.

You have my sincere sympathy.

C.

Jacqueline slipped the note back into her pocket, feigning indifference in case Callone was watching. It had removed any last hope that there could have been a mistake in identification: Camilla had been with him when he died. It really was Marco's body they had just placed with his ancestors in the Calitri family vault.

Camilla must have slipped the note into her pocket as she waited for her to pass with Francisco, behind the coffin. It had been kind of her.

Vaguely she wondered why Camilla had thought subterfuge was necessary.

December 1942 – September 1943

Now hatred is by far the longest pleasure;
Men love in haste, but they detest at leisure.

Lord Byron, *Don Juan*

CHRISTMAS HAD been a ghastly ordeal. Jean-Jacques had been transferred to a camp further south, too far to be allowed leave for the holiday. Jacob was at Calitri, Ernesto at home with his family. Anna tried hard to make Christmas lunch as bright and normal as possible, pulling crackers with the children and wearing a paper hat. Francisco was quite lively, but Katarina had long, solemn spells. Jacqueline had pushed the food round and round her mouth finding it very hard to swallow; while Sergio, the unwelcome guest who refused to wear a paper hat, sniffed.

Jacqueline realised that in a way the fact that Marco had not lived at home for two and a half years did make it easier for the children as well as herself. They had had a chance to become accustomed to his absence. As the weeks and months passed, the sudden waves of grief came less frequently and she was able to concentrate more consistently on the mundane tasks of daily life.

An official of Marco's Rome bank came out to see her one day by appointment; he wished to familiarise her with the terms of Count Luzzi's will.

The Calitri estates naturally went to the new count, Francisco, to be habited and controlled by the late count's estranged wife, Camilla, until she was sixty-five and Francisco twenty-four, at which time Camilla would retire to the east wing and the young count would take over the rest of the castle and the estates. At twenty-five, Francisco would become a director of the banking corporation, and ten years later, the president. He would also be the major shareholder of the banks, and throughout each of their lifetimes, he would pay Camilla and Jacqueline twenty percent each of his dividends.

Jacqueline became president of ten various companies of which she knew nothing, but for which she was later handed a pile of documents, accounts and balance sheets. She was also chief shareholder in four manufacturing companies in and around Milan. It was also requested that she pay Camilla twenty-five percent of the dividends on these. She received his shareholding in a jointly owned company whose registered office was in Panama . . . she gave a half smile; *Ocean Dreamer*, sitting in Miami.

'The Villa Mendose and the motor car factory at Vicenza are left to his daughter, Katarina, to be held in trust with you, Contessa, and myself as Trustees, until she is twenty-one. And finally, his last major bequest is the Milanese fine gold and precious jewellery manufactory to Jean-Jacques Tyroler, a splendid and lucrative company, if I may say so.' He was a pleasant, if overly serious man.

There were other generous bequests to family retainers including Giuseppe and Rosita.

They sat together after the reading, drinking coffee substitute and discussing various aspects of the will.

'You do realise, don't you, that I am under house arrest as an enemy alien, because I have an American passport, and therefore I cannot take part in any practical way in the running of the businesses or companies bequeathed to me, much as I would like to.' She thought how much it would help, to be able to continue the work Marco had been doing until he took up his military duties.

'Of course, Contessa.' He smiled over his spectacles. 'I must tell you that the Count spoke highly of your business acumen and I do look forward to the time when we can work together on projects to which Count Luzzi had devoted himself for many years. He had an excellent business brain, you know, and everyone who worked with him was grateful for the experience. He gave confidence and inspiration to us all.'

She smiled at him. 'Yes,' she agreed. 'To us all.'

Jean-Jacques had taken to writing quite regularly. Much of his time off duty was devoted to sport, at which he apparently excelled. He was moved by the generosity of Marco's will and looked forward to visiting his property in Milan. He expected to have leave to visit home around Eastertime. Jacqueline enjoyed his letters, though she wished they were not always signed, 'Frederick'.

Her latest concern was the education of Francisco, Katarina and Bobo, which she had intended to discuss with Marco at Christmas. Due to lack of regular transport into Rome they were attending the local village school, but the tuition was quite inadequate by private school standards. Capitano Callone had given permission for a private tutor to be engaged, provided that he approved her choice, but so far her advertisement in *Il Popolo* had produced only one elderly drunk.

Anna helped. Every time she visited Rome with Sergio she took the children with her and treated all four to visits to museums, the Vatican, the Coliseum and other places of historical interest, giving history lessons which she had swotted up the day before.

'You wouldn't believe it,' she told Jacqueline. 'Sergio puts up his hand to answer questions just as though he were still at school.'

'I sometimes wonder if we have been fair to him,' Jacqueline commented. 'Perhaps if we had been kinder and less critical, he might have been a nicer person.'

'I doubt it.' Anna was dubious. 'He is just one of those people who are born on the wrong foot . . . or whatever the expression is,' she added as her daughter burst out laughing.

The Sunday before Easter a smart little horse-drawn

317

vehicle drew up by the front door. Jacqueline ran to the window and saw Teresa step down.

'Teresa! What a lovely surprise,' she called, and hurried out to greet her ex-secretary.

'How are you, Contessa?' Teresa hugged her. 'I am so sorry . . .' she flushed.

'I know, everyone was. We are just getting used to the fact that he won't be returning.' She sighed. 'Now, to what do we owe the pleasure of this visit?'

'First,' Teresa whispered. 'Tell me what your guard is like. Can you trust him? I mean, is he a staunch Fascist?'

'Ernesto? Good heavens no, he's not a Fascist. Why?'

'This is why.' Jacob's head appeared from under a blanket.

'I wanted to bring my husband to see you,' Teresa announced.

'Husband? Oh, Teresa! Jacob, how lovely. When were you married?'

'Four weeks ago.'

They trooped inside to tell their story to Anna and the children.

Jacqueline felt uplifted for days after their visit. The transparent happiness of the young couple who owned nothing, had no prospects and no future other than their love for each other, heartened her. If they could feel so happy, surely she should not grieve as she did. She was still losing weight, was short-tempered and moody for long periods. She sat alone in her room for hours, brooding, remembering. But Marco was a chapter in her life which was now closed. Was she being overly morbid? Selfishly indulging in grief and making everyone around her miserable? Wasn't it time she thought of making Anna and the children happy? She spoke her thoughts to her mother one morning as they worked together in the kitchen.

'Two years, my dear. It takes two years for the pain and the grief to ease, despite all the positive and noble thoughts you might have. Claude was a comparatively brief page in my history, but even now, after nearly three years, I still get a lead weight in my stomach from time to time, thinking of him. It doesn't seem to follow any reminiscing or morbid thoughts. I am sure it is quite subconscious.' She peeled dough from her fingers and kneaded the bits into the large lump in her bowl. 'I am in my fifties, remember. There is little chance for me to start again. But you! You are only just thirty-two, beautiful and fabulously wealthy. When the war is over you will have all the eligible men in Europe at your feet . . . and a few who are not, too!'

'I suppose I should try to count my blessings, but I'm afraid the art of breadmaking is not one of them,' Jacqueline added as she removed a tray of unhealthy looking loaves from the oven.

'You were not born to make bread, my dear.' Anna's tone became haughty. 'You may not have made a brilliant marriage yet, but you were a superb wife to Marco in all but name, as well as a good mother and an astute business woman. You carry your title regally and I am proud of you. Your future may be obscure at the moment, but you certainly have nothing to fear. Oh, dear!' She looked down at her bowl. 'I don't think I was born to breadmaking, either.'

Jacqueline smiled to herself. Strangely, despite knowing how successful she had been, she did so enjoy her mother's words of praise. Did everyone want, need, their parents' praise and admiration all their lives?

Jean-Jacques didn't arrive home until May. More than ever he seemed to be a confused half-man, half-child. Taller than herself now, Jacqueline thought he looked extraordinarily healthy and athletic, considering the rigorous neglect of army life. He followed her around the villa, talking about football, athletics, his friends, his promotion to junior corporal.

'I won't be corporal in the senior army units, you cannot get senior promotion until you are over eighteen. This is pre-embarkation leave, did you know?'

'No. Where are you going?' She was horrified. What possible chance had this fifteen year old to survive actual fighting against British or American troops, men experienced and toughened by their victorious campaign in North Africa?

'We are not supposed to know, but everyone says it will be Sicily.'

'Why Sicily? And when will you go?' Some of her fear abated, as there was no fighting in Sicily.

'I don't think anyone knows that. They are very disorganised at headquarters. Now that the enemy have taken the whole of North Africa, I suppose we can expect them to attack Italy, the coast must be guarded. Mother,' he added, 'I hope you don't mind, but I have reassumed my Rumanian nationality. Rumania is an ally, and it would be very unpleasant if it was discovered that I have American citizenship.'

'I think in the circumstances that was very wise of you. By the way, what do you call yourself in camp? I see you always sign yourself Frederick, now.'

'I have always been known at school as Roli, from my last name, and they still call me that.'

He also spent a great deal of time with Anna, questioning her about Rumania and the royal family. She was happy to talk for hours on the subject. Jacqueline had not mentioned that she thought he now regarded himself as a prince. It might cause embarrassment between them, and anyway he would grow out of it.

When his leave ended he hugged Jacqueline tightly, which was most unusual these days. She guessed he was as nervous about being involved in battle as she was for him.

'Do remember, if you should be captured, you must try to contact Admiral Stevenson of the United States Navy. He might not be in the Mediterranean area, but if you insist they may let you write him a letter and he will eventually get it.' She felt sure that Bill would make every effort to help his grandson, even if he had been fighting on the wrong side. It would in fact be the best possible thing if he was taken prisoner. So much better than . . . oh, she could not bear to lose him as well as Marco. He saw the tears in her eyes.

'I am not going to be captured. Don't worry about me, Mother.' His tone was almost avuncular. 'I won't be hurt. I shall be quite safe.'

Nevertheless she was terribly worried a couple of months later when the British and Americans landed on Sicily. She had heard nothing of him since his departure and prayed he might have been wrong about their intended destination . . . until army police stormed into the villa searching every room, the stables and sheds. Jean-Jacques had deserted. They cross-examined her very roughly and it was lucky that Ernesto was there to vouch that the boy had left, apparently to join his new unit, and they had not seen him since.

Jacqueline and Anna were stunned. He had always seemed so enthusiastic about the army – they could not imagine what had suddenly changed his mind.

Before the end of July, Ernesto brought them the electrifying news about Mussolini. The two guards had become quite casual in their duties now, and the older man often went home to spend the evening with his family, returning as early next morning as transport would allow. On this occasion he was late, hurrying in flushed with excitement.

'Contessa, Contessa! Madame! Have you heard the news? Il Duce is under arrest. Finished. Marshal Badoglio is in his place.'

'What will this mean, do you think?' Jacqueline asked. 'Will he fight off the British and Americans with any more success?'

'He says he will. But many of us have our doubts. We will have to wait and see.'

Only three days later it was announced on the radio that the Italian Fascist Party was dissolved. They never saw Sergio again. Even Ernesto only spent an occasional day with them.

'I really don't know what the position is now,' he told them. 'Capitano Callone has gone away and the office is closed. Nobody seems to know what will happen next.'

'What is happening in Sicily? The war news on the radio is very vague,' Anna complained.

'My niece is a nurse and she says some of the soldiers in hospital were wounded in the mountains right up north around Mount Etna. I doubt it will be long before our troops are hurrying back across the Straits of Messina.' He shook his white head. 'What a mess. What a mess.'

The news, on 8 September, that Italy had signed an Armistice with Britain and America, following the fall of Sicily, relieved Jacqueline's mind about Jean-Jacques. Now, presumably, he would be able to return home without fear of the military police coming for him. But he still had not appeared when Ernesto came out to the villa to say goodbye.

'Don't worry about the boy, he will soon be home, Contessa. Look, I have brought you a little gift to say thank you for being so kind, sharing your home and your family with me.' He produced a bottle of brandy, a very precious gift indeed, from behind his back.

'Ernesto! You are the one who has been kind.' She hugged the old man and kissed his cheek.

The telephone rang.

'Hello?' Jacqueline answered in the drawing room.

'This is the Palazzo Venezia. There is a message for the Countess Tyroler. Is she there?' It was the voice of a young girl.

'Speaking.' She frowned. This was odd.

'It has come through on ship-to-shore radio with instructions to telephone you.'

'Yes. Yes, what does it say?'

'It just says, "With you soon. Stop. Bill."'

'Is that all? Nothing more?'

'No, nothing more.'

'Thank you very much, then. Goodbye.' She couldn't

help feeling disappointed. It would have been a relief to hear that, after all, he had found Jean-Jacques among the prisoners in Sicily.

Anna came down the stairs. 'Who was that?' she asked.

'Mama, it was a message from Bill. He says, "With you soon." It will be good to see him.'

'Marvellous, darling.' Anna forced a smile. 'Have you made up your mind what you are going to do next? Will you stay here, or do you want to go and live in America?'

'I think it would be better for us all to go to the United States for a while. The children can learn to speak English properly, and go to proper schools. It will take a long time for things to get back to normal here. I shall have to spend quite a lot of time travelling back and forth because of the businesses, but we should live over there. You will come with us, won't you?'

'No, I don't think so. I think it might be rather embarrassing for Bill and Louise, and myself, don't you?' Anna grimaced.

'Oh, dear, I suppose it would. I wasn't thinking. But still,' she brightened, 'we won't have to live with them. We can go to Miami and live on *Ocean Dreamer*. I don't know what the money situation will be. I might not be able to get any income from the businesses for years. Thank heavens Badoglio has agreed to an Armistice. At least the factories won't have been destroyed by bombs and shelling, even if the economy is in ruins. We might have to sell the yacht. Well, we must wait and see. In any case, you will love the States; it's a wonderful country. You will come, won't you?' she begged.

'My darling girl, what a dear, sweet, forgiving person you are!' Anna's eyes shone with tears again. 'How can I say no?'

So, what to take, what to leave behind? How long before she would return to Italy? It could be as long as a year.

In the end it was not difficult to decide about clothes. Nearly every practical garment they possessed was faded

323

and darned. Everything, in fact, except the ball gowns, worn only once, relics of another era . . . She closed the doors on them. Even if she had been able to get into Rome there was little in the shops to buy. Eventually she selected very few items for herself and for the children.

Now it was just a matter of waiting.

The weather was hot and sultry, as if, despite the sunshine, a storm was brewing. The children were bored.

'How about a picnic, up in the woods?' Anna suggested.

'Splendid idea, Mama. It will be a relief for them to get away from the house for a while. I had better stay here, though, in case there is another message from Bill.'

After they had gone, Jacqueline took a sunbed and a book out to the swimming pool. It was empty, of course, fuel and labour being too short to keep it clean. But it was a beautiful sunny area and she relaxed in a sunsuit, reading and dozing.

She shivered as a shadow passed over the sun. Surely the clouds weren't building up already. She looked up . . . and stopped breathing. The ice blue eyes of Heinrich von Reinikker were staring down at her.

She was speechless. Fear. Anger. Curiosity. Her mind spun; her mouth was dry and her lungs empty.

'Good afternoon, Countess.' Von Reinikker clicked his heels.

Jacqueline scrambled to her feet, fastening her towelling robe around her waist. 'Good afternoon.' It seemed a stupid thing to say.

'There are some matters we should discuss. Shall we go inside?'

The walk back across the lawn to the glass drawing room doors gave her time to think. What on earth was he doing here? Italy had surrendered. The British and US forces were already invading the Italian peninsula, as far as she knew. Was he going to appeal to her for help in escaping? She must say something.

'Surely Italy is no longer a very safe place for German

soldiers, since the Armistice?' She didn't look at him as she spoke.

'On the contrary, it is the Italian forces who are being rounded up; those who do not continue to fight with Feldmarshal Kesselring against the invaders. Armistice? That was only a traitorous plot by Badoglio. We have released Mussolini and he is now cooperating with his German advisers to bring the country back under control.'

'German advisers?' she queried. What was he saying? Mussolini . . .

'Yes. The Führer considers that Signor Mussolini needs assistance from the Fatherland to control the disloyal elements in all the major cities. Now,' he changed the subject, 'I see from the lists at the Passport Office that the Countess Tyroler is an American citizen. Therefore I must ask you to accompany me to Rome. There are several questions to be settled in accordance with our new regulations.'

'Questions? What about? You have no jurisdiction here. Under Italian law I am free to leave the country as soon as transport is available.' She tried to look dignified, but it was difficult standing there, bare-footed, her hair blown about by the wind.

'I don't think you understand. Italy is under German control now, and therefore it is German law which matters. Now, if you would care to put some clothes on before we leave . . .'

'But I am not going anywhere!' She would not dare to leave the villa with him; her heart pounded with terror at the thought.

'I assure you, Countess, you are, willingly or otherwise. Also, I understand that Madame Dumesca and your children are here. Where are they?'

Her brain worked quickly. 'They were staying with friends in Sicily before the invasion, so are presumably in American hands.'

He frowned. 'There was no record of this.'

'Of course not. They are not enemy aliens. Their movements were not restricted as mine were.' She prayed that the weather would remain fine and Anna would stay out until Reinikker left.

'Well, if it is so important I will get changed and come with you,' she told him.

She forced herself to walk up the stairs slowly. How to get a message to Anna? She must be warned. A note. Where was her pen? Here, a pencil would do. She sat at her dressing table.

There was a knock on the door. 'Colonel von Reinikker asks you to hurry, Countess.' It was one of his soldiers.

'Just coming,' she called. Grabbing a piece of paper she scrawled one word, 'Reinikker!!!' and screwed it up in her hand.

She pulled a skirt and shirt over her sunsuit and slipped her feet into sandals. At the bottom of the stairs she turned abruptly to the kitchen, calling to the soldier behind her. 'I must just tell the maid I am going out,' she said, and heard his feet following her.

Rosita was at the sink.

'I am going out for a while,' she said, grasping the old woman's hand and pressing the paper into it. 'Don't forget the note for the baker.'

'Eh?' Rosita looked at her in amazement.

'Yes, the baker,' she repeated, desperately hoping that the woman would realise she should give the paper to Anna, who was the one who baked their bread now. 'Goodbye.'

Reinikker didn't appear to have left any men at the villa. Jacqueline sighed with relief. Perhaps he had believed her story about Anna and the children. Now, she wondered, what does he want with me?

They climbed the stairs of a tall building in the city centre, past three floors of offices.

'There is insufficient electricity to power the lifts at present, but we have people working on it,' Reinikker explained.

It was the first time Jacqueline had been in Rome for nearly two years; she was amazed at how little it had changed. From the villa she had often enough seen Allied bombers flying inland, and had supposed Rome must have been one of their targets – but the Eternal City had so far been spared.

Reinikker opened a door. 'You will wait in here.'

Jacqueline did not like his tone, it was very abrupt. She looked around the small, bare room. It was like a doctor's waiting room; a few hard, straight-backed chairs and a table with some old magazines. Reinikker disappeared through the only other door in the room into what she thought was a general office, judging by the voices and the clatter of typewriters.

It was four-thirty by the clock on the wall. She wondered if Anna and the children had returned yet. Would Rosita give her the note? Oh, yes. The old woman had been so surprised at her odd behaviour that she would be sure to report it to her new friend, Anna. She wondered if she was being overly cautious. Even if the Germans were technically in control here, there was surely some limit to their powers. But on the other hand, Reinikker was a dangerous animal. Instinctively she wanted to keep her mother and children away from him. How would Anna react to the one word on the note? She might take the children down to the village until she returned home.

The magazines were old political issues, full of the wonderful part Italy was to play in the 'New European Order'. She thumbed through them, looking at repeated photographs of Duce with various ministers and groups of glorious soldiers and airmen. What a great big, stupid dream it had all been.

She became restless. It was now five-thirty. This was downright rude. What attitude should she take, bold or submissive? Could it help just to sit here by the hour, patiently awaiting von Reinikker's pleasure? Pleasure! No, surely not that. This was an office. He only wanted her here for some petty official business. He was trying to irritate her.

She walked to the inner door, hesitated a moment, then swung it open. There were several men in German uniforms sitting at desks and a table. One looked up and raised his eyebrows at her without speaking.

'Colonel von Reinikker seems to have forgotten I am here. Will you tell him that if he cannot see me in the next five minutes I wish to go home. I will have to see him another day when he has more time.'

All the men raised their heads and looked at each other, grinning. Still, not one of them spoke, but the nearest pointed the end of his pen at the door through which she had just entered, in a gesture of dismissal.

Either she 'backed down' and obeyed or headed for the door at the far end of the room through which Reinikker had obviously gone. Retreating was no longer in her nature. She walked straight to the door and opened it without knocking, hearing men hurrying after her. Reinikker sat alone, at his desk.

'I have been waiting for over an hour,' she tried to speak calmly. 'I have no intention of waiting forever. Either you see me now or I will return home and we will have an appointment for a more convenient time.'

He ignored her.

'Why have you let this woman come in here?' he demanded of the men behind her. 'Get her out!'

'How dare you be so insolent, Reinikker.' She was furious. 'If you cannot be civil . . .'

He strode across the room and, while her arms were held, hit her across the mouth. 'Take her away!'

She was dragged backwards through the doorway, while he coolly returned to his desk. They pushed her back into the waiting room and closed the door.

She was paralysed with shock and fear. She tasted blood on her lip, then panic hit her. Get out! You've got to get out, quickly. She turned the handle of the outer door; it wouldn't open. She shook it. The heavy, panelled wood didn't move. She was locked in.

Help. Get help. She ran to the window and pulled open the casement. In the street fifty feet below were a few German soldiers. But surely there must be other people, Italian people, within hearing, behind all those windows.

'Help! Help me!' she yelled. 'Help! Please help!'

Some of the soldiers looked up, laughed, and walked on. No one else appeared.

She sat biting a fingernail. Got up and tried the outer door again . . . sat down.

At a quarter to seven a man opened the inner door and beckoned her with a jerk of his head. She followed him to von Reinikker's door which he opened and stood aside for her to enter.

Reinikker didn't look up; he just left her standing there while the door behind her closed. A mixture of fear and anger welled up again. He really couldn't behave like this. Whatever he said, the war in Italy was over.

'Are all Germans as rude or are you an exception?' She tried to look dignified, arrogant, but was horribly aware of the ill-matched clothes hastily pulled on over her sunsuit, her flat sandals.

The angry question brought no response – he might not have heard.

Two could play at that game. She strolled over to a cabinet where brandy and glasses stood ready on a salver, poured herself a drink, and turned, holding it to her lips. It was plucked from her fingers and replaced on the salver; he had followed her across the room.

'Sit down,' he ordered.

'I prefer to stand . . .'

She was pushed into a leather chair, bruising her hip on the wooden arm.

'Will you stop behaving like a childish bully and tell me what you want?' She tried to keep the fear out of her voice.

Silently he poured a drink for himself, lit a cigarette and fitted it meticulously into a gold holder.

'Kindly be civil enough to answer me. What do you want? Why are you keeping me locked in like a prisoner?'

He blew smoke at the ceiling. 'I will ask the questions. First, where is Count Luzzi?'

She pressed her lips together.

'You received a message through the Palazzo Venezia a short while ago. Tell me, who is Bill?'

She stared at a point just above his left shoulder.

'Very well. You will remain here overnight. You will be quite comfortable. You may take a bath and there are clothes in the wardrobe.'

He rang a bell on his desk and a white-coated manservant limped into the room. Reinikker looked at her and moved his head in the direction of the open door.

'I have no intention of staying here all night.' She made one desperate last stand. 'Kindly allow me to return home.'

She might as well have saved her breath.

She was pushed through a charming sitting room, then a small foyer, and into a bedroom. The door was closed behind her and she heard the key turn. Another door beyond the four poster bed led into a beautiful marble bathroom. It really was a magnificent apartment. She wondered who had been deposed to accommodate von Reinikker.

A thought struck her. Was this his room? Was he going to try to make love to her again, after all these years? She looked around, opened cupboards and drawers. No, there was no sign of anything that looked as though it might belong to him. There were masculine clothes, yes, but not his style or size.

The mirror over the dressing table gave her quite a shock. She looked a frightful mess. Right, she thought. She would take up his offer of a bath and fresh clothes.

The water was hot, and she soaked for a while. Wiping condensation from the bathroom mirror she studied the bruise and cut on her lip and pulled her comb through her hair. She walked back into the bedroom wrapped in a huge towel, and found two white-coated men waiting for her. They said nothing but seized a wrist each and, as the towel fell away, forced her, naked, towards the bed.

'No! Stop it! Leave me alone!' She swung and brought her knee up into a groin.

'Bitch!' the man yelled. He was in considerable pain, but not sufficient to prevent him twisting her arm up her back.

She screamed . . . but stopped struggling.

One of the men held her down while the other tied the free wrist to the nearest bedpost. An ankle was tied to one of the footposts despite her kicks. Then she was pulled on to her back and the other wrist and ankle tied to the other posts. The men left the room. She was lying naked, with arms and legs pulled wide across the big bed, unable to move.

At last the full truth of what was happening dawned on her. It was amazing how it had taken so long, but perhaps subconscious fear had prevented her from believing the obvious. She was completely and utterly in Reinikker's power. And he was going to avenge himself! He wanted revenge for the fiasco of his advances in Berlin, for her escape from him and his blackshirt bully boys, and for the scene at the British Embassy Ball in Rome.

When the door opened, she didn't need to raise her head to know it was him.

She couldn't hide a searing blush and tears of embarrassment as he gazed down at her body. He stood, with a faint smile on his lips, looking at her for a full minute. It seemed like an eternity.

She turned her face away.

'Well, well, my proud Countess. Don't tell me you are speechless for once,' he sneered.

He was right. For once she was speechless. Had she been able to force words out, there was nothing to say: even to relieve her feelings. She was no longer angry – just terrified. A heavy weight lay on her chest, making it

331

difficult to breathe. What was he going to do? Rape her? Beat her? Was he that savage? She remembered Jacob's account of Reinikker's attack on their home in Munich, the murder of Herman, Sarah and Ruth, for which he was responsible. Yet, although she had been terrified of the very thought of him for years, still she found it difficult to associate the suave, cultured, meticulous German officer with those atrocities.

'What a pity you didn't learn to hold your tongue and curb your arrogance years ago. We might have been good friends. Instead, you chose to be so unpleasant. You made me very angry, you know. Very, very angry.' He moved to study her body from another angle, held his head on one side. 'Very unwise of you,' he added quietly.

He placed a forefinger on her shoulder and drew it down, slowly, softly, to circle a nipple. She shivered and went rigid, the nipple hardening to a point.

'Ah! I see you respond to touch,' he commented.

'I am cold,' she murmured.

'You always were. You are a cold woman. However, we will see if we can warm you.' He pressed a bell.

A door opened.

'Brandy and glasses, Otto.'

He held a glass to her lips, then tipped it too fast so that she gagged. He waited and gave her more, sipping from his own glass at the same time. She felt the alcohol radiate heat from her stomach right through her body.

'Better?' He placed both glasses on the table.

She nodded.

With the back of his finger he stroked the flesh under one breast, then under the other. Then he moved it slowly, barely touching, down her stomach to circle softly through the curls on her mound.

Again she stiffened.

'Still cold? You need more brandy. Here.'

She raised her head to sip again. Not that she really wanted to drink; she had not lunched before he arrived at the villa so it was nearly twenty-four hours since she had

332

eaten and already the brandy was making her feel dizzy. But at least it kept his hands off her body. He continued to hold the glass for her, silently sipping from his own.

Suddenly the tension left her and she felt quite relaxed. That was better, now she could think, plan how best to react to him, though somehow it didn't seem to matter. Her eyes were closed and she lay wondering if Anna and the children were at the villa. Anna would be worrying . . .

A delicious sensation quivered up through her stomach and she realised he was stroking very gently through the hair on her groin.

'So! The cold Countess is warming up!'

'No!' He must not know of the spasm of response he had roused.

'Then a little more brandy, I think.'

She turned her head away from the glass. She should have known that was why he was urging the liquor on her.

'Come, come, you don't want me to force you to drink, do you? I can, you know.'

She obeyed, taking minute sips at a time, frightened of making him angry. He was patient and persistent.

When he put down the glass she let her head fall back on the pillow and closed her eyes. She could feel his gaze on her, then the finger again, lightly tracing lines and circles over her skin: arms, breasts, stomach, thighs . . . back to her groin. A feather-like touch, teasing, tantalising . . .

It was so long since she had been touched, nearly four years. Long enough to lose the desire and response, she had supposed.

Suddenly she realised that she was shaking, that her back was arched reaching up for more. No, stop it. Think of something else. The boat, the children. Anna. Marco . . . no, no, not him. Not now . . .

Just pretend to be asleep.

He was no longer touching her, but her body still quivered. She knew he was still in the room, heard him moving.

Then he was on her, pressing into her.

She tried to prevent herself moving with him, reaching up to his thrusts . . . but could not prevent her body convulsing in reaction to the sensation.

No! Oh God, no! Not with Reinikker! Tears of helpless rage trickled out from under her lids.

Taps were running in the bathroom. Twice a door opened and closed. The second time it was Otto and his assistant, come to untie her. They left a tray of bread, antipasta, and tepid coffee.

Her legs felt almost too weak to carry her. She swayed into the bathroom and tried to swallow some water, her throat was so dry.

She rolled herself in a sheet on the bed and drifted through a brandy haze into sleep.

The sleep hadn't lasted long. She lay, waking and dozing through terrifying nightmares and distorted pictures until daylight.

Her head throbbed and she felt sick. In the bathroom she pushed her fingers down her throat, forcing herself to retch up the bitter, stinging bile from her stomach.

A bath made her feel a little better. The lady's clothes in the wardrobe were far too small, the skirt not reaching to her knees, but a man's shirt and trousers, belted well in at the waist, were quite comfortable.

She wasn't hungry, but as the morning wore on and no one came near her she knew she should try to eat some of the stale food from last night's tray.

The doors were locked, as she knew they would be. Why was he keeping her here? To play with, torment as a cat torments a mouse . . . before killing it? Was that what he intended? Was he so angry for what she had said and done in Berlin and at the British Embassy Ball? Angry enough to kill her?

The memory of last night made her sick with anger at herself. Imagine being stupid enough to drink so much brandy that she allowed her body to respond to the beast.

She would never have believed it possible that she would react so. It was horribly humiliating.

There were no books in the room, nothing to occupy her mind. Only the little fanlights above the windows would open, so she was unable to look down into the street. No one moved in the building opposite.

The rumpled bed irritated her. She re-made it. Flushed the remaining food from the tray down the toilet, washed the plates and brandy glasses. Wiped, tidied, dusted.

She lay on the floor to do her daily muscle-toning exercises.

When daylight faded, she switched on the light.

Long afterwards the door opened and Otto came in with a tray. Spaghetti and tomato sauce.

She ate it all.

She could not remember how many days and nights she spent in that room. It was probably only four or five, but it felt like weeks.

Then one day Otto led her into Heinrich's office.

'Sit,' Heinrich ordered, as though she were a dog, she thought.

She obeyed.

'Now, if you answer my questions it will be easier for you, for both of us.'

It was hard to believe what feelings he had aroused in her only a few days ago.

'Who is Bill?'

'A family friend.' How much of the truth would it be safe to tell him? Could it do any harm for him to know all about Bill?

'What nationality is he?'

'American.'

'His full name?'

'William Stevenson.'

'What service and rank?'

She hesitated. 'What makes you think . . .?'

'Service and rank,' he snapped.

'Navy . . . I don't know.'

335

He pressed a bell on his desk. Immediately two soldiers came in and stood behind her chair.

'Rank?' There was a threat in his voice. He would no doubt set his bully boys to beat it out of her.

'Er . . . Commander.'

Reinikker got up, walked round his desk and hit her hard across the face. 'Rank?'

God, how she hated this man! 'Admiral, you savage bastard.'

He hit her again. 'Ship?'

'I have no idea.' That was the truth.

Again her head was knocked sideways; she could no longer hold back the tears. 'Are you deaf?' she sobbed. 'I told you I didn't know . . . I have no idea. Years ago I went on his ship but I don't know what sort of a boat it was, nor what it was called. Beat me to a pulp if you like, I know you'll enjoy it, but I cannot tell you what I don't know, can I?'

'It is surprising what some people can remember . . . when they are . . . persuaded.'

'Duce is a friend of mine, you know. You wait until he hears about this,' she threatened.

He burst out laughing. 'So! The Countess has a sense of humour! Ha, Duce might have been a friend of Count Luzzi, but I am told that Luzzi is dead. So Duce is no longer a friend of yours. Anyway, I assure you, he is in no position to help you now, even if he was interested.'

She was silent.

'Where is your other son, the one you had with you in Berlin?'

'Jean-Jacques? He is in the army.'

'What army?'

'The Italian Army.'

'Italian!' he exclaimed. 'But he has an American passport, like yourself. How can he be fighting with the Italians?'

She sighed. 'Does it matter? He is only a child.'

'How old is he?'

'Fifteen.'

'And you say you don't know where he is? Come, come, I cannot believe that.' He grabbed her chin and shook her.

Something snapped inside her. She leapt at him, hitting, scratching, kicking . . .

The two men grabbed her, their fingers pinching hard into her arms.

'That was stupid,' Reinikker remarked quietly as he dusted the scratches from his boots. 'I see you need to be taught another lesson. Into the other room,' he told the men, who turned and frog-marched her back into the bedroom.

Otto was waiting with the other white-jacketed man. They stripped her and tied her to the bed as they had done the first night. The soldiers stayed to watch, laughing and joking, fingering her breasts and groin.

'Don't mark her,' Otto warned.

She lay there for hours after they left, feeling dazed and confused, weeping.

It was dark when Otto came in and she didn't know what he was doing until she felt a needle jab into her thigh. Then he was gone.

The effect was quite quick. Pleasant waves of relaxed euphoria swept over her. The bed seemed more comfortable and her wrists and ankles no longer hurt.

The door opened and shut but it really didn't matter who it was. Let them get on with whatever they wanted to do, as long as they didn't hurt her.

She had no idea how long she slept. Her arms and legs were free, a coverlet thrown over her. Her mouth was dry, so dry. She wobbled into the bathroom and drained three tumblers of water. Standing under the cold shower her brain began to clear.

The swine, the swine, the swine. Twice he had used her body, twice brought her to reluctant orgasm. How long would this go on? How often would he want this 'act of sex' with her before he let her go? She had not been clever. He was right, in fact; she had been very stupid. She should try to match his cunning. Surely she could fight off the effects of the drugs if she concentrated? Not if she was starving, though. They had again left a tray for her, more spaghetti with tomato sauce. Wrapped in a towel she sat at the table, cut forkfuls of the cold pasta and forced herself to eat. She drank the cold coffee. Half the spaghetti was left so she washed out a pin tray from the dressing table and used it as a dish to store the remainder in the bathroom cupboard, to eat later just before the time Reinikker had come in on both evenings. She must do this every day. Then the drugs would have far less effect. She must not allow herself to show any response, then he would no longer want her and would probably throw her out.

It had been ridiculous to lose her temper during the questioning. She must control herself, keep cool, in command of her thinking if not her situation.

First, she must maintain a sense of time, otherwise she would lose orientation, even go off her head if Reinikker kept her here long enough. It was difficult without a clock, but she would have to gauge the time of day by the sun's arc and divide each day into a programme; portion the food out, plan active and inactive periods. But at the same time she must pretend to deteriorate.

Four nights later she was again tied to the bed, again injected. She fought the waves of dizziness, concentrating on hating Reinikker. She tried to add columns of figures in her head . . . nearly impossible.

When he came in she feigned sleep, careful, though, not to relax. The routine was the same, the soft stroking of her body. The attempted arousal.

She pictured his open hand across her face, his shouts and sneers. But the light stroking persistently drew her mind, her awareness. She thought of Rosita and Giuseppe; about the contents of her larder; tried to estimate the number of bottles of fruit and conserves in the pantry . . . while all her feeling was drawn to his hand. She had a sense of floating. What was she struggling for? Why not relax? Let the beautiful thing happen, just once more.

But the stroking had stopped.

A door opened.

'You fool, Otto, you gave her too much,' Heinrich snarled.

'It was the same dose as the last time, Herr Colonel,' Otto whined.

'Halve it the next time.'

They left the room together.

She had won that round.

Two days later they tried it again. Because of the smaller drug dose it was easier to resist his touch, to transfer her mind to mundane matters. Again she was feigning sleep when he stopped stroking and she heard him strike a match, pause, and drop it in the ashtray.

Without warning a searing pain shot through her breast. She screamed.

'Did that wake you? Or were you awake all the time?' He stood over her, wearing a silk dressing gown.

She could smell the scorching flesh where his cigarette had burned her. She watched him inhale, causing the cigarette end to glow red. Saw his hand move across her.

'No! No!' She screamed again and again as the stub bit through the skin of her other breast, then back and forth from one to the other.

She sobbed and moaned in agony. 'Why, Heinrich? Why are you doing this? What do you want of me?'

He walked round the bed, untying her. 'I want you to cringe, to cry and beg my forgiveness for the insults you have given me. That is what I want!' He grabbed her wrist and pulled her off the bed with a bump. 'On your knees, woman. On your knees and beg, pray to me for mercy.'

Anger pounded in her head, agony seared through her chest, fear fought the drug in her brain. She couldn't think. All she wanted was to fight off this depraved animal and run. Get away, anywhere, away, away.

The bedside table was a delicate thing on spindly legs.

339

She grabbed one of them, sending the lamp, ashtray and his brandy glass crashing as she swung it at him.

She hadn't realised how useless her drugged limbs were. It was a feeble effort in which she lost her balance, falling forward from her knees on to her face. Heinrich had only had to take one step to avoid being touched.

'On your knees, I said.' He snatched a handful of her hair and jerked her up.

She screamed in anguish as his hand slapped across her face, back and forth. 'Shut up, you damned bitch. Stop your screaming and speak. Speak,' he shouted. 'Come on, beg me to forgive you.'

With one last effort she swung her hand at his face, and felt her nails drag through his flesh . . . before a violent pain shot through her whole body. Then blackness.

January 1944 – May 1944

> And now in age I bud again,
> After so many deaths I live and write;
> I once more smell the dew and rain,
> And relish versing: O, my only Light,
>   It cannot be
>   That I am he,
> On whom Thy tempest fell all night.

George Herbert, *The Temple: (The Flower)*

JACQUELINE HAD no idea where she was; it could have been the same building or a hundred miles away. She had remained unconscious for an immeasurable time, surfacing only when the drug wore off and the agony in her breasts woke her.

Thinking clearly again had hurt. In a state of mental and physical shock, she still couldn't believe what had happened . . . expected to wake from the hideous nightmare safe and warm in her own bed. But the burns were too real, her whole body seemed bruised and she was cold, shivering. She tried to wash out all awareness, drift into a vacuum, but pain and discomfort fought back.

She was in a cellar, lit only by a shallow grille just below the ceiling. A small pile of sacks in one corner and the coverlet in which she must have been carried served as her bed. Someone, Otto and his friend perhaps, had pulled her into the shirt and trousers she had worn on her last day in the bedroom.

There were wooden steps beside one wall with a door

at the top which opened inwards, so anyone or anything standing on one of the top three steps when it opened would be knocked down eight feet to the stone floor. Twice each day the door opened and food was placed one step down, either bread and soup or bread and pepperoni. She discovered that if she placed the chipped enamel jug on the fourth step down it would be taken away and filled with water. If the stinking latrine pail was left beside it, it was taken and emptied.

She found it hard to estimate how long she had been there. If she had had a knife or a pencil she could have marked the wall to record the days . . . if she could remember. But the days were so long one might notch three times, forgetting each time that the previous notch was made only hours before. Some of the burns had healed, but others still wept yellow fluid; one oozed pus and it hurt to move her right arm.

When she first recovered her senses in the cellar, she tried hard to nurse herself back to health, mentally and physically. When she was strong enough she tried to do her exercises again, those that did not require her to use her right arm. She tried to divide up the day, ration out the hours of thinking into set subjects. But it all became pointless . . . too exhausting. In constant gloom or darkness, on a diet which frequently made her vomit, she found herself drifting more and more through dreams and nightmares, not knowing where she was when she awoke. Images of Jean-Paul, in Rumania, in Paris and even coming to her in the cellar, recurred over and over. Sometimes he was in army uniform, sometimes in civilian clothes. Once he was without clothes at all, making love to her – then he became confused with Marco and Reinikker and she screamed and screamed until she awoke exhausted. She knew she had lost weight, her arms and legs were so thin, though her stomach seemed distended by hunger.

She couldn't understand why Reinikker kept her locked up. He never saw her now so he could no longer gloat.

Hah! She never did beg him to forgive her, but would she be here now, if she had? Might he have let her go?

She scratched her head. It itched like mad, but it hadn't been washed for . . . how long? She had bathed or showered twice a day all her life. She supposed she must smell pretty awful, though she couldn't smell anything herself. Even the latrine bucket was no longer offensive. The shirt and trousers were filthy, but it was so cold she never took them off, and anyway there was no means of washing them and nothing else to wear. One of the sacks made a good top-coat. There was plenty of warmth in sacking. The British and Americans seemed to be taking a long time coming. Or had they been thrown out of Italy as Reinikker had vowed they would be? If only he had told her how long she would be imprisoned. She curled up on the sacks under the filthy coverlet and scratched herself to sleep.

Days, or weeks, later, during pitch darkness, she heard voices. It was a long time since she had heard anyone speak.

'Gott! The stink! I am not going down there. Bring her out and let me look at her.' It was Heinrich's voice.

Oh no! Not more burns.

'Come. Up the stairs,' a man's voice ordered.

Better do as he said, then they might not burn her. The stairs seemed to have become higher and steeper recently. Perhaps they had come in the night to alter them while she was asleep. Just to make it more difficult for her . . . to test her. The light through the doorway hurt her eyes so she shaded them with her hand.

Heinrich stood in the corridor. He seemed to have grown bigger. No, he couldn't have, he was too old to grow any more. She had just never noticed before.

'That is the Countess? Are you sure?' he asked.

Silly man. He knew perfectly well she was a countess.

'We will be moving all the prisoners in a few days. They are being assembled so you may receive others here to be held until transport is arranged.' He turned to look at her again. 'So, Countess, you look and smell rather different from the occasion of the British Embassy Ball in Rome, remember? I did tell you it was unwise to anger me, didn't I? Now, are you going to beg forgiveness?'

She cringed back against the wall, the bright light hurting her eyes. What was the beastly man talking about? Of course she looked different in a ballgown. What was he asking her, forgiveness? Forgiveness!

'No. How can I forgive you? The burns still hurt. Perhaps one day. You can't help being the way you are, I suppose.' Her voice sounded slurred and distant.

'She is too far gone, Herr Colonel. She cannot understand what you are saying.' Jacqueline tried to focus on the other man, but failed.

'Perhaps. Perhaps.' Reinikker beat the side of his boot with his baton. 'Put her back.'

Some days later someone was pushed down her cellar stairs. He fell heavily, his hands tied behind his back, and lay very still.

Jacqueline sat near him on the floor for a while, watching. Eventually she touched his arm. 'Are you one of them?'

'Uh?'

'Are you a German?'

He clearly did not understand what she was saying, therefore he was not Italian. She tried German, and then French, with no better success, save that he seemed to understand a word or two of French. That meant he had to be English.

'Are you a German?' she asked again, in English.

'Great Scot, no! Hello.' He blinked at her. 'Are you English?'

'Of course not.'

'But . . . what are you doing here?'

'This is my cellar,' she told him. 'I have been here for weeks. You are English, aren't you?'

'Yes. Look, do you think you could untie my hands, please?'

'How do I know you won't hit me . . . or touch me? Have you got any cigarettes?'

'Cigarettes? No, why? Do you need to be paid in cigarettes?'

'No, silly, I don't smoke. I just don't want you to burn me.'

'Burn you?'

'Yes. Cigarette burns hurt so much, and one of them has gone bad. I think that is why I cannot use my arm much. But I will try to untie you if you promise not to burn me.'

He looked at her long and hard. 'I promise.'

Her nails were very long and got in the way. Her fingers were weak.

'My name is David Broughton. What's yours?'

'Jacqueline Tyroler.'

'What nationality are you?'

'Why do you want to know? You are one of them. I won't untie you because you're going to burn me.' She moved back to her sacks.

'I am a British Royal Air Force pilot . . .'

'You're lying!' Suddenly she started to scream at him. 'Don't come near me. No, no more, please, no more.' She lay on the sacks, weeping.

He sat looking at her in horror, hands still tied behind his back.

After a while she got up, scrambled up the first few stairs, and sat watching him as though he were a dangerous animal. Moments later the door opened and a tray was placed inside.

She looked puzzled, frowned at the second bowl of soup, then carried the tray down to the floor. It smelled horrible, but he was starving, as she obviously was. She dipped a chunk of bread into the greasy liquid and sucked it, over and over, finally lifting the tin bowl to her lips.

David's mouth was watering. 'May I have some? I am very hungry.'

'I do apologise. I should have helped you first.' She held the full bowl to his lips.

He was almost too surprised to drink. She sounded so gentle and cultured, so different.

'Wouldn't it be better if I released your hands?' she asked. Apparently she had no recollection of her first attempt.

'I would be most grateful, if you are sure you don't mind.' He spoke quietly.

'Of course not. You must be feeling so uncomfortable.' She started working on the knots. 'Oh dear, they are very tight, aren't they? And your wrists are bleeding. I think you had better eat first or he will take away the bowl before you have finished.' She dunked the bread and fed it to him like a baby.

When he had finished she took the tray and bowls back to the top of the stairs and returned for the jug and the pail. It was a major operation; her limbs dragged heavily and she had to sit on each stair, lifting each item separately, step by step. She turned to stare at him. 'You are not Jean-Jacques,' she accused, pointing a clawlike finger at him.

'No, I'm David.' He smiled, praying her mind would not slip back into terror.

'David? David! I don't know a David, do I?'

'Yes, you know me, Jacqueline. I'm David from England.'

'Oh, well, if you say so.' She sighed, and relaxed.

The door opened. Hands removed the tray, jug and pail. The key turned and turned back a few minutes later. The jug and pail were replaced.

Slowly she brought them down and held the jug to her mouth. 'I suppose you want some of my water?'

'Yes please.'

When he was finished she set the jug carefully in a corner, then, without hesitation or ceremony, dropped her trousers and sat on the pail. He looked away, wishing she would hurry up and release him. He needed to use the pail, too, but he could hardly ask her assistance for that.

She worked on the rope intermittently. The trouble was she kept forgetting what she was doing.

'I don't really know why I bother,' she muttered. 'It won't be any use for tying Christmas presents. It's too thick.'

She must have been shut up in here alone for many weeks, he thought, to be in this state. He longed to ask her questions but was afraid she would imagine he was cross-examining her and take fright again.

It was nearly dark when he felt the bond on one wrist slacken. Painfully he eased his hand out of the widened noose.

'Thank you,' he smiled at her. 'That was very kind. Now I think I can undo the other myself.' His fingers were stiff and numb. He just hoped she would now remove her malodorous body back to her sacks in the corner.

David couldn't sleep. The stone floor was cold and damp, but he didn't fancy lying on one of Jacqueline's sacks, even if she could be persuaded to part with one. The stink from her corner caught his breath. He listened to her throat rasping. Twice she cried out, muttered to herself, whimpered. Only once could he follow the words.

'Marco, Marco my darling, why did you leave me? Please come back,' she was sobbing, in French.

He must have dozed off, briefly. He woke to pale light and running water. She was on the bucket again. He had used it twice himself so it must be getting pretty full. He would carry it up the stairs himself, today.

She pottered about the floor, talking under her breath, looked up, saw him, and screamed. 'What do you want? What are you doing here?' She backed away into her corner.

'I am a prisoner here, like you. They have captured me.' He spoke softly.

347

'Oh, thank God. I thought you were one of them. What is your name?'

'David.'

'I think I have heard that name before, and your face is familiar. We must have met somewhere. Can we be friends?'

'Of course we can.' This was better.

'Will you be staying long?'

He wished he knew. 'Until they move me on.'

'Let's go together, shall we? It has been very lonely here all by myself.'

'Have they kept you here very long, then?'

'I don't know. I lost count of the days. It seems a long time, at least a month or two. It is very worrying. The children will wonder where I am.'

'They captured me three weeks ago. When did they get you. Can you remember the date?'

'Not exactly, but I think it was about the end of September. It was very hot. How long will it be before Christmas? I must get the children's presents.'

Christmas? Christmas was two months ago! Had she been alone here for five months? No wonder the poor thing was demented. 'Long enough to give you time for your shopping,' he assured her. There was no point in distressing her with the truth.

They were only confined together for a few days, but in that time David was pleased to note a slight improvement in her mental state. Although he had had some rough treatment himself during cross-examination, he was mentally and physically fit, and tried to help her think logically.

Early one morning they heard sounds of activity. Their food came in early, and not long after, armed guards ordered them out into a big courtyard where other prisoners were waiting in groups. More kept appearing until three or four hundred were assembled.

Heinrich von Reinikker arrived in a jeep around noon. He spoke to the guards in charge of each party of prisoners. 'Where is the Countess?' he demanded in a loud voice.

'Countess?' David exclaimed, as Reinikker approached.

'Yes.' The German answered for her, in English. 'Didn't she tell you she is the famous and beautiful young socialite, Countess Jacqueline Tyroler? How are the illustrious fallen!' he added with a sneer. 'Mein Gott, Jacqueline, not even Il Duce's cat would look at you now. Ugh! You stink!' His expression was one of triumph mingled with disgust as he moved away.

They were all herded out of the gates in a column, chivvied by boots and rifle butts. Like Jacqueline, many of the prisoners had been confined for months and found walking painful, and in some cases impossible for their useless muscles. After only a hundred yards David dragged Jacqueline's arm over his shoulder, held the wrist with one hand while supporting her round the waist with the other. Her eyes, weakened by the dim cellar, hurt in the bright sunlight. They were moving through a dirty, built-up area of warehouses, sheds and occasional blocks of cheap tenements. People who looked scarcely better off than themselves stared silently at the line of human scarecrows.

'David, I cannot walk any more.' His burden slid on to the roadside and lay in a filthy heap. Before he could pull her up again a boot crunched into her ribs.

'You bloody idiot! Can't you see she's finished?' David shouted at the young soldier. A rifle butt caught him across the face, spurting blood down his shirt. Two other prisoners shouted and other guards ran up to encircle the group.

Von Reinikker's jeep screeched up. 'What is it?'

A corporal told him what had happened.

The colonel caught the young soldier by the front of his battledress. 'You were detailed to escort them, not kill them,' he hissed. 'You are responsible for getting them to the station. So carry her.'

They waited in a wire-enclosed compound for two blistering days and icy nights. Buckets of water were passed round with one tin cup. Chunks of bread were shared out the first day and on the second the buckets were filled with a greasy, evil-smelling mess called soup. Sanitation was an open trench beside the wire.

A steam engine drew up on the third day, trailing a variety of goods vans and cattle trucks, all already full of prisoners, into which they climbed, or were pushed and thrown rapidly before it moved on.

The train laboured very slowly. Jacqueline lay motionless for a long time and David was relieved when, at last, very painfully, she sat up; he doubted she could survive much longer, anyway. And what had she to live for? Could this pathetic hag ever have been beautiful? A countess? It was hard to believe.

They were in a goods van, the view limited to thin slits between worn timbers. David guessed they were moving up the valley of the River Tiber into the mountains. By nightfall they passed through a station where he glimpsed a signboard stating 'Terni', wherever that was; he knew very little of Italy. After fifteen hours without food and water, even he was feeling weak. It was very cold and in a way they were grateful for the warmth of strange bodies packed so close together. Some lay, some sat, a few still stood. One died. The smell was appalling.

Jacqueline drifted through a haze varying in density with her level of consciousness. She murmured something.

'What did you say?' David asked.

'Are we out of Rumania yet? Don't let the king get him, will you.' Her mind had drifted back fourteen years. She could hear the train wheels carrying her through Hungary into Germany, but no! Not there. Reinikker would find her. Better to go on to Paris, but that would not do either. King Carol would be waiting to sit her on the piano; but surely Jean-Paul would be at the party and he would take her away to Marco? They couldn't leave Anna behind, though, and they must get to the ship in time.

What was that explosion? And gunfire! The Germans were firing on them again. Poor Claude. God! The pain. She had tried so hard and now there was nothing. If she closed her eyes tight and prayed perhaps God would end it all . . . take her . . .

'Quick! Come on, old girl, we're getting out of here.' David dragged her to the open side of the van.

'No. No more, I am at the end. It is all finished. You go.' Feebly she tried to resist.

'Nonsense, you are a countess. Countesses cannot give up, they have responsibilities. Now make an effort.' But she was too weak to move.

'Want help?' a strange voice asked.

'Yes. She is pretty far gone, I'm afraid,' David answered.

'You don't look too good yourself. Come on, let's go.'

Jacqueline was only aware of agony in her ribs and breast and another immense pain in her back and stomach as she was lifted over someone's shoulder, before she passed out again.

Wooden walls? Of course, she was on *Ocean Dreamer*. That was why she felt sick. Not that she had ever been seasick before. It was broad daylight, but she still felt weary. She yawned.

'She yawned!' someone shouted.

Jacqueline turned her head towards the voice.

'Who are you?' She could hardly hear herself speak.

'Just a friend. We are all friends, here. You are quite safe now.' It was a woman talking.

She must have fallen asleep again because the next thing she knew someone was turning back the sheet and blanket to tend the sore on her breast. She recognised this woman immediately.

'Camilla?' What on earth was Marco's legal wife doing here?

'Hello, Jacqueline, you have had a long sleep,' she smiled. 'Yes, this is looking much better.'

'I don't understand . . .' Jacqueline reached out to touch her, but her arm felt like a lead weight and fell back on the bed. 'Where . . .? Am I still alive? I wanted to die.'

351

She closed her eyes and opened them again. 'This is not the yacht, is it? But you . . . why you?'

'Don't worry about anything, my dear. You are quite safe, no one will harm you any more. We will look after you.' She finished applying the fresh dressing. 'Now, I will go and fetch some broth. You have been awfully ill and we must start feeding you up.'

Camilla waited another three days before telling her what had happened. 'I am afraid you lost the baby.'

'Baby?' Jacqueline shook her head, mystified. 'I wasn't pregnant . . .' she hesitated. 'Was I?'

Camilla nodded. 'You didn't know?'

'I had no idea. I do remember thinking how bloated my stomach was, but supposed it was the lack of food. I thought my period had stopped for the same reason.' She lay back and closed her eyes. Even talking was exhausting. Then the realisation struck her. 'Heinrich von Reinikker! I was pregnant by Reinikker! Oh, Holy Mother of God!'

'Von Reinikker! Well, we knew he had taken you prisoner . . .'

'How?'

'Anna told us.'

'Anna? Where is she? Are the children all right?'

'Everyone is fine, except you. You are still very weak and tired. Sleep again and I will tell you all about them later.'

Jacqueline was too weary to argue, but she couldn't sleep. Her mind was disturbed by surges of relief that she had miscarried, alternating with guilt at the certainty that had she not, she would have hated Reinikker's child. What an admission, to hate a child one bears. But even if it hadn't resembled him, she would always have seen its father's cruel eyes every time she looked at it.

She put up her hand to run fingers through her still itchy hair. Her hair! What had happened to it? She had to wait until she was brought a mirror the next day to see what had indeed happened: she had been shorn to within half an inch of her scalp.

'It was a filthy, tangled mat, I'm afraid, full of bugs. I

just had to clip it off and paint your scalp with paraffin to kill them all,' Camilla explained. 'I will fetch your breakfast. Back in a minute.'

Jacqueline was hardly listening. She was gazing at a strange, elderly looking woman. A woman with sunken, red-rimmed eyes, a blotched, bony face, yellow teeth and dry, brown skin stretched taut. The woman blinked when she did! It was incredible to believe that this was herself. She looked down at her body. Skin hung from arms and legs, empty of flesh and muscle, her breasts lay flat and scarred.

What a hideous sight. She was scarcely human. Wrecked. She lay back, letting the mirror fall on her bed. Oh, God, she thought. Is this my punishment for living in adultery with Marco? For Jean-Paul? For running away from Rumania? Should I have stayed with Ion Tyroler, accepting the consequences of my wickedness with Jean-Paul, and allowed Jean-Jacques to be brought up as 'Prince' Frederick? Is that what he would have preferred? As if it mattered. The Rumanian Fascists had forced Carol to abdicate back in 1940, and he had as usual fled without a backward glance, again, as usual, taking his Madame Lupesca with him into exile in Portugal. Where Prince Peter, the genuine heir to the throne, now was she had no idea. And now Jean-Jacques was lost, anyway. And Marco was dead. Legally, Francisco and Katarina should live with Camilla; better for the ten-year-old Count and his sister to be brought up at Calitri, their ancestral home.

So, the Countess Jacqueline Tyroler was finished. Destroyed. At thirty-three years old, the society beauty was reduced to a hideous, wretched hag. The bombs and guns were destroying the wealth of Europe. Certainly her wealth would be gone. She had played for high stakes – and lost. Lost everything: Marco, the children, her home, business, money and looks. All gone. She was young in years, too young to die, but who would want to live, alone and penniless, locked in this hideous, painful body?

Camilla came in, set a tray on the bed, and sat down.

'Now, I have a little time to spare before my next job, so let me explain all about Anna and the children, and how you come to be here.'

Jacqueline could hardly see the point in hearing the story, it was all history. It couldn't affect the future – because she hadn't one. But she tried to appear interested, out of politeness.

Apparently a number of Italians, from all sections of the community, who had become disenchanted with Duce's policies and alliance with Germany, had banded together in small groups, loosely linked, hoping eventually to oust him from office.

'We had such a group centred at Calitri at the time of Marco's funeral, which was why I told you to keep my note secret, remember? We didn't want the Fascists nosing around because they thought we were in contact with an enemy alien.'

Jacqueline recalled how Capitano Callone had picked the note up from the floor of the train. But she said nothing. It couldn't matter now.

After Badoglio's surrender, in which he had been encouraged by the knowledge and support of these groups, they had banded together more closely. Their German ex-allies were rounding up the Italian troops, shooting many as deserters for refusing to continue fighting, and taking thousands of them prisoner, sending them north by train to Austrian detention camps. On these trains there were also various political prisoners, as well as British and American prisoners-of-war and so-called 'subversives' . . . amongst whom had been Jacqueline and David. Guerrilla groups were blowing up railway lines to stop the trains and release the prisoners whenever and wherever they could. Through friends in strategic places, Camilla and Jacob, who was the radio telegraphist for their group, had known when Jacqueline was to be taken from Reinikker's office out to the suburbs, when she was no longer of use to him. But she was put in an area of German troop concentration where they knew they could not rescue her.

354

Camilla went on to explain how Anna had received the note for the 'baker', from a very mystified Rosita. She had realised immediately the danger to herself and the children, and had hurried them down to the village where Giuseppe and Rosita's daughter had driven them, dressed in peasant clothes, in her donkey cart to a contact point with the guerrillas. Anna had left the children in good care and joined the guerrillas, cooking, nursing, and sometimes even laying bombs with them. She had been to see Jacqueline once while she was still unconscious, but would return again as soon as she could.

David came to see her. She had been carried out to sit under the trees and when she looked up she had no idea who he was at first.

'David? Oh, yes! We were locked up together. I'm sorry, I'm afraid the recent past is very vague.'

'Just as well,' he said, speaking in halting Italian with a nervous grin; he had apparently been busy during her illness. 'Nothing of it is worth remembering, I assure you.' He sat on the pine needles beside her. 'I was lucky only to have been a prisoner for a few weeks. I just don't know how you survived so long alone in that cellar.'

'You call this surviving?' She spread her hands. 'Look at me.'

'You will soon be back to your old self. You don't know how much better you look already. On the train I really thought you had had it.'

'Train? Yes, I remember the wheels . . . train wheels. Do you know, David, I seem to have spent my life escaping, searching . . . once, I thought I had found the nearest thing to paradise a human being could ever hope for, but it was only temporary. Now I am escaping again, but it's too late. I have lost all I ever had and I just don't have the strength to go on running and searching any more.' Her weak eyes stared up through the branches, seeing nothing.

'Never mind, old girl, you'll soon feel better.' He patted

355

her hand. 'I'll come and see you again soon.' He strolled away, looking back once, pensively.

Jacqueline was in the same place a few days later when she heard soft footfalls under the trees. Again she found it difficult to recognise who approached. Wearing a workman's blue trousers and check shirt, his blond-grey hair ruffled by the breeze, he didn't look much like a worker, his walk was too effeminate. When he came close and grasped her hand she smiled weakly. 'Mother! What do you think you look like!' She put her arm up to hug Anna.

'You're hardly in a position to talk! Look at yourself,' Anna teased.

'I have and I don't ever wish to do so again,' Jacqueline replied solemnly.

'That's understandable, but you are already looking very much better. You should have seen yourself when they first brought you in. Few of us believed you would ever recover; certainly not as quickly as you have.' She sat down beside Jacqueline's chair.

'Tell me about the children, and how you escaped,' Jacqueline asked.

'Well, it really was rather funny. When we returned from our picnic, remember, we found Rosita standing in the kitchen looking quite stunned. I asked where you were and she said you had gone off with some Germans in a car, but you had told her to leave a note for the baker! She hadn't an idea what you meant but I realised immediately and asked her for the note. I think that was the first time she realised there was anything clutched in her hand. That one name got me moving, I can tell you.' She went on to describe the details of their flight into the mountains. 'Camilla has been wonderful,' she continued. 'She really is a remarkable woman. Do you know she has been helping with the setting up of these camps all through Northern Italy and establishing communications between them? And do you know who the head radio technician and operator is?'

'Camilla said something about Jacob.' Jacqueline's voice was colourless.

'Yes, isn't it marvellous that he and Teresa have become involved in something so worthwhile?'

'I suppose so.'

Anna found it hard to conceal her alarm at Jacqueline's indifference, her blank, listless eyes. Certainly she wasn't recognisable, mentally or physically, as the brave young woman who had driven across France to fetch her four years ago. Understandably. The poor thing had gone through hell, but hopefully the damage wouldn't be permanent. However, it was going to take a determined effort from someone to revive the old spirit. She had seen so much of this among released prisoners during the past six months.

'How are your muscles?' she asked. 'Are you walking well now?'

'No, hardly at all.'

'Well, there's no point in sitting there letting yourself deteriorate still further. Come on, let's get you started.'

Anna got up and took Jacqueline's hand to draw her to her feet, but the girl held back.

'Oh, no, Mother, please don't. I really don't feel up to it.'

'Of course you don't, and never will until you really get going again. It's a vicious spiral, you know, which is still leading down. We have to reverse that and start you spiralling up again.'

Anna could have wept as her arm went round her daughter's waist and she felt how terribly thin and wasted she was. Every bone protruded. 'That's fine, splendid, keep it going.'

Anna remained at the camp for three days, insisting on various exercises for Jacqueline, three times a day. Before leaving she left instructions for an increasingly strenuous rehabilitation programme. Jacqueline felt obliged to cooperate, sometimes with David and Camilla, sometimes with strangers who kept appearing, taking her for longer and longer walks through the woods.

The day Anna returned, a fortnight later, Jacqueline broke down and wept. 'Please, Mama, no more. I know you are all trying to be very kind, but there is no point. I am a wreck. Finished. There is nothing left for me and I no longer want to struggle, to survive. I only want to lie here in peace, until I . . . fade out.'

'Will you shut up and stop being so damned blind and selfish.' Anna forced herself to shout the cruel words. 'It is you, and people like you, and Jacob, and me, people who know, who have suffered from the dictates of that confounded Austrian paperhanger, people who have the incentive of anger and hatred and revenge, who must lead. Lead, not armies, but ordinary men and women, civilians, in ridding Italy and all of Europe of the evil plague of Fascism and Nazism.'

Jacqueline's eyes and mouth were wide in amazement at the outburst, but Anna continued. 'You think you've suffered! Just a few cigarette burns and single rapes two or three times followed by solitary confinement? You have no idea. We are in contact with the Maquis, the French Underground Movement. The horrors, the atrocities in France make your experience seem like a holiday. How would you like to be raped by a dozen soldiers one after the other? How would you like to have your breasts cut off? How would you like to have seen your whole family, children included, lined up and shot in front of you? Whole villages have been wiped out by the machine-guns of these animals.'

Jacqueline still sat staring in astonishment; Anna drew breath. 'We, you and I, and all those who have suffered, must put our experiences to good use,' she went on. 'Otherwise it will all have been for nothing. A total defeat not only for ourselves but for generations to follow. A victory for Fascism and the depraved politics it represents. Are you really prepared to sit there and let Reinikker win? He hasn't yet, you know, not while there is still breath in your body and the will to get up and destroy him, before he destroys your children. Will you let him defeat you? Or are you going to get up and kill him. Kill him for what he has done to you and to hundreds like you. And he is not the only one. There are thousands of these evil creatures who have become drunk on Hitler's venom. Every day they are torturing and killing the decent and the innocent. But they can't win,' she struck a fist into the other palm, 'because we won't let them. All of them, every last evil man and woman, yes, there are women Fascists who are just as bad, they must all be wiped off the face of the earth, their poison obliterated, so that our children, my grandchildren, can grow up in peace and freedom.' She sat down beside Jacqueline's chair and took her hand. 'I know, "vengeance is mine, saith the Lord". We are taught from childhood not to be vengeful, vindictive. But if ever there was a time for Christians to get up and smite them it is now. God, if there is a God, and I for one am fast coming to the conclusion that there is, cannot exterminate this plague without using the hands and hearts of decent people. And you are one of the many He has prepared for the task.'

There was a long silence.

'Do you think all Germans are bad?' Jacqueline spoke at last.

'Heavens, no. Mostly they are as good and wholesome as we hope and believe we are ourselves. The majority are only guilty of allowing Hitler the power to destroy so much that was good. No, it is only the von Reinikkers we are after.'

Slowly the invalid stood up and smiled. 'Right, when do we start?'

'Jacqueline, my darling.' Anna's eyes filled with tears. 'Thank God, oh, thank God.'

Life suddenly became more organised than she had ever known it. The camps were small, only ten to fifteen people in each, and mobile. Jacqueline's camp had risked remaining in the same place for four weeks, a risk taken for her benefit as she had been so ill. After she recovered it was a matter of caves or bivouacs, digging latrines and building new fires within hours of removing all evidence of their previous pitch.

In each camp everyone contributed to the well-being of the group as well as to the advancement of their purpose. Among them was a cobbler, whose skills were constantly in demand, an ex-hospital orderly and an army cook. Being multi-lingual, Jacqueline taught simple English and German for an hour each day.

They rose at dawn, ran, breakfasted, and did chores. They were taught weaponry and unarmed combat, did physical training and finished the mornings with classes on map-reading, tracking, use of radio and camouflage. The programme continued after the lunch break until dusk, when they ate by the fading glow of the fire. No lights were permitted, but they were all too exhausted to sit up long. Jacqueline, especially, wondered if she could possibly keep it up. It required endless willpower not to fall asleep after lunch, and the afternoon schedule was torture. But she was no less amazed than the others at the speed of her recovery after Anna's lecture. Dear Anna, it must have hurt her to speak like that, but it certainly did the trick.

Guards were posted throughout the night. Twice they were alerted, silently packed and covered tracks in just over ten minutes, and were away to another hideout before the German patrol discovered any sign of them. Of the progress of the war itself they had little information, but they knew that the British and the Americans were bogged down south of Rome, held there by determined German resistance; they would be on their own for a while yet.

David had remained in the same group with Jacqueline. He took pride in her recovery, was always gentle and attentive. He had fair, freckled skin which reddened in the sun, pale ginger hair, curly and receding from his forehead, and green eyes under blond lashes. He was a quiet, thoughtful person, quick to assist her, perform kindnesses and bring her little luxuries.

Before very long Jacqueline was aware that he was becoming very attached to her, although she couldn't imagine why. Her mind was as hard and flat as her body, her looks gone; it was difficult to conceive of a less attractive woman. Perhaps he was one of those deep, sensitive Englishmen of whom she had read, who perceived, or imagined he did, some inner beauty in people. A soul reader. But he obviously hadn't read deep enough to find the woman who would have hated her own child if she hadn't miscarried, whose sole reason for living was revenge, whose motivation was hatred.

She liked him. He was an immensely likeable person, with a great sense of humour. Everyone in the group enjoyed his company, though most could not freely converse with him as his progress in Italian remained slow. He told her that he had married at the beginning of the war, but that his wife had fallen in love with another man while he was away and had asked him for a divorce, to which he had agreed.

'You are the only special person in my life, now,' he told her.

'Not too special, I hope, David,' she warned him. 'I don't think I could ever be really special to anyone again.'

'Don't worry, Jacki, I'll never push it, I promise. Our friendship will remain only as special as you want.' He had heard most of her story about Heinrich and knew about the baby, so she presumed the 'only as special' must be a veiled reference to a 'degree of sexual involvement'. He had never attempted to touch her or make a suggestive remark, seeming quite content to keep their friendship on a purely platonic basis, which did not help her feeling of embarrassment, almost guilt, that he aroused no spark of sexual interest in her whatsoever. To the extent that she wondered if she was being fair in allowing their close friendship to continue. But how could she become even more distant without hurting his feelings?

*　　*　　*

Anna and Camilla were treated with the respect of rank. They moved freely between groups and were always welcomed and questioned regarding war news. It was they who brought information about the British and American landings in France on 6 June, causing great excitement. David was thrilled. He knew the Normandy coast quite well and described it to the others. Even better news arrived immediately afterwards, that Rome had at last fallen to Field Marshal Alexander and his Allied army. Even Jacqueline was smiling, although they were warned that this did not mean the war in Italy was over. Far from it, the Germans were still occupying well prepared defensive positions in great strength, and Alexander had to send all his best troops to sustain the assault in France. But it was still possible to feel that the end was coming closer, step by step.

Anna was happy to see the extent of her daughter's recovery. She knew Jacqueline would never be the same again, but how many people involved in this war would be? Experience affected everyone to some degree. Jacqueline cetainly looked different. The graceful, rounded curves and soft skin, gentle, smiling eyes and full lips, the long, silky, honey-coloured hair were gone. Now her body was lean, hard and muscular, her hands calloused with rough use. Her hair was still cropped short and her face had not been made up since she had left the villa nine months before. But despite the coldness around her eyes and mouth, Anna knew she still had one weak spot. She longed to see Francisco, Katarina and Bobo. She had begged to be taken to them, but it had always been impossible, for one reason or another. Now she was asking again.

Anna and Camilla looked at each other. It was the Italian woman who answered. 'There are two reasons against it, Jacqueline. One is that they are happy and settled in their present adopted way of life, and the other is that you have been selected to go on an assignment which will take you away from this area, probably for several weeks, if not months. If you visit them, and I know they are just as keen to see you as you are to see them, it will only be for a few hours; surely a painful and upsetting experience for all four of you.'

Jacqueline gave her a long, searching look, not realising how quickly Camilla would read it.

'No,' Marco's estranged wife went on. 'I am not trying to exercise my legal prerogative. Nice children they may be, but I am not the maternal type. I am not trying to get them away from you, and I honestly believe the best possible thing for them, after the war, is for you to take them to America, educate them and bring them back to Italy only for holidays until they are old enough to decide what they want to do. I will do my best to look after Calitri, if there is anything left, and I will welcome Francisco back to take over the estate and Marco's businesses if that is what the boy chooses. And, of course, you would always be welcome there yourself. But the Italian educational system will not recover in time to be of any use to your children. Far better for them to go to good schools in the United States. Don't you agree?'

'I apologise for doubting your intentions, Camilla. You are so very kind, and wise. Of course I won't upset the children by visiting them yet.' Jacqueline smiled at the older woman who patted her shoulder and winked.

'Good girl. Now, Rico,' she called. 'Are you ready to give the briefing?'

Jacqueline thought that Rico was probably in his sixties, though to the casual eye he would appear much younger. Medium height, solid build, his curly grey hair framed a wide forehead and light brown eyes, and although, like the others, he wore dungarees and an open-necked shirt, he obviously held authority.

'War is not a simple matter of one side against the other,' he began. 'It is also a matter of who sides with whom. I may fight with you against the Germans, not because I dislike the Germans, but because when the war is over I want your protection against a different enemy of mine, with whom you have no quarrel. This is not a simple war. There are extreme right-wing Fascists, moderate right-wing elements, middle-of-the-road and moderate socialists involved, and on the far left, the Communists. All these different groups have their following in every country, and every single man and woman is hoping that, after the war, men with their own political leanings will govern their country.' He paused to look around his listeners. 'Here, today, we are not only Italians, but also British, Jewish, Yugoslavian and Rumanian. In other groups we have French, Greek, Hungarian and Czechoslovaks. Generally speaking, I think we are none of us extremists. We hate extremism. We believe it leads to oppression. We who are here have all seen what Fascism can do and I think most of us know that Communism can be as bad. But, unfortunately, there are considerable factions all around us, working for both these extremist policies, while still fighting on our side.

'In Yugoslavia, for instance, Josip Broz, who calls himself Marshal Tito, heads a considerable force of guerrillas who are determined to turn their country into a Communist state. Another force of partisans, the Chetniks, are determined to prevent the Communists from gaining power, and are fighting for King Peter's return. They were, and still are, headed by Draza Mihajlovic, but when he collaborated with the Fascists, many of his followers were disillusioned and formed their own moderate group, a group with whom we are now working and with whom some of you will link up, shortly.'

He took a hip flask from his pocket and drank before continuing. 'We don't just want to rid Italy of Duce's extreme policies and of foreign troops. We want to feel that around us we have peaceful, moderate friends and neighbours. To that end we work with both tongue and gun. We have agents throughout Italy and the Balkans, talking, coaxing, explaining to the people what we believe, that extremists will always destroy those they claim to represent. But we cannot fight bullets with words, nor will we gain support unless we are prepared to protect our followers with arms. Our whole network is a combination of information and action. We assess the information we receive and send people to talk, fight, lay bombs, or kill as necessary. Here in Italy we have worked with some success to prevent the deportation of both military personnel and civilians to German detention camps. In particular we have sought to rescue those same moderate politicians, thinkers, leaders, whom the Nazis want to destroy. But it is our work abroad for which we need you now. There are hundreds of islands off the Yugoslav coast which the Germans have not occupied. We maintain communications bases amongst them. Unfortunately, the Gestapo caught some of our operatives recently, so we must replace them. The head of operations there was lost. You, David, as an RAF officer, will take command, please. Anna, you and Berto are now experts on explosives. You will take a store over with you, look after it, and when necessary, take it to the mainland and put it to use. Jacki, you are the linguist. You will be based on the radio, working with Jacob, and interpreting for David when he attends meetings on the mainland. As with everyone else, you will fight if necessary.' He looked around the group and added grimly, 'Live enemies are dangerous. Already we have many enemies. They seek us out ruthlessly. Remember, if you need to shoot anyone, shoot to kill. Otherwise you are risking many lives besides your own. Tonight you will follow guides down towards the Adriatic coast. They will encamp you for a few hours' sleep during the day, then tomorrow night you will be taken to a seaside village near Ancona, where a sailing yacht awaits you. David, you are an enthusiastic yachtsman, I am told.'

David nodded.

'You will be the only experienced man, so it will be up to you to get the party across the Adriatic. Here are the charts.' He took them from his satchel. 'Let me show you the course and bearings.' The two men laid the charts out on a makeshift table.

Rico had talked for a long time. It would soon be dark, so a fire was started for the evening meal, while those who were leaving collected their belongings and weapons.

Jacqueline was happy: action at last. Now she would have an opportunity to work against the Heinrich von Reinikkers of this world, and hopefully destroy some.

May – September 1944

It is better to fight for the good, than to rail at the
  ill;
I have felt with my native land, I am one with my
  kind,
I embrace the purpose of God, and the doom
  assign'd.

Alfred, Lord Tennyson, Maud

THE TREK down to the coast was uneventful, until, creeping
cautiously from doorway to doorway down the narrow
seaside village street towards the waterfront, lit only by
the stars, they saw a German soldier silhouetted against
the sky. He was pacing up and down the little quay where
dinghies and small fishing boats were tied by their painters,
stern anchors holding them in line.

David left his gear with the others and edged across to
enter the water below the road and move silently along
under the quay. They couldn't see him climb up, but
suddenly the guard was alerted, turned, aiming his rifle
. . . and dropped it with a clatter, folded up and fell over
into the water with a splash. David had learned to throw
his knife with deadly accuracy.

They washed away the traces of blood and pulled on the
bow warp of a small sailing sloop, drawing her close enough
to enable them to clamber aboard. A rope was tied round
the soldier's body, lifting it clear of the water and against
the gunwale, and David hurriedly set the foresail. There
was little wind inshore, but as they drifted slowly out into

the Adriatic it was possible to fill the mainsail and with the wind astern the shadowy Italian coastline was lost behind them. Not until they were miles out did they allow the soldier's body to glide down into the depths.

Anna, Berto and the two other men who had joined them were not good sailors. Their stomachs protested in the usual fashion as the wind gained strength towards noon on the following day. Jacqueline found herself trying to understand David's shouted instructions as she hauled on sheets while attempting to keep her balance on the heaving deck. Twice, when the little craft shipped water, she was nearly sluiced away, but both times she got up soaked but smiling, enjoying the danger and the challenge. Having only ever sailed on a large, professionally crewed motor yacht, she had never before understood the exhilaration of pitching over green, watery mountains under canvas.

Wind and sea had dropped considerably by the time the first islands were sighted. There were two more hours to go until sunset, so David tacked in the soft breeze, planning to land at dusk. The accuracy of his navigation delighted even himself as they slid quietly under the high cliffs into the bay described by Rico. A small rowing boat left the shingle beach to ferry them ashore. While they were led up a cliff path they saw the yacht taken in tow.

'What are they doing with her?' Jacqueline asked David in a whisper.

'Getting her out into deep water before pulling out the bung,' he said ruefully. 'Can't risk her being found.'

A momentary twinge of sadness pierced the hard shell of her mind and she paused to watch the yacht moving out between the headlands, before turning back to the climb.

Their hideout was a small derelict dwelling. It had been built across the front of a natural cave which provided a large storeroom at the rear with a floor sloping up to a narrow exit amongst the rocks and brush – a useful escape route if unwelcome guests knocked on the door. The larger of the two rooms was a living-cum-workroom where the radio and a stove were the most important features. In the other, too small to allow segregation of the sexes, they slept.

Jacob, Teresa and their two companions gave them a warm welcome, congratulating Jacqueline on her quick recovery; only later did they privately express to Anna their shock at the change in her.

The four had only arrived on the island a few days earlier, after a lucky escape from a shoot-out with the Gestapo on the mainland. Instinctively Jacqueline and Anna wanted to help Teresa make the place more habit-able – but David forbade it.

'The more derelict and disused this place stays, the better our chances of remaining undiscovered,' he ruled. 'Also, I am told that patrol boats and reconnaissance aircraft check these islands quite regularly, so no one must go out in daylight unless they are close to cover, nor must we wear or carry anything shiny which would reflect the light.'

Only a week after their arrival, Jacqueline was on radio duty when she picked up a coded German message in Morse. She and Jacob went through his code notes together and worked out that 'X' would bring goods to Slav 10 on the following Friday.

'Slav 10 is the German unit we tangled with two weeks ago,' Jacob explained to David. 'They are based on the coast and the "goods" are probably ammunition and gen-eral supplies to replace what they lost.'

'We should try to prevent those supplies from getting through, I think, don't you?' David always couched his decisions in the politest possible terms. 'What transport do they use, Jacob?'

'Trucks. They use different routes each time, but in-variably in rotation. So this . . .' he pointed to the map, '. . . is the one they will probably use this time.'

'Wizard. We'll leave you, Jacki, Teresa and three others to hold the fort while the rest of us go over on Wednesday night to see if we can mess things up a bit for them.'

Jacqueline was rather alarmed at the thought of her mother going off on an ambush, but Anna was delighted.

'I haven't seen any real action for weeks. Not since we booby-trapped a truckload of explosives on their way to the Gustav Line.'

For a moment Jacqueline's mind drifted back to the balls and dinners, cocktail parties and receptions of the past, pictured the Cotroceni Palace with her mother in veil and gloves . . . and chuckled. If only Queen Marie could see and hear them now!

Their food was mainly fish and vegetables supplied by local sympathisers. Wednesday lunch was quite a feast, after which the ambush party went to bed for a few hours until dark.

Jacqueline was sitting outside watching the sunset when David joined her. 'Do be careful, won't you, old thing. Don't relax your guard for a minute. Remember those blighters are looking for us all the time.'

'You watch out, as well. We can't afford to lose two COs in one month.'

He took her hand and looked at her. She knew he wanted to kiss her, which made her feel awkward and confused. She liked him very much, but only as a friend. Yet wouldn't friends kiss goodbye even on a far less significant parting? She turned her face towards him. Immediately his arms slid round her and he kissed her, tenderly at first, then hungrily.

She waited to feel some response inside, a warm rush of wanting spreading from her stomach, but there was nothing. His tongue sought hers. She felt him harden against her thigh.

A wave of regret swept over her. She would have liked to respond to this man; wanted, just for a few minutes, to enjoy his arms, his niceness, his affection. But apparently her sexuality had been killed stone dead. Poor David; she hugged him in a last farewell gesture. She really shouldn't have let him touch her. Now he would begin to think . . .

They sprang apart as the door opened behind them.

'Oh, there you are,' Anna murmured. 'I just wanted to say *au revoir*. Look after yourself and we'll soon be back.' She kissed Jacqueline on the cheek. 'Can you just hitch my backpack a little higher while I tighten the straps, please? Thank you, that's much better.'

The six stepped quietly away into the gloom, to rendez-vous with the fisherman who would take them across.

The mission was a great success. They all returned un-scathed having seen one of the trucks completely burnt out and the other blown off the road into a ravine.

As Jacqueline had anticipated, David expected to take up their relationship where they had left off. She knew she must bite the bullet and tell him that it was hopeless.

'I am so sorry, David. You are such a terribly dear person and I do enjoy your friendship so much, but I'm afraid that that "special" relationship is a thing of the past for me. Perhaps it is the result of what Reinikker did to me, but I think that I am now so consumed with hatred and a longing for revenge that there is no room left for loving. Whatever it is, I hope you will forgive me and we can just go on being good friends, please?'

David smiled sadly, then nodded. 'Yes, of course, always. And maybe when you have been on a few missions and killed off a few Huns? But please,' he added, 'don't let the fact that I love you interfere with our friendship.' He stood up. 'Funny thing, my love. Don't know why, but I've always been a loser. Dorothy and I were only married a year, you know, before she asked me for a divorce . . . come on, duty calls.'

Throughout the following weeks the radio was their main source of work and interest, stimulated their long evening discussions.

When the battlefront was pushed further up the Italian Peninsula, many of the groups working under Rico were contacted by the Allied Intelligence and asked to remain north of the fighting, including Rico himself, where they could do more damage to the Germans from behind their lines. He was asked to arrange a meeting on the mainland between David and a breakaway group of Chetniks, during which Jacqueline acted as interpreter. She was surprised at how little evidence they saw of German occupation, but as David observed, the Nazis now needed every available man to fight the Americans and British who were already deep into France.

The Chetniks seemed gloomy and angry. Tito's Communist Movement was gaining popularity all the time, which in itself was alarming, but mainly they were irate that Mihajlovic was cooperating so much with the Fascists, splitting their own movement and thereby, they believed, playing right into Tito's hands.

David reported the results of the Chetnik meeting to Rico as soon as they returned, commenting that although their own moderate policies were gaining popularity with an increasing number of Chetniks, they seemed to be losing ground generally in Yugoslavia to the Communists. Also, Mihajlovic, who was maintaining his footing with the help of the German Occupying Forces, had been joined by a Rumanian Group who considered the policies of their King Michael to be too accommodating to the Socialists, and who wanted to set up an extreme Right Wing Monarchy in their own country.

Rico had heard these comments from other sources and was disturbed by them, but as conversation was limited and made tedious by the need for ciphering and Morse code they did not discuss the matter further. He had no other instructions for them, other than to post lookouts to guide in other agents who were joining them from a now obsolete Greek base. They were to expect four: two ex-Free French fighters, a Britisher, and a Rumanian.

On the second night Jacqueline and Berto were on watch on the clifftop, when a pinpoint of light flashed on the horizon and disappeared. They waited. Exactly five minutes later the light flashed again. Jacqueline immediately answered with her torch . . . one flash and off, then looked at her watch to repeat the flash five minutes later. Berto slipped away to find the top of the winding path down to the shingle beach, while Jacqueline stayed to give two more flashes at five minute intervals, and then sat back to wait and watch.

She was totally unprepared for the sudden explosion of light. A brilliant flare shot into the sky and a searchlight beamed across the black water. Rivers of fear ran down her back and thighs, her lungs seemed paralysed. The loud thumping noise in her ears proved to be her own heartbeat, but the necessary adrenalin was flowing. Her training brought her to her feet and soundlessly she ran back the way she had come to warn David and the others.

'Okay. Operation Abandon,' he ordered quietly.

They all knew their rôles. Jacob set about dismantling the radio equipment, Anna went through to the cave storeroom. David and Jacqueline put their few possessions into haversacks and left them for the others to carry away whilst the two of them set off for the clifftop with machine-guns.

To darkness and silence.

They waited behind a rocky outcrop, ears straining. A single cicada shrilled nearby, another answered.

A nightbird cried down on the shore. It was a signal. David pulled at her sleeve for her to follow him down the cliff path, pausing every few moments to listen again.

And again the birdcry. Despite hours of effort, Jacqueline had never mastered the art of mimicking these calls – so it was David who replied, hands cupped over his mouth. Immediately two more cries came from below, in quick succession.

David hurried forward until they reached the final rock-fall over which they clambered, feeling for unseen toe-holds, down on to the shingle . . . which crunched loud enough to be heard for miles. The searchlight immediately beamed from across the water into the left-hand corner of the bay and began moving steadily towards them. They fell flat on their faces, not daring to breathe as the powerful light washed over them and continued silently to their right. David jumped up pulling her after him and together they dived at a group of rocks to the left, displayed by the searchlight a few moments before. Their footfalls sounded like a regiment of tanks in the still night air, bringing the beam back to illuminate them four yards short of their objective. Several machine-guns spat at the same moment. The noise was deafening, bouncing and echoing from one cliff to the other. Then they were behind the protective rocks, the light now stationary, pinning them down. The gunfire ceased, leaving a different din. Hundreds of sea-birds had been flushed from their nightly roosts to swirl overhead, screaming protests.

'You all right?' David mouthed the words in the eerie light.

There was a burning sensation in her left calf and a chip of flying rock had cut her forehead, letting a trickle of blood run down her cheek. Nothing serious. 'Yes,' she answered. 'Now what?'

He pressed his mouth to her ear. 'I think the others are further down the beach to our left. Berto is probably with them. They haven't been spotted yet, so we'll let them make the first move.'

It came as he finished speaking. A single rifle shot and the sound of breaking glass as the searchlight was extinguished.

They stood immobile, and the sound of scraping pebbles came nearer, waiting for the new arrivals to join them.

Jacqueline never knew what had alerted her to the fact that these were not friends approaching. Had she, during that period with Heinrich last year, learned the exclusive smell of Nazis? Or had the sensitive computer in her brain perhaps recognised something which she had no ability to analyse? Wedged into a slight rock crevice she waited until she could hear a man's breath beside her. She guessed rather than saw the position of his gun muzzle as she thrust it upwards with her left hand, pushing her own gun butt into his side.

374

She felt his breath on her face as he shouted, 'Sheize!' His muscles surged against her thrusting arm; she smelled his fear as he tried to twist away from her gun. She didn't feel any fear herself, only anger and hatred. Adrenalin flowing, she enjoyed this first opportunity to hit back at Reinikker's obscene world. She squeezed the trigger hard, turning the gun with her body to follow his attempt to avoid her fire. Blood spurted over her as he started to fall. She grabbed him and held him in front of her as two shadows appeared behind him, tried to bring her gun back towards them and felt bullets thud into the German's chest. David's gun barked beside her, followed by screams, a low moan, distant firing, then silence. Not even the birds made a sound any more.

Briefly a boat engine coughed and throbbed away to the open sea.

Jacqueline allowed the limp body to slither down on to the shingle. She was soaked through to the skin with his blood. Her hands, arms and gun were sticky. The fight hadn't lasted more than a minute but her mind had recorded every move in slow motion and it seemed to have lasted an hour. She felt drained, longed to lie on the pebbles and sleep.

'You okay?' David whispered.

'Fine,' she lied. There were a thousand adjectives which might have described her feelings at that moment, but 'fine' was not one of them. And David knew it.

'You were magnificent, darling,' he whispered, his mouth pressed into her hair, an arm round her shoulder.

She leaned heavily against him and sighed.

A seabird shrieked nearby.

'Here they are,' he hissed, releasing her, and sent an answering call.

Shadows appeared, gently crunching the shingle.

'Come.' David led the party back up the cliff path but turned away from the cottage, down into a rocky valley. More nightbirds called from the darkness, and Anna with some of the others joined them on their trek across the island, into another valley which sloped gently down to a narrow inlet.

Jacob was waiting beside a rubber dinghy full of equipment. 'Quick,' he snapped, 'or the tide will turn and we will be here until tomorrow morning. Strip off and put your clothes in the dinghy.'

Another time and place, stepping naked into the cool night waters of the Adriatic might have been a delightfully sensuous experience, Jacqueline thought, remembering another time she had swum naked, with Jean-Paul in the mountain pool high in the Carpathians. She stumbled over the stones, bearing her share of the loaded dinghy's weight, wondered how a woman of Anna's generation must feel, walking naked among a group of equally naked men. Probably as indifferent as she was herself, the sense of purpose and camaraderie, and the intimacy in which they had all been forced to live over the preceding weeks overcoming any embarrassment.

'Anyone here unable to swim?' David asked.

There was no reply.

'Good. Here are some buoyancy corks from fishing nets; they will help you to rest if you get tired. Anyone who finds they cannot keep going must be assisted into the boat, but we cannot tow people, they would act like sea-anchors and we would make no progress. The strongest swimmers will take turns towing with these ropes. The others can push from behind. Don't speak unless you have to get in the boat; remember, sound travels miles across water.'

Jacqueline wondered how far David expected them to swim. Diving off the swimming-platform of *Ocean Dreamer* to drift lazily around the stern with the children was very different from towing a dinghy an unspecified distance in the darkness.

Anna and Teresa didn't get very far before being heaved into the boat by unknown shoulders thrust into their rumps, but the others all managed to keep going until their feet touched rocks and boulders below the surface.

376

David, who had mapped out these islands in detail for himself weeks before, led them rock-hopping and swimming round the northern cliffs of the next island towards the more gently shelving east shore.

They were all frozen.

'Not far now,' David whispered, while they fought to prevent the dinghy from swirling away from them as water eddied around the rocks. 'Just thank heaven the sea is so calm. They tell me that in a Mistral ten foot waves would be crashing on these rocks.'

On her other side one of the newcomers bumped against her. '*Pardon*,' he whispered in French.

Despite her chattering teeth, Jacqueline grinned to herself in the dark at the ridiculous situation, swimming naked beside a total stranger, whose face she had not even seen . . . and actually welcoming the warmth of his flesh against her goosepimples.

'*Entendez!*' her companion hissed.

They strained their ears and faintly detected the throb of an engine. It was coming closer.

'Back! Back to that islet we just passed,' David ordered. 'There is a shallow cave on the landward side.'

The sloping cave floor was strewn with boulders, submerged at the entrance, dry further back. Wearily they scrambled out of the water, tugging the ropes, Anna and Teresa and their possessions floating after them. It was colder out of the water than in it and as the sound of the engine drew closer they grabbed at the heap of clothes, pulling them on regardless of ownership, both to cover the whiteness of their skins from a prying searchlight and for warmth. In the pitch darkness they slipped and slithered on the seaweed covered stones.

'Either they have repaired their light or they have another boat,' Berto remarked as the pale beam hit the rocks nearby, wavering with the roll of the sea, then swinging away.

They waited half an hour after the engine's throb had ebbed into the darkness.

'Better risk it now, or we won't be ashore before dawn. Let's go.' David stripped off again as he spoke and reluctantly the others followed.

When dawn did eventually break they were all asleep on piles of straw in a barn, to which a friendly islander had led them. The man had thought it only proper that the three women should have a place apart in a rather smelly horse-stall, and at noon sent his wife to fetch them to use the humble washing facilities in their farmhouse.

Their outdoor life and physical fitness had certainly helped them through the night's ordeal, but they still felt very cold and shivery. It crossed Jacqueline's mind that part of her shakiness might be due to her first killing, though she would not dream of admitting it. Somewhat refreshed, she stepped outside with Anna and Teresa into the warm sunlight, to cross the yard and rejoin the men who were by the barn door, eating.

'*Mon Dieu!*' One of the Frenchmen dropped his enamel plate with a clatter and stood staring at her.

She stared back, eyes and mouth wide.

Slowly, as though mesmerised, they started towards each other, then ran, arms outstretched, oblivious of the amazed stares around them. They clung fiercely together, then held back at arms' length. Jacqueline saw the grey hairs at his temples, the little lines forming at the corners of his deep, dark eyes . . . and for the first time in years she felt a surge of passion swelling from the pit of her stomach down her thighs and up into her chest until she thought she would choke.

Again they hugged and laughed. 'Jacqueline, my darling, I cannot believe it,' he whispered.

'But it is true, Jean-Paul. It has to be true.'

Neither of them noticed David turn away and walk back into the barn.

They didn't talk for a long time. They just sat apart from the rest staring at each other in amazed disbelief. They ate, unaware of the taste, joined in the work of sorting and drying out the gear, eyes constantly lifting to each other.

Later, towards dusk, Jacqueline led Jean-Paul to where Anna was sitting with Jacob and Teresa. 'Mama,' she said formally, 'I would like to present Major Jean-Paul de Busonniere.'

'Jean-Paul . . .?' Anna frowned. 'You don't mean . . .?'

'Yes,' Jacqueline nodded. 'Jean-Jacques' father.'

Anna looked from one to the other, shaking her head in astonishment, then smiled and held out her hand.

'Jean-Paul! I am very happy to meet you at last.' She turned to Jacqueline. 'And for you, my darling, I am very, very happy.'

Jacob and Teresa were introduced too, and Jacqueline left Jean-Paul with them while she went to find David.

He was sitting at an improvised table in the barn, papers strewn in front of him.

'May I speak with you for a minute, please?' she asked.

He looked up and forced a smile. 'Yes, of course. Sit on that box. Afraid the furniture around here is a bit sub-standard.'

Knowing how hurt he must be, his effort to be bright and cheerful only made her feel worse. She had been dreading this moment for some hours. Poor David. Always the loser in love.

'Jean-Paul is the father of my eldest son,' she announced.

David stared at her in surprise, but said nothing.

'We met by chance and went riding together in the mountains. The day before I was to be taken away to Paris we made love. I was sixteen. We had meant to meet again in France, but . . . well, I had to return unexpectedly to Rumania. Years later we met again at a trade fair in Paris. We . . . spent two days together and . . . well . . . we agreed to go our separate ways and never contact each other again. That was ten years ago.' She was flushed and confused. 'I . . . I do want you to understand, David. I have loved Jean-Paul all my life.'

He raised his eyebrows. 'And Marco?'

'Yes, and Marco. It was because of Marco and Jean-Paul's wife that we agreed never to meet again.'

'After you had had a rollicking two days together in Paris. Very noble of you.' His eyes had become hard and angry. 'And then, I suppose, you went back to Marco's bed and dreamed of this French fellow while he made love to you?'

Jacqueline opened her mouth to speak and closed it again. She was hurt and angry. Damn it, she was only trying . . .

'De Busonniere has been drafted into our unit because he has a first-class reputation in radio, both coding and mechanics, though I doubt if he can be better than Jacob, but I am advised that he has had no guerrilla training. We must pray he knows how to fight when the time comes. Now, I think it's time to forget our childhood romances and get to work. We leave here in half an hour.' He turned back to his papers with an air of dismissal.

She stood staring at him, uncertain whether to voice the furious retorts seething in her mind, or wait until she had simmered down. Really, this was ridiculous. So, he had saved her life and she had once let him kiss her, but surely that did not give him the right to speak to her in that tone? She wanted to say, you are only the CO of this outfit, remember, not God Almighty. I came in here to explain about Jean-Paul, not ask for a judgment.

Instead she said, 'I will collect my things,' in a cool, colourless voice, and left the barn.

She didn't do as she had said she would. Instead she slipped behind the old stone building to be alone and think. She was suddenly overwhelmed by an awareness of feeling. Not just the immense animal need to make love to Jean-Paul again – surges of elation and weakness coursed through her at the mere thought of it, and she was thinking of it constantly – but also of her other feelings; concern about David and Anna; anger, of which she had thought herself incapable. Apart from cold hatred of Nazism she had felt no emotion whatever for . . . a year? No, but nearly. Now, within hours of meeting Jean-Paul again she was emotionally overwrought.

But she was also aware of another change: control. She remembered the numerous times her tongue and temper had made trouble for her and was surprised that, despite her anger, she had not lost her temper with David.

'What on earth are you doing? Come on, we are leaving.' Berto's gravelly voice made her jump.

'Oh! Right, I'm ready.' She followed him back to the others.

David was addressing the group. '. . . the night patrol leaves the mainland at five p.m. and will probably head in this direction as this is the area where we were last seen. Our friend here, whom we will call Bob,' he indicated their host, 'is taking us out to sea to meet up with another boat so that we can complete our circuitous journey to the mainland.' He glanced around. 'All you chaps ready, then?'

Only once did they see a patrol boat in the distance. Their skipper cut his engine and they drifted until it disappeared. Once ashore, they hoisted each other's packs while straps were tightened, and set off in single file behind David – who seemed to know where he was going.

It was an exhausting journey, at times on roads where they had to be constantly alert, ready to jump into hedges or ditches for concealment, at others on rough, stony tracks where each step could twist an ankle. They waited at the edge of a forest for dawn to give them sufficient light to enter. Well concealed, they were able to eat and sleep.

Jean-Paul came and lay near Jacqueline. Though he didn't touch her she was aware, through closed lids, that he was staring at her, willing her to get up and walk away with him to a private place. She longed to open her eyes and receive his call, felt physically sick from the aching demand in her stomach. Every fibre within her mind and body screamed for him to fill the waiting void.

But she resisted. Feigning sleep until exhaustion made it real.

They ate corned beef and dry biscuits, washed down with stale water. A horribly indigestible diet, but it did stem the hunger for a few more hours while they moved on, always climbing, into the mountains.

David held up his hand. 'Right, this is where we wait until we are collected by the bods who are expecting us. We are bang on time so they shouldn't be too long. Anyone fancy some more grub?' He glanced around expectantly. 'Oh, well, I'll eat alone.' He opened his knapsack and took out a tin plate. But they were all hungry and soon even the smell of the dreaded corned beef made their mouths water.

Three hours later David looked anxiously at his watch. Four, five hours. They were all feeling restless, tired and nervy.

'What happens if they don't come at all?' Berto asked.

'Another case for plan B, I'm afraid. Get everyone close in and I'll explain. Now,' he started, 'we are meant to be linking up with another group, some of whom were supposed to meet us here. As there seems to have been some foul-up we will have to press on to a friendly farm marked here on the map. We are told the farmer will organise a meeting later. When we are nearer the farm we'll divide up into twos and threes and circle the buildings, just to be sure there are no unpleasant strangers preparing a welcome. We had better conceal our equipment first so that we can approach with guns and knives at the ready. Naturally, if we can cope with any emergency with knives only, all the better. We don't want to broadcast our arrival.' He went on to detail instructions to them all, pairing Jacqueline and Jean-Paul without comment.

It was past three in the morning when they made a cache of their supplies and equipment. David had not been able to give them any idea of the actual terrain or layout of the buildings, they just had to edge in quietly and unseen. Jacqueline and Jean-Paul wriggled up a rocky gully to a clump of bushes from where they could see the vague shape of the buildings across an open field.

There was no glimmer of light, and except for the high-pitched whistle of cicadas, so incessant that it seemed more like a feverish headache than actual sound, the silence was absolute.

Keeping to long grass and bushes at the edge of the field they worked their way closer. It was eerie to think that twelve other people were approaching too, yet they heard and saw nothing.

It was as they passed some high trees and neared the gate beyond that they heard a distinct footfall. They lay flat, side by side, listening, and Jacqueline was surprised to feel Jean-Paul shaking. Cautiously they looked up, and at the same moment both saw a shadowy figure standing by the gate.

Jean-Paul yelled, half ran, half crawled back to the sheltering trees, firing wildly. The figure at the gate jumped and bellowed, again and again, obviously in great pain . . . it was a cow.

Suppressing an immediate desire to laugh, Jacqueline wriggled forward on her stomach to the gate, and, seeing nothing but the cow moving, continued towards the buildings, Jean-Paul following. Nearing an outhouse they saw a light from a window.

A bird called. It was all clear.

The scene in the house was terrible. The farmer, his wife, two teenage children and a younger child, must have been sitting at dinner when their murderers had burst in. The man was still in his chair, sprawled forward across the table. His wife had run to him; she was on the floor, her head twisted up against his chair-leg, her blood a pool at his feet. Their daughter had fallen sideways to the floor. Their son lay by the far wall, an ancient fowling piece still hanging from its nail above a brown splatter of dried blood, the trail he had left as he slithered to the floor. There was terror still in the wide brown eyes of the youngest child when Berto rolled the pathetic little body on to its back.

David was moving from room to room, looking through doors and windows.

'I don't imagine that whoever did this will be back in a hurry; we should be as snug here as anywhere.'

'You cannot be serious!' Ugo exclaimed. 'Stay here with them?' He glanced briefly at the macabre scene and turned away.

'Of course not. We'll bury them.'

The bodies already stank horribly. David detailed Ugo and Philippe to produce makeshift stretchers to carry them outside, others to find spades. Logs were brought in to light the stove and Anna put pots of water on to boil for cleaning up. David took four men out to place on guard duty.

It was daylight before the rest of them were able to seek sleep, and it eluded Jacqueline completely. Her mind kept returning to the incident of the cow. At first the full implication hadn't really registered. Not until she was lying on a straw mattress on the floor, listening to Anna's heavy breathing, did she realise just what had happened, and it came as a shock. In his terror, Jean-Paul had left her lying there to face whatever danger there might have been, alone. He had scuttled away risking all their lives by firing unnecessarily in his anxiety to save his own skin.

Her mind was immediately crowded with a thousand excuses, reasons for his apparent . . . cowardice? The very word was abhorrent, causing conflict with her love and urgent physical need of him. She turned from left to right, was first too hot, then too cold. The straw itched and her head ached.

She got up, and went into the kitchen. David was there, alone.

'Hello, you're up early. Couldn't you sleep?'

'No. I think my stomach yearns for something other than corned beef,' she quipped.

'Don't we all! But we certainly can have some fresh beef if anyone knows anything about butchery. Afraid I had to

384

put that cow Jean-Paul shot out of its misery. She looks a bit long in the tooth, but we should get something out of her.'

For a moment she was worried . . . but then realised that although David and the others all knew that Jean-Paul had shot the cow, only she knew all the circumstances.

'Jacki.' David reached out and touched her arm. 'I'm sorry I was so rude to you about him. It was inexcusable of me. Please forgive me, one day.'

She blushed, couldn't think of what to say. 'Oh! Er . . . yes. Don't think about it. Forget it. I quite understand,' she stammered.

He pumped up a beaker of water from the well and handed it to her. 'His appearance came as quite a shock, you know,' she added, sipping the water. 'I still find it hard to believe. I never dreamt we would ever meet again . . . at least, no, that isn't true, I did sometimes dream, years ago, a sort of makebelieve fantasy. There was no way I would ever have hurt Marco . . . you see, I really did love him. I still do. He was a wonderful, most remarkable man . . .'

David watched tears spill down her face.

'Dear Jacki, I'm so glad for you that Jean-Paul has turned up. He has already done for you, in a few days, something that I was unable to do in all these months. Tears are a fairly normal part of a woman's make-up, but this is the first time I've seen you cry.'

'Dear, sweet, kind David.' She put her forehead on his shoulder and let the tears flow. She didn't honestly know what they were about. For Marco? For Jean-Paul? Or David himself?

She pumped some more water into a bowl and splashed it over her face. 'Thanks, David. Seems I just needed a shoulder to cry on.'

'Any time, old girl. Be my guest!'

And it was David who engineered the moment they both so desperately wanted.

They had been at the farm for four days, had buried the dead, cleaned up the living room, explored the countryside and made radio contact with the group who were waiting for them and were arranging for someone to fetch them. Apart from those on guard or radio duty, the rest had little to do but wait. They were sitting around a drinking trough in the yard one morning when David pointed to the highest hill in sight. 'There should be an excellent view from up there. You could see anyone approaching from miles away. Maybe someone should reconnoitre.' He turned to Jean-Paul. 'Would you go up there with a pair of binoculars, old chap? Take Jacki with you. Keep watch for two or three hours, then let us know if you think it is worthwhile posting a permanent lookout there until these people come for us.'

Jean-Paul was not apparently aware what David was offering him. But Jacqueline knew, and suspected that some of the others guessed too. The pit of her stomach knew – and leaped with excitement.

She jumped to her feet. 'I'll just put some food and water into a rucksack,' she called, disappearing into the kitchen.

They walked in silence, keeping to wooded areas. They had to walk in single file, but even side by side there would have been nothing to say. Two people, thinking the same thought, propelled by the same need and knowing exactly what was in the other's mind. Words were meaningless.

Her jacket caught on a briar and he came back to help her disentangle it. She turned to thank him . . . and then he was kissing her, fumbling with her rucksack, her clothes.

They didn't wait to undress. Just slipped to the ground, releasing the vital buttons. Then he was in her, filling her. She nearly fainted as the blood drained from her head, arms, legs, to swell and tighten her around him. A few brief moments and they climaxed together and lay breathless with excitement rather than exertion.

Later, on the hilltop, they lay naked together, warmed

by the autumn sun, scanning the panorama with binoculars, making love, eating and making love again.

He told her how he and Veronique had both joined the Resistance, the FFI, and how she had died during SS interrogation. Their two daughters were living with his parents in Bordeaux. His eyes filled with tears as he spoke and when he finished his face was a mask of bitter hatred. They remained so as she told him about Heinrich. He sympathised over Marco's death, but sprang up in concern when he heard of Jean-Jacques' disappearance.

'What have you done to find him?' he asked.

'Nothing. What could I do? Even if I had not been under house arrest, if the Italian authorities had found him he would have been shot as a deserter, and if the Germans had found him they would either have sent him to the front to be killed or to a detention camp in Austria. You know, he must have been planning his desertion during his last leave, or even before. He is a deep, serious boy and I don't believe he would have deserted unless he had something more important to do . . . although I cannot imagine what. Of course I worry about him, about them all, but Jean-Jacques knew he could go to Rosita and Giuseppe. They would take care of him. Anyway, he must surely be safe now, with the British and Americans as far north as Firenza. He is probably living in solitary state at the villa, being waited on hand and foot.'

Far below them a man was herding goats up a narrow track which wound out of the forest. From the valley beyond, smoke drifted lazily from a cluster of buildings. Jean-Paul sketched a rough map of the area.

'Better to have more than big, wide smiles to take back with us,' Jacqueline laughed.

'Why, do you think they'll guess?'

'Guess! Darling, they knew what we were going to do before we left.'

'Will you be embarrassed?' Jean-Paul asked.

'Of course not. I have loved you since I was sixteen. We are adults, for heaven's sake. I can make love with you if

I want to and I really don't give a damn who knows or whether they approve. It's nobody's business but our own,' she asserted.

'I don't know how you can say that. It certainly matters to me.'

But he soon recovered. In fact they romped down through the grass and rocks more like teenagers than soldiers, until Jacqueline suddenly stopped. 'Sssssh!' she hissed.

They rolled into a hollow and lay still. It was the noise of an aircraft flying low over the trees in the valley below. Peering through a crevice they could see quite clearly right into the cockpit.

'Whew! That was close. We really were being stupid. Come on, let's go, but we will have to be more careful.' Jacqueline was annoyed with herself for allowing her guard to drop.

Nearing the farm she was extra cautious, and Jean-Paul became impatient. 'We are all right here. They have posted guards all round.'

'Ssssh. Keep your voice down.' She frowned at him. 'We don't want to lead anyone into our hideout.'

From an island in the Aegean Jean-Paul and his group had helped in the rescue of British escapees and maintained a radio link with the Royal Navy, passing them information of enemy movements. Valuable work, but he had never been trained as a guerrilla. 'Surely we won't have to play Cowboys and Indians all the time?' he whispered.

She ignored the remark, remembering David's comments, and moved stealthily forward.

Leaves rustled behind her and she swung round to see Ugo's hand clapped over Jean-Paul's mouth, a knife pointed at his throat. 'You came through there like a herd of elephants,' he growled. 'Have you forgotten all you were taught?'

Jacqueline whispered an apology. Jean-Paul looked furious and Ugo faded into the bushes with a grunt.

David examined the map on the kitchen table.

'Excellent,' he remarked. 'You're an expert, Jean-Paul. If these bods don't come and get us soon we'll need several more like this one to plan our next move. Could you do some further afield we could link up with?'

'No problem.' Jean-Paul looked pleased. 'I'll start tomorrow.'

'Please, if they don't turn up by then.'

But they did. The other Englishman, Bill, brought two Chetniks in at gunpoint just before lunch.

David and Jacob cross-examined them through the Yugoslav interpreter for several minutes before extending hands of welcome. 'Sorry to have to grill you,' David said, not knowing whether to address them direct or continue using the interpreter.

'Don' to worry. We do *même chose*,' one of them replied in a jumble of broken English and French. ''Ere we 'ave papers.' He produced a sweaty envelope from inside his shirt.

David's eyebrows lifted as he read the contents. 'Hm. Better digest this with lunch, I think. What do you reckon, cook? Can you raise two more platefuls?'

The visitors seemed to like cow stew with homegrown onions, swedes and boiled corn. They belched impressively afterwards and then, having journeyed through the previous night, requested the use of beds.

When the bedroom door closed, the others grouped round David at the table to hear his news.

'I think we had all better discuss this matter before we go any further.' He struck a match and held the paper until it burned through and fell in his plate. He mashed it up with his fork and continued. 'As you know, we don't get orders from Rico any more. We are all working for British Intelligence who are themselves working with the Yanks. And somewhere along the line our original purpose in coming here, you know, all those ideals Rico spoke to us about in Italy, well, they seem to have been overtaken by some far bigger and more important matters. Judging by the Allied advance in France and Italy and the Russian successes on the Eastern Front, nobody except Hitler has much doubt about an ultimate German defeat. What does seem to be bothering the Allies now is Communism. As we heard on the radio, the Russians have moved into Rumania and two days ago, when they crossed the Danube south of Bucharest, the Rumanians swopped sides and joined them. Now the British doubt that the Russians will ever get out of the countries they claim to have liberated, so they are desperately hoping to prevent them linking up with Tito and taking over Yugoslavia. Thus they want our groups to link up with the Chetniks to fight together against the Communists, even more than the Germans. How do you all feel about that?'

He paused and looked around, but nobody spoke.

He went on. 'The point is that from here on it's going to be difficult to decide who is a friend and who is an enemy; we may well wind up fighting alongside pro-German groups, you must realise that. And another thing I had better mention is that this Tito fellow doesn't like people who try to interfere with his operations. He doesn't take prisoners and has been bumping off all the Chetniks he can lay hands on, so if we join the Chetniks I daresay his attitude will be the same towards us.' He sat back and waited.

Ugo was first to speak. 'If I find myself in a ditch with a bloody Kraut I'll kill him. I don't give a damn whose bloody side he's on.'

''Fraid I have to agree,' Bill nodded.

'Will it really come to that?' Teresa asked.

David shrugged and remained silent.

Anna pushed her chair back from the table. 'Now just a minute, let's not forget the purpose we had in mind when we started. Rico used to describe our mutual enemies as extremists. People who torture and kill those who even passively disagree with them. Like Fascists and,' she struck the table with her palm, 'Communists. We don't know who killed this farmer and his family, but judging by what

David was just telling us about Tito's mob killing the Chetniks, it probably was Communists.' She drew breath and continued. 'Does it matter if we use the Germans to fight Communism? They are going to lose the war anyway.'

'True,' Berto agreed.

'No! This is crazy.' Philippe, Jean-Paul's compatriot, exploded. 'It is too mixed up. First we fight this one, and then that. The Germans are our enemies, then our friends. Now the Bulgarians who supported the Germans have changed sides and fight alongside the Russians. The British and the Americans and the Russians were all fighting the Germans. Now the British are asking us to stand and fight against Tito on one side of us, Russians on the other, with our worst enemies, the Krauts, at our backs pretending to be our friends!' He threw his arms wide. 'I volunteered to be part of an underground strike force – not a suicide squad!'

Nobody spoke until David leaned forward. 'This is politics,' he sighed. 'It has always been this way throughout history. However, I honestly believe that British Intelligence, that Churchill and his government, must know more and understand more than we do. And if they think the Communists are a genuine threat to the Balkans, and feel there is a chance of preventing this link-up between the Russians and the Yugoslav partisans, I for one am prepared to assist in any way I can.' He stood up. 'None of us is committed. We have signed nothing. We are all volunteers to do as we wish. Personally, I am going to join the Chetniks to fight against Communism, whatever their politics and whoever their friends may be.' He picked up the papers in front of him and walked out into the afternoon sun.

Anna and Berto, Jacqueline and Jean-Paul, Jacob and Teresa immediately followed. Others joined them after more discussion until finally Bill, Ugo and Philippe emerged, grumbling, but agreeing to stay with their unit.

* * *

The Russians were moving rapidly west towards the Rumanian-Yugoslav border only fifty miles from Belgrade, where the Germans were anxiously strengthening their defences in the hope of holding out until General von Weich could arrive with reinforcements withdrawn from Greece. Tito's forces were spreading north from his head-quarters at Uzice in the mountains of Serbia, and the Chetniks and Allied units were being used in an attempt to hold him back, so preventing a Communist encirclement of Belgrade.

David's group was obliged to make their journey on foot, so it was the third week of September before they were in a position to make contact with the enemy. They were camped in the plains south-west of Ruma, between the Danube and its major tributary the Sava, moving through swamp-grass, reeds and muddy streams.

Twice Tito's men moved up to try to take the Ruma to Belgrade road. Twice they had been repulsed, and now Ugo reported that on his scouting patrol he had seen them bringing up heavier supplies with bazookas and shells.

'Where the hell did they get those?' Jacqueline asked.

'Stole them from the Krauts. That's where most of their supplies come from,' Jacob replied. 'I've heard the Germans reporting lost equipment on the radio for weeks.'

'Well, we haven't the men or the arms to face a real battle with that lot,' David mused. 'All we can do is sneak in and try to destroy it before they put it to use. Pity we've no more grenades.'

'Couldn't we make petrol bombs?' Jean-Paul asked. 'The FFI used them all the time.'

'How do you mean? What are they?'

'Simply beer or lemonade bottles filled with petrol. You put some paper or a rag in the top of the bottle and light it immediately before throwing it. They are very good incendiaries, providing you are quick, but there is a right and a wrong way of making them. I can show you.'

'Where do you suppose we will get the petrol?' Anna looked dubious.

'We saw a truck in a ditch by the road back there this morning. There may be something in its tank,' David suggested. 'No, it's the bottles that are going to be difficult to find.'

'There is a village up ahead. Where there are people there are usually bottles,' Jacqueline chipped in.

The trouble with carrying two dozen empty bottles in a sack is the extraordinary amount of noise they make. Jacqueline finally arrived back with bottles in her sleeves, down her shirt, in pockets, and even in her pants. Bill had done the same. David and Jacob had been lucky to find a long piece of rubber tubing for syphoning in the garage of an abandoned house.

'That is very fortunate,' David remarked. 'Have you any idea how far it is from the petrol cap of a truck to its actual petrol tank? A long way.'

Under Jean-Paul's instructions the bombs were made up.

They had moved to a waiting position at dusk and closed in as darkness thickened. The thin drizzle would have soaked them, had they not already been saturated by the mud through which they had squelched for the past week. Teresa had had to be left behind as she had caught a cold and could not stop sneezing.

The enemy were assembling in three groups around a cluster of buildings and trees on slightly higher dry ground. Each man appeared to be carrying a rifle or machine-gun, but David guessed the bigger weapons and ammunition were in the trucks parked in a central courtyard.

Jacqueline had discovered that with practice it was possible to see quite well in the dark and to tread as stealthily as a cat. Darkness seemed to quicken all the senses . . . as now, when suddenly she was aware of smoke . . . cigarette smoke. She signalled Jacob and they circled around the guard until she could jump from a good vantage point and clamp her hand over his mouth while Jacob slit his throat. She held on until the body went limp, then together they pulled it into the bushes.

Jean-Paul beckoned them on until the three stood together, backs pressed against the wall of a building. They could hear voices. Jean-Paul edged past a doorway and as Jacqueline started to follow, it opened. She stepped backwards into Jacob as two men emerged. As one man turned to close the drop latch the other saw her and she tried to stifle his shout as Jacob swung round her with his knife to kill the sound at source. Seeing the second man's gun come up, Jacqueline dropped his friend and lunged at him. Her hand hit the rifle, sending an excruciating pain up her arm, but she had thrown him off balance, leaving him a sitting target for Jean-Paul's knife . . . but Jean-Paul just stood flattened against the wall, not moving. It was Jacqueline who stuck a knife into the waiting chest, though not accurately enough to forestall his scream.

They heard an inner door open and footsteps running.

Jean-Paul came to life, grabbed one man's feet and dragged him rapidly behind a water butt. Jacqueline and Jacob pulled the other in the opposite direction round the corner of the building and waited. Men rushed out, shouting.

Jacqueline tugged her knife out of her victim, wiped the blade on his clothes and slipped it back into its sheath. It was time for guns now.

Peering round the side of the house she saw a group of men beginning to scatter. Better to fire into the lot before they disperse, she thought. The gun shuddered violently in her grasp as it spat death. Jacob joined her, both careful to fire not too close to the water butt in case Jean-Paul emerged.

Anna and Berto must have acted immediately they heard the shots. There was a tremendous roar and rush of hot air as the trucks exploded within seconds of each other, lighting the whole area and sending debris hundreds of feet into the air.

Not one of the group of enemy soldiers who had rushed from the doorway remained standing. They were either dead, wounded, or escaped. But where was Jean-Paul? Was he hit?

Jacqueline ran to the water butt. It concealed only the man they had killed. She ran on to peer round another corner.

'Psst!'

She swung towards a clump of bushes and a low wall.

Jean-Paul stood up. 'Thank goodness you are all right,' he whispered.

'Of course I am all right,' she hissed. 'Come on,' and ran back past the water butt to the door where Jacob waited, flung it open, and together they burst in, firing.

There was no one in the hallway, but they heard movements behind a door. Jacqueline pulled a bottle of petrol from her pocket, drew the cork and pushed a paper spill into the neck. Jacob struck a match. She opened the door with one hand, flung with the other, closed the door immediately and stood waiting for what seemed like a full minute, but was probably only a split second, until the explosion and shouts. The door opened and Jacob fired as people tried to get out.

The fire took hold quickly and smoke billowed out. They went on through the house but saw no one.

'Okay. Let's go,' Jean-Paul called.

'You two go that way.' Jacob indicated the way they had come. 'I'll go out through the back into the courtyard.'

Jean-Paul reached the door first, opened it cautiously and rapidly closed it again. 'There is a whole bunch of them out there,' he shouted above the noise.

'We can't stay here!'

'Follow Jacob.' Jean-Paul grabbed her arm and started to run down the hallway past the door where flames were already licking the paintwork. Through streaming eyes they saw the back door open and a figure appear.

Jean-Paul shouted.

Jacqueline fired.

Another figure took its place and fired back. They had dropped to the floor just in time to allow the bullets to whine over them, and crawled to the cover of the stairway. Their assailants must have thought them dead and advanced with an amazing lack of caution. Jacqueline killed them both in one short burst. They appeared to have been alone.

Outside, a gun battle was in progress beyond the trees. Jean-Paul hesitated, but Jacqueline jerked her head impatiently and they ran down an alleyway between two buildings. A figure appeared at the end and peered at them.

'David, it's us,' Jacqueline called.

He beckoned. 'Come this way. Better avoid the courtyard. We'll head round the perimeter.' As they caught up with him, he added, 'We're fanning out now and heading back to base.'

Jacqueline had looked at her watch in disbelief. The actual assault had lasted less than fifteen minutes. Now, two hours later, they lay wet and shivering on the soaking grass, waiting for the last of the party to join them. Her body and mind were numb, partly with cold but partly with sheer exhaustion. She must have burned up every last drop of adrenalin. Jean-Paul lay beside her, curled up in a foetal posture. Her brows drew together; for the first time since they had met again she felt nothing. No urge to draw closer to him, touch him, feel his warmth. Despite her desperate need for sleep her mind went back remorselessly over the details of the raid. Unwillingly she counted the number of times he had put their lives at risk by failing to strike, to kill. He had even run away. Wasn't it the instinct of a normal man to fight in such circumstances? She remembered fighting side by side with David on the beach the night Jean-Paul and the others had arrived. David – who had saved her life.

Teresa was passing round hot broth. Jacqueline reached out to take the mug with her left hand, gasped, and nearly dropped it.

'What is it?' Teresa asked. 'Are you hurt?'

'Just a bad bruise, I think. I'll look at it properly in daylight. Is Anna still not back?'

'No. Nor Berto, Ugo, and three of the Chetnik boys. Philippe was shot in the arm, but I think the bullet went right through. And a couple of people were a shade too close to their petrol bombs when they exploded and got a bit scorched, but nothing serious.'

Another hour passed before Anna and Ugo turned up, half dragging Berto between them. He had taken a row of bullets down his right side: shoulder, hip, chest and thigh. His head arched back in agony between bouts of unconsciousness.

'We had reached the long grass and were wriggling towards the trees when they saw us. Bill drew their fire while Ugo and I dragged him away. Bill is still there; I think they killed him.' Anna's voice was toneless.

Teresa and David worked on Berto together while Anna sipped a mug of broth, watching. There was little they could do except inject him with painkiller, cover the wounds with antiseptic dressings and wrap him in dry clothes.

'Any chance of finding a doctor?' Anna spoke quietly.

Berto heard her and shook his head. 'Too risky,' he whispered. 'And it is not worth it. He would be too late.'

'Nonsense. You are going to be all right.' Anna's voice was harsh with determination, but her face was drawn and anxious.

'Sit by me for a while.' His left hand fluttered towards her.

Jacqueline fell asleep, still shivering, and was woken an hour later by someone coughing. It was Berto. In the dim light of Anna's torch she could see blood on his mouth. Her mother was kneeling beside him, whispering something. Between spasms he smiled faintly up at her and for the first time Jacqueline realised how close the two had become. A wave of sadness swept over her. Berto was obviously dying.

By dawn he was in a coma. The rain had stopped and the sun rose slowly into a clear sky over the distant outline of Belgrade. Anna maintained her vigil, held his hand, stroked his forehead. Jacqueline warmed the remaining broth and handed it round. They could hear Berto's breath rattling in his chest, gradually getting quieter. Then there was silence. Anna pressed down his eyelids.

September 1944

Here is my journey's end, here is my butt,
And very sea-mark of my utmost sail.

William Shakespeare, *Othello*

EVERY DAY they scouted, and were pleased to see that the Communist unit they had attacked was not replaced. On the other hand, there was now a constant rumble of heavy guns from the east, denoting the Russian advance.

They were joined by two groups of Chetniks, led by a short, wiry young man with a broad, serious face, called Primo. He had orders to hold the road open from Ruma. Chetniks also held the main road further north, from Novi-Sad. This was an important wedge to hold because the German General Freissner was forced to retreat west over the Rumanian border when, out of his four armies, the two consisting of Rumanian troops changed sides.

However, the whole picture was changing all the time, and only a few days later Novi-Sad fell. At the same time Tito's forces attacked in strength northward across the Sava.

David conferred constantly with Primo and his officers, who insisted they fall back along the road towards the capital, holding it as long as they could.

Their final stand was watched with interest by men of the German garrison and as they withdrew across the bridge over the Sava they were allowed through unchallenged. It felt very strange to most members of David's troop, and they had to resist the temptation to look back

399

over their shoulders, almost expecting a hail of bullets to follow them.

Looking around, they were amazed at the extent of the devastation; huge mounds of weed-covered rubble stood as monuments of Hitler's 1941 Blitzkrieg.

It was obvious that the city had been prepared for a siege, but of the German troops there was remarkably little evidence. The townspeople were quite blatant in displaying their divided allegiance. The poorer folk met them with stony faces, and there was little doubt that if the Communists moved in they would greet them with open arms, whereas the merchants and professional men were eager to offer the Chetniks their assistance. It was also obvious that opinions differed on the outcome, some believing the city would remain impregnable, others fearing at least the bombardment if not the arrival of Communism, and these were still piling up cars and carts, even wheelbarrows, preparing to evacuate.

Food was hard to find. The remains of depleted stocks had been traded for valuables far beyond their worth. Eventually the group were fortunate to be taken into what remained of a once beautiful mansion overlooking Kalemegdan Park, in the past an old Turkish fortress. It was owned by a wealthy royalist sympathiser who offered to feed them until they were assigned new duties.

It was the first time in nearly a year that Jacqueline had enjoyed the luxury of lying in a real bath, washing her hair and retiring to a glorious feather bed. She stretched each limb to ease the aching muscles and examined the still painfully bruised hand, at last free of mud. Anna was already asleep in the next bed, but despite her weariness, Jacqueline wanted just to lie and think. She wanted to think about the war and her confusing role in it. Even when Marco was alive it had been difficult to sort out her feelings, being an American citizen and yet the adoring mistress of a member of a political party she hated. She had almost felt herself to be Italian until Duce had elected to join Hitler in his oppressive policies. Yet all that seemed so simple when compared with present-day issues. It had all become too ridiculous. Far too many conflicting factors, interests, needs, demands, ideas and ideals.

Six months ago Anna had fired her with a desire for revenge against the Fascists, the extremists, the Communists. So she had fostered her hate, trained with determination . . . and killed both Fascists and Tito's Communist partisans. Yet for what? It was becoming obvious to her that these factors were part of the normal consistency of any country. The rich, the poor, the haves and the have-nots, the keen and the disinterested, the hard-working and the lazy. There would surely always be people who wanted to lead, rule, hold power and sway over the masses. And for a while they were usually good for the masses. But power corrupts, and inevitably they would become tyrants and have to be deposed.

Most people would claim that all they wanted was peace, adequate provision, a home. Or was it human nature to find that enough was not enough? Always to want more than one has . . . and, when a sufficient number of others agreed with one, be prepared to kill for it? Murder, in the name of patriotism? Were all soldiers just hired assassins – like herself? Except that nobody paid her; she killed for revenge, hate. And even that reason, or excuse, no longer applied. It had become increasingly difficult to work up a hatred when going on a sortie. The men she had to kill had ceased to be the weak-minded puppets of a despised political system. They were just men: husbands, sons, lovers. In fact she had not felt the old hatred for weeks, not since the arrival of Jean-Paul . . .

And what about Jean-Paul?

Was he peculiar in some way that he was unable to kill? Or had he, like herself, found it difficult to hate enough? Or was he simply a coward? She wondered what had been in his mind when, on repeated occasions, he had failed to use his knife or his gun? Was he aware that he had put their lives at risk more than once? A conscientious objector? Hardly, or he wouldn't be here at all.

Could she love a coward? Her mind drifted back. First, to Marco: she still loved the memory of his strength and dependability, always there to offer encouragement, guidance and reassurance. She couldn't imagine him being weak – and yet had it been weak of him to continue to fight for Duce long after he had ceased to believe in the Italian dictator's policies?

And then she thought of David. In many ways David was similar to Marco. Calm, steady, undemanding and reliable, he had been the strength of their group, driving them on when they were tired, always ready to point them in the right direction.

If they all survived the battle for Belgrade she knew there would be two men who loved and wanted her, waiting only for her acceptance. One, who would quietly take the lead in all things, though no doubt be prepared to stand back with a wry smile if she wanted a turn on the helm.

But would there be the glorious, passionate ecstasy? No matter what adventures they might share, storms they might sail through, would life always lack the spice of sexual exhilaration she had experienced with the other man, Jean-Paul? Could they ever sit at a candlelit table gazing at each other with the passionate awareness of what was to follow?

Could her lack of response to David be because she had always resisted, consciously or subconsciously, the temptation, the luxury of loving another man? Surely the more likely reason was that when David first showed his feelings for her, she was still sexually numb. She might have remained numb, too, had not the first sight of Jean-Paul revitalised the memory of their ecstatic Paris interlude, stirred and stimulated the dormant feelings that surged back into life the moment their eyes met. She rolled on to her back and stretched her aching muscles. The memory, past and recent, of lovemaking with Jean-Paul still roused her. Yet, for the first time, she found herself wondering if 'love' was the correct term to apply to that arousal?

Worried and confused, she sighed and turned again.

Should she consider which would be the better father for her children?

The children. Oh, how she longed, ached to see them again. To think it was a whole year now since Anna had taken Francisco, Katarina and Bobo picnicking on that fateful day. How many times in that year had she pushed thoughts of them out of her mind lest the tears and longing should weaken her resolve to fight on. They would have grown a lot. Pray God they were happy.

And Jean-Jacques? She sighed. Poor, confused boy-man. Where was he now? She would scour Italy for him when she got back . . . if she got back.

At last, the feathers and soft linen lulled her into a dreamless sleep.

She slept for a long time. When she awoke her filthy clothes had been laundered and returned, and by the time she went downstairs David had gone for a briefing on their next move.

Most of the others were up; Jean-Paul was one who was not.

Jacqueline and Anna sat alone together sipping coffee, obviously a black-market purchase, finding very little to talk about. Anna was trying hard not to make her sadness over Berto's death too apparent, so Jacqueline did not refer to him. Silly, she thought, for a mother and daughter to sit here almost speechless, when within the next couple of days they might both be dead, never having said the million things they had to tell each other.

Anna looked up and smiled, Jacqueline thought, as though she had read her thoughts. Despite having slept well the older woman was looking very drawn and tired. Her skin was greyish yellow and she had become very thin. Jacqueline felt concerned about her but knew that nothing could be done about it at the moment.

'I am sorry I talked you into this mess,' Anna sighed. 'I can only pray that you survive. I must have been mad, but it seemed so right at the time.'

'Don't talk like that, Mama, it was right. I would probably be a chronic invalid by now, or dead, if you hadn't shaken me out of my self-pity, made me get up and fight.' She put a hand over Anna's. 'Let's be truly honest, when we talk about fighting tyranny and oppression for the sake of our children, aren't we in fact seeking an aura of glory to boost ourselves in our own eyes? I only got up from that wheelchair to kill Reinikker. It was a personal vendetta, and I have lost count of how many men I have killed in revenge for what he did to me. So many that the hate has dwindled, ebbed away. I don't feel anything now, when I think of him, but at the time I was pulling a trigger or thrusting my knife I wasn't thinking of my children, just indulging in gut hate.'

Anna was nodding. 'I know, I agree we all do delude ourselves about our motivations, but that doesn't mean we are all entirely selfish. For instance, why did you come to fetch me from Le Mans in 1940? In a savage bout of self-criticism *you* might call it "self-glorification" – but you would be wrong. You could say that one only gives love so that one may be loved in return . . . but surely that is a fair bargain? You have given me so much love and happiness in these past few years . . .' she smiled gently at her daughter. 'I cannot believe it was purely for self-gratification and for what you could get out of me in return.'

'It wasn't anything I had planned, it just happened.'

'Can you imagine how disgusted I feel with myself over my attitude to you as a child and a teenager?' Anna's eyes filled with tears. 'I was a monster!'

'Can you imagine what a boring life I would have had if you had been the traditional, cosy sort of mother!' Jacqueline laughed; she wanted Anna to feel no reproaches, nor did she want her own emotions to overspill at this moment.

Shellfire boomed monotonously in the distance, becoming steadily louder and nearer.

When David came in he was full of news.

404

'Some of the German forces are retreating into the city, but the main body of Freissner's troops are reported to be further north. They're a pretty mixed bag, from what I've seen of them. Hitler is obviously throwing all his best divisions against the Allied armies in France.

'The point is that there is now no hope of stopping the Russians taking Belgrade, or indeed all of Yugoslavia; they're expected to reach here within twenty-four hours. Because of this, British Intelligence has ordered that all fighting must cease. Under no circumstances must we be found opposing the Reds in any way. Also, because some of us may have been identified as having fought with the Chetniks, we've been ordered to go to the Swedish Embassy and claim political asylum until London can sort out our exits from the country. This is what we are therefore going to do.'

'And the Chetniks?' Jean-Paul asked.

David sighed and shrugged. 'Must do the best they can about making their peace with Tito. I know it seems like deserting them, and I also know a lot of them are going to wind up against a wall, but we didn't make the decision to back them in the first place, and we aren't taking the decision to abandon them now. We're soldiers, and we obey orders.' He looked from face to face, but no one said anything.

'There is, however,' he went on, 'one last and apparently urgent assignment for . . . certain members of the group. You all know that London is aware of the composition of this unit; they seem to have files on us all, covering our names and backgrounds. They want me to detach the two . . .' he paused, glanced at Anna and Jacqueline in some embarrassment, '. . . Rumanian members of my group for an urgent assignment.'

Mother and daughter looked at each other.

'It will not take long,' David said. 'You are still instructed to get to the Swedish Embassy as soon as you can. The danger lies in the Russians actually entering the city before you make it. Believe me, Jacki, Anna, if there was anyone else . . .'

'What do you want us to do?' Anna asked, quietly.

'Well, you will recall that I told you of this group of Rumanian right-wingers who are planning to set up an alternative king to Michael, in the hopes of holding back the Russians. Frankly, they are as Fascist in their beliefs and behaviour as any Nazi, but, while there was some chance of holding Communism in the Balkans, London was prepared to go along with them, even if they also knew they were receiving support from the Germans. Now that's all over as well. London wants these people told that they can expect no further support from the West, and will be opposed even if they do manage to pull off some sort of coup. They are to be told they must disband like everyone else, and accept the Russians as their friends.'

'Do you think they will listen to two women?' Jacqueline asked.

'Not exactly two women, Jacki. You are still the Countess Tyroler. You were friends with the royal family. So was Anna.'

'Friends? My God!'

'Anyway, I have no one else to send,' he said. 'You also speak Rumanian. And Jacki, it doesn't matter to London, or to me, whether they listen to you or not. You'll have delivered the message, and if they want to commit suicide after that, it's up to them. Will you do it? I'm afraid I've already arranged for a couple of the Chetnik boys to pick you up this evening, but I'd still like you to volunteer. Believe me, I'd come with you, but I'm under orders to round up all of my group and get them to the Swedish Embassy.'

Anna gazed at Jacqueline. 'Politics make me sick,' she said.

'Agreed,' David responded. 'But when the chips are down, it has to be us against them. And "us" includes the Russians at this moment.'

'How do you feel, Mama?' Jacqueline asked. 'Shall we

406

go and try to talk some sense into this pseudo-prince?'

Anna shrugged. 'I suppose I am quite curious to see who he is.'

'Okay,' Jacqueline said. 'We volunteer, but we'll be with you at the Swedish Embassy by midnight. You can set your watch on that.'

Jean-Paul had come into the room and overheard the discussion. 'Can't I come with you? I do speak a little Rumanian. Frankly, I don't like the idea of just you two women going. I could pose as your husband.'

'Not if I'm to convince them I am the Countess Tyroler. Ion may still be alive.' And what assistance could we possibly expect from you, if there were to be trouble, she wondered.

'Come on, they've got some food ready for us. You can discuss that later.' David led them out of the room.

It was a frugal meal, but they were very grateful for whatever they could get.

'Do you realise this could be the last meal we shall ever have together as a group?' Anna reflected. 'It seems odd that after having lived so close together for all these months, in a day or two we will go our separate ways and maybe never meet again. David, what do you intend to do when this is over?'

'The powers-that-be have asked me to stay on in Intelligence,' David said. 'But . . . perhaps I'm just tired, but I have the feeling that I want to get away from killing, fighting, death. I have an increasing desire to be up and away as soon as this is over. Seek fresh fields. My wife and I are divorced, my parents are dead. I no longer have any ties in England, and I have a sudden urge to start all over again. What about you?'

As the conversation continued, Jacqueline was aware of Jean-Paul's gaze, willing her to look at him . . . knew there was a question in both their minds for which he wanted her answer. Instead she turned to Teresa.

'What about you and Jacob? What will you do?'

'We are both going to try to get to Palestine, if we can.

We have been told the British Government may help us.'

Jacqueline listened intently to Teresa's plans until the meal was finished.

Afterwards she went up alone to the room she had shared with Anna to put her few things together and think. She frowned when someone knocked on the door.

'Come in.'

It was Jean-Paul.

'I have been waiting for an opportunity to speak to you. Can we talk now?'

'I suppose so. What did you want to talk about?' As though she didn't know. 'Coming with us this evening?'

'No, well . . . that too, but . . . Oh God, where do I begin? I have botched everything, haven't I?'

She frowned. 'What do you mean?'

'You think I am a coward, don't you? Weak. Timid.' He threw himself on the bed and gazed at the ceiling.

So this was why he had come. With explanations, excuses. He looked pathetically miserable.

She sat beside him. 'I'm not in a position to think anything. I don't know what is going on in your mind. Why don't you tell me?'

He paused for a few moments. 'I don't really know what to say. I suppose it just comes down to the basic fact that, for all my bravado, I am hopelessly over-sensitive. I have an absolute horror, not only of violence, but even of discord. That's why I got out of the army years ago.'

'What about the Underground Movement, the FFI? What were you doing with them?'

'With the Maquis I was in Intelligence. I never had to look a man in the eye and kill him. When I escaped and joined the FFI I was in a similar unit. Only since joining your group have I been asked to kill . . . and found I cannot.'

Suddenly she felt a great sympathy for this man's reservation. She had an urge to put her arm round him, comfort him like a mother – but resisted and said nothing.

He got up and walked to the window. 'It is a basic weakness in my character, I suppose. It was the same in business before the war. I used to track down superb antiques and I built up a splendid stock, but it was my father who had to beat down the price. Then it was something similar with our employees. I could find excellent staff and I was able to work very well with everyone, but my father had to do all the hiring and firing. I just could not be tough enough.'

'A pity I am not a bit more like you,' Jacqueline commented, almost to herself. 'You must think I am a very hard, murderous bitch.'

'No, no! On the contrary, I admire you. I envy you. I am not happy to be the way I am, constantly to have a feeling of inferiority because I lack aggression. I long to be strong and decisive, but on the few occasions when I have been it has been a disaster, or I have not slept for weeks worrying about what I have done.' He turned to face her. 'What makes me so miserable is knowing what a person like you must think of me. I so desperately wanted your love and respect, but . . .' He shrugged.

Jacqueline looked into the dark eyes, the gentle face with its softly curved mouth, and saw the same deep, brooding personality as their son, Jean-Jacques. Then she knew she could not love him in the unreserved way of a wife or lover.

This was no Marco, no empire builder she could look up to and revere. Nor a David, a leader whom she could follow or go with, side by side. However much she might once have loved him, or even love him still, she realised that this man would turn theirs into a mother–son relationship, that if they were to make anything of their lives she would have to lead, organise, dominate. And however much he might love and want her now, he would grow to resent that domination. Certainly the basic animal attraction existing between them up to now would soon be worn away within the abrasive confines of their unbalanced relationship.

He was watching her, waiting . . . and she had no idea how to frame the words.

'Dear Jean-Paul.' She shook her head wearily, the words faltering. 'Our love affair, stretching over the years, has been a fragile thing, built on dreams and fantasies. It has never had the substance of reality. I don't think it ever could; we are too different. I love and admire your gentleness and sensitivity, but I don't understand it any more than you could be expected to understand my . . . aggression. When our different characteristics are applied to matters outside our relationship, we can admire or criticise them in a detached way, which need not affect our feelings for each other. But if those characteristics are applied to our joint daily lives . . .' She hunched her shoulders and ran a hand over her cropped hair. 'I'm afraid the friction would destroy our love.'

Jean-Paul was gazing out of the window, his back stiff and motionless. 'Can't you picture our little home together in south-west France, surrounded by our children, vineyards, sunshine?' he asked. 'I would go back into the antique business . . .'

'I can picture it, Jean-Paul, but it is not what I want. I intend to take my children to America. There they will finish their education in good schools and learn a new, modern way of life.'

He turned to face her as she spoke.

'I want to start my own business again,' she went on. 'Build it up, expand and develop my ideas, my life. A house among the vineyards sounds marvellous after all this . . . but I know I couldn't endure it for more than two or three weeks.'

'*Pas de problème*.' Jean-Paul returned to sit beside her, taking her hands in his. 'I will come to America with you. We will start up a business together. I . . .'

Jacqueline shook her head. 'That is not what you want, is it? You hate fighting, and there will be just as much fighting, business competition, struggle and effort as we have had here; the only difference will be in direction.

You will hate it. You will hate me for wanting it and I will hate you for not wanting to carry on when the going is hard.'

'All I want is you, chérie.'

'Which was wonderful as long as our affair remained within the bounds of fantasy, but in reality it is not enough. We have lived separate lives for too long. We are very different people, too different.' She felt dreadfully conflicting emotions surge through her in waves as he gazed at her, flat and dispirited, eyes filled with pain and sadness. She wrestled with the urge to put her arms round him and say, 'Forget it, we'll give it a try. We'll stick together for as long as we can.' But when she thought of the continued disruption of their respective children's lives, quite apart from their own, she knew she must not give in. She must consider the children. Jean-Paul might be fine with his own daughters, but as a stepfather to her lively and tempestuous tribe he would be a disaster.

He stood up with an effort, touched her shoulder lightly. 'We'll talk again, later,' he muttered, and left the room before she could summon the courage to say 'No.'

Two Chetniks whom they had not previously met called for them that evening. They were obviously very friendly with the householder and his wife, pausing to drink and chat briefly before hurrying the two women and Jean-Paul away towards the palace.

In quite good Italian, one of them made it clear, in a roundabout way, that they had enough problems on hand at the moment and the Rumanian prince could prove to be a considerable embarrassment to them. The Germans, who were also supporting the Prince, had been convinced that Belgrade would stand against the Russians, leaving it very late to get him out safely now that they saw the strength of the Soviet onslaught. Even now they were arguing on whether or not to leave and if so, where they should go. It had not been possible to find sufficient Rumanians in the city to make up a force strong enough to consider slipping back into the Transylvanian Mountains where they could form the nucleus of a future revolution.

A series of shells crumped into buildings only a few streets to the east of them, sending up more smoke and dust to add to the heavy clouds turning pink in the sunset.

Jacqueline felt comforted by the thump of her machine-gun against her hip. She was aware of passing beautiful, or parts of what must once have been beautiful, buildings. It must have been a lovely city before this senseless devastation. How the people of Belgrade must hate the Germans, she thought, yet it was just history repeating itself. Belgrade had changed hands so many times over the centuries. Hadn't it once been a great trading centre for the Ottoman Empire? What would happen to it when all this was over?

The interior of the palace looked far from regal. It had been used by the Germans as offices, with hastily erected plywood inner walls, desks and cupboards installed, in the once noble halls.

Waiting in a corridor, they all became aware at the same moment of the change in background noise. The heavy thump of artillery shelling ceased and was replaced by small-arms fire. They looked at each other in alarm.

'The Russians are in the city! They are fighting in the streets,' one of the Chetniks exclaimed. 'Come, we must leave.' And with a brief 'goodbye' they ran off down the corridor.

'There is no point in standing here,' said Jean-Paul. 'Which way did they go? How do we get out?'

'They went down there. Should we head straight for the Embassy?'

'As fast as possible, I should say. David showed me where it was on the map. Now we'll see if it's still standing.'

The corridor ended in a long, wide hallway with double doors at each end. They turned right and, reaching the doors, flung them open.

To stop short.

They were in a large, lofty room, ornately decorated with pillars and frescoes, and hung with giant chandeliers, tapestries and gilt-framed portraits. The room was crowded, mainly with outlandishly smartly attired people, considering the situation outside. They seemed to be split into several groups, all arguing, voices raised and arms waving; all except for the largest group standing around a magnificent ebony table inlaid with brass and mother-of-pearl.

The newcomers were ignored, so Jacqueline approached the table to inquire the way out. Elbowing between two gentlemen, she opened her mouth to speak, but only emitted a strangled gasp.

The three people seated at the table behind files of papers looked up at the same moment. And they, too, gasped. Because, despite her shabby dungarees, short-cropped hair and lean, mannish bearing, the Countess Jacqueline Tyroler was still easily recognisable to her eldest son, Jean-Jacques, to her husband's *cher-ami*, Bruno Balanel, and to Colonel Heinrich von Reinikker.

Instinct, born of weeks of training and months of guerrilla warfare, carried the gun down from her shoulder and slipped the safety catch in one motion, which was fortunate, because her mind was in a turmoil. The relief at seeing Jean-Jacques alive and well, horror at the circumstances in which she found him, amazement at confronting von Reinikker, converged in an immense resurgence of the hatred she had thought was gone.

'Hands on the table!' she snapped at Reinikker in German.

He obeyed, colour draining from his face.

Bruno, on the other hand, turned puce. 'Damn you, woman,' he blustered. 'How dare you interrupt Prince Frederick when he is in conference?'

Something hard jabbed into her back. 'Drop the gun!' a voice threatened.

Fear shot through her. She hesitated a moment . . . but

before she could obey she heard David's voice. 'No, you drop it!'

The pistol clattered to the floor behind her.

'Put your hands up, everyone,' Anna shouted in Rumanian. 'Over to that wall. Quick, Quick. Move. Place your hands on your heads.'

She and David stood side by side, their guns covering the group.

'No, not you three.' Jacqueline spoke quietly as Bruno and Reinikker started to rise. 'You stay right where you are.'

'Do not worry, Your Highness,' someone called from across the room. 'She doesn't realise who you are. Someone explain it to her.'

'Mother . . .' Jean-Jacques gasped, rising.

She almost wanted to weep at the shame and embarrassment in his face. He stood tall and immaculate in a dark, pin-striped suit and starched collar. A crested pin held his tie, matching cufflinks were just visible beneath his coat-sleeves. His hair had been slicked back with cream, but it was his eyes that held her. Big, dark eyes, wide with confusion, sensitive and anxious.

She must not soften now. She must be hard, even cruel, if the day was to be won.

'I do not require an explanation.' Her voice was firm and clear. 'I am quite capable of recognising my own son.'

There was a gasp from his supporters.

'Jean-Jacques Tyroler,' she added loudly.

Several voices were raised at once. There were shouts of 'Prince Frederick of Rumania!'

Bruno pushed back his chair and stood up.

'That's right,' he shouted. 'You may be his mother, but you know full well that his true father was King Carol.'

Everyone was suddenly silent, waiting.

'Rubbish,' Jacqueline replied quietly, and without moving her eyes spoke over her shoulder. 'Jean-Paul, will you come round and stand beside our son. Now, Jean-Jacques, at last I can introduce you to your real father.'

Jean-Paul did as he was asked.

Every pair of eyes in the room watched as the slim, black-haired man with the deep, dark eyes moved round the table to stand beside the youthful but perfect replica of himself. There was no doubt, they could have been brothers. There were gasps from behind her and whispered comments.

'Why don't you take your son to the mirror over the fireplace,' Jacqueline said. 'Let him see the proof for himself.'

Bruno sat down again, mouth opening and shutting in impotent rage.

Throughout the drama Jacqueline's eyes had never left Reinikker's face. Now she saw his eyes flicker. With her gun aimed at his stomach, fear was driving him . . . to what? He remained deathly pale, as though he had seen a ghost. He had not attempted to speak so far, but now made an effort. 'My dear Jacqueline, may I congratulate you on your recovery.'

'No, you may not.'

'We felt sure that you would be delighted at all we are doing for young Frederick. We look forward to seeing you in your rôle as Queen Mother. I see the idea pleases you,' he added, because she had smiled.

But her smile had nothing to do with his words. The old, burning anger she used to feel when confronted with him was gone. Now all she felt was cold hatred, together with pleasing comfort emanating from her trigger finger. And the satisfying anticipation of what she knew she was going to do.

'In three sentences, you have made four mistakes, Reinikker,' she observed. Because she was still smiling he responded with a tentative widening of his mouth. 'You see,' she went on, 'for one thing, far from being delighted by my son's situation, I despise the way you and that creature . . .' she inclined her head towards Bruno, 'have attempted to manipulate the boy for your own ends, filling his head with nonsense about becoming king.'

'But, Mother . . .' the boy protested.

'Don't interrupt, Jean-Jacques.'

'My name is Frederick . . .'

'Your name is what I chose to call you. Nobody had any legal right to interfere with that . . .'

'Grandmother,' Jean-Jacques called across the room. 'Wasn't I christened Frederick? Didn't my other grandmother, Queen Marie, choose my name?'

'Queen Marie, who is not your grandmother, did interfere,' Anna replied. 'With my help, I regret to admit. She was always inventing schemes to try and manipulate her playboy son. Her head was full of fantasies about forcing him to live up to his responsibilities.'

There was an angry hiss from the Rumanian Royalists lined up against the wall.

'Secondly,' Jacqueline continued, staring at Reinikker. 'As you can see by looking at father and son, Jean-Jacques bears no resemblance whatever to any royal family, Rumanian or otherwise. He is the son of a French businessman.'

She paused, heart pounding with exhilaration.

'Thirdly, you will never see me in the rôle of a Queen Mother. Partly because I have no intention of interfering, or allowing my son to interfere, with the reign of King Michael, who is doing the best he can, I am sure, during a very difficult period. And also partly, and this is your fourth mistake, because you won't be alive to see anything at all.' His eyes widened as he drew a quick breath. 'I am going to kill you.'

'Mother!' Jean-Jacques shrieked. He started towards her, but was grabbed by his father. 'Mother, you cannot be serious. The Colonel and Monsieur Balanel are my friends, my aides. They have been helping me . . .'

'Using you, my darling. And I am serious, as Reinikker well knows.'

Reinikker started to his feet. 'No,' he shouted. 'For God's sake, somebody stop her.'

Jacqueline lifted the gun to aim carefully and deliberately at his groin, and fired.

He fell backwards, hitting the chair behind him before rolling on to the floor. His hands, already covered in blood, clutched the front of his once immaculate riding breeches.

He was screaming.

Masked by the table, Jacqueline failed to see his right hand reach for his holster and draw out the pistol. As she moved round the table, he aimed at her. She threw herself sideways, firing, but missed. His pistol barked once, twice, then before she could renew her aim a machine-gun chattered behind her.

Jacqueline rolled over to see Jean-Paul crouched behind a chair . . . and David moving up to see that his bullets had lodged in Reinikker's chest. She got up and stood beside him, looking down into those icy blue eyes. There was no cruelty in them now, only amazement and pain. Memories flashed through her head. She realised that he had probably loved her at first, in Berlin, and in his arrogant way had tried to force her to love him. But his love had turned to anger at her rejection of him, and later to cold fury when she had escaped to Italy. It wasn't until after the British Embassy Ball in Rome that he had hated her. Sought and taken the opportunity to humiliate her in return.

Heinrich had hit her and made love to her, brought her to orgasm and then raped her. And, when she no longer responded to him, malice and cruelty had flared in his twisted brain. He had disfigured the breasts he had so admired and thrown her into a cellar to go mad.

His breathing became shallow. Blood trickled from the corner of his mouth. Watching him die, she wondered if perhaps something had happened in his childhood to twist his mind to cruelty and evil. She could feel her hate evaporate.

Suddenly her legs felt weak, shoulders drooped, the gun barrel pointed at the floor. She sighed.

Reinikker's lips moved and she bent forward, straining to hear.

'It could have been so different,' he whispered.

She shrugged. 'Perhaps. But you understand, don't you? You had to die.' Her voice was as low as his.

There was an almost imperceptible nod of his head. He exhaled. Then she saw the coldness leave his pale, staring eyes.

All at once the room was in pandemonium. With attention centred on Jacqueline and the dying man, Anna had dropped her guard and some of the younger men sprang to take advantage of the situation. Anna, Jacqueline and David were seized, and now the three guns were pointed at them.

'Murderers!' one man exclaimed.

'Yes, cold-blooded murderers!' Others took up the shout.

Jacqueline and David were thrown to the floor, everyone crowding round in a circle.

The gunfire outside was very close now. Some people in the room were looking agitated. One of the men holding a gun stepped towards Jacqueline. 'We should kill them both now, to be sure they don't get away with it.'

'Yes, yes,' others agreed.

'Yes, I agree my daughter is a murderess.' Anna's voice was raised above the increasing din outside. Faces turned to her in surprise. Jacqueline gaped in horror.

'But how can you be so sure she killed in cold blood?' Anna shook off the restraining hands and walked across the floor. 'Look!' She knelt down to remove the dungaree straps from Jacqueline's shoulders, tore her shirt wide open, exposing the scarred breasts.

Some of the onlookers were curious, others appalled by the lack of decorum. Jean-Jacques was blushing with embarrassment.

'Before you pass final judgment, I think you should know that that . . .' She paused and pointed at Reinikker's body, '. . . that animal over there took my daughter from her home, had his soldiers tie her to a bed, where he proceeded to rape her. Several times. And when she ceased to please him, he did this, and this.' She pointed to each scar. 'Look, and this . . . with his burning cigarette.'

She looked up at the silent, staring faces, her eyes filled with tears. 'She was beaten and left almost starving in a cellar for several months, alone. And when the Allied forces might have released her, he . . .' She pointed at the dead man again, 'personally watched her thrown with that man,' she pointed at David, 'into a cattle train when she was even too weak to walk, to be taken north to one of the Nazi prison camps.'

She sat back on her heels, her voice dropping to a whisper. 'When we rescued them from that train six months ago she was a mental and physical wreck. It is a miracle she is still alive.'

She leaned over to close Jacqueline's shirt.

The uproar outside was deafening. Inside, nobody moved a muscle.

Anna got up. 'Now you can decide whether or not the Countess Jacqueline Tyroler acted in cold blood.'

No one seemed to notice Jean-Paul, ashen-faced, crawling away on hands and knees. From the corridor he stood peering through the door slit as the crowd stepped back from Jacqueline and David, allowing them to rise together. Then quickly he closed the door.

It was Jean-Jacques who broke the silence. 'Colonel von Reinikker . . . did that to Mother?' he asked.

'Yes.' Anna went to the boy and put her arm round him. 'You see, he was a Fascist, and Fascists use torture and murder to enforce their ideas. They believe they are justified, but unfortunately the movement attracts the very worst kind of men: sadists, people with sick and twisted minds, the arrogant, the avaricious, and the evil. It gives a *carte blanche* to their warped and twisted desires and protects them against retribution from just and decent people.'

The boy was pale and dazed. His adolescent mouth sagged open. Jacqueline got up and went to him. 'Don't worry, darling. You are only one of hundreds, perhaps thousands, who have been duped by von Reinikker's charm. I was once, myself. Do you remember the gentleman who escorted you and I to the Zoo in Berlin all those years ago?'

He thought for a moment. 'Yes. Yes, I do. He wore riding breeches and shiny boots . . . Ah!' His hand came up to his mouth. 'No! Not him! Not the Colonel? And he did that to you?' The big dark eyes filled with tears.

'Judge not, lest ye yourselves be judged,' a voice murmured in the background.

One of the men crossed the room to Jacqueline. 'Here, you had better keep this in case you need it again.' He thrust her gun into her hands.

'No!' a voice wailed. Bruno Balanel ran to the door.

David beat him to it, barred his way. 'What do we do with this one?' he asked.

'Nothing. Let me go. I have done nothing,' Bruno whined, thin wisps of peroxided hair falling over his face.

'Nothing?' Jacqueline queried. 'Trying to blackmail me on the threat of abducting my son when he was only seven years old, is nothing?' For a moment she again felt angry. 'You are just a scheming little rat. One of my poor so-called husband's many problems.'

'That is not true. I was his only . . .' he hesitated, and looked furtively around the room.

'And where is Ion Tyroler?' she asked.

'He died. Two years ago. And I have been alone ever since,' he moaned.

Dead! Her pathetic 'husband', who had never even kissed her, was dead. She was free. 'Oh, let him go,' she said. 'He is nothing.' She felt limp and exhausted.

Bruno's hurried exit seemed to release the tension in the air. But in the silence that followed, everyone became suddenly aware of the greater drama being enacted outside.

They all moved to the window, but it was dark and they could see nothing except flashes and buildings burning a short distance away.

Then doors slammed somewhere in the palace. There were shouts and shots, followed by the thunder of several pairs of heavy boots.

'Quick! Give me those guns.' David snatched them up, laid one on the table and dropped the other two, with the pistol, into an ornate Ottoman.

He turned to Jacqueline. 'Tell them they must all cheer the Russians as though they are our rescuers. They must be told that Reinikker was holding us at gunpoint and we overpowered him.' He spoke rapidly in French.

She repeated his instructions in Rumanian, praying there would be no argument. Moments later the doors were flung open and soldiers burst in, brandishing machine-guns.

She needn't have worried. The Rumanian Royalists, who hated Communism and the Soviets above all things, cheered and cheered the Russian soldiers. Several moved forward, hands extended to grasp a Russian hand, to hug and kiss them.

Fortunately, one of the Russians spoke a little Rumanian.

'Look,' Jacqueline explained, pointing to Reinikker's body. 'The Kraut wanted to kill us all, but my friend here,' she hugged the arm of the nearest Rumanian, 'he is very brave. He jumped on him and we were able to get his gun and turn it on him.'

The man interpreted and their officer smiled and nodded. And held out his hand.

She had noticed a little gilt calendar on the mantelpiece which read 20 October 1944.

They were all politely asked to show their papers, though most people shrugged and said they had never had any. The soldiers eyed the clothes Jacqueline, Anna and David were wearing with some suspicion but said nothing. Having advised them all to remain in the palace until the fighting was over, the Russians continued their search of the building.

There was a buzz of chatter when they left the room, mainly speculation on what would happen next.

'I thought you were going to the Swedish Embassy,' Jacqueline said to David. 'What on earth are you doing here?'

'As soon as I had reported, I doubled back here,' he replied. 'Something told me you might run into trouble.'

'You were dead right. And so you have saved my skin again. Thank you.' She smiled.

'Mother,' Jean-Jacques came with Anna to stand beside her.

'Yes?'

He looked directly into her eyes for a moment before lowering his gaze. 'I . . . I don't know what to say . . . I . . .'

'You don't have to say anything. I am just so happy to have found you again.' She had a great desire to take him into her arms but knew it would only embarrass him further, so gently she touched his hand.

Anna watched, smiling.

'What are you going to do now?' the boy asked.

'Wait until the firing stops and then go to the Swedish Embassy.' She glanced over her shoulder, still aware of the body by the table at the other end of the room.

'No, I mean, now that Count Marco is dead, where will we live? Are you going back to your business . . .?'

'Not in Rome. Not in Italy. I want to take Francisco, Katarina and Bobo to the United States. Will you come too? Please?'

'Where would we live? With that Admiral we met who took me on his ship?' His eyes were guarded.

'*Ocean Dreamer* is over there. We could live on her for a while. Cruise in the Caribbean.'

Jean-Jacques' whole face lit up. 'Oh, Mother, that would be great. Yes please.'

Jacqueline caught Anna's eye and both women smiled. At last Jean-Jacques showed signs of becoming a boy again.

'And Jean-Paul is coming too, I presume,' Anna said.

'No,' Jacqueline replied quietly. 'No, that is not what he wants to do.'

David's head came up with a jerk. He looked around the room. 'Where is Jean-Paul?' he asked.

Anna and Jacqueline turned, their eyes scanning the crowd. Jean-Jacques flushed. 'He left ages ago, before the Russians came in.'

'Are you sure?' David frowned.

'Yes, sir. He watched you and Mother for a few moments when you got up from the floor, and then he disappeared.'

Anna saw the brief, expressionless glance that passed between David and her daughter. She could only hope.

The firing continued for most of the night. David left them to explore the palace and came back to lead them to a small sitting room he had found empty upstairs. Jacqueline had taken one last, shuddering glance at Reinikker's body before closing the door of the reception room, relieved to be removing herself from the scene at last.

The little sitting room contained two sofas. Anna lay down on one, with Jean-Jacques on the floor beside her. David insisted that Jacqueline have the other one. 'Please take it, you look exhausted. I'm going to sit up and keep an eye on what's happening outside for a while.' He locked the door, moved a bureau across it, and snuffed out the single candle, leaving the room lit only by the pale pink glow of fires across the city.

Jean-Jacques and Anna were soon asleep, but when Jacqueline eventually drifted into unconsciousness it was to dream hideously. Reinikker had only pretended to be dead and now had them imprisoned in this room. He was pacing up and down in the corridor, a lighted cigarette in its holder, waiting for Anna to bare her breasts and bring her to him.

'No, no,' she wept. 'Please, no more.' She saw Anna coming towards her, hands outstretched to grasp the straps

423

of her dungarees. 'No, Mama, please don't! Da . . . vid!'
She was awoken by her own sobs, found she was sitting
bolt upright, pouring perspiration . . . and saw David
sitting on the edge of the sofa beside her. Anna and
Jean-Jacques stirred in their sleep, but didn't awake.

'Oh, David,' she gasped. 'It was horrible.' She leaned
forward, her head flopping against his shoulder.

'My poor Jacki,' he said gently, putting both arms round
her. 'You are exhausted.' He stroked her hair.

They sat together in silence for a few minutes, then she
raised her head. 'Why are you being so kind to me after
the way I have behaved towards you?'

'You know why,' he answered, and in the dim light their
eyes met. 'Because I love you.'

Jacqueline shook her head. 'How can you, after seeing
me with Jean-Paul?'

'Jean-Paul was a childhood passion, a spectre from the
past. I never believed he could become a real part of your
life. Not a woman like you. I just hoped that if we remained
together long enough, perhaps you might come to love
me. Not as you loved him, though. More in the way you
loved Marco.'

She didn't need light to see his strong, square-set jaw,
skin weather-roughened like her own, the ginger hair
which was always combed back straight against his head
every morning and which, in the slightest breeze, sprang
up into unruly curls, the green eyes . . . she remembered
his leadership over the past few months, his strength and
determination, his understanding and consideration for
every member of the group, his ability to make rapid
decisions, to act fast under fire . . .

She felt a glow of respect and admiration warming the
cold misery in her chest, was aware of his hands touching
her, his breath on her face . . . and for the first time she
allowed the glow to spread through her body. Yes. Yes
indeed, this was a man she could love as she had loved
Marco, but this time there would be no spectre of a girlish
passion lurking in the background to distract from that

love. Now she was free, and ready for a love without reservation.

Jacqueline smiled into David's eyes. 'There's no perhaps about it,' she told him. 'I do love you, David. I think I must have loved you for a long time without realising it. Now that the ghosts of the past have been laid, I feel free to love again.'

David had held his breath as she spoke. Now he inhaled, slowly and deeply. 'Jacki! Oh, my dearest, darling Jacki!' This time he was not gentle. His arms held her fiercely and passionately . . . and the moisture on her forehead proved the depths of his emotion. Then they kissed, and for the first time Jacqueline felt a warm response to him building in her body.

Soon she fell into a deep, untroubled sleep.

It had been another beautiful summer's day at sea. The old liner, still bare and austere after five years pressed into service as a troop carrier, nosed through a long, gentle swell.

A woman stood against the bow-rail, wind ruffling her honey-coloured hair to reveal a few grey streaks. Her figure was lean, boyish, giving her clothes a casual look. She smiled at her husband, her face calm and relaxed, eyes warm and loving.

He was slightly taller than herself, his fair, reddish hair receding at the corners of his forehead. His eyes were sea-green under thick brows. He was smiling back, adoringly.

Each held a cocktail glass in one hand, the fingers of the other twined together.

Her younger children had been bathed, fed and put to bed. The youngest was an adopted refugee orphan girl. Next was a ten-year-old girl with blonde hair and grey-green, dark eyes . . . who adored her brother, only a year her senior, the young Count Francisco Marco-Gregorio Luzzi di Calitri.

The husband and wife turned to greet a couple strolling towards them.

425

The silver haired woman was in her late fifties, tall, slender, and very elegant.

The young man smiled at his mother and stepfather, causing wrinkles of happiness at the corners of his deep, dark eyes.

The setting sun blazed a path of light across the western sea for them to follow.

Together they gazed over the bow as the glorious red ball sank beneath the horizon ahead. They raised their glasses in a toast to the future, and sauntered away to the dining room.

> It may be that the gulfs will wash us down:
> It may be we shall touch the Happy Isles,
> And see the great Achilles, whom we knew.
> Tho' much is taken, much abides; and tho'
> We are not now that strength which in old days
> Moved earth and heaven; that which we are, we are;
> One equal temper of heroic hearts,
> Made weak by time and fate, but strong in will
> To strive, to seek, to find, and not to yield.
>
> Alfred, Lord Tennyson, *Ulysses*

JANTHINA

Diana Bachmann

Canadian born Janthina is only sixteen years old when the relationship with her father becomes so difficult it is imperative that she leave the comforts of the farm on which she grew up and be sent to live with her maternal grandparents at Glenfalk Castle in Scotland. With the enthusiasm characteristic of youth, Janthina eagerly embraces her new life. But all too soon the dream is shattered. At seventeen she finds herself pregnant and in disgrace, once again uprooted and in France.

Janthina returns to visit her relations in Scotland who arrange a suitable marriage. All that remains for her is a long struggle to achieve emotional and financial security. But a life time of striving must have its rewards, and Janthina still has to find the love that could fill her heart.

MORE GOOD READING

FROM NEL

NANCY CATO

☐	04400 9	All The Rivers Run	£3.95
☐	05651 1	Forefathers	£3.95
☐	04932 9	North-West By South	£2.95

RUTH HARRIS

☐	05735 6	A Self-Made Woman	£2.95

LOLA IRISH

☐	05760 7	And The Wild Birds Sing	£2.95

KAY McGRATH

☐	05632 5	The Seeds Of Singing	£2.25

ANN TOLSTOI WALLACH

☐	05460 8	Women's Work	£1.95

All these books are available at your local bookshop or newsagent, or can be ordered direct from the publisher. Just tick the titles you want and fill in the form below.
Prices and availability subject to change without notice.

Hodder & Stoughton Paperbacks, P.O. Box 11, Falmouth, Cornwall.

Please send cheque or postal order, and allow the following for postage and packing:

U.K. – 55p for one book, plus 22p for the second book, and 14p for each additional book ordered up to a £1.75 maximum.

B.F.P.O. and EIRE – 55p for the first book, plus 22p for the second book, and 14p per copy for the next 7 books, 8p per book thereafter.

OTHER OVERSEAS CUSTOMERS – £1.00 for the first book, plus 25p per copy for each additional book.

Name ....

Address ....

....